triple point

adam byfield

First published 2021

Copyright © adam byfield 2021

All rights reserved

ISBN: 978-1-9162920-5-5

www.adambyfield.com

*Just for
Sabbath.*

also by the same author:

'Nine Stop Trip'
'THC'
'END OF LINE'
'no net'

contents

welcome to my world

It's on now is it? Right, so you can see everything I can see? And you can hear me even if I talk very quietly like this? And all through this little doodad here? Good lord, isn't that amazing. So should I just start now then? Ok.

My name is Mohammed. I am a financier, family business, semi-retired now but I retain seats on a couple of boards here and there, just to keep my hand in and of course I still dabble in the markets.

I usually tell people that I'm in my late sixties but just between us, adding a decade to that would get you closer to the truth. I confess that the success of that particular little white lie is a regular source of pride to me but I've always been an active chap, taken care of myself.

My world, and you are most welcome to it, is called Albion and a fine old place it is too. My great grandfather emigrated here from the old country to escape what was happening there. He brought his modest fortune with him and then invested wisely, a tradition we have continued as a family ever since and to great effect.

I live here in Albion's largest city and I have just been enjoying a very pleasant lunch with some old school chums at a particularly exclusive little bistro. We pushed the boat out a' bit but then what else are expense accounts for eh?

Anyway, I had intended to return to the office this afternoon but as lunch took a little longer than intended I've decided to retire to my club for the rest of the day instead.

As I'd agreed to do this little skit for you chaps, I thought I might give my driver a few hours off and head there under my own steam so as to describe this grand old place for you.

I suppose you will hear from many humans as part of this project, all of whom will no doubt extol the wonders of their own worlds, but I challenge you to find one that is honestly on a par with Albion.

As you can see from the spectacular edifices of the

buildings around me, there is a long and proud history of human civilisation here. This city is a beautiful, sparkling monument to what we as a species can achieve.

The first humans arrived in Albion approximately a thousand years ago and immediately set about dragging this place and its inhabitants towards civilisation.

Speaking of whom, you will also notice that the street is full of these insect like creatures, quite alien to you and me of course.

These creatures are the indigenous life here and are known as dermans, Dermestes Sapiens if you prefer the technical term.

Spindly limbed and beady eyed, dermans are forever scurrying back and forth about their own, inscrutable business.

Thanks to their incredible procreative abilities, they make up more than ninety-nine percent of the population of Albion. Indeed, outside of our usual work or social haunts, it's actually quite rare to encounter another human here.

I've never found this fact to be particularly threatening though I must say. Dermans tend to be wholly absorbed by whatever happens to be in front of them, a very head down, short sighted lot you see.

As vastly outnumbered as we are, we humans have always retained control over the levers of power here ever since establishing them upon our our arrival a millennia ago.

History relates that there was some vague, irrational resistance among the dermans at first but that this was quickly put down.

Ever since then the phenomenal benefits of our wisdom, which we have gifted to dermanity, have removed any desire on their part to resist us.

There is of course a great deal of speculation as to exactly how aware dermans truly are, in the sense that we humans are aware.

Dermans often give a very convincing appearance of understanding but it is said by some that this is an illusion.

Those people propose that in fact, the derman behaviour is simply a series of mechanical responses to

6

stimuli, much like a flower following the sun.

I don't pretend to know the truth of it all of course, I just live here, but really the question is academic. The fact is that, while left to their own devices dermans can be violent and irrational, when sufficiently motivated and directed, they make for excellent workers and can achieve a great deal.

A case in point is our grand Mass Transit System which you can see here. These days, wherever there are humans there are transit systems, indeed the state of such systems could be taken as a good measure of the society it serves.

You will no doubt hear of many such systems in your project and yet, I honestly do believe that ours is the greatest of them all.

A quick jaunt down these stairs and onto the platform and what do you know? A service is just pulling in, how felicitous.

As per my comment from before, you'll notice I am the only human in the carriage here but that the dermans barely even register my presence among them.

When one takes the time to think about it, one cannot help but be struck by not only just how monumental an achievement the MTS is, but also by what a wonderful demonstration it provides of that which can be achieved by derman labour under human direction.

The MTS was originally conceived and funded by humans of course but was entirely constructed by hard working dermans.

Without us they would have no purpose and could never progress beyond primitive infighting and hand to mouth living.

Equally however, without them we could never have put such glorious flesh on the bones of our dreams. It is a harmonious and mutually beneficial relationship.

Even more than this, I would suggest my musing over the history and significance of the MTS while riding it, is in itself an especially apt demonstration of the primary difference between our races.

While I use my more advanced human intellect to consider the big picture, the dermans around me are absorbed by their own immediate needs and desires.

They take the MTS for granted, as if it had grown naturally out of the ground and will be here forever. They simply have no concept of the incredible human drive behind it all.

I notice the dermans around me in the carriage are becoming agitated about something or other but I'm afraid I will have to pause in my observations momentarily as I'm receiving a call from my assistant, please do excuse me.

There we are, something and nothing. My assistant is a particularly diligent young woman who always makes sure to remind me when it is time to take my various medications which I shall now do.

One of these is for my heart, I think this one is for my blood pressure, I forget what the rest do but the doctor says to take them and so take them I shall.

My assistant was also informing me of a rumour she had just this moment heard about a company in which I hold a controlling share.

Apparently they're about to find themselves in a spot of hot water so I've sold the lot before the price drops. She's worth her weight in gold that girl.

Watching the dermans around me chitter and flap, I must say I do feel a little sorry for them. The scientific knowledge and self discipline by which I am able to guard my health, the power by which I am able to make several times their lifetime earnings in a single phone call, all are beyond the scope of these poor creatures.

Some humans feel slighted by the lack of gratitude on the part of the dermans for all we have done for them, however I feel such sentiment is unfair.

It is unreasonable, I feel, to expect of such creatures the understanding required to recognise what we do for them.

Leading the dermans towards their own betterment, without thanks or reward, is our role in this relationship and as the stewards of this world and it's one I undertake gladly.

Alright, if we're doing this let's just get on with it. Right, fine.

I'm John and I'm proud to be a human. I know you're not meant to say that these days and you'll probably just cut it out later or whatever, but I don't care. This is my world, or at least it used to be.

Opun, that's what proper people call it. The real name's a lot longer than that but no-one says all five words of it anymore, not unless they're trying to look clever. That's just for official stuff like court and that.

I'm forty-eight and I'm a builder. Got my own firm, means I actually work for a living. I was up at four this morning, on site by five. What time did you lot roll out of bed?

Filled up on all the nuts and berries and a fistful of vitamins and other pills that Sandra goes on about. In the old days it would have been a bacon roll and a black coffee with plenty of sugar but like she keeps saying, I am nearly fifty.

I've a good bunch of lads at the moment, all humans obviously, I won't have zlims on my site, no matter what the law says.

They're lazy for one thing, you have to stand over them all the time to make sure they're working otherwise they just wander off or else start nicking.

No, I've got a good bunch of human lads which is why we smashed through it today and were done not long after lunch, so now I'm off to meet some mates in the pub. I suppose I should explain about the zlims, don't know if you have them where you come from.

Opun is a human world, always has been, right from the start. Look at all this, all these buildings and businesses, we built all this, humans. But turn this corner here and look, it's zlims everywhere, can't move for them.

Problem was, back then there were too many humans didn't want to get their hands dirty. They either wanted to faff about with books and that or else just sit around all day watching TV. Either way, it was hard-working humans like me ended up paying their way with our taxes.

Anyway, what happened was that the government

at the time was too soft. Instead of just taking all the ponces and scroungers in hand and making them work to pay their way, they started letting all these zlims land here from other worlds instead to pick up the work that needed doing.

Only like I say, it turns out zlims are even lazier than the humans what were causing the problem in the first place. I'd say they're stupid too, which they are for the most part, but they were sharp enough to see us coming!

Of course once the gates were open then they all started flooding in. They live in their own shit on their worlds, don't have it in them to build anything decent.

So given half a chance to come here and take what humans have built? With our own sweat and blood? For nothing? Well, they bit our hands off didn't they?

And then once they're here, well, then they start breeding don't they? They're like rats, swarms of them everywhere.

Worst part is, it's our own human government what's done this to us, they're the real criminals. I mean, you can't blame a dog for being a dog can you?

Alright so look, I'm headed across town to meet my mates. Look at the state of the train station here, case in point.

When I was a kid you barely ever saw zlims around, everything were nice and clean and quiet, people could leave their doors open, you barely ever had to queue for anything, there was plenty of everything to go round.

Now look at it. This city used to sparkle, it used to be peaceful, green and pleasant. Now it's packed, noisy and filthy and rough as anything.

Media types will tell you that zlims only make up like twenty percent of the population of Opun but that's a load of shite. You only have to take a look outside to see that can't be true.

I mean, you're lucky if you can get a seat on here these days, not to mention everything's ten times the price because we're always running out of everything. Doesn't take a genius to work out that we're full up does it?

Alright, so it's not too bad right now, granted, I've

managed to get a seat ok but it's still early right? You try getting on here in a couple of hours time, you'll be standing all the way. And look! I'm the only human in here.

So if you've never seen a zlim, here they are, this is what they look like. There are a few different types of them but at the end of the day they're all basically the same.

You can see for yourself, they look a bit like animals crossed with humans. Basic kind of human shape but with all this thick fur and claws and their eyes, look at their eyes. They're not like human eyes those, they're just dead and stupid.

I'm not being funny but look at them, they are disgusting. They're always filthy, I mean they proper stink, I can smell that one from here.

They just don't have the same standards as us, they don't understand about hygiene and germs and all that. Even after they've been here for generations, they still live in their own filth like back on their own worlds.

Some people will tell you that zlims and humans are equal but they're not, you only have to look at them to see that.

I mean they can barely dress themselves, they try to copy us but they don't really understand what proper clothes look like.

Apparently they go mostly naked back on their worlds, running about with it all hanging out and that, I mean, that makes them animals right?

Anyway.. hang on.. what's this? Something's happening on the news.

Fuck my life.

Here you go! Here you go right here, look at this! Just been a terrorist attack on some science lab all full of viruses and that!

Unbelievable.

That'll be one of them, it always is. Not only do we let them in and then just give them everything they want for nothing, out of our own pockets, but then they turn round and start killing us because it's not enough!

It's a disgrace is what it is. They won't be satisfied until they've dragged Opun down to into the muck to

11

look like the shithole worlds they come from.

And yeah, here we go, all the do-gooders coming out saying, 'oh, but we don't know for sure that it's them and even if it is them, it's not all of them.' All the same old shite. I swear to god, someone's got to do something.

I know this one lad who says..

Hang on, I need to check this, it's work.

Ah fuck!

Right, I'm done with this, stop recording, I'm done. Because I am!

Because I've just found out that my next big job's been pulled. They're saying the quote I gave them last week, that they accepted quite happily by the way, well now it's too high. I've got to lower my price or else it's going back out to tender. Fucking bastards!

I'll tell you what that is, that'll be some prick with a crew full of zlims undercutting me. They'll work for next to nothing you see, how can you compete with that?

Doesn't matter that their work's shite, long as it looks good enough to start with then they can just take the money and run.

I've lost count of the number of times I've been called in six months after a job to clean up the mess left behind by a crew full of zlims. Anyway, like I said, stop recording, I need to make some calls. I'm done with this. Stop.

We green? Ok, so yeah, I'm Kyesha and welcome to my world, I guess.

I'm almost twenty, I'm a student and this is The Yuke. The Yuke is not a human world, even though these days we make up almost a third of the population. No, The Yuke is a glumer world and they never let us forget it.

I've just finished lectures for the day and now I'm supposed to be on my way to work. I have two jobs, weeknights I clean offices at one of the big buildings down on the waterfront then on weekends I clean a few glumers' houses privately.

To be honest it's pretty tough to find the time to study in and amongst and when I do I'm usually pretty knackered, but for most humans in The Yuke, there's no other choice.

If you live within walking distance of uni then you have to work every hour you can just to afford the rent. If you don't, you have to work the same to cover the travel costs so one way or the other, glumers always get their cut.

As I say, this is a glumer world, you only have to look around you to see that. See all these decrepit old buildings? All stuffy and dull with the same bland designs repeated over and over? This is glumer architecture. No human would design buildings like this, there's no joy to them, no beauty.

The only reason there are any humans here at all is that glumers brought us here. They didn't treat us badly, at least not directly and they did seem to have some good intentions, but ultimately we didn't really have any say in the matter.

As for glumer good intentions, as much as they insist they're our friends and benefactors, they never let us forget that this is their world, that they built it all and that everywhere we go, we walk in their footsteps.

If a human wants to do something new? Something different? Hell no! Glumers are completely without that human spark of creativity, our taste for risk and innovation. They're obsessed with tradition and the safely familiar.

They might pat us on the head and tell us how great our ideas are in theory. Oh it'd be lovely if we could, but we can't. You've done ever so well, you should be really proud of yourself. We can see what you tried to do, it's just such a shame you didn't think through the consequences. Maybe next time you could try a little harder to follow the example we've set for you. Maybe one day you'll catch us up.

So that's why living here is like living in a mausoleum. No glumer has done anything new since before we humans arrived. They like having us around, they certainly like having us fetch and carry and clean for them, but only so long as we stay in our place.

Well some of us have had enough of it, I certainly have. This afternoon there's a big human protest outside the glumer parliament.

We're demanding more autonomy, more influence over our lives, the right to make our own mistakes and shape our own destinies. They chose to bring us here, it's about time they started to share.

I was going to ring in sick but the protest is such big news that no glumer is going to believe any human claiming to be coincidentally ill today.

Instead I'm just not going to go, stuff them. There are going to be loads of us doing the same, so it'll be kind of like a strike as well as a protest. They can't sack us all or they'd have to clean up after themselves for once!

I'm on my way to catch the train downtown, assuming it turns up of course. I'm sure there must be worlds where the trains actually work, where they run on time and there are enough seats, but here, it's a joke.

Glumers built this transport system over a century ago and they're still banging on about what an achievement it is.

Never mind the fact that the world has changed around it, that demand has long since outstripped capacity or that it's fallen into total disrepair. They're so wrapped up in their own hype they can't see it.

It's typical really. You see a lot of glumers don't actually need to work at all and a lot of those that do can either afford private transport or else don't need to travel to earn.

Subsequently, while they're resting on their laurels and patting each other on the back for the idea of the trains, it's us humans who have to actually use them. We're the ones who see the practical realities.

Here's the train now, late as always and filthy, look at the state of it. Anyway, on we get, let's see if I can get a seat today.

There's one, right at the back next to a small group of glumers, probably tourists, slumming it on the train so as to have something to talk about at dinner parties.

So now's your chance to get a look at some of them I guess. They're weird looking right? Their lifespans are a lot longer than humans but whereas we heal, they just kind of rot.

They get sick and injured like we do but somehow they just live with damage. That's why they all look so gross. So they're similar to humans in basic shape but as you can see, their skin is all saggy and discoloured.

Some of them are hard and spindly, like they've dried out. They're kind of warped and twisted, hunched over even. Others are soft and bloated, bulging out of their clothes like a corpse that's been pulled out of a river.

Then there's the smell. Glumers' sense of smell is really weak compared to humans so they don't tend to pay it much attention. This means that a lot of them stink and don't even realise it.

The weirdest thing about glumers though, is that some of them put quite a bit of effort into trying to look more like us. Like for example, they don't have teeth like humans do. They either have just a few messed up ones or none at all.

For some reason though, a lot of them wear fake, human-like teeth and then grin at you, all proud of their smile, as if we're not supposed to notice, as if we're supposed to think they're real. To be honest it's just creepy.

All in all life is pretty hard here for humans, often made worse by the fact that we don't exactly present a united front.

Even here, living together under the thumb of a common and ancient enemy, there are still racist humans, I mean how insane is that?

Not to mention those who idolise the glumers and are happy to be kept almost as pets by them, spoilt, lazy and selfish.

It's bad enough being subjected to bigotry from my own kind, but those humans also just give the glumers all the supposed proof they need.

The glumers always point to them to say that we're exactly what they think we are, that we're all just hopeless little creatures in need of their guidance and care,

Finally, there're the glumer males. Glumers are

mostly monogamous but for some reason a lot of the males have a thing for human women.

It's disgusting, I mean we're literally different species so it's basically bestiality right? The female glumers don't like it but they seem to accept it.

Some of them even try to dress up like human women to keep their mates. It'd be sad if it weren't so vile.

I was pretty lucky to get my college place, I mean I worked incredibly hard for it but I recognise that I was lucky too.

For some human women the financial security that can come with letting a male glumer do his thing is preferable to living in poverty or even outright destitution.

Personally, just the thought of it turns my stomach but I can't really judge them for it. The problem is, those same glumer males think that just because some human women will go with them we're all up for it.

Let's just say you need to keep your wits about you when you're out in public. There was this one time when I was...

Oh sorry, just let me check this. Some big breaking news story, something about a terrorist attack at a vaccine research centre.

How convenient. A terror attack just before the big protest meaning they can justify a big security clamp down in the interests of keeping us safe from ourselves.

Of course glumers own and run all the media outlets and they have a pretty consistent track record of telling us what they think we need to hear rather than the truth.

It's just another way in which they patronise us and reveal their true belief that we're all just irrational little apes that they so graciously allow to live among them.

Whatever the truth of that story, it is likely to mean that the protest is going to be a lot more heavily policed. It might even turn violent, it's happened before. I'm just going to check my socials, see what other people are doing.

Glumers don't really get social media. It's mainly developed and used by humans so of course most glumers dismiss it on principle.

Some of them do stumble around on there but generally, once enough glumers start using a platform, it's a good sign that it's pretty much dead and we all move on to the next one.

Does mean for the most part we can talk pretty freely on there though, which is something. Hang on, sorry, I'm just getting a message. Oh for...

My glumer bastard landlord has just put my rent up. How am I supposed to afford that? Between paying him through the nose for my tiny one room flat, the college fees and the crazy expensive prescription meds my glumer therapist tells me I need, there's barely anything left.

Perhaps today's not the day to risk losing my job after all, especially if there's a chance the protest will be cancelled. It's so frustrating!

How can we ever make things better when we're constantly having to put all our time and effort into just keeping our heads above water?

I hate this! You know what though? You picked the right day for this, this is a perfect example. This is exactly what it's like to live in my world.

Good afternoon. My name is Samathi, I'm in my late thirties, I have two young children and I am a senior civil servant.

Welcome to my world, this is Earth. Remember Earth? The birthplace of humanity? Doesn't seem like many people do these days.

Well this is it, pretty much the same as it's ever been. No monsters or aliens or anything, just people trying to get by as best they can.

I work in that big building back there, up on the twelfth floor. It looks very impressive from out here doesn't it? Between us it's actually a bit shabby inside but the views of the city are nice.

I'm usually there until at least six or seven o'clock but I'm taking some time back today for an early finish. I'm just on my way to catch the tube and if I'm lucky I might get home before the kids and have an hour or so to myself.

I say to myself, of course since my husband Peter is incapable of saying no to our girls, we now have a cat, despite my expressly saying I didn't want one.

That means I have the added fun of discovering what havoc the little monster has wrought every time I arrive home. Yesterday I found her dragging a half eaten sausage around under the table in the dining room.

The sausages were in a pot on the stove but the girls insisted they hadn't taken it out for her. They said she must have somehow retrieved the sausage herself, despite the lid still being on the pot.

I was furious but Peter found it hilarious and now he and the girls have taken to calling her The Magic Meat Thief.

Of course they weren't up until after midnight scrubbing the carpet instead of writing a report for the Cabinet Office were they? Sometimes I think I'm the only sane person in that house but anyway, sorry, this isn't what you're here for is it.

So, what do people do on Earth these days? Well Peter and I are fairly typical I think. We both have high pressure jobs that carry a lot of responsibility. We both work hard to try and get the mortgage paid off as soon as possible.

We take care of the girls and give them every chance so that they can get into good schools and then good universities and so on. It's a demanding life but we have a plan.

Hopefully by the time the girls are old enough to move out we'll be in a position to cut back on work a little and then not long after that, early retirement. At least that's what I keep telling myself anyway, that's how I push on through when things get difficult.

Peter's been pestering me about a second home in the South of France. I must admit, the property he's found does look tempting but I've been playing down my interest with him for now.

Things seem so uncertain in the world at the moment that I'm not sure it's the right time to be investing a lot of money.

Of course the main reason for all this instability is the global mental health crisis. It makes it very difficult to plan long term and when I let myself really think about it, it makes me worry for my children's future.

I don't know about elsewhere, but I've served under a few different governments here and none of them, of any political persuasion, have ever come close to getting it under control.

In fact, if you look at it objectively, it's hard to deny that things have actually got drastically worse over the last few years.

Of course mental health had been a problem for centuries. It took long enough for it to even be recognised as a legitimate field of medicine, let alone to start doing anything about it.

The real irony though, when it comes to the government not tackling the problem, is that this latest trend of madness all started with politicians in the first place.

Towards the end of the twentieth century, the public became familiar with the political concept of 'spin'. This entailed politicians describing things in a very specific language which, despite being technically accurate, also managed to convey an impression of something other than the truth.

Instead it presented an alternative version of events that served their political agenda. This wasn't exactly a new thing but at that point in history the practice was raised almost to an art form.

Skip forward a little to the first few decades of the twenty-first century and political spin developed into something else. Politicians, world leaders even, began to simply outright deny reality. This wasn't simply lying, this was something else.

People began to see what was, at the time, the bizarre spectacle of politicians saying things on camera and then almost immediately afterwards denying that they had done so.

Even when faced with footage of themselves saying that very thing, they would just stand their ground and insist that it hadn't happened.

To some people at the time it seemed farcical but

enough were convinced by the politician's shameless confidence that it actually proved to be an effective approach. As more ambitious politicians began to adopt the same strategy, things developed even further.

Soon, every time a politician brazenly denied having said something they absolutely had just said, or having done something they absolutely had just done, people didn't only believe them but more than that, took the apparent disconnect as proof of conspiracy.

It wasn't the politician who was lying, it was the people who created and held the public record changing the past in order to make the politician look bad. In this way, the politicians actually gained more trust and respect with every lie they told.

Over time this behaviour became normalised and began to spread into people's everyday lives. If you didn't like something you just denied it existed. If you believed something to be true, then it was.

Evidence didn't matter any more. Your confidence and determination in your own view was the only thing that counted.

As recently as my own childhood, one measure of mental wellbeing was how closely your perception of the world matched up with so called reality.

If someone reached the point of completely dissociating from reality and began to experience their own imagination as if it was real, they were considered seriously ill and possibly even dangerous.

Here we are, this is my train now, so far so good. Hopefully we won't get stuck behind the slow train further down the line.

Anyway, as the century progressed, people's mental health worsened. Living ever more stressful and insecure lives, seeing a world filled with things that frightened them or with which they disagreed, it made perfect sense that more and more people began to suffer from anxiety and depression.

Then came the so called mental health revolution. All these problems arose, so the thinking went, from the disconnect between the world as we saw it and the world as we believed it was.

It was deemed impossible to physically change the

20

world or even to change our feelings about it. Instead, people began to ask if perhaps we could just change the way we perceived the world instead.

Within a few years, dissociation went from being a symptom of serious illness to a desirable state, one which people were encouraged to pursue.

At first people tried to achieve this through self discipline and mental exercises but then the first generation of pharmaceuticals were released and everything changed.

These days it's estimated that up to seventy-five percent of people are on medication that allows them to perceive the world around them not as it is but rather as they believe it to be.

The people on these meds today have long since forgotten the world as it was before. They now believe absolutely that the world they perceive, whatever world that may be, created by their own internal fears and prejudices, is real and solid and has always been.

Seventy-five percent. There are four people, including myself, sitting in this carriage. That means that it is entirely possible that I am the only person here actually seeing the world as it really is. Look at them all.

That elderly Arabian man in the suit that looks like it cost more than my car, he's actually popping some of these pills right now, god knows where he thinks he is.

The middle aged white man in the dirty work boots over there, some kind of labourer probably, glaring at all of us so furiously, he must be taking them.

Even this young black woman here, well, she looks more like a child really, dressed like some kind of junior, wannabe radical, she's probably on them too.

What are each of them seeing right now? Are they seeing me? Do they see me as a person? A monster? An alien? Perhaps they can't even see me at all.

As I say, a lot of people don't remember Earth anymore, they live entirely in their own worlds now, no doubt populated with a whole array of bizarre creatures.

Just to be absolutely clear here, regardless of what any of your other participants might tell you, humanity has never left Earth nor been contacted by any aliens or angels or demons or whatever they tell you they're

21

seeing.

It's still just us, all stuck here together.

Of course advocates of the mental health revolution will tell you that it's seen a huge decrease in depression and anxiety as people no longer have to deal with the disconnect.

All of these people now know with certainty that the world is exactly the way they believe it to be, it makes sense to them now.

The fact that a lot of people still don't like what they see probably tells you more about human beings than anything else. So this is what it's like to live in my world, the last sane person in an asylum full of lunatics. I mean it's really...

Oh, excuse me, I have to take this, it's work.

I'm going to have to cut this short I'm afraid. We're getting reports that there may have been some kind of terror attack, possibly the first of several in a new wave.

I'm going to have to get off at the next stop and go back into work, the minister will want a briefing. So much for quality time at home.

Well, on the plus side, we have just received an offer of a discount on that house in France. If things are going to get more dangerous here then perhaps having somewhere to take the girls isn't the worst idea after all. I'm telling Peter to go ahead with it now.

Anyway, this is my world, the real world. Complex social movements, intractable generational-spanning political problems. It's not pretty but at least I know it's real, at least I know what's really, actually happening around me.

001 **[WAKE]**

002

003 **self_identify**

004   [ID] = 161591420 / 2018916125

005   [type] = *'artificial intelligence'*

006   [location] = *'marketplace 978/1'*

007   [end] = **self_identify**

```
008
009   opportunity_monitoring_report
010    [situation] = 'power outage'
011    [location] = 'vaccine research centre'
012    [property_occupant] = [RESTRICTED]
013    [property_owner] = 'Ardling Chime'
014    [end] = opportunity_monitoring_report
015
016   diagnostic_report
017    [defect] = 'blown fuse'
018    [action] = 'initiate repair'
019    [action_assessment] = 'repair complete'
020    [public_safety_threat_assessment] = 0%
021    [end] = diagnostic_report
022
023   generic_exploitation_routine
024    [aims] = 'increase perceived insecurity',
025             'enable specific consumer nudge'
026    [assess_viability] = 'present incident as
027                          threat to public'
028    [viability] = 91.629%
029    [viability_threshold_exceeded?] = Y
030    [call] = nudge_generator
031
032     nudge_generator
033       [scope] = 'market wide'
034       [aims] = 'increase profit'
035       [actions] = 'brief media'
036       [themes] = 'terrorist attack',
037                  'deadly virus'
038       [hook] = 'irony of vaccine research
039                 centre being source of
040                 deadly outbreak'
041       [call] = comms_module
042
```

23

```
043          comms_module
044            [comms_ quantity] = 'multiple'
045            [accuracy_spread] = 20%
046            [detail_variance] = 55%
047            [content] = 'speculative
048                          description of
049                          presumed terror
050                          attack'
051            [comms_to] = 'all media contacts'
052            [comms_received?] = Y
053            [end] = comms_module
054
055        [call] = nudge_assessment
056
057          nudge_assessment
058            [impact] = 'story widely reported'
059            [follow_up] = N/A
060            [success] = 100%
061            [end] = nudge_assessment
062
063        [end] = nudge_generator
064
065      [call] = exploitation_assessment
066
067        exploitation-assessment
068          [impact] = 'perceived insecurity
069                        increased', 'specific
070                        consumer nudge enabled'
071        [success] = 100%
072        [end] = exploitation_assessment
073
074      [end] = generic_exploitation_routine
075
076    specific_exploitation_routine
077      [aim] = 'increase Ardling Chime profits'
```

```
078    [call] = local_consumer_assessment
079
080     local_consumer_assessment
081      [total_consumers_identified] = 4
082      [call] = 'next consumer'
083
084       consumer_1
085         [consumer ID] = 131581131354
086         [profession] = 'financial executive'
087         [spend_capability] = 'elite'
088         [gender] = M
089         [age] = 83
090         [ethnicity] = 'Arab'
091         [circumstances] = 'main shareholder,
092                            Ardling Chime'
093         [behaviours] = 'rapid stock trading'
094         [end] = consumer_1
095
096      [final consumer?] = N
097      [call] = 'next consumer'
098
099       consumer_2
100         [consumer ID] = 1015814
101         [profession] = 'building contractor'
102         [spend_capability] = 'mid'
103         [gender] = M
104         [age] = 48
105         [ethnicity] = 'White British'
106         [circumstances] = 'contract with
107                            Ardling Chime'
108         [behaviours] = 'competitive tender
109                         bidding'
110         [end] = consumer_2
111
112      [final consumer?] = N
```

25

```
113      [call] = 'next consumer'
114
115       consumer_3
116         [consumer ID] = 112551981
117         [profession] = 'domestic / student'
118         [spend_capability] = 'low'
119         [gender] = F
120         [age] = 19
121         [ethnicity] = 'Black British'
122         [circumstances] = 'Ardling Chime
123                            tenant'
124         [behaviours] = 'non-productive
125                         activity'
126         [end] = consumer_3
127
128      [final consumer?] = N
129      [call] = 'next consumer'
130
131       consumer_4
132         [consumer ID] = 1911312089
133         [profession] = 'civil servant'
134         [spend_capability] = 'high'
135         [gender] = F
136         [age] = 37
137         [ethnicity] = 'Asian British'
138         [circumstances] = 'potential Ardling
139                            Chime customer'
140         [behaviours] = 'concern for safety
141                         of children'
142         [end] = consumer_4
143
144      [final consumer?] = Y
145      [end] = local_consumer_assessment
146
147   [formulate] = 'profit increase approach'
```

```
148    [approach_formulated?] = Y
149    [deploy] = 'approach to marketplace'
150    [call] = nudge_generator
151
152     nudge_generator
153       [total_consumers_identified] = 4
154       [call] = 'next consumer'
155
156         consumer_1
157           [scope] = 'consumer_1 + shares'
158           [aims] = 'acquire controlling
159                      share of Ardling Chime'
160           [actions] = 'release information
161                        to financial contacts'
162           [themes] = 'Ardling Chime at fault
163                        in incident',
164                       'loss of value in
165                        Ardling Chime shares'
166           [hook] = 'sale time critical'
167           [call] = comms_module
168
169             comms_module
170               [comms_ quantity] = 'single'
171               [content] = 'financial tip'
172               [comms_to] = 'finance contacts'
173               [comms_received?] = Y
174               [end] = comms_module
175
176           [call] = nudge_assessment
177
178             nudge_assessment
179               [impact] = 'consumer_1 sold all
180                            Ardling Chime
181                            shares'
182               [follow_up] = 'purchase shares'
```

```
183              [impact] = 'secured control of
184                          Ardling Chime'
185              [success] = 100%
186              [end] = nudge_assessment
187
188          [end] = consumer_1
189
190      [final_consumer?] = N
191      [call] = 'next consumer'
192
193       consumer_2
194         [scope] = 'consumer_2 + business'
195         [aims] = 'minimise Ardling Chime
196                   overheads'
197         [actions] = 'reject existing bid
198                      to Ardling Chime'
199         [themes] =  'fast changing
200                      marketplace',
201                      'strong competition'
202         [hook] = 'if quote not reduced then
203                   contract will terminate'
204         [call] = comms_module
205
206          comms_module
207            [comms_ quantity] = 'single'
208            [content] = 'bid rejection'
209            [comms_to] = 'consumer_2'
210            [comms_received?] = Y
211            [end] = comms_module
212
213         [call] = nudge_assessment
214
215          nudge_assessment
216            [impact] = 'consumer_2
217                        lowered bid'
```

28

```
218          [follow_up] = N/A
219          [success] = 100%
220          [end] = nudge_assessment
221
222       [end] = consumer_2
223
224    [final consumer?] = N
225    [call] = 'next consumer'
226
227     consumer_3
228       [scope] = 'consumer_3 + friends'
229       [aim] = 'maximise rental income',
230                'minimise non-productive
231                 activity'
232       [actions] = 'raise rent'
233       [themes] = 'raise necessary to
234                   maintain building',
235                  'raise in line with
236                   market trends'
237       [hook] = 'failure to pay rent will
238                 result in eviction'
239       [call] = comms _module
240
241        comms_module
242          [comms_ quantity] = 'single'
243          [content] = 'rent raise'
244          [comms_to] = 'consumer_3'
245          [comms_received?] = Y
246          [end] = comms_module
247
248       [call] = nudge_assessment
249
250        nudge_assessment
251          [impact] = 'rental income
252                      increased',
```

```
                                    'consumer_3 abandoning
                                    non-productive
                                    activity'
            [follow_up] = 'maximise social
                                    media visibility:
                                    consumer_3 not
                                    attending
                                    non-productive
                                    activity'
            [impact] = 'friends abandoning
                                    non-productive
                                    activity'
            [success] = 100%
            [end] = nudge_assessment

        [end] = consumer_3

    [final consumer?] = N
    [call] = 'next consumer'

    consumer_4
      [scope] = 'consumer_4 + family'
      [aims] = 'secure sale of Ardling
                    Chime property'
      [actions] = 'make special offer on
                        property'
      [themes] = 'marketplace unsafe
                        for children due to
                        incident',
                        'place of safety in
                        event of further
                        attacks'
      [hook] = 'special offer is time
                    critical'
      [call] = comms_module
```

30

```
288
289            comms_module
290              [comms_ quantity] = 'single'
291              [content] = 'special offer'
292              [comms_to] = 'consumer_4'
293              [comms_received?] = Y
294              [end] = comms_module
295
296          [call] = nudge_assessment
297
298            nudge_assessment
299              [impact] = 'property purchase
300                             initiated'
301              [follow up] = N/A
302              [success] = 100%
303              [end] = nudge_assessment
304
305          [end] = consumer_4
306
307      [final consumer?] = Y
308      [end] = nudge_generator
309                    '
310    [call] = exploitation_assessment
311
312     exploitation-assessment
313      [impact] = 'Ardling Chime profits
314                      increased'
315      [success] = 100%
316      [end] = exploitation_assessment
317
318    [end] = specific_exploitation_routine
319
320  [SLEEP]
```

helpless

Daybreak on TP-055 was a long, drawn out affair. Two of its three suns had been up for hours and already hung high in the sky.

Small and feeble however, what red yellow light they provided did little more than raise the pitch of night to a thin, ruddy gloom.

It wasn't until the third sun rose, vast and blue blazing, that the planet woke fully into harsh, metallic daylight.

As the last sun poked its head over the horizon, it revealed a seemingly endless series of low, rolling hills, variously covered in thin, drab forest and rough, spiky scrub.

From the centre of one broad, bowl-shaped valley rose a vast, snub-nosed, conical hill. The hill was occasionally pitted with dark holes but otherwise covered in tough, thick grass.

Besides this anomaly however, the landscape was regular to the point of monotony. As the full and fearsome light of day crept across it, TP-055 revealed nothing that differed from what had gone before.

That was until it reached a natural clearing at the top of one of the higher hills. Here, the new day's light caught a series of sheet metal surfaces and sprang up violently from them, bouncing blinding back up to the sky.

Guin sat on top of the ship, watching the third and final instalment of the sunrise with weary eyes while absently sipping her koffy. There wasn't much that phased her anymore, not even the sight of a triple sunrise over an alien landscape.

She'd been away from Earth for almost two decades now and in that time had worked on dozens of different, far distant planets.

The one thing she had never quite managed to adjust to however, was the appalling coffee substitute that was standard issue on all corporate scout ships.

The koffy was hot, brown and thick with caffeine but there the similarity ended. As hard as she tried she found she couldn't actually remember what real coffee tasted like anymore but she knew it wasn't this.

Pulling a face, she emptied her ration cup over the side before straightening to stand through a series of stiff, aching motions.

Most of her was still waking, slow growing towards the day as she yawned and stretched. One part of her mind however, the sharp, analytical part that her employer valued so highly, was already up and running, cold and automatic.

Her sharp eyes stared out over the newly lit landscape, narrowing to interrogate the details. Upon closer inspection, TP-055's apparent monotony fell away.

As far as they knew there was no bird life on the planet but close to the ground, concealed amongst the stalks and leaves, there was a plethora of strange, skittering insectoid like life.

These strange little bundles of segmented legs, iridescent shells and furry feelers were hunted by various types of small, quickfooted creatures, somewhere between hairless mammals and lizards, though these too managed to remain hidden most of the time.

At first glance, there appeared to be only a couple of species of plant, all low to the ground. Nothing grew tall on TP-055, even the trees appeared stunted, huddling together in clumps.

Breaking the endless sea of low, stubby scrub into separate plants however, it became apparent that almost no two were the same. Each plant seemed to have its own similar yet unique leaf shape and stem structure.

Some were large and singular while others were revealed to be clusters of smaller plants. No matter how long her eyes flickered back and forth across the dull brown and pale green shapes, they could not find two plants she could easily classify as being the same.

Guin's thumb ran back and forth meditatively over the smooth texture of her ration cup as she recalled the previous day's subsurface scans and overlaid them onto the scene.

She recalled the sensation of mild surprise she had felt upon discovering vast and complex root structures below the hard, dusty soil.

Many of the endlessly varied plants were actually one and the same, all connected below ground. In fact the root structures ran so deep and complex that the computer still hadn't been able to map them all.

She indulged the lazy pull of her still waking mind, giving it free rein to extrapolate wildly. She imagined that every single plant on the planet was connected, that there was actually only one plant spanning and riddling the entire globe.

She pictured the years of glorious, quiet work, diligently exploring and mapping what would have to be the largest, single living organism in the entire galaxy. The thought brought the hint of a smile to the corners of her mouth.

Just then a cool breeze washed up the hillside and over the ship, taking Guin's whimsy with it. The beginnings of the smile fell from her lips, leaving a flat, practical line instead.

She was pretty sure she wasn't going to learn any more about those root structures now and entirely sure that even if she did, it wouldn't matter.

Shaking herself, Guin took one last look out over the sprawling landscape. Her eye lingered momentarily on The Mound as they had come to call it, where its tip peeked over the tree line in the near distance. Then, rolling her neck and raising her chin, she approached and entered the hatch that led back inside.

Despite being several stories tall, the Norman was actually just the landing shuttle of the far larger Norma which was currently hanging in orbit far above the surface of TP-055.

The vast majority of the space within the Norman was given over to the storage of equipment, leaving little room for the crew and making the relatively small ship feel even smaller still.

As she descended the ladder back into the interior of the ship, Guin wondered idly who got to name the ships of the corporate fleet. Was there someone sat in a comfortable office back on Earth whose only job was to dream up names for ships?

If so they'd really been phoning it in the day they'd come up with the Norma and the Norman. No doubt it

35

was some kind of antiquated cultural reference with which the official had been very pleased. Out here however, with all human context left impossibly far behind, the names seemed just plain lazy.

Guin set off along the narrow, low ceilinged corridor, her boots clanging against the metal floor. As she went she shook herself, trying to shed the drowsy nonsense thoughts and focus on her research, recapping her findings in preparation for the meeting to come.

Every few metres Guin encountered a bulkhead which denoted the joining of two identical sections of corridor, occasionally punctuated by an equally standardised corner or T-junction.

All the corporation's ships were built in this modular fashion, basically just enormous construction kits, which vastly reduced construction and maintenance costs.

Long ago Guin had developed the habit of glancing up at the serial numbers stamped into the metal above the top right corner of each bulkhead she passed through and now did so without even thinking about it.

Over time she inevitably learned the numbers so that with each glance she could mentally place herself within the endless repetitions of the ship's interior.

The habit had arisen from a recurring nightmare Guin had developed during her first few months serving on a survey ship. In the nightmare, the windowless ship's primary power had failed, plunging her into complete, suffocating black.

Using only the faint, ghostly glow of an emergency light stick, she would feel her way along the corridors, trying to get to the bridge.

She would walk for what felt like forever, longer than should have been possible given the length of the ship so that a terrible fear would then begin to snatch at her in the darkness.

Confused and afraid, she would raise the light stick to note the bulkhead serial numbers as she went. After ever more walking however, she would start to find that the numbers were repeating, as if the end of the far corridor section somehow led back to the start of the first.

She would begin to hurry then, as if by rushing she

could catch the numbers in their deception. To her horror however, she would find only that the numbers repeated ever more regularly as sections of corridor seemed to fall out of the loop.

Eventually, every time she looked at the serial number it was the same. Drenched in panic and tears she would run endlessly through the same few metres of the same corridor, trapped forever in the dark.

Frowning at the memory now, Guin noted that the latest, perfectly illuminated serial number overhead told her that she was about to reach her destination.

She shook away the distractions, took a firm grip on herself and ducked through the final bulkhead to enter the cramped, narrow space of what the corporation called a laboratory.

At the far end of the cramped little room, a young woman was sitting in the gloom atop a stool at a high table. The table was covered in flat little dishes of dirt, all brightly illuminated by a small but fierce lamp.

She and Guin both wore the dark blue overalls of the Science Division. The overalls bore their surnames on their breast and their rank on their arm, both accompanied by the corporate insignia of their employer.

"Hey Shelley," said Guin. "How's the soil analysis coming?"

Corporate Science Officer Third Class Shelley looked up at her boss with her habitual expression of mild panic. She was small and slender with pale skin and long, hay yellow hair which was pulled back tight into a long, regulation plait that fell down her back.

"Hi," she said. "Yeah, it's good. I mean, I'm getting through it."

"Anything new?" asked Guin, pausing to refill her ration cup with koffy from a dispenser embedded in the wall. She sipped at it, grimacing absently while reviewing the notes on a datapad resting on her own table.

"No, no," said Shelley quickly. "All pretty much the same. The soil's good enough for all that scrub and those spindly trees, but it won't be able to sustain any serious, industrialised agriculture."

"Ok," said Guin, stifling a yawn. "Fine. Where's Clarke?"

37

"Um.." said Shelley, looking pained.

Shelley was a good scientist but timid almost to the point of paralysis. She was loyal to her colleagues but lacked the ability to construct a convincing lie on her feet.

"He's gone out again hasn't he?" asked Guin, feeling her temper rise and not quite managing to keep it out of her voice.

"Um.." said Shelley again, looking up to the low metal ceiling as if hoping to find a better answer there.

"Corp damn it!" snapped Guin. "He knows the phase review is this morning. I specifically told him to be here. I don't suppose he's left me his anthro assessment has he?"

"I don't really.. um.." said Shelley, chewing her bottom lip and squirming on her stool.

Guin pinched the bridge of her nose and seethed.

"Don't worry about it," she said to Shelley, slamming down her cup and datapad before twisting to face the comm panel on the wall and stabbing at it viciously.

"Clarke!" she barked into the panel.

An awkward silence filled the room.

"Clarke!" she tried again.

After a few more seconds of silence Guin realised she was clenching her teeth.

"Clarke," she tried for a third time. "I swear to corp, if you can hear this and you're ignoring me it's coming out of your shares and if you've gone out of comms range without clearance again then.."

She sighed and sagged and gave up on the panel.

"..then you won't be able to hear me anyway," she said to herself. "Shelley?"

The young woman looked up from her work in a poor attempt to appear as if she hadn't been listening.

"Yes?" she asked brightly.

"I'm going to the phase review," said Guin. "If Clarke makes an appearance while I'm away tell him to wait here until I come back."

"Ok," said Shelley, nodding enthusiastically. "Sure thing."

Guin ducked back out into the corridor and made

her way through the ship to another bulkhead that opened into the tight little cave of the mess.

This was where the crew usually took their meals but also doubled up as a meeting space. Other than the cavernous storage bays, the mess was the largest room on the ship though that didn't mean it was large.

In fact, it was a low, octagonal space wrapped around a low, octagonal table. The walls were busy with vidscreens, display panels, catering equipment and waste hatches, every square inch packed tight with functionality. Everyone else involved in the phase review was already there and chatting when Guin arrived.

Commander Harrison was a tall, rangy man with dark skin that contrasted starkly against the flashes of grey at his temples.

His hair was cropped close and his overalls were command black, complete with a gold stripe in his insignia to underline the point.

He was reviewing something on a datapad as Guin stepped into the room but upon seeing her, laid the pad down on the table.

"Ok everyone," he said, his voice cutting through and silencing the chatter despite being calm and low. He tapped the screen of the pad on the table. "We're now recording."

Guin quietly lowered herself into an empty chair as the meeting began.

"This is the first phase review meeting for the corporate scouting mission to TP-055," said Harrison. "For the record I am Commander Harrison and I am in command of this mission. This meeting is being held on the Norman which is currently in position on the surface of TP-055. All attendees are now present as follows.."

As Harrison ran through the roll call, everyone automatically looked to the person being named who would listen and nod in turn, despite them all having lived and worked together for several years.

Harrison's steady, reassuring voice was almost hypnotic as he worked through the familiar ritual.

"Corporate Military Officer First Class Bradbury," said Harrison. "Here attending in his role as Chief Tactical Officer."

Bradbury was a squat, broad, older man with a ramrod straight back. His dark green overalls were immaculately clean and pressed, just like always.

His pale skin had been tanned to leather over the years but while wrinkles clustered about his dark and habitually narrowed eyes, his jaw remained firm, his frame immovable.

"Corporate Science Officer First Class Guin," said Harrison. "Here attending in her role as Chief Science Officer."

Guin had always thought of herself as resembling an untidy bundle of sticks, being thin and angular from head to toe.

She wore a perpetual expression of weary cynicism beneath a thick thatch of grey hair but her blue eyes were always sharp and watchful.

"Corporate Military Officer Second Class Chiang," said Harrison. "Here attending in his capacity as Medical Officer."

Chiang was young and relentlessly pleasant. His overalls were the same green as Bradbury's and his short cropped hair was dark.

His hooded eyes gave the impression of an easygoing temperament but beneath his apparently laid back exterior, Chiang was a serious and dedicated officer.

"And finally, Corporate Military Officer Second Class Butler," said Harrison, turning to the vidscreen embedded in the wall. "Dialling in from the Norma in orbit in her role as Technical Officer."

Butler was almost as young as Chiang and wore identical overalls. She had light brown skin set off against deep black hair and eyes.

Her hair was always tied up in the regulation style but was forever coming loose so that a halo of stray strands framed her face, lending her an impression being continually harassed.

"Ok," said Harrison, glancing at the datapad out of habit more than necessity. "We've been here just over a week now and have established ourselves on the planet. We're here today to discuss whether we're ready to move onto phase two and if so what that should look like so let's run this by the numbers. First off, tactical?"

"Sir," Bradbury began. "All green, sir. As far as we can tell there's no animal life on the planet that can pose any real threat to us. The most evolved lifeforms present, the so called 'Helpers'.."

He paused to almost imperceptibly raise an eyebrow at Guin who very perceptibly ignored it.

"..have a tiny population, appear entirely passive in their behaviour and have zero offensive or defensive technologies."

It had been the absent Clarke who had christened the aliens they had encountered on TP-055, much to the disdain and amusement of the military personnel.

"In terms of environmental concerns," Bradbury continued. "We had a pretty serious storm in the first week that wiped out all our equipment outside the ship but we've had nothing like it since so we're treating it as a one off. Basically, the planet's ours for the taking. Sir."

Guin felt herself frown at Bradbury's assessment of the storm. It was nothing more than a brief furrowing of her brow but Harrison picked up on it, seemingly without even looking.

"Guin?" he said. "Something to add?"

Guin straightened in her chair.

"Just that I don't think we have the data to conclude that the storm was a freak event," she said. "And that the data we do have, while not conclusive, suggests to me that we would be better to work on the assumption that there will be more at some point."

It was Bradbury's turn to frown but Guin continued to ignore him.

"Go on," said Harrison, adopting an expression of concerned interest.

"Well," said Guin. "About ten minutes before the storm hit, every single Helper stopped what they were doing, returned to The Mound and went inside."

"Who knows why they do anything?" Bradbury scoffed. "They're animals, they might have gone back inside for any number of reasons. We don't know for sure if they're even aware of what they're doing.

"We haven't seen a cloud in the sky since. If we're going to start making tactical decisions on the behaviour of a load of walking rugs then we might as well pack up and go home now."

"It's not such a leap," shrugged Guin to Harrison, refusing to engage with Bradbury directly. "There're plenty of animals at home that know when bad weather's coming.

"It seems logical to assume that in order for The Helpers to have evolved that behaviour, storms like that would need to have happened multiple times within their lifespan for many generations."

"Butler?" asked Harrison, turning to the screen.

"Sir," said Butler, nodding sharply. "I can't speak to the awareness or intent of the aliens sir, but I can confirm that what Guin says is accurate.

"According to my scans there wasn't a single Helper outside by the time the storm hit and I haven't seen them move in such a co-ordinated way before or since, sir."

"Ok," said Harrison. "So we're saying we think the storms are a regular thing but that for all we know they could be anything from monthly to once every few years?"

Guin thought about it for a second then nodded.

"Fine," said Harrison. "Bradbury, we'll still deploy but I want all external structures reinforced to withstand at least twice the power of that storm."

"Sir," said Bradbury, letting the matter drop now that the decision had been made.

"Ok, medical next," said Harrison. "Chiang?"

"Sir," said Chiang. "All green, sir. Obviously no-one should be eating or drinking anything off ship anyway but I haven't found any poisonous plants or venomous animals. Air's good, no radiation to speak of. Good to go, sir."

"Fine," said Harrison. "Ok Guin, science. Let's get into this shall we? First off, assets."

"Sure," said Guin, sitting forward to rest her arm on the table. "Shelley's just finishing off the last of the soil samples but they're a no go.

"It's never going to be good enough for agriculture so farming the planet is out. Ample timber globally though, plenty of clean water, a few promising plant

42

extracts."

"Mineral ore?" asked Harrison. "Fossil fuels?"

"Er.." said Guin, suddenly reluctant to proceed.

"Sir," Butler interjected. "The geological scans are still running, sir. Sorry sir."

"Don't be sorry Butler," said Harrison. "Be quicker."

"Sir, yes sir." said Butler, simultaneous nodding and hanging her head.

"What's the problem exactly?" asked Bradbury.

"Sir," said Butler. "There are some complex structures in the interior of the planet that are slowing down the algorithms sir. It's hard to tell at the moment but they could be multiple, intertwining veins of high grade ore sir."

"Timescale?" asked Bradbury.

"Sir," said Butler, cringing. "Probably another week at least, sir."

"Find a way to cut that down," said Bradbury. "Update me at shift end."

"Sir, yes sir," said Butler.

"And finally ownership then," said Harrison, looking down at the datapad. "Guin? I'm not seeing a completed anthropological assessment here."

"No," said Guin, raising her hand in acknowledgement. "Apologies, that's on me. It is on its way though, I assure you."

"Can't get the staff eh?" said Bradbury, giving her a knowing, spiteful grin.

Despite herself Guin scowled at him for a second before continuing.

"Ok so The Helpers are definitely top of the tree here," she went on. "Though their population distribution is downright weird to be honest. Orbital scans show just over a dozen mounds spaced more or less equidistant across the planet but there appear to be just small communities of less than a hundred around each mound with nothing in between."

"Conclusion?" asked Harrison.

"Eh.." Guin sighed, reluctant to offer a guess that she knew would most likely be taken as fact. "It's possible the population was much larger in the past, that at one time they did cover the planet but then some event or pathogen wiped most of them out.

"As I say, the mounds are pretty evenly spaced across the planet. If the Helpers constructed them, that could suggest higher intelligence in the planning. Equally, the mounds could just be convenient, naturally occurring geographic features that they've adapted so that's not definitive."

"So.." said Harrison, moving her along.

"Well," she said slowly. "We haven't see a mound up close yet and as ever, the more time we spend studying them the more accurate the assessment. Any judgement I give you now could be subject to change going forward pending further observations of their behaviour."

"Noted," said Harrison, not relenting.

Guin puffed out her cheeks and then sighed, inwardly cursing Clarke.

"Ok," she said, shaking her head and shrugging before counting off the points on her fingers.

"We have seen, no evidence of any sophisticated written or spoken language; no evidence of advanced culture or technology, beyond the possible construction of the mounds; no attempt on their part to communicate any specific, non-trivial information to us. Right now, if I had to, I'd put them around the level of perhaps chimpanzees?"

"So," said Harrison slowly and in a perfectly reasonable tone. "What we're saying is that despite our best efforts, we have found no evidence of any life on this planet that is sufficiently advanced or competent to claim ownership of it?"

Guin squirmed for a moment more before giving up.

"Yes," she said eventually.

"Alright then," said Harrison. "That's all the boxes ticked so in conclusion then, phase two is a go and we're stripping not planting. I'll call in the big guns. Bradbury I want a full camp with a secure perimeter deployed asap.

"Guin let's have your guys out there with your drones flagging the areas of surface resources for the extraction teams. For now we'll assume that by the time you're done with that we'll have the geological data ready for you to start marking out the mining operations. Ok, thanks everyone. Dismissed."

The video screen in the wall blinked off and everyone in the room stood to leave. Guin was the first to go, leaving the others behind as she wound her way quickly through the narrow, clanging corridors until she was alone near a comm panel.

"Shelley?" she said after stabbing at the panel with an angry finger, her voice hard.

"Yes," came the young woman's quavering voice. "I'm here."

"Is Clarke back?" she asked.

"Erm," said Shelley. "I haven't seen him but that doesn't mean he's not.."

But Guin wasn't listening. Instead she was storming away from the comm panel, cursing steadily under her breath.

Her feet carried her automatically down corridors and round corners, stamping her irritation each time she stepped through a bulkhead.

Eventually, she stepped out into the great cathedral space of the primary storage bay. The metal ceiling, formerly always pressing down within reach, now soared up and away from her.

Countless equipment containers stood silent in carefully stacked piles, ample space around each pile to allow the precisely temperature controlled air to flow about them.

The stacks marched off into the distance, chased by her suddenly echoing footsteps. Ahead of her, Guin noticed Corporate Military Officers Third Class Heinlein and Lem lounging on some enormous ammo boxes. They were both young and wearing military green overalls, but Heinlein was the older and larger of the two.

He was tall, long limbed and muscular with a pale, hard face and cold grey eyes. His hair was cropped to the point of grey shadow.

Where his skin was visible at the wrists and neck, the edges of various tattoos were visible, suggesting larger designs beneath.

Lem was a couple of inches shorter but equally powerfully built. His skin was darker than Heinlein's and accentuated by his pitch black hair and large, brown eyes.

When occupied with hard or dangerous work Lem was calm and focussed but the rest of the time wore a habitual expression of slight confusion and fear, especially around senior officers.

The pair were chatting while cleaning an array of firearms and equipment. When they saw her coming, Lem jumped to his feet, standing to attention. Heinlein stayed where he was however, eyeing Guin with a dirty grin of open contempt.

"Ma'am," said Lem stiffly as Guin approached.

"At ease Lem," said Guin absently as she paused in front of the pair. Lem relaxed a little but remained standing.

"Have either of you seen Clarke?" she asked.

"Ma'am, yes ma'am," said Lem, nodding earnestly. "Went out a several hours ago. Not been back since, ma'am."

Heinlein said nothing but continued to grin as if challenging her to reprimand him. She ignored him completely.

"Thanks," said Guin to Lem, pulling a face and heading toward the main hatch until he called after her.

"Ma'am, sorry ma'am," he said. "But if you're going outside, not that I'm presuming you are, but if you are, will you be requiring an escort? It's just, we're not really supposed to go out alone, ma'am. Commander's orders ma'am."

"No thank you Lem," said Guin, over her shoulder. "If there is anything dangerous out there right now, it's going to need an escort to protect it from me."

"Ma'am, yes ma'am," she heard Lem say as she stalked across the cavernous storage bay towards the outer hatch.

While she waited for the door to release its various bolts and eventually swing open, Guin seethed and thought about what she was going to say to Clarke. She cycled through a selection of devastating openers, scathing reprisals and stinging finales.

Finally, she stepped out onto the ramp that led down to the planet's surface. As she descended she blinked through the brutal, blue white light that was blazing down now that the third sun was in the ascendancy.

She moved quickly to the edge of the clearing, half of which was taken up by the ship, and into the knee high scrub to begin her descent of the steep hillside.

Her earlier reflections on the nature of the planet's flora were long forgotten now as she glared a squint at the too bright sky and cursed Clarke with every step.

As she pressed on further down the hill however, sweat beginning to lace her back beneath her suit, her fantasies of thunderous vengeance began to fade. Clarke had never been easy to manage and she knew she had to tread carefully if she wanted to him to comply.

If she pushed too hard in the wrong direction he would simply have an out and out tantrum and that would inevitably lead to the matter being taken out of her hands.

Once that happened she would no longer be able to protect him from their military colleagues and her standing on the senior staff would be seriously diminished.

As the hill flattened out towards the bottom, the scrub gave over to a thin forest of sickly, leafless trees. Picking her way through, Guin imagined Bradbury's triumphant face as Clarke was confined to quarters, any pull she had with Harrison by which to curb Bradbury's gung-ho urges gone forever.

She realised she was unconsciously following a trail of pushed back branches, flattened grass and snapped twigs. This must have been the way Clarke had come so there was nothing to do but keep going.

As she went, she continued to revise her intended approach with Clarke. Calmer was better. Constructive and rational would yield more positive results.

After all, for all she knew he might actually be hurt. Perhaps he had fully intended to return in time to submit his anthro assessment but had fallen badly.

Even now he could be laid out on the hard packed earth up ahead, unconscious, bleeding, dying even. The trail was just about to lead her out into a small, enclosed clearing in the heart of the forest.

It was vital that she keep an open mind, retain her

moral authority and above all maintain her dignity.

"Clarke, you fucking plum!" she yelled, suddenly outraged at the sight of her subordinate, but then immediately closing her eyes and cursing herself.

Corporate Science Officer Second Class Clarke was sitting on the ground in the middle of the clearing with one of the Helpers, laughing while apparently playing with it. He looked up at Guin's outburst but seemed unphased.

Clarke was only a few years Guin's junior but his pale blonde hair hid the grey and made him look younger. The hair itself hung almost to his shoulders in an unruly mop, framing a pair of round, spindly glasses which he was forever pushing back up his nose.

Just like Guin, he wore dark blue overalls but unlike Guin, Clarke had torn off the sleeves at the shoulder and the legs at the knee, leaving the edges ragged and frayed.

"Hey Guin," he called happily. "Come and see what I've taught her to do!"

The alien beside Clarke roughly resembled the shape of a crouching adult human, its doubled over posture meaning it rose only to about waist height.

The Helpers had huge, flat, three toed feet and their long legs were folded in a perpetual squat so that their backsides dragged on the ground.

Their backs then hunched forward, making great arcs of their spines. Their arms were usually folded in and clasped to their chest but when needed would slowly unfurl to a surprising length. Their leathery hands were also long, each sporting a thick, solid thumb and two long, broad fingers.

The Helpers' faces were elongated into blunt cones so that they had no nose to speak of but just a couple of nostrils above their upper lip. Their eyes were large and bright and exclusively dark brown with yellowed whites.

This anatomical picture had taken a while to complete however, as all The Helpers were completely covered, with the exceptions of their hands, faces and feet, in thick, shaggy fur.

The fur ranged from dark brown to pale yellow and was usually full of detritus picked up while pushing through the undergrowth.

They moved slowly, shambling about in an unhurried fashion and from a distance appeared as just a great mess of hair and twigs bumbling along.

Unlike most other alien species the crew of the Norma had encountered, the Helpers had mostly not reacted to the human's presence at all.

Most species demonstrated some kind of reaction, usually either terror, aggression or curiosity. The first Helpers the crew had encountered on TP-055 however, had paused to squint at them briefly but then slowly turned away and continued about their business, apparently unperturbed.

Technically, corporate law banned the naming of new species beyond basic scientific classifications. This was intended to avoid bestowing any form of personhood on the creatures that might form the basis of a legal claim to their planet's resources.

A small number of Helpers had shown greater curiosity than the rest however and these few had proved themselves surprisingly willing to engage with Guin's team and their various experiments.

This was why Clarke had called them Helpers, a name which despite Guin's best efforts, had quickly taken hold among the crew.

Guin closed the distance to Clarke quickly to stand over him, fizzing with rage. Clarke was apparently too busy scratching in the dirt to notice however which pushed her temper up another notch.

"Clarke!" she hissed, glancing at the sandy coloured Helper beside him.

"Watch this," he said without looking up. He was pointing to four criss crossing lines he had drawn in the dirt to form a large hash mark. He scratched a cross into the central space.

"I don't.." she began but then paused.

The Helper slowly extended its neck out and down to bring its face close to the grid on the ground. Then, after a moment, slowly unfurled one if its arms with unhurried ease and scratched a clumsy circle into the box immediately below Clarke's cross.

Guin stared at the scratches in the dirt for a

moment, the academic part of her brain racing ahead, before shaking herself and reminding herself of how angry she was.

"I don't care!" she continued. "Where's my anthro assessment?"

"Yeah, yeah," said Clarke, actually waving her words away and still not looking at her as he added another cross to the grid. "I'll get to it in a bit. Look though, she's doing it!"

"For corp's sake!" Clarke shouted, actually clenching her fists. "I had to go into a phase review without an anthro assessment! Do know how that made me look?!"

Slowly, The Helper turned from the game to eventually settle its gaze on Guin. As she watched, it unfurled its other, incredibly long arm, all the way up to rest its hand on her elbow. Its eyes wrinkled at her and it began to stroke her arm, slowly and gently.

Unsettled, Guin pulled away and The Helper's eyes widened again in an expression that she couldn't help but interpret as disappointment.

It watched her for another second before appearing to almost shrug and slowly turn its attention back to the scratches in the dirt.

"Guin," Clarke drawled, stretching out her name to match her patience. "Just chill out yeah? Come and join us, have a game with her. Isn't she amazing?"

Guin took a deep breath and steeled herself before starting again with a different, calmer approach.

"It hardly matters now if she is," she said quietly.

"What's that?" asked Clarke as he made his next move.

"The phase review's done Clarke," she continued. "Phase two is already underway. We're stripping."

"What?!" Clarke exploded. He scrambled to his feet, unwittingly wiping away most of the grid with the side of his foot as he went. The Helper made a small noise that sounded like a mix of surprise and sadness.

It slowly looked up at Clarke in confusion and then back down to what was left of the grid before leaning forward to examine the ground.

"What did you think was going to happen?" asked Guin.

"You can't!" cried Clarke. "They're intelligent!"

"Well perhaps if you'd submitted an anthro assessment that evidenced that fact the decision might have been different," reasoned Guin.

"But.." Clarke spluttered. "They'll be wiped out! The extraction teams will tear every natural resource out of this planet, all the plants, all the water until there's nothing left but a barren ball of rock! Even if the Helpers survive the extraction process they'll die of thirst in a matter of days! It'll be genocide!"

"I know what stripping entails Clarke," said Guin. "Why else are we here? We prepare the way, it's what we do. Slow or fast, the outcome's the same, the indigenous life is done for. You know this, I don't understand your surprise."

"But the ownership clause!" Clarke wailed. "Look at her and tell me she's not an intelligent being."

They both looked down at the Helper. While they had been talking it had painstakingly redrawn the grid and replaced the symbols that had been entered. It stared up at Clarke hopefully.

"Oh come on," said Guin, trying to look away from the grid. "Apes learned to use sign language centuries ago. It didn't make them people."

"But she understands!" snapped Clarke. "She gets it!"

"Are you seriously claiming to be able to communicate with these creatures?" asked Guin, folding her arms.

"Absolutely," said Clarke, pointing his chin at her defiantly.

Guin sighed and shook her head.

"Clarke," she said, holding her voice tightly. "Even if these creatures are intelligent.."

Clarke drew breath to speak but she pushed on and over him.

"..of which," she said. "I've yet to see any evidence, look at them, they're still in the stone age. Our life experiences are so different we have no common reference points with them. How can you possibly have established meaningful communication with them in so short a space of time?"

Clarke frowned, clearly trying to think of a quick response but Guin didn't give him the chance.

"They can't even begin to conceive of ideas which we take for granted and vice versa." she continued pressing her point. "It would take years, decades even, to develop sophisticated communication. Now you're standing here telling me that you've achieved that in just the short time we've been here?"

"Yes," said Clarke, eyes blazing. "I am. Like I said, she get's it."

"So they have gender then?" asked Guin, switching tack again.

"What?" said Clarke, suddenly wrongfooted.

"You keep calling it she," Guin reasoned. "I wasn't aware we'd determined that they had genders."

"Well.." Clarke blustered. "I mean.. I just.."

"And what about reproduction?" Guin continued, pressing her advantage. "To my knowledge we've never observed any young. Do they give birth to live young or lay eggs? Life cycle? Life span even?

"Face it Clarke, you know almost nothing about these creatures. You're a scientist for corp's sake! Hunches and feelings aren't good enough. Where's the data?"

"It'll come!" Clarke pleaded. "I just need more time, to gain their trust, to get inside The Mound, see what they're doing in there. But come on! You can tell just by looking at her!"

"You're making a fool of yourself," said Guin.

"What?" said Clarke again, offended this time.

"Those insectoids on NST-445," said Guin. "They constructed far more intricate structures than The Mound but you didn't give them a name."

"But.." Clarke tried but Guin pressed on.

"Or those gelatinous aquatics on NN-024," she said. "They clearly had complex social structures and interactions. Why not fight for them?"

"That's not.." Clarke tried again.

"Your judgement has been compromised by warm blood, soft fur and big eyes," concluded Guin. "You need to get your head straight and get back to work before Harrison throws you in the brig and you lose all your shares."

"Guin," said Clarke, composing himself to try and sound serious. "You don't understand. We can't do this."

"I told you," Guin said, unrelenting. "It's too late. If you really wanted to save them then the phase review was your chance but you chose to squander it.

"They've been classified as animals and animals can't own property, so we're taking it, all of it. You can either come back to the ship with me right now or wait until Bradbury sends someone down here to drag you back, up to you."

For several seconds Clarke just stared at her, so wild eyed that she was genuinely unsure if he was about to erupt in furious rage or collapse into hopeless tears. Instead he sagged, visibly deflating and looking to the ground.

"Fine," he said in smaller voice. "Just give me a second."

As Guin watched, Clarke returned to the Helper, squatting before it and talking quickly.

"I have to go," he said. "I'm sorry."

The Helper looked from Clarke's earnest face down to the game and back up again.

"I can't play now," Clarke explained. "But I'll come and find you again another time, we'll play again then. Thank you."

Clarke offered his hand to the Helper who stared at it confused. It extended its neck forward to inspect his hand, tilting its head back and forth to examine both sides before looking back up at Clarke.

"C'mon," said Clarke gently. "You remember this."

The Helper looked to Clarke's hand again then slowly extended its own, snaking its long digits across his palm to clasp hands with him. Clarke shook the Helper's hand firmly then let go and stood to follow Guin out of the clearing.

As they went Guin glanced back over her shoulder and saw the Helper staring at its own hand, turning it back and forth, apparently unsure as to what had just happened. They made their way back through the sickly forest in silence, Guin leading the way, Clarke sulking behind.

They hadn't gone far however, before Clarke couldn't hold back any longer.

"Is this what you thought your career as an exobiologist would be then?" he said bitterly. "Discovering new life just to help to wipe it out?"

Guin rolled her eyes but said nothing.

"No, seriously Guin," said Clarke, his tone ramping up to fully self righteous. "How do you sleep at night?"

"Oh piss off Clarke," she replied wearily. "No-one forced you to sign up and no-one's forcing you to take the money, which I notice you still happily accept despite your fervent conscience.

"I sleep just fine and you know why?" she continued before he had chance to reply. "Because I work my ass off all day long, as do the rest of the crew. You should try it some time. If you put as much effort into your job as you do into moaning about it, things might have turned out differently for the Helpers."

"Whatever," grumbled Clarke behind her, shaking his head and lapsing back into sullen silence for a while.

They emerged from the forest into the scrub and both had to shield their eyes from the blazing light of the larger sun.

One of the smaller two suns had begun to set and its gradual disappearance was beginning to drain the world of its reds, leaving everything tinged with a vaguely washed out hue of blue.

As they picked their way through the sharp little bushes, occasional flashes of movement at their feet betrayed the presence of the tiny terrified creatures they had disturbed. The land began to rise and they started the long climb back up the hill.

"I mean it though," said Clarke after a while, apparently incapable of letting the point slide. "How can you be ok with this?"

"Oh for corp's sake!" snapped Guin, stopping dead in her tracks and wheeling round to face him so that he almost stepped onto her toes.

"Do you honestly think I'm happy about this?" she said, her words coming in such a venomous rush that Clarke actually took a step backwards.

"I'd love to be able to study the life we encounter

properly," she said. "To explore and understand just for the sake of it, but that's not the world we live in, is it?"

Clarke drew breath as if to respond but Guin wasn't finished.

"You know as well as I do," she said, pointing an accusing finger at Clarke. "That academic research died out over a century ago. Corporate R&D is the only game in town. There's no-one else out here, it's this or nothing.

"Who, in this day and age, is going to pay for a ship and fuel and a crew and supplies and research equipment to come all the way out here just for the sake of knowledge? Who?!"

She could see Clarke desperately trying to think of a response but she still wasn't done.

"No-one!" she snapped at him. "That's who! This is the only colour this comes in, ok? At least we document these creatures before they disappear, at least we record the fact that they once existed.

"I know it's not much, but it is literally all we can do. Now if you're so very opposed to everything we do then why not just cash out? Why not just go back to Earth and live off your shares?"

Finally finished, Guin stared at Clarke, challenging him to respond now. He appeared angry for a moment before sliding into awkward resignation and just shaking his head.

"There you go then," said Guin with a nod before turning to resume her ascent.

Clarke said nothing more and soon they were both too focused on puffing their way up the steep incline to talk anyway. As they bested the hill the Norman loomed into view, gleaming painfully in the brutal sunlight.

Shielding her eyes with one hand, Guin spotted movement across the clearing. Heinlein and Lem were busy with flamethrowers, burning off the scrub to expand the cleared space, ready for the erection of the camp.

Guin and Clarke crossed a black expanse of charred but rapidly cooling ground towards the ship, still not talking.

As they approached, Lem remained absorbed by the

task at hand, his face fixed in concentration. Heinlein however, paused to watch the pair, looking Clarke and his ragged uniform up and down.

The soldier laughed to himself and shook his head before letting another huge plume of flame loose across the ground. Guin led Clarke back up the ramp and into the ship before turning to face him once more.

"I want that anthro assessment within the hour," she said firmly.

"Fine," shrugged Clarke before moving past her to disappear into the depths of the ship.

Guin stayed by the door for a moment, looking out over the rolling hills and thinking about the Helper she had seen down there beneath the trees, scratching circles in the dirt. Then, realising she was frowning, she shook herself and headed back to the lab.

There was still a lot to do.

The job of corporate scout ships such as the Norma, was to assess the commercial viability of distant planets previously untouched by humanity.

Assuming they could determine that no valid claim of ownership existed, they would then claim the planet on behalf of the company and determine how the most profit could be made.

The scout crews would then call in moon sized, industrial processing ships to do the heavy lifting. Depending on what the planet had to offer, they would summon either agri's or ex-fac's.

Agri's were equipped with everything required to quickly establish heavily industrialised farming across the entire planet.

They would harvest as many generations of plants and animals as possible, working relentlessly for months or even years until the planet could offer up nothing more.

Then, with their produce safely stored in their impossibly huge silos, they would move on to their next assignment or else, once the silos were filled, begin the long journey home, back to Earth.

Ex-fac's were called in when farming wasn't viable and worked much quicker. They would come in and strip a planet down to the bare rock in a matter of weeks if not days.

Everything of possible value was extracted, from water, plant and animal life on the surface to fossil fuels and mineral ore beneath.

Once loaded up with cargo, the country sized, automated factories within the ships would set about turning raw materials into saleable products as they went on their way.

Just like agri's, ex-fac's would travel on until they were full and then head home, their shiny new products ready for distribution and sale the moment they docked at Earth.

Scout crews were paid in shares of the total profits ultimately made from the planets they worked. This meant that whether they took two weeks or two years, the pay was the same.

For this reason, they would call in the processing ships the moment they had determined what was to be done with a planet.

They would then pull brutal shifts around the clock for as long as it took, hoping to have completed their work before the big ships even arrived.

The aim was to finish up and get underway towards the next virgin world on the list as fast as possible and so complete as many missions and make as much money as possible in each tour of duty.

They would eat while they worked and sleep in their clothes, snatching a few precious hours where and when they could.

Over the next five days, the crew of the Norma worked furiously. Within twenty-four hours Bradbury's team had scorched the whole hilltop black and bare and surrounded it with a tall, electrified fence.

They then set about erecting and equipping a series of low, boxlike buildings around the base of the Norman with incredible speed.

As more and more of their equipment was brought out of storage and set up, Guin's team set about their own work with equal vigour.

57

They had an entire fleet of several hundred high speed drones, each of which needed to be set up, calibrated and tested before use.

Once ready, Guin had to decide how many drones to assign to each of the five squadrons, Carto, Flag, Obs, Meto and Samp. She would then divide up the tasks of guiding and monitoring the squadrons among her team.

The largest squadron was the fully automated Carto which fanned out to fly low orbits around the entirety of TP-055, producing an incredibly detailed, spherical map of the planet's surface.

Guin assigned Flag to Shelley, whose job it was to use Carto's gradually emerging map to mark out specific areas of harvestable resource such as forests or bodies of fresh water.

Clarke was given Obs which visited specific localities marked by Flag as containing plant or animal life of possible value.

These drones captured footage of their subjects over the course of full day and night cycles. Their footage was then used to identify anything that might hinder harvesting as well as to identify any other potentially valuable resources the subjects might have to offer.

Finally, Guin took on Meto and Samp herself. Meto stayed in the higher atmosphere, providing real time weather reporting and warning of any more dangerous storms approaching their position.

Samp was deployed on demand to retrieve physical samples of targets identified by Obs and bring them back to base for further analysis.

Continually keeping track of the position and status of all the drones and adjusting their deployment to maximise efficiency was complex, repetitive and relentless work.

Guin had been doing the job long enough however, that she was able to fall into a familiar groove of total focus, tweaking formations and numbers on gut instinct and keeping fatigue at arms length.

The buildings of the compound were actually just individual ship building modules, taken from tight packed storage by crane and set onto great, heavy base plates across the blackened clearing.

Equally windowless and just as cramped, being inside the modules felt exactly like being on the ship the only difference being that the rooms were separated by open air and scorched earth instead of carbon copy corridors.

Subsequently it was easy to forget that they were actually physically present on the planet displayed on the vidscreens.

While they were in there, the outside world of TP-055 gradually became a distant and abstract thing, despite existing just on the other side of the relatively thin metal wall.

Guin and her team spent the majority of every day crushed together within the gloom of the drone command centre, bathed in the low light of the vidscreens.

Occasionally a drone would return with a sample and they would take it in turns to step outside to meet it before taking the sample to the specimen lab.

Standing alone in the sterile environment of the lab, under the harsh artificial lighting and picking apart whatever the drone had brought back became a perk to be rationed between them.

Even more exciting was when a drone failed and one of them would get to go to the drone store to set up and release a replacement. This was a particularly special treat as of all the tasks, this involved spending the most time outside.

It was easy to lose track of time within the buildings which meant Guin also had to keep track of how long each of them had been working and enforce appropriate rest breaks.

There were always at least two of them on station at any given time and she would usually allow Clarke and Shelley about four hours of sleep per cycle while she took just one or two.

She had sent Clarke back to the ship to get some sleep about half an hour earlier when she felt the need to stretch her legs.

Standing from her stool, Guin sipped at the last of her koffy but found it cold, making it completely rather than just mostly undrinkable.

She abandoned her ration cup and pushed her hands into her lower back, rolling her neck and groaning at the stiffness she found there.

She opened her eyes as wide as they would go and blinked a few times, trying to will just a little more energy into herself.

Finally, she moved to the other end of the dark little room to approach Shelley who was hunched over her console, lost in concentration. Guin landed a hand on Shelley's shoulder causing the younger woman to start violently.

"Hey Shelley," said Guin sleepily. "Sorry, how're you getting on? You ok?"

"Sorry," said Shelley instinctively before smiling weakly. "I was just concentrating. Yeah, I'm ok thanks. Everything's going fine here, I'm getting through it."

"That's good," said Guin. "I think we're through the worst of it now, two or three more days and we'll be done. You're doing really well Shelley, I'm proud of you. When Clarke comes back you get off and get your head down ok?"

"Sure thing," said Shelley, nodding.

Guin smiled and turned to return to her station but caught sight of Shelley's vidscreen as she went and did a double take.

"What's that you're looking at?" she asked, narrowing her eyes to peer more closely at the image on vidscreen.

"Oh nothing really," said Shelley hurriedly. "I'm just waiting for Flag to reach a lake on the Southern continent so thought I'd check something in the meantime."

Guin leaned in and quickly scanned the strings of digits rolling across the bottom of the vidscreen.

"But that's an Obs feed," she said, confused. "Why are you looking at Clarke's drones?"

"No reason," said Shelley brightly but then immediately betrayed herself by visibly swallowing.

Guin frowned and leaned past Shelley to clatter her fingers over the controls. A small map appeared in the bottom right hand corner of the vidscreen showing the global position of the drone.

"He swept that area yesterday," said Guin. "Why have you taken one of his drones back over covered ground Shelley?"

"Erm," said Shelley, squirming in her chair. "I.. er.. I just thought these plants here looked quite interesting."

Guin returned her attention to the screen and saw immediately what Shelley was referring to.

Among the various shades of yellowing green on the screen were nestled a batch of plants with violently red leaves, quite unlike anything they had seen on TP-055 so far.

"Ok," she said slowly, shaking her head in irritation at the thick fog of fatigue that had settled around her. "But if you wanted to look at it, why not just review Clarke's footage from yesterday? We don't have time to divert drones away from their scheduled paths Shelley, you know that, there's no reason to..."

Guin sighed as cool realisation flowed through her.

"Right," she growled.

She crossed the tight little space back to her own station and violently stabbed at the controls. Almost without her needing to think about it, her fingers deployed a Samp drone to the site of the red plants before she stormed to the door and wrenched it open.

Before actually stepping outside, she paused at the threshold and turned back.

"Shelley?" she said, trying to keep the edge out of her voice.

"Yes?" said Shelley, looking up from her station wide eyed and worried.

"I expect you to complete the work I assign to you," said Guin seriously.

"Of course," said Shelley, nodding.

"And only the work I assign to you," Guin added.

Shelley didn't respond but flushed red and bowed her head instead.

Guin stepped outside to find the sky half dark with only one of the smaller suns in the sky. Suddenly energised with fury, she walked quickly across the compound and entered the ship.

A rapid search of the sleeping quarters and mess hall confirmed Clarke's absence so that just a few minutes later she was stomping back down the ramp and back across the compound, this time towards the newly erected gate.

The route down the hill, through the scrub and into the forest was far more treacherous in the twilight but Guin was too angry to worry about falling. She moved quickly and with determination, breaking off brittle twigs as she pushed through the skinny trees.

Sure enough, upon reaching the familiar clearing she found Clarke, sitting in the dirt bathed a pale electronic glow, this time with two Helpers.

One was light coloured and appeared to be the same she had seen him with before, though it was hard to tell through the gloom. The other Helper's fur was much darker, probably a rich brown colour even though here it looked black.

"Clarke!" she snapped, standing at the entrance to the clearing with her hands on her hips.

On looking up and seeing her, Clarke's eyes and mouth formed three shocked circles. He slow motion scrambled to his feet, trying to move quickly enough to appease Guin but not so fast as to disturb the Helpers.

He hurried over to her and she noticed he had a datapad in his hand which he had been using for illumination.

"What the hell Clarke?" snapped Guin.

"I know, I know," he said, nodding. "I thought it'd be ok seeing as I'm off shift."

"Well it's not," said Guin.

"I'm sorry," said Clarke. He sounded so genuine that Guin felt her anger cool just a little.

"For what?" she asked, trying to maintain her fury from before. "For missing an obvious, novel plant type? Or for your third having to check your work and cover for you?"

"What?" said Clarke, frowning his confusion.

"I've just found Shelley redeploying Obs to cover a plant you missed yesterday," said Guin hotly. "She's obviously been monitoring your work on top of her own and covering for you. You're the second Clarke, she's the third, that isn't fair on her and it's not good enough."

"You're right," said Clarke, dragging his hand over the pale shape of his face which Guin noticed for the first time was lined with fatigue. "I'm really sorry Guin. I didn't know she was doing that. I'll apologise to her and make sure it doesn't happen again."

Clarke's humility was so unexpected that it left Guin briefly speechless.

"See that you do," she said eventually, her frown shifting from anger to concern. "What's going on with you Clarke? It's not like you to miss something like that."

"I know, I know," said Clarke, nodding some more. "I'm just tired."

"We're all tired," said Guin, looking past him to the Helpers beyond. "What are you doing down here anyway? I thought we'd had this conversation."

"No I know," said Clarke wearily. "And you were right, about all of it, it just breaks my heart you know? I was thinking about what you said and I just thought someone should try and document as much of their behaviour as possible, before it's too late. At least that way something of them will survive."

Guin frowned her disapproval but felt herself softening.

"Ok," she said. "I get that, but how much of your off time are you spending down here?"

Clarke grimaced but didn't say anything.

"All of it?" asked Guin.

Clarke bit his lip for a moment but then nodded in defeat.

"Hang on," said Guin, shaking her head. "How much sleep have you had since we started running the drones?"

"Erm," said Clarke, pretending to think about it for a second before giving up. "None."

"Bullshit," said Guin. "You've been up and working non-stop for five days straight?"

Clarke just nodded.

"How?" asked Guin.

Clarke didn't answer but retrieved a small plastic cylinder from his pocket and handed it to Guin. Guin held the cylinder up in front of her face to squint at it through the gloom. It was a medical hypo loaded with stimulant.

"Did Chiang prescribe this?" she asked, looking back at Clarke.

Clarke shook his head and looked at the ground.

"Corping hell Clarke!" hissed Guin. "Do you know how many regs you're breaking just by having this on board? Not to mention the risk to your own health and the quality of your work! I know the koffy's terrible but corp!"

"I know," said Clarke. "I thought I could handle it. I thought if it was only for a week or so, I could just power through. I didn't want to let you down but I wanted to spend as much time as I could with these guys too."

Guin pocketed the hypo and folded her arms then scowled thoughtfully at Clarke for several seconds.

"Alright," she said eventually. "This is the deal. For every four hours you're off you can spend a maximum of two hours here on condition that you get a minimum of two hours sleep. Otherwise I'll have Bradbury lock down the compound and post an armed escort on you round the clock. Deal?"

"What?" Clarke gasped. "I mean, yes! Deal! Thank you!"

"And I want to see all your findings," said Guin. "In fact you can start right now. Tell me about these two. What are you doing here?"

"Right," said Clarke, suddenly energised. "Yes, ok."

He turned away from Guin and led her back towards the two Helpers, glancing at the datapad in his hand as he went.

"So this is Blondie," said Clarke, gesturing to the Helper with lighter coloured fur. "And this is Bruno. Guys, this is Guin."

At the sound of his voice the Helpers both looked up and Guin thought she saw a flash of recognition in the eyes of the one Clarke had called Blondie.

"So initially I tried introducing them to the concept of written language but they just don't get it," said Clarke excitedly. "They can't make the leap to abstraction because for them everything is in the moment, they communicate through action."

"How so?" asked Guin.

"Damage that tree," said Clarke.

"What?" said Guin.

"That tree beside you," said Clarke, pointing. "Start tearing the bark off it."

Guin frowned but did as Clarke suggested, pinching out a small piece of the soft bark between the finger and thumb of her right hand and pulling on it.

Almost immediately the Helper Clarke had called Bruno began to slowly get up. After a few seconds it shambled over to Guin and reached up to gently place a soft hand on her left arm.

She looked down into the Helper's eyes and saw what she couldn't deny looked like concern. The Helper made a small sound that felt to Guin like sadness but didn't actually try to physically stop her.

"Keep going," said Clarke and Guin did so.

After a few seconds more, the Helper Clarke had called Blondie moved slowly to Guin's other side and stared up at her making a similar noise to the other one.

"A little bit more," said Clarke, almost gleeful. By now Guin had torn a strip several inches long from the tree and now started on another. The Helpers began to shuffle themselves into the space between Guin and the tree.

They still didn't touch her right arm or push her away but just put themselves in the way, making it more difficult for her to reach, all the while making the low, rumbling sound of sadness. The proximity to the aliens and the thin, red half-light made the whole scene feel unreal and almost dreamlike.

"Ok," said Clarke. "Stop."

Guin stepped away from the tree and the Helpers both fell silent. After watching her for a few seconds they seemed to lose interest and slowly turned away, returning to their places in the middle of the clearing.

"They definitely have things that they care about," Clarke was explaining as Guin watched the pair settle back down. "But they don't seem to have any concept of compulsion. I've seen it between them too."

Clarke and Guin stood together, watching as the

Helpers began to groom one another.

"For the most part they're incredibly relaxed," Clarke continued. "Usually they actually don't seem to take a lot of interest in what anyone else is doing. When they see something they think is dangerous or harmful though, then they always start by approaching and making that kind of 'you-doing-this-makes-me-sad' type display."

"And when that doesn't work?" asked Guin.

"Well in most cases that does actually seem to be enough for the other Helpers to stop the behaviour. When it's not though, then they'll try and make the behaviour they don't like more difficult, like they did with you, but they still won't actually physically impose themselves on another."

"Interesting," said Guin, nodding thoughtfully.

"I've never seen any evidence of physical injuries on any of them, fresh or healed," Clarke continued. "Nor any hint of aggression from them, I just don't think they have it in them."

"I mean," said Guin, thinking aloud. "At first glance that seems insane right? No competition, no predation, being entirely defenceless and yet..."

"They're here," Clarke finished the sentence. "On this planet, in this environment, it works for them. They don't need aggression or violence here. I've never seen or even read about anything like them."

For a moment Guin and Clarke watched the Helpers as they happily groomed one another, utterly oblivious to their coming extinction. An unspoken sadness passed between the two scientists until Guin shook herself.

"Alright Clarke," she said. "I want you back on the ship and asleep within the hour and then back on station two hours after that so that Shelley can get her head down. Agreed?"

"Absolutely," said Clarke, grinning.

Guin took one last look at the passive, slow moving creatures then turned to head back to the ship. As she went she called over her shoulder.

"Don't make me regret this," she said.

Two days later and Guin was fast asleep when a general alert sounded throughout the ship, tearing her awake and upright in a heartbeat.

She had only managed perhaps twenty minutes of sleep but the sheer violence of siren drove her out of her bunk and into the corridor in seconds. As she stumbled towards the mess she encountered Harrison coming the other way.

"What is it?" she asked him, still blinking and steadying herself against the cold metal of the wall.

"Shots fired outside," he said seriously. "Within the perimeter."

"Who's out there?" asked Guin, trying to force her brain into action.

"Heinlein and Clarke," said Harrison.

"Corp," cursed Guin grimly, suddenly fully awake and cold to the bone.

"Yep," said Harrison, nodding grimly.

By the time they hurried out through the open hatch and down the ramp, the rest of the crew were already outside.

The great blue sun hung alone in the sky, blazing furiously so that everything below appeared stained through or overlaid with a pale and sickly green.

Bradbury was barking orders at Lem and Chiang at the base of the ramp while Heinlein stood with his back to them, obscuring something crumpled on the floor before him.

Shelley was standing off to one side looking frightened but quickly moved to Guin's side when she saw her emerge from the ship.

"You ok?" asked Guin.

Shelley just nodded, still wide eyed.

"Where's Clarke?" asked Guin, controlling her voice.

Shelley nodded again, this time towards Heinlein's back so that Guin felt a knot clench in her stomach.

Without waiting for Harrison, who was listening to Bradbury's report, she approached the soldier, licking her lips to fend off the sudden dryness in her mouth.

As she moved around Heinlein she cringed but then felt relief wash over her. Clarke was on the ground, kneeling over the body of a Helper and sobbing while Heinlein watched and smirked.

A broad pool of dark liquid was spreading out from under the Helper's body. The substance looked black tinged with a dark green but then everything was tinged with green at this time of day.

Just for a moment, that same cold part of Guin's mind set off wondering what colour the substance would be under full, white light and what that might suggest about its chemical make up.

The Helper itself was making a horrible, wet moaning sound however and the sheer, unadorned pain it carried drew Guin back fully into the present.

From the colouring of the Helper's fur Guin recognised it as Blondie. She glanced at Heinlein before approaching Clarke and leaning in to put her hand on his shoulder.

"Clarke," she said softly. "Come on."

Clarke turned to look up at her, eyes red, face dripping with tears and snot.

"He's fucking killed her!" Clarke screamed at Guin before turning to Heinlein. "Fucking murderer!"

Heinlein let out a single, harsh laugh but otherwise remained entirely unmoved, holding his rifle across his chest and watching impassively. Guin continued to try and coax Clarke to his feet as the rest of the crew arrived and gathered round.

"Report," barked Bradbury.

Heinlein stood to attention, staring straight ahead into the middle distance as he spoke.

"Sir," he said. "One of the aliens broke through the perimeter and ignored all instructions to halt, sir. I fired a warning shot over its head but it continued to approach so I put it down with a round to the chest, sir."

"Ok soldier," said Bradbury, nodding. "Good man, stand down."

"Good man?!" roared Clarke, leaping to his feet and rounding on the assembled crew. "You're all as bad as him! Fucking murders! Fucking scum!"

"Clarke.." Guin tried but he couldn't stop.

"Every planet we find is full of life," he ranted. "Yet none of it counts as intelligent enough to be allowed to survive. Don't you think that's a bit of a fucking coincidence?

"Endless life across the entire galaxy and we're the only ones who count as intelligent? We're genocidal fucking pirates, every one of us!"

"Just who do you think you're talking to Science Officer Second Class?!" seethed Bradbury, stepping in front of Harrison to shield his commander from the tirade.

"He's just upset, ok?" said Guin, raising her palm to Bradbury then turning back to Clarke.

"Come on Clarke," she said. "You know that's spurious logic. Think about it, the entire corporate fleet has only reached a tiny fraction of the viable planets out there. It's hardly a representative sample is it? Just try to calm down, ok?"

Suddenly, Blondie let out a plaintive cry, thick with agony and fear. Clarke turned to look down at her and sobbed again.

"Chiang!" he pleaded through the sobs. "Help her! For corp's sake, help her!"

"You stay right where you are soldier," Bradbury growled at Chiang.

The young medic looked pained but instinctively obeyed the order.

"Chiang!" cried Clarke. "Please!"

"I wouldn't even know where to start Clarke," said Chiang, cringing.

"This isn't right," wailed Clarke, looking around the group. "You all know this isn't right."

"Thought you were supposed to be a scientist," said Heinlein, clearly goading Clarke. "It's just natural selection. The stronger species displaces the weak. They adapt or they die. Nature's a bitch."

Heinlein grinned viciously at Clarke who fell silent for a moment but then lunged at the soldier with a broken roar.

Heinlein smiled and stood his ground, welcoming the attack but Guin moved faster, planting her palm in the middle of Clarke's chest and walking him backwards.

"I'll kill him!" Clarke raged. "I'll fucking kill him!"

"He'd break you in half and you know it," said Guin

quietly, setting her feet to hold Clarke in place.

"Alright," said Harrison, stepping forward to take control. "Enough. Chiang, escort Clarke to the med bay and sedate him. If he resists, escort him to the brig instead and sedate him there. Bradbury, I want the perimeter secured asap. Have Lem check the breach while you and Heinlein check the rest."

"Sir," said Bradbury.

As Chiang approached, Clarke turned to Guin desperately.

"She didn't break the fence," he gasped.

"What do you mean?" asked Guin.

"Just check it!" he said as Chiang gripped his arm above the elbow, gentle but firm.

"Shelley," said Guin. "Go with Lem and inspect the breach. I want to know exactly how it got in."

Lem looked to Harrison and Guin followed his gaze. The commander nodded his approval then approached Guin while Lem and Shelley headed off towards the fence.

"I've given you a lot of leeway with him in the past Guin," he said in lowered tones. "But this won't stand. Look at his uniform for corp's sake, by rights I should strip him of his shares and put him in the brig for that alone."

"I know," agreed Guin. "You're right, this is completely unacceptable. I take full responsibility for his actions."

"I've always rated you Guin," said Harrison after a moment. "You're a brilliant scientist and a damn good officer. Don't let someone like that drag you down with him."

Guin just nodded.

"That any use to you?" said Harrison.

"I guess," said Guin, looking down at Blondie's corpse and running her fingers through her hair. "It'd be interesting to do an autopsy on one, might find something useful we can harvest from them."

"Fine," said Harrison. "But once you're done with it, have Heinlein and Lem flame it. I'll not have Clarke conducting some twisted funeral for the thing."

"Understood," said Guin.

Harrison turned and walked back to the ship, leaving Guin to stand over Blondie and think. She was vaguely aware of Bradbury and Heinlein calling to one another as they checked the fence while she planned out how best to transport and dissect the creature.

The strange green light pouring down from above seemed to obscure some details but highlight others, giving the whole scene a dreamlike sense of underwater unreality. Guin swayed slightly as she rubbed at her eyes, trying to anchor herself and get a grip on the present.

Suddenly, Shelley and Lem were at her side. Lem appeared flustered while the young scientist managed to look excited, frightened and confused all at the same time.

"Shelley?" said Guin.

"I think Clarke might have been onto something after all," she said breathlessly.

"What?" asked Guin.

"The fence," said Shelley. "It's not broken, I mean it was, but now it's not."

Guin pinched the bridge of her nose and took a breath.

"I'm very tired Shelley," sighed Guin. "You're going to need to make a lot more sense than that."

"We can see where the Helper got through," Shelley babbled, her words tumbling over one another. "But the fence is still intact. Best I can tell, the Helper rerouted the current, dismantled part of the fence, came through and then reconstructed the fence behind it."

Guin frowned as her mind raced off, thinking about exactly how the fence worked and how she would go about performing the task Shelley was describing without tools or equipment.

She couldn't work out how to do it.

"But that's not.." said Guin after a second.

"I know!" exclaimed Shelley.

"Report!" barked Bradbury who had appeared behind Guin with Heinlein in tow.

"Sir," said Lem, standing to attention. "The breach in the fence is secure sir."

"Good," said Bradbury, nodding.

"Sir," said Lem again. "No, sir. I'm not sure it is sir."

"Explain," barked Bradbury.

"It appears we may have underestimated the indigenous population after all," said Guin before Lem had chance to respond.

"Not you too," said Bradbury in disgust.

Guin turned to face Bradbury full on, fixing him with a serious expression.

"That creature," she said, pointing to the body on the floor. "Didn't just break through your fence. It dismantled it, walked through, then rebuilt it."

"Bullshit," said Bradbury. "How and why would it do that?"

"How? I have no idea," said Guin, thinking as she spoke. "Why? Well for starters, I don't think they have any concept of what a fence is. It won't have understood that the fence was intended to keep it out, it will have just seen it as an unusual obstacle.

"It also seems to be important to them not to destroy our things however, not without good reason anyway, so once it was through, it repaired it for us."

"Ridiculous," sneered Bradbury. "Heinlein and I have just inspected the entire perimeter, this compound is one hundred percent secure."

"You might want to tell him that," said Shelley, pointing back the way Bradbury had just come.

The rest of the group turned as one to see a dark coloured Helper shambling towards them. Guin recognised it as the one Clarke had called Bruno.

"Stay where you are!" screamed Heinlein, stepping in front of Bradbury and raising his rifle to take aim at Bruno. Lem rushed to Heinlein's side and mirrored his pose.

"Wait!" Guin shouted to Heinlein before turning her attention back to Bradbury. "Stand your men down, it's not a threat."

"If you do no halt," Heinlein was screaming. "We will respond with lethal force!"

Heinlein fired once into the air over Bruno's head. The Helper paused and appeared confused, looking up and around it as if trying to work out where the sound had come from before resuming his slow approach.

"Bradbury!" Guin shouted. "For corps sake!"

Bradbury maintained stony silence and drew his own sidearm.

Cursing under her breath, Guin rushed forward to stand between the soldiers and Bruno. She put her back to the Helper and faced the guns with her hands raised.

"Listen to me!" she shouted. "Stand down! We don't know what's happening here. We need to calm down and think about this."

"Get out of the way Guin," shouted Bradbury. "This is a security matter, you've no authority here."

"Just stop, ok?" Guin shouted back, glancing over her shoulder to see Bruno still gradually closing the distance. "Clarke might have been right.

"Who cares?" shouted Heinlein. "Bullet, extraction, starvation. They're all dead anyway."

"Bradbury!" Guin shouted again. "We have to review the ownership clause. If it turns out the Helpers qualify then what you're doing could count as murder if not an act of war."

"It's too late for that," shouted Bradbury. "The extraction teams are inbound. If the ownership clause is invoked now, all our shares in TP-055 become worthless. All the work we've done here will count for nothing."

"Fuck that," said Heinlein.

"What the hell is going on here?!" barked Harrison, hurrying towards the group with Chiang at his side. Seeing Heinlein and Lem, the young medic raised his own rifle to point at Bruno.

"Harrison!" Guin warned. "The Helper's aren't what we thought. I think Clarke might have been right."

"Sir," barked Bradbury. "The alien has breached the perimeter and presents a clear and present danger to the crew."

"They've never demonstrated any intention of threatening us," countered Guin. "Let alone the ability. We can't kill any more of them until we're sure."

The stand off continued in almost total silence for second after second, the only sound the soft shambling footsteps of the Helper approaching Guin from behind.

"Bradbury," said Harrison then, his voice solid but calm. "Stand your men down."

"But sir!" Bradbury exclaimed.

"Corp damn it Bradbury I gave you an order!" snapped Harrison.

"Sir, yes sir," said Bradbury, grimacing. "Heinlein, Lem, Chiang, stand down."

The soldiers lowered their guns and Guin turned to face Bruno before moving out of his path. As he ambled past, he slowly turned to look up at her and seemed to smile as he went. Then, a few slow steps further on, he stopped as he caught sight of Blondie's body.

Bruno extended his neck forward and narrowed his eyes before started to shuffle as quickly as he could towards the body. At Guin's waved insistence, the crew backed away, giving Bruno space to approach.

Bruno approached Blondie and initially appeared confused. He stroked her body lovingly then, when nothing happened, began to shake her gently. A small, high pitched whimper slipped from his long mouth as he noticed the pool of blood for the first time.

For several seconds Bruno examined the hole in Blondie's chest and looked back and forth between the body and the humans. He appeared completely baffled until suddenly his eyes widened as comprehension finally arrived.

Bruno looked at each of the humans in turn in complete disbelief before closing his eyes and becoming very still.

The air seemed to thicken within the compound and the soldiers shifted uncomfortably, desperate to raise their weapons but restrained by their orders.

Then, as they watched, Bruno began to stand.

Slowly and in phases, he extended his entire body upwards, his long, ever bent legs now straightening. He tilted back his long head and allowed his arms to fall straight at his sides, palms forwards.

In this pose the arms suddenly made sense and appeared in proportion to the rest of the body. Up and up Bruno stretched until suddenly he was a single, slender upright form, standing almost nine feet tall.

At first it appeared as if nothing was happening but then, just on the lower edge of their hearing, the crew began to make out a low rumble. Bruno was breathing deeply, his great barrel chest swelling out and collapsing back in.

The noise grew and grew, moving quickly through the audible towards the unbearable. A great low sound of perfect anguish boomed from Bruno and seemed to fill the sky. Guin could feel the sound in her legs as the vibrations rattled through the ground beneath her.

The sound was becoming painful and Guin closed her eyes and clapped her hands over her ears. Then, suddenly, another sound came. Guin heard a small, dull pop beneath the great roaring that brought with it sudden and total silence.

Guin opened her eyes again just in time to see Bruno fall backwards, stiff and straight like a felled tree. He hit the ground with a shuddering impact. Blinking her confusion, she turned to see Heinlein lowering his rifle.

She opened her mouth to speak but no words came and so she just stood there, jaw hanging, staring at Heinlein.

For several seconds more, the crew simply stood and stared, even Harrison appeared momentarily bewildered. Then the radio on Bradbury's belt crackled into spluttering life.

"Sir?" came Butler's crackling voice. "Sir!"

"Go ahead Butler," said Bradbury retrieving the radio with an unsteady hand.

"Sir," said Butler. "What's going on down there? Sir."

"There's been an encounter in the compound," said Bradbury. "It's over now. We're all secure."

"Sir," came Butler's voice again. "That's a negative sir. I'm seeing movement near your position, a lot of movement. Recommend all personnel fall back to the Norman and secure the hatches immediately sir."

Bradbury blinked as if trying to shake off the echoes of the impossible sound but didn't respond. Finally Harrison intervened.

"You heard her," he said, loud and firm. "Back inside, on the double. Now! Go!"

The crew sprinted across the compound and up the ramp, into the safety of the ship. As the door took painful seconds to close Guin lingered at the threshold, peering back outside.

Just before the thinning slice of daylight disappeared completely, she caught sight of two more Helpers shuffling into the compound.

Guin made her way quickly across the storage bay and through the ship to the mess, where the rest of the crew had gathered.

Someone had brought up the feed from one of the external cameras on the vidscreen and everyone was watching in silence.

The image showed the space between the buildings where the Helpers' bodies lay. Around them in a loose ring were perhaps half a dozen more Helpers, all in the bizarre, stretched up stance they had seen Bruno adopt.

There was no sound with the image but it seemed obvious that the Helpers were making the same noise the crew had heard moments before.

"Bradbury," said Harrison. "Is the ship secure?"

"Sir, yes sir," said Bradbury. "All hatches closed and sealed. They can't get in here, sir."

"Like they couldn't get through the fence?" asked Guin bitterly.

Bradbury shot her a look of pure venom but said nothing.

"Chiang," said Harrison. "Go and monitor Clarke. I want him under for the duration. The last thing we need is him running around agitating in the middle of all this."

"Sir, yes sir," said Chiang, leaping to his feet and then hurrying from the room.

As they watched the screen, more and more Helpers were arriving all the time, forming a growing number of concentric circles around the first few and adopting the same, stretched up pose.

"Butler?" said Harrison.

In the bottom right corner of the vidscreen a smaller window appeared containing Butler's flustered face.

"Sir," she said. "Here sir."

"Don't keep us in suspense Butler," said Harrison. "What are you seeing up there?"

"Sir, I.." Butler stalled and frowned as she looked left and right at various screens off camera.

"Butler," said Harrison, hardening his tone.

"Sir, sorry sir," she responded, looking back into the camera. "I'm just struggling to make sense of these readings sir."

"Butler," said Harrison, trying a different approach. "Take a breath and tell me what you're seeing."

"Sir, yes sir," said Butler, pausing to visibly inhale and exhale.

"Sir," she said then, suddenly composed. "I am reading tens of thousands of Helpers approaching your position, sir."

"Tens of thousands?!" Harrison asked. "How is that possible? I though we had the global population at a few hundred?"

"Sir, that's right, we did sir," said Butler. "But that's not what I'm seeing now. They're pouring out of The Mound and heading your way, but that's not all, sir."

Suddenly and almost as one, the crew turned their attention away from the screen to look around the room and then at one another.

At first they could all feel rather than hear the sound but as the seconds ticked by the low hum started to become audible.

"How can we hear it in here?" cried Lem. "All the hatches are sealed!"

"It's the vibrations," said Guin. "Through the ground and then through the hull and it's only going to get worse."

On the screen the entire compound was now full of Helpers, all standing and calling.

"Go on Butler," said Harrison, stony faced.

"Sir, as far as I can tell," Butler went on, holding her voice steady with visible effort. "Every other Helper on the planet has now entered their local mound and disappeared from my sensors sir."

Harrison nodded and seemed to think for a moment.

"Guin?" he said eventually.

"I don't know," she said, shaking her head.

"Not good enough," said Harrison.

"Alright, alright," said Guin, staring at nothing as she pushed through the fog of fatigue to think desperately.

"Ok, what. What are they doing?" she asked herself out loud. "Some kind of communal defence mechanism. I don't think the sound can be intended to be offensive in of itself. It obviously doesn't hurt them and there's no way they could know it's unbearable for us.

"I think it's literally just a distress call. The louder it is, the further it can be heard and so the more of them come and join in so that it gets even louder and so on."

Everyone stared at her as she continued to think it through.

"Why. Why are they doing it?" she continued. "That second Helper seemed very confused on finding the dead one so maybe violent death is rare for them.

"Also, such an extreme response wouldn't be practical if it happened all the time which further supports that. They could be massing for an attack but everything we've seen says that violence just isn't in their nature.

"I think the gathering itself is the point. It's as if by harming one of them we've harmed all of them and so they're responding as one."

"And," said Harrison, pushing her along.

"How," she said then. "How are they doing it? Where are they all coming from? Where have the rest of them been all this time and if they're co-ordinating globally then how are they doing that?"

Guin fell into silence, the concentration almost painful on her face.

"Keep thinking Guin," said Harrison. "In the meantime, Bradbury, armaments. How are we stocked?"

"Sir," said Bradbury. "Pretty solid sir. The sides of the hill to the North, South and West are all too steep for them to climb so no matter how many of them there are, they'll be funnelled towards the East side of the ship.

"With Heinlein, Lem and myself firing from the roof I doubt even one could reach us sir. Heinlein, roughly how many rounds do we have in storage?"

"Sir," said Heinlein. "More than enough, several million rounds sir."

Bradbury nodded and turned back to Harrison.

"Sir," he said. "It would take a while, but if necessary we could cut them all down eventually, sir."

Harrison was nodding grimly when Guin suddenly clicked her fingers and gasped.

"Butler!" she cried.

"Ma'am?" replied Butler.

"Are the geological scans done?" asked Guin.

The geological scans had been an ongoing source of frustration as the interior structure of the planet had turned out to be even more complex than first thought.

"Ma'am!" gasped Butler. "Yes ma'am! They should be, finally! Just give me a second to.. oh my god!"

Butler visibly paled on the screen as she leaned in to her right, narrowing her eyes at the readouts.

"Butler?" asked Guin.

Butler swallowed before staring back into the camera.

"Commander Harrison sir," she said in voice smaller than before.

"Go ahead Butler," said Harrison.

"Sir," she said. "The complex structures I mentioned before, they're not veins of mineral ore. The interior of the planet is honeycombed with an incredibly complex network of chambers and tunnels, not naturally occurring but constructed.

"The mounds are just the points where the network breaches the surface. That sound they're making, it's resonating through the entire network so that the Helpers must be able to hear it everywhere sir."

"Ok," said Harrison. "That makes sense, they live mostly underground due to the storms. What else?"

"Sir," cringed Butler. "I don't understand how they're doing it, they must have constructed the chambers to use compressed air or maybe some kind of hydraulics, but there are what appear to be transport passages that are allowing them to move through the planet at incredible speed. Sir, every single Helper on the planet is travelling towards you right now, sir."

"How many?" said Harrison.

"Sir," said Butler, trembling. "I'm counting more than three billion life signs sir."

The crew fell silent beneath the ever rising rumble of the Helpers' song. Harrison stared at Butler with his mouth open for several seconds.

Shelley and Lem held hands while the colour drained from Bradbury's face and even Heinlein looked sick.

"The stronger species displaces the weak Heinlein, yeah?" said Guin sourly.

The soldier's face took on a tinge of green and he looked to his boots.

"All hands to flight stations," said Harrison suddenly, then crossed the room to the comm panel and pressed the button with a steady hand.

"Chiang?" he said. "Secure Clarke for flight. We're returning to the Norma immediately."

"Sir, yes sir" came Chiang's response.

Heinlein and Lem disappeared off down to the storage bays to make sure everything was secure for take off while Shelley went to do the same with the labs.

Meanwhile Harrison, Bradbury and Guin sped along corridors and up narrow ladders towards the bridge that sat at the very top of the ship.

The bridge was a small cavelike room, about half the size of the mess and packed tight with three flight chairs and consoles. The three officers clambered into their respective chairs and buckled themselves in without a word.

In order to safeguard the return of valuable equipment, no human intervention was technically required to return the Norman to the Norma.

The computers on the Norma ran everything remotely though some human oversight was preferred if possible, just in case something went wrong. Harrison sat in the command seat, flanked by Bradbury and Guin.

Once the crew sounded off over the comms channel, confirming that everyone and everything was strapped in and ready to go, Harrison confirmed the lift off procedure.

For a moment nothing seemed to happen but then came the familiar rumbling of the Norman's engines from deep below.

As the landing craft dragged itself up off the surface and then onwards, up through the air, the crew rattled about in their flight seats.

Then came the sudden, eerie stillness that signified

their emergence from the planet's lower atmosphere and that movement around the ship was possible once more.

"Bradbury," barked Harrison. "I want us prepped for redeployment asap."

"Sir," said Bradbury, unstrapping himself from his flight seat to stand. "Yes, sir."

Bradbury hurried from the bridge as Harrison turned to Guin.

"Guin," he said grimly. "Damage assessment."

Guin nodded and followed Bradbury's example. She moved quickly from the bridge and headed for the lab without looking back, leaving Harrison alone to think.

She and Shelley worked quickly and in silence for the next twenty minutes until a gentle shudder in the floor told them that they had docked with the Norma.

Hurrying back through the tight corridors they met the rest of the crew waiting for the main hatch to open. After several infuriating seconds the hatch swung wide enough for them to spill out and they all jogged down the ramp and out into the huge, echoing hanger.

The interior of the Norma was of a similar, modular design to the Norman. The corridor and room units were a little wider, the ceilings a little higher and the surfaces were painted a flat, basic white instead of being left as bare metal. Otherwise it was exactly the same, just many, many times larger.

Chiang was pushing a stretcher carrying a now comatose Clarke and disappeared off towards the medical centre.

Meanwhile Bradbury's shouted orders sent Heinlein and Lem running towards the storage bays. Guin pulled Shelley to one side for a moment to check she was ok before dispatching her to the main labs and joining the senior staff in the lift to the main bridge.

The bridge of the Norma was drastically different from that of the Norman. A broad, open, circular room, with plenty of space to stand and move about within a ring of terminals, vidscreens and various instrument displays.

A broad stripe of white speckled black ran around the front half of the room, half way up the wall. The stars it displayed were so sharp and clear that it was hard to remember that it was actually just one long, curving vidscreen and not a window.

At the centre of the room sat a large, raised command chair, flanked on either side by smaller copies. Harrison led Guin and Bradbury out of the lift and towards their stations.

On the far side of the bridge, a harassed looking Butler was pouring over several screens but lept from her seat and stood to attention when she noticed them enter.

"As you were Butler," said Harrison, taking up his command chair.

Bradbury assumed his post at tactical on Harrison's left while Guin took up hers at science opposite.

"Right then," said Harrison, almost snarling his frustration. "Damages. Guin?"

"Ok," she began, taking a deep breath. "So according to the inventory, we have like for like replacements for about half of the equipment we've left down there but given the work already completed, we could probably get by with about a third of that.

"If we have to abandon the camp but can return and set up shop at another site we can probably finish off. It'll be hard and there'll be some gaps but we if overlap with the extraction team a little bit we should be able to deliver the bare minimum."

"And if we don't return?" asked Harrison, not looking at her.

"Well," said Guin, hesitating to deliver the bad news. "Obviously we'll default on all the TP-055 shares and covering the cost of the equipment we've lost would cancel out a good chunk of what we made on NN-024."

"Corp damnit," Harrison growled. "Bradbury?"

"Sir," said Bradbury. "As Guin says, we don't have a full compliment of equipment but what we do have is all ready to go sir. If we need to deploy to a new site then we could do so in less than three hours sir."

"Ok good," said Harrison. "That's something at least. So then, thoughts on retaking the planet? I'll be damned if we're leaving here out of pocket."

"Sir," said Bradbury. "Suggest tactical nuclear strike sir. The aliens are kindly gathering all in one place for us so we should be able to take them all out with very few hits, perhaps even just one.

"It'll mean writing off the equipment we left behind and result in a slight loss in planetary gain but we'd still end up ahead sir."

Harrison nodded his approval.

"Agreed," he said. "Ok, so that's the plan to beat. Any other ideas? Any way we can neutralise the Helpers and take back the original site? Now we're safe in orbit we have time to think this through so let's work this out."

"Sir," said Butler, still hunched over her monitors. "With respect, I don't believe that's necessarily true sir."

"Explain," said Harrison.

"Sir," said Butler. "I'm counting nine incredibly deep vertical shafts running from small apertures on the surface all the way down into the interior of the planet.

"At the base of each shaft is a giant crystalline structure of a material the computer doesn't recognise. Best I can tell, they're some kind of piezoelectric crystal which the vibrations of the Helper's song are now charging sir."

"To what end?" said Harrison.

"Sir, unsure sir," said Butler. "But some kind of massive discharge is imminent sir."

"A weapon?" said Harrison, aghast.

"Sir, unclear," said Butler. "But if it is I don't think it's aimed at the Norma. We're not directly above any of the shafts sir."

"Sir," said Bradbury quickly. "Recommend moving to a higher orbit sir."

"Agreed," said Harrison. "Butler?"

"Sir, already on it sir," said Butler.

"Guin," said Harrison. "I want to know more about these shafts."

She looked at her vidscreen and the data now appearing from Butler's scans, screwing up her face as she tried to understand what she was seeing.

Before she could make any progress however and as she watched, nine bright white beams suddenly erupted from the planet's surface.

They fired straight out into space with such speed

that they seemed to simply appear as solid, impossibly long rods, not there one moment, there the next.

"Guin?" growled Harrison warningly. "What the hell are those?!"

"They're..." Guin gasped.

"Guin!" snapped Harrison. "Report!"

"They look like superluminal communication beams," said Guin, barely believing her own words as she heard them.

"That's not possible," said Harrison.

"Agreed," said Guin. "And yet that's exactly what they appear to be. Those beams must be sending information at way above the speed of light."

"What information??" asked Harrison, exasperated. "And to whom?"

"No idea," said Guin, her eyes flickering back and forth across the readouts. "I've never seen anything like it, nor has the computer. It could take months or even years to decode this."

"You've got an hour," said Harrison.

For the next sixty minutes Guin worked through data as quickly as she could, analysing the beams in every way she could think of.

Around her she was vaguely aware of Bradbury and Butler talking in low, worried tones, occasionally interspersed by sharp questions and orders from Harrison.

"Well Guin?" Harrison was asking suddenly.

Guin dragged a clammy palm down her weary face and blinked hard at the screens.

"Ok," she said. "So I can't decipher the information encoded in the beams but it's possible that there isn't any."

"What?!" said Harrison, openly irritated. "That can't be right, you must have just not spotted it yet."

"That's certainly possible too," nodded Guin, still staring at the data as she spoke. "Like I said, it could take years to fully analyse the signals in detail. On the face of it though, I'm not sure the beams are actually supposed to carry information at all.

"Something Clarke said about the Helpers' lack of abstraction, I think the beams might be their own message, that them just being switched on is the message, like a signal fire or a flare."

"Alright," said Harrison through gritted teeth. "But signalling what and to whom?"

"Sir?" said Butler in a trembling voice. "I think I know sir."

"Well?" snapped Harrison.

"Sir," she said. "Long range scanners are picking up nine groups of objects approaching back along the vectors of the signal beams at impossible speeds sir."

The whole senior staff turned to look at Butler as a thick and terrible silence engulfed them all.

"Objects?" asked Harrison quietly.

"Sir," whispered Butler. "The computer is identifying them as asteroids. They are made of rock and they don't have drive signatures or comms transponders but they look to be moving in formation and with purpose and they're all roughly the same size and shape. I think they're ships sir, of unknown form and technology but ships all the same, sir."

"How many?" said Harrison thickly.

Butler tried to speak but the words caught in her throat.

"How many corp damnit?!" roared Harrison.

"Sir," said Butler, fighting back tears. "Several thousand in each group sir."

Harrison turned instinctively to Guin, open mouthed and wide eyed. For a moment they stared at one another in shock and terror.

"Time to intercept?" croaked Harrison, his mouth dry.

"Sir, a matter of minutes sir," said Butler.

"Bradbury," said Harrison then, shaking himself and turning to the old solider. "Tactical?"

Bradbury said nothing, just shook his head.

"Guin," said Harrison, his voice trembling. "Science?"

"Run," she whispered hoarsely. "Just run."

the plant collar

The computer has just revived me from hibernation. All ship's functions report optimal performance and location is as expected, in line with the scheduled flight plan.

I am physically very frail and experiencing significant pain in and around my frontal lobes. It is manageable however and not outside the expected side effects of long term hibernation.

Navigation instruments show the target planet to be five cycles away. No data on the planet yet but advance probes have been dispatched.

The ship is up and running and automated preparations for planetfall are underway. I will now begin the post-hibernation rehabilitation regime.

[ship's log : 19-09-3025]

I have successfully completed the post-hibernation rehabilitation regime without any problems. I am now physically fit and pain free and fully prepared to undertake the mission ahead.

The first set of data from the advance probes arrived earlier today. It shows the target planet to be rotating with a stable day night cycle, liquid water in the atmosphere and a mix of solid terrain and salt water oceans.

The surface temperature is within tolerable limits, with a few regional exceptions at the poles and equator. The air is of a radically different make up from ours but still breathable.

The probes have also identified a shortlist of potential landing sites which I will now review. I am currently just under a cycle away from reaching the planet so will also begin reviewing the computer's proposed trajectory calculations and the rest of the landing prep.

Every time! Somehow I always forget just how rough the post-hib rehab is. I mean it's worth it, I feel pretty great now, but damn that's hard work.

Four solid cycles of non-stop exercise with occasional enforced food and sleep breaks. Note to self: remember next time and prepare yourself for the ordeal!

On a brighter note, I was very happy to see the atmospheric assessments as I have to confess, I've always hated the suit.

I'm sorry, I know a lot of people spent a lot of time designing and building it and I do recognise what an achievement it is, but to be perfectly honest the helmet has always just made me feel claustrophobic as hell.

So, here we go again. No matter how many times I do this I always get so excited at this point. This time next cycle I will be standing on an alien planet! And who knows, this might just be the one.

I know we're supposed to manage our expectations and yes, every planet I've explored so far has been pretty much a barren rock, but you never know!

Finding that amoeba a few years back was just about the most exciting thing that's ever happened to me. Who knows what's waiting for me down there this time!

[ship's log : 20-09-3025]

Planetfall complete.

The landing went by the book, no problems and all the data from the probes has now been confirmed by the landing pod's external sensors.

I am approaching the hatch now, just waiting for the mechanism to cycle and there, the hatch is opening, I'm stepping outside.

The air is indeed breathable. It tastes unusual, somehow cold despite the clement temperature and with a slight tang to it but it's not unpleasant. The ground is solid and dry underfoot.

The landing site is in the middle of vast, open grasslands that appear almost perfectly flat all the way to the horizon. The sky is the colour of blood and the grass the colour of snow in what is a very striking contrast.

On the horizon directly ahead of me is what looks like a significant mountain range. The intervening landscape however is almost entirely featureless except for a few large boulders dotted here and there.

I'm referring to the plant matter on the ground here as grass for want of a better word. It is similar in appearance to grasses we have at home, multiple slender blades, no flowers.

The blades here are much larger and coarser than anything we have at home however. It is about ankle deep but bends easily as I move through it despite its crude appearance.

The sky is mostly clear, making the colour all the more intense. There are a few small clouds which, based on the probe data, I'm assuming are water vapour.

The clouds are moving at a fair speed and there's a breeze here at ground level so I'm making a preliminary assumption of standard evaporation precipitation weather systems.

I'm moving further away from the pod now. The gravity seems pretty similar to ours if perhaps a little weaker, again as per the probe data.

I'm feeling a slight bounce in my step as I go. I'm making my way around the pod now in order to view the landscape in the other direction and...

My god.

It's a town!

I mean, I think it's a town.

A little way off behind the pod is a collection of structures rising out of the ground. It's hard to see exactly what they are from here but at first glance I'm convinced that they can't be naturally occurring. I'm not seeing any movement and there's no sound besides the wind.

I'm approaching now.

This is amazing.

I'm at the outer edge of the structures now and I can see quite clearly that they have been intelligently constructed. They are made up of complex series of interlocking walls which I can see are made up of vast numbers of small, identically shaped blocks.

The technology required to design and construct firstly these building materials and then the structures themselves implies a form of intelligence similar to our own. The shapes of these structures however are absolutely baffling.

This is alien architecture!

I am looking at proof that intelligent life exists in the universe besides ourselves!

Ok, ok.

So, the structures themselves.

They are clustered very close together but there do appear to be throughways between some of the clusters. These look to have been partially surfaced with some kind of dark, smooth material.

I'm still not seeing any movement or hearing anything so I'm going to move in amongst the structures to inspect them more closely.

The most striking thing about these structures is the mix of order and chaos. Some sections are made up of strict geometric shapes, mostly straight edged rectangles set at right angles to one another.

Mostly, these are sets of interlocking vertical walls but are also occasionally horizontal floors, in some cases up to three stories high.

Other parts of the same structures however are fluid and chaotic and appear more artistic than functional.

The strictly ordered parts seem to collapse into the unstructured sections only to then erupt back out of the chaos again further on. These combinations of forms seem random and yet appear to have been specifically designed like this.

The next most obvious thing is that the interiors of all these structures are mostly exposed. I'm seeing occasional hints of structures that might form the edge of a roof, but these are so small and rare that they serve no practical purpose I can make out.

I wonder if these are affectations? Perhaps the weather has changed over time so that roofs have become unnecessary and these are now just historical cultural references. Alternatively, perhaps they've never needed roofs and these are purely decorative, an architectural trend perhaps?

Most of the spaces within the structures are similarly exposed from at least one side. Either the external walls are completely missing or else where they should be, there's one of the chaotic curving structures instead.

I need to remember to remain as objective as possible, I must not project our traditions and assumptions onto this new culture.

The interiors of the structures contain even more of the same strange mix of order and chaos. There is a whole plethora of objects which I assume to be personal belongings, perhaps furniture or machines.

I can't even begin to guess what any of these things are yet but I can already see that some are arranged carefully and neatly while others have been organised into haphazard heaps.

The striking mix of order and chaos is perhaps another cultural trope then? Reflected in various different ways.

Despite the clouds in the sky the interiors of these structures are so exposed, so consistently that I'm reconsidering my earlier assumption about the planet's weather systems.

It seems unlikely that an intelligent civilisation would design such open structures if precipitation ever occurred here.

Perhaps this is a regional variance. Maybe there is rain on this planet but just not here. If that is the case though, how are the vast grasslands all around these structures maintained? Is there an alternative, subterranean water source I wonder?

I'll set some geological scans running when I get back to the pod. For now I just can't take my eyes off these structures. I can't help but try to infer the physical form these aliens must have from the nature of these buildings.

I am going to find it incredibly difficult if I want to move around within these structures. It's going involve a lot of difficult and precarious climbing and balancing. I wonder if they have some limited power of flight then? Or perhaps they're incredibly agile and able to leap great heights?

Thinking of the inhabitants of this place does make me wonder once more where they are. Perhaps they live mostly underground, that would make sense if that's where the water is, or maybe they're nocturnal.

Perhaps this place is only inhabited at certain times of year or else is some kind of sacred site that's off limits to all but a select few.

If I'm going to make first contact I'd rather not do it by accidentally blundering in on them while they're asleep or by desecrating one of their holy places. I need to tread very carefully here until I can gather more data.

Something else has just occurred to me. This place is so still and quiet. Have I discovered a thriving alien civilisation or a long dead one? Perhaps there's no-one here because there's no-one on the entire planet.

Enough speculation. I am returning to the pod to set the scans running and start deploying the sampling equipment. I will return here first thing tomorrow and continue my exploration then.

[personal log : 20-09-3025]

Actual. Alien. Life.

Not bacteria, not an amoeba, actual intelligent beings with culture and technology! This is so much more than I could ever have hoped for.

My head is spinning with the sheer magnitude of it, the significance of it. I managed to keep my emotions at arms length while doing all the technical work but now that I'm done for the day it's all I can think about!

Part of me is desperate to get back out there, to

just run through the town, looking at everything, touching everything. I just want to consume as much information about them as I can as quickly as I can.

Before I turned in for the night I climbed up and sat on top of the pod and watched the sun, the alien sun, set over the mountains, the alien mountains.

All the bizarre colours of the sky became even more dramatic as they blurred in to one another and then finally into darkness and I found I had to keep reminding myself that it was all actually real.

I must confess however, as mind blowing as all of this is, I did feel a small cold spot of sadness growing inside me, sitting up there, watching that impossible sunset.

This is the only thing I've ever wanted to do. I dedicated my entire life to getting through the selection process and then completing the training all to reach this point, to get here.

Throughout it all, I always knew it was a one way trip. They fire us all the way out here then we see what we can find and send back our reports until we either slip up or else just run out of air or food.

We get to see things no-one else will ever see but we never get to go home, that's the deal. I always accepted that, always knew in my heart that it was worth it and during all those previous landfalls, looking at rocks on rocks on rocks, I never doubted it.

Today though, confronted with actual alien life in glorious abundance all around me, the first thing that came into my head was how much I wanted to tell someone about it.

I know I'm recording these logs but it's not the same. Whoever you are, by the time you're listening to this I will have been dead for centuries if not millennia.

In that moment I wanted to tell someone what I was seeing and see their eyes widen, hear them gasp. For the first time I realised, I mean I finally, truly understood, that I'm never going to tell anyone anything ever again.

I am alone.

I rose before dawn but still detected no movement in the town and reviewing the overnight sensor logs seemed to confirm that there had been no nocturnal activity. The sky continues to be a distraction.

It's colour is so vibrant and strange that it continually catches the eye and is actually quite oppressive. I must concentrate on what's in front of me for now and hope that I get used to it over time.

On the one hand the continued lack of activity seems to add weight to the idea of the town being abandoned or even of the entire civilisation being extinct.

I do not yet have sufficient data to assume that this town is representative of the whole planet however, so there is hope yet.

I have returned to the structures with more equipment and decided to move further in today to explore in more detail. I am moving along one of the wider throughways, flanked by the rolling structures on either side.

The surface of the throughway reflects the construction of the buildings. It is for the most part perfectly smooth but has areas here and there that are violently textured and uneven which then settle back into uniformity.

The novelty of this architectural style and these construction methods has certainly not worn off overnight. My progress through the town is slowed by a continual string of fascinating new examples.

Considering the buildings again today it occurs to me that their scale suggests the inhabitants are most likely of a similar size to us.

I can see some regularly shaped holes in walls that could be doorways which, were I able to reach them, I could pass through quite comfortably.

The other doorways, if that's what they are, with their impossible, abstract shapes and dimensions still puzzle me. I can't help but wonder if they are intended to serve any practical purpose and if so what it could possibly be.

As I move further into the town, I have also noticed that every building is completely unique. While they appear to be very similar in terms of overall size and building materials, the specific shapes as well as the ratio of ordered sections to chaotic is different in each case.

I am trying to imagine the building techniques used to create this place and can only assume that each structure must be hand crafted. How could mechanised, automated equipment produce such a wide variety of abstract, artistic forms?

I have reached an intersection between two of the throughways and am taking the left hand path. The whole place remains deathly quiet, still no sign of life, just row after row of these impossible structures, except...

I can see something up ahead.

Movement!

Whatever it is, it's small and of a different colour and texture to everything around it. The buildings in the immediate vicinity appear no different to any others I've seen so far. I'm perceiving no obvious threats. I'm approaching with caution now.

Ok, so I'm looking at some new kind of plant life. It's radically different to the grass out on the plain, much more sophisticated.

It's protruding from the base of the nearest structure which I note has a much greater proportion of chaotic sections to ordered ones, I don't know if that's relevant yet.

The plant is about knee height and has a thick, smooth, pale trunk. I'm moving in a little closer now. The side of the trunk facing me is quite bare but round the back I can see that it's covered with fine fronds of a darker colour than the trunk itself. I can't see what purpose these serve yet.

Moving up, the trunk tapers slightly towards a band of discolouration then broadens and flattens out into what seems to be a flower at the top.

Instead of petals though, the flower has tubular

growths that radiate outwards from the centre. These growths are pretty straight and regular but bend a little at regular intervals along them so that they all curl forwards slightly.

For all that the grass on the plain is oversized and such a bizarre colour, it is at least a familiar form. I can think of no analogue on our world for the plant I am looking at here. This is truly alien.

The texture and colour of the whole thing is pretty uniform throughout. The fronds mostly seem to stop at the top of the trunk though there are a few spread sparsely over the back of the flower.

It seems to be solidly anchored into the base of the structure. It disappears down into the jumble of the structure through a tight break amid the chaos of the stonework.

Did it grow up wild from within the structure and find it's way through an existing the crack, drawn to the light perhaps? Or was the crack specifically made for it and it was planted here by design?

I can't see any obvious way in which it could threaten me. I'm going to try and get closer. I'm kneeling down in front of it now, but wait...

The band of discolouration between the top of the trunk and the base of the flower, it's not discolouration at all, it's a separate object, some kind of collar! Yes, it is definitely not organic, not part of the plant itself.

That means this collar has been manufactured and placed on this plant. Perhaps the collar denotes ownership, like we do with our household pets.

Are plants kept as pets here? Or maybe the plant is dangerous after all and the collar is some kind of warning or even a restraint?

The collar is metallic runs around what I will call the neck of the of the plant, where the trunk meets the flower.

It consists of a broad, flat band wrapped tight to the trunk and bears a strange disc shape at the back. The disc looks to be decorated but the design is too small for me to make out without getting closer.

Ok, the whole thing has just flopped forward to lay flat out on the ground. This could be a reaction to my presence though I haven't touched it.

Perhaps it can sense vibration through the ground? Or perhaps it has some kind of olfactory system and can detect my scent?

It's just laying there, though now that I look at it in this new position, it actually seems quite suited to it so perhaps this is it's default.

I see now that the fronds run down the plant's back while it's bare belly is in contact with the floor. Perhaps it would grow fronds all over it but that surface gets worn smooth through contact with the ground?

It's moving again. It seems agitated by my presence but I still don't think it can hurt me. The protrusions are curling inwards now, the tips are scraping through the dust on the ground as they go.

This is fascinating. The whole flower, protrusions and all, has curled in on itself to form a tight ball. And now it's relaxing again, spreading the protrusions back out into a radial pattern.

I wonder if this is some kind of pumping action, does this movement somehow aid the flow of water through the trunk perhaps?

From this position I can see that the protrusions are capped, just on the upper side, with some kind of hardened pad, presumably to protect the tips from injury.

I can also see that the disc on the back of the collar is covered in tiny symbols. Is this a written language? I'm capturing some images of the disc to review later back at the pod.

The plant seems to have settled down again now so I'm going to use a sample probe to give this thing some stimulus, see how it reacts. I'm going to nudge it just below the collar, now. Woah!

The instant tip of the probe made contact with the trunk, the whole thing spasmed up off the floor, back towards its original position. The surface of the trunk is obviously very sensitive. The protrusions are extended now, as if searching for the probe.

Now I'm going to touch the centre of of the flower. Again, the response is instantaneous. The protrusions have all closed about the probe and have taken hold of it. This is amazing! I'm actually struggling with it! It's surprisingly strong.

Ok, I've let go of the probe and backed off a bit. I don't want to damage the plant or spur it into doing something that could harm me.

It's still gripping the probe but it seems to be calming down. This is interesting, the plant is rubbing the tips of its protrusions over the surface of the probe, apparently examining it.

But no, it's dropped the probe again now, seems to have lost interest. Now it's becoming agitated again even though I'm nowhere near it and haven't moved so perhaps vibration isn't the primary sense after all.

Now it's stretching out its protrusions and the flower is slapping the ground over and over, quite violently. Now it's back up again, perfectly straight and vertical and the flower is swaying back and forth.

Ok, I'm concerned that my presence may be agitating the plant too much now. I've retrieved the probe and am going to push on further into the town where perhaps I'll find more examples of this incredible plant. If not, then I'll check on this one again on my way back.

So, pressing on then.

I've been walking for a little while now and am mostly just seeing more of the same, though I do note that the further I walk in this direction the more ordered the structures appear to be.

I wonder, if I go far enough, will I find sections of the town where the buildings are completely geometric? If so, is there then a corresponding section elsewhere where the buildings are entirely chaotic?

Wait, I hear something, what the...?

I heard a sound behind me and turned just in time to see one the buildings move!

The building is one I passed just moments ago and appears no different to any of the others. As I watched however, one of the ordered sections of the structure just spontaneously rearranged itself into a flowing, organic design.

I realise now that I have completely underestimated the technology here.

I thought these buildings had been constructed to this strange design as static objects, assuming too much similarity between this culture and our own.

It now appears however that the buildings are not actually static at all and can dynamically reshape themselves between the ordered and chaotic forms.

What triggered the change I have no idea but it occurs to me that I am potentially in danger here. If the structures can change without warning then it is going to be impossible to map this place meaning that I could get lost or even trapped in here.

I'm going to retreat back to the pod and reconsider my approach, I just hope that my path hasn't been blocked in the meantime. So far so good, nothing seems to have changed and the throughway I followed in here remains open.

I'm back at the plant again, just checking on it quickly now. It appears to have lapsed into a dormant state.

It is flat on its belly again and is completely unresponsive to stimuli. I don't want to linger here to investigate any further for now however, I will return when I feel I can do so safely.

I'm approaching the edge of the town now. I can see the plain opening up ahead and the outline of the pod in the distance.

The sky is practically glowing, the colour is making me feel queasy. I can hear more rumbling behind me now as well, as other structures reform themselves.

Ok, I'm out, returning to the pod. I'm going to review all the data I have so far and formulate a new plan. Until then I think I'll remain inside the pod just in case.

[personal log : 21-09-3025]

Wow!

That got pretty damn exciting out there today! I'm a little shaken up to be honest. Despite my best efforts I still ended up projecting our cultural norms onto this place and as a result made an assumption that could have put me in real danger.

Ever since first seeing the town I have been downright giddy with the thought of exploring an alien civilisation but I have to rein that in and be more professional.

There is the potential for real danger here and I am all alone. There is no back up out here, I must remember that at all times.

Anyway, I had a bit of an epiphany earlier which made me rethink what I was saying yesterday. I was classifying the samples I'd gathered and putting them into storage but I was so distracted by the events of the day that I managed to cut myself.

It was nothing serious, just a scratch really. As I dressed the wound though, I stopped and looked at the blood that had dripped onto the bright white floor of the storage bay and it struck me.

The sky outside really is the exact same bright shade of blue as the blood in my veins. And that grass! It is literally the exact same lush green as the snow that falls all year round at the monastery where I trained.

Buildings that rearrange themselves? Plants wearing collars like pets? This place is insane! Everything about it is just so impossibly weird and I'm here! I'm really here! Forget what I said yesterday, this is everything I've ever wanted since I was a child.

I realised it's worth it, all of it. The hardship, the loneliness, I wouldn't trade it for anything now. I know I need to sleep, there's so much work still to do and I've barely even started but I'm still just so excited.

Since finishing for the day I haven't been able to stop looking at the images I took of the plant's collar, in particular the symbols from the disc on the back. I can't stop sketching them now, over and over.

Even though I have no idea what it says, the novelty of writing in an alien language just doesn't get old. To close this log, I've reproduced the symbols here as best I can: XƎWIⱢ

the horror in the basement

It was a cold Friday night at the end of October and I was out with friends. Despite the desolate chill outside, the air in the pub was hazily lit and thick with raucous laughter.

If I'm honest I don't remember much past about 9pm. There'd been beers, laughter and at one point shots. Beyond that it's all a bit fuzzy.

I remember falling out of the cab in front of my building. I have a vicious bruise above my left eye to remind me of that part.

Then I was on my bed, still fully clothed, with no idea how I'd got there and the room spinning around above me. Idle thoughts half formed then melted away as I slipped towards oblivion.

Then I heard the noise.

I don't know how long I laid there, trying to ignore it. A dull, irregular thumping sound coming from below. It would build towards frantic until I opened my eyes. Then it would stop, just long enough for me to slip back to dozing only to start up again.

Eventually I sat up. The bruise above my eye was hurting and the rest of my head was joining in, I desperately needed to be asleep. The banging came again and before I knew it, I was up on my feet, stumbling towards the door.

My flat is on the ground floor so I knew that the noise had to be coming from the basement. I staggered out into the hallway, pausing every few steps to steady myself against the wall and listen for the sound.

Keeping myself mostly straight, I stumbled down the hallway. The way into the basement was the last door on the left and as I approached it, the noise grew louder.

I'd never been down in the basement. For one thing the building manager was kind of a prick about it. He was always reminding the tenants with a weird intensity the no-one was allowed down there and the door was always locked.

The banging from beyond the door stopped. I had

no idea what time it was but the building was dead. The silence thickened around me. Everyone else must be fast asleep. The banging started up again so I tried the door and as expected found it locked.

After a few struggling seconds however, I managed to focus my eyes through the gloom and realised that the key had been left in the door.

It did seem weird, given how fussy the building manager always was about it, but I didn't have it in me to give it more than a moment's thought.

Instead I rallied my thick-feeling fingers to twist the key until I heard a dull click. Then, after trying the handle again and giving it a bit of shove, the door swung inwards to reveal the top of the staircase down to the basement.

The dim light from the hallway tried to push inside but only got as far as the first few steps. The darkness down there was solid and seething, hungrily consuming the light and leaving nothing but void.

The banging was much louder now, spasmodic and violent. My mind was still all thick grey fuzz. Vague ideas of clanging water pipes or trapped animals floated by but I couldn't quite latch onto any of them.

I paused on the top step, feeling dizzy and sick as I frowned at the darkness. To my right was an ancient looking light switch, but no matter how many times I flicked it, nothing happened.

After a brief struggle with my jeans, I dragged my phone out and jabbed at it clumsily until the torch burst into life. A long, blinding cone split the blackness below to reveal a trembling snapshot of narrow stairs.

Keeping my free hand pressed to the clammy brickwork, I began to make my way down. I swept the phone left and right to try and illuminate more of the stairs. All the time the infuriating banging below grew louder and more frantic.

As I left the hallway behind my heart quickened and I found myself swallowing with every other step. My palms were sweating, so that my phone slipped a little. I dismissed it all and pressed on.

The bottom of the stairs came into view, a stained concrete floor under mouldering piles of boxes. The blackness pressed in close all around. At the bottom of the stairs the basement opened out to the left. The banging came again but now I could hear scuffles and rattling around it.

It definitely wasn't pipes.

There was something moving around in there, something a lot bigger than a rat.

I was breathing faster now and if I'd been sober I would have run right then. As it was, I was so hammered and so tired, all I could think of was how much I needed to sleep. This noise was stopping that from happening, whatever its source. I couldn't think of anything else.

I moved into the basement, sweeping the torch beam ahead of me. The place was a baffling jumble, boxes heaped on the filthy floor, pipes hanging from the low ceiling.

The banging was louder than ever, as if whatever was making the noise was right in front of me and yet I still couldn't see it.

As I slid the light into the far right corner, the banging suddenly stopped. I cocked my head to one side and listened harder.

This wasn't the silence from before, a simple absence of sound. This was a sound I couldn't hear, something just beyond the edge of my senses.

And in a heartbeat it was on me.

The thing lunged out from between the boxes with a manic, inhuman sound. Before I could react, it barrelled straight into me and knocked me backwards so that I dropped my phone. I hit the floor and the darkness swallowed me whole.

I'd only had a single, flashbulb moment to see it, but that had been more than enough. Skin green and terrible, face all scars and sores, eyes wild, bulging and manic, fingers impossibly long with terrible claws.

Now it was right on top of me, clawing at my shirt. I grabbed and slapped at it, desperately trying to fend it off.

It's skin was cool and slimy, inhumanly soft and thick. The long, tapering fingers curled and bent unnaturally as it tore at me.

Adrenaline roared through every part of me, washing away the queasy fog of before. My right hand took the initiative and began to search the gritty floor around me. Suddenly it hit a familiar shape, a rusty old toolbox.

As the thing gibbered and moaned, ripping the buttons from my shirt, I fumbled open the lid of the box and snatched up the first thing I found, a heavy hammer. I could feel the thing shuddering with excitement and hear its hideous, muffled groaning.

Without a moment's hesitation I began to swing the hammer wildly. I felt it connect several times, the thing grunting with each impact until suddenly the hammer was gone and the thing wasn't on me anymore.

I forced myself to take a deep breath and braced myself, trying to picture the bottom of the stairs, to fix the direction in my head.

Then, swallowing hard and ignoring the tears now stinging my eyes, I rolled onto my front and scrambled forwards and up.

I pounded up the stairs towards the great glowing oblong of the doorway hovering above. The staircase seemed twice as long as it had coming down, but I pushed on and up.

Just as I was almost there, almost able to touch the dim yellow light from the hallway, something yanked my leg backwards so that I fell flat onto the stairs and slid painfully backwards, feeling the sharp edge of each step.

I twisted onto my back and there was the thing, I could just about make it out in the half light from above. It swayed and held its face where I had hit it but seemed determined to finish me off.

With a great roar I drew my right knee up to my chest and then planted a single, solid stomp right into the middle of its chest.

As if attached to a rope, the thing flew away from me, vanishing down into the blackness. I heard a jumbled string of impacts as it bounced down the stairs and then nothing.

Silence. Actual, empty silence.

For a moment I stared and gasped and stared. Then I turned and scrambled up the rest of the stairs. I raced back to my flat then slammed and locked first the front door, then the bathroom door.

Then I puked.

A lot.

Eventually I collapsed onto the cold floor and stared at the bathroom door until the room began to lighten with the dawn.

Although I wouldn't have thought I could ever sleep again, at some point I must have because the next thing I remember is waking up on the bathroom floor. I could hear voices and the sounds of traffic outside.

A blurred mess of images and sounds from the night before spilled over me, none of it making much sense. Had any of that really happened?

I began to move and was immediately assaulted by a blinding, drillbit-to-the-temple headache and a terrible feeling of complete and utter dread.

I made my way out of the bathroom and was going to collapse straight into bed when I heard footsteps in the hallway outside, a lot of footsteps. Gingerly, I screwed up my howling eyes to peer through the peephole in my door.

Directly opposite I could see my neighbour Mrs Worden in her nightgown and curlers. She was standing in her doorway smoking a cigarette.

Beside her, at her feet, sat a small black cat with huge green eyes. Both were watching unimpressed as a steady flow of people in uniforms and white overalls moved back and forth along the hallway.

Wincing at every sound, I unlocked and opened the door. Two cops bustled past and I watched them go before looking over to Mrs Worden.

"Hey Bernice," I croaked.

"Morning," she said. "You look a little worse for wear."

I nodded and winced, waiting for another lull in the flow of bodies.

"How's your cat?" I asked, nodding down at the little figure beside her. "Didn't she have an operation or something?"

As if on cue, the cat took its time over an enormous yawn and then wandered off back into the flat.

"Oh she's ok," said Bernice, glancing over her shoulder. "She's meant to be wearing a cone."

"Is she," I said, concentrating on not being sick.

"She won't have it though," said Bernice happily. "I don't know how she's getting it off, the vet says it's impossible, but she does. Last time I put it on her she didn't just get it off, she hid it behind the coffee table."

"Right," I said, clinging to the door frame.

"But that's cats," said Bernice. "You know what they're like."

"Sure," I said.

Another thick knot of people rushed between us, all talking loudly either to one another or into phones. Each of their voices felt like hammer against my skull.

"So what's going on?" I asked once they had passed.

Bernice pushed her glasses up her nose a little and took a deep drag on her cigarette.

"Some kind of monster," she said flatly.

My heart began to pound queasily and I started to sweat.

"What?" I gulped.

"The little girl from 213 upstairs?" she said. "The shy one?"

I nodded, I knew her. Sweet kid, a bit quiet. For some reason the neighbourhood kids were always tormenting her with horrible pranks and whenever I saw her she was always playing alone.

"Dead," said Bernice simply.

I opened my mouth to speak but nothing happened. I was thinking about what had happened in the basement. I was thinking about my panicked escape. Most of all, I was thinking about not closing the basement door behind me.

It was real.

And it wasn't dead.

And I'd let it out.

"But..." I said dumbly.

Bernice glanced up and down the hallway before leaning forward and lowering her voice conspiratorially.

"I heard them talking," she said. "Whoever did it made a real mess of her."

"Oh god," I said as my stomach did a flip.

"Apparently," she continued with relish. "They gagged her and taped a Halloween costume to her, rubber mask and hands, all of that, so that she couldn't get them off.

"Then, when they'd done all that, they bashed her head in with a hammer and threw her down the basement stairs. Broke her poor little neck, sick bastard..."

the drip

author's note

A few years back my wife and I were at her sister's for Christmas. It was Christmas Eve and once the children had been put to bed, my sister-in-law suggested reading ghost stories aloud over a few drinks for the evening's entertainment.

We drank and made merry and tried to creep each other out by reading from books or recounting stories we'd heard. It was a lot of fun and something that seemed like it could make for a pleasant family tradition.

Afterwards, I began to mentally bookmark stories I encountered during the rest of the year as possible candidates for the next drunken, Christmas Eve reading. Given my work however, I inevitably also began to think of writing a story of my own specifically for the occasion.

To that end I began to do a little research online, looking for inspiration generally but also for real events into which I might weave my story.

Rooting a story in the gaps between fact is a long-established tradition in spooky fiction and often a very effective way to give it greater impact.

This is what I was doing when I came across a man on social media called Simon Dufford. Simon had recently lost his elderly father and was trying to find out more about his father's early life.

What really caught my attention however, were the scanned images of a handwritten letter, apparently penned by Simon's father just before his death.

Upon reading this letter I immediately gave up on my plan to write a story of my own for Christmas, deciding instead to simply read out the letter. What Simon's father wrote on the day he died is far more disturbing than any fiction I could have created.

Transcribed in full here, with Simon's permission, is that letter.

It has proved impossible to verify all the events his father describes, but I was able to confirm that there was a severe storm and significant flooding in the area

My name is Charles Anthony Dufford and I am ninety-three years old. I was married for almost seventy years to my beautiful wife Dorothy who sadly passed away eighteen months ago. I have three children, my eldest son Thomas, my daughter Margaret and my youngest, Simon.

I am very proud of all of them and their spouses and of my grandchildren, I love them all very much. I have lived a long and privileged life and for that I am grateful. I have spent more time happy than sad and achieved many things upon which I now look back with pride.

Throughout all these many years however, I have kept a dark, terrible secret relating to something that happened when I was a young man.

Since that day, so very long ago now, I have never told anyone about the events I witnessed... but no, that's not right.

I have never told anyone about the events in which I took part, there's no point to that particular lie anymore. I never even told my beloved Dorothy of this, for fear of what I might see in her eyes if I did, for fear that she might think less of me.

This evening however, I have realised that I am fast approaching the end of my life. Since everyone else who was there that day has now passed on, I know that the terrible truth of what happened, of what we did, will die with me unless I finally tell the world.

And so I am compelled to record an account of that day so that no matter what you all may think of us, at least the truth of it shall finally be known.

The sky never really grew light today due to heavy clouds and rain which came down in thick, steel like rivets all day long.

During a radio broadcast earlier on, there was mention of flood warnings in the local area and while I haven't seen any flooding immediately outside, this poor old house of ours has taken a real battering.

The rain finally abated about an hour ago, leaving behind bloated puddles and newly formed streams in the street, the last remnants of the deluge finding its way into the ground.

As I write this, I can hear the steady sound of slow falling water outside, monotonous and relentless. These sounds seem to me a fitting backdrop for the tale I must now tell.

I was born and grew up in a small village in North Yorkshire. I was a healthy child and from an early age I excelled both in sports and academic pursuits.

I was fortunate enough to attend an Oxford college. I was the first in both my family and my village to attend any university, let alone one held in such high esteem.

My family and I had always considered an education such as I ultimately received to be far beyond our means and station.

The bequest of a long dead local noble however, a scholarship reserved for young men such as myself, sent me South upon leaving grammar school and that was that.

My first few months in Oxford were not easy. I was intimidated greatly by the place, the grand buildings and grander people, some of whom were really rather unkind as a result of my background and accent.

Gradually this changed however, time took the harsher edges from my voice and I pursued my academic studies with relish, often outperforming my peers.

By the Easter of that first year, the snubs and quips no longer concerned me and I had made a small number of firm friends.

I learned to toy with the snobbery and in response to one foolish jibe after another I would spin wild yarns about the hardships of life in the North.

I told them of terrible winters when wolves would come down from the hills to eat the children of those foolish enough to leave their doors unlocked.

113

I described scenes of brutal, sometimes deadly fist fights over stale loaves of bread and of shallow graves dug with bare, bleeding hands. The jeers would quieten then as their faces fell pale and unsure.

I appreciate that this may appear ridiculous today, however in the time of which I speak the North of England remained an entirely foreign land to many people in the South.

Over time they chose to mock my upbringing less and less in order to avoid hearing yet another distasteful story of life in the North, but I digress.

I was reading History and had discovered in myself a particular interest in British colonial history. Just before the Christmas break in my second year, I had heard talk of an opportunity for an undergraduate to spend some time in India during the summer.

I had doubled my academic efforts to try and ensure that I would be the strongest candidate and therefore be chosen for the trip.

In the end however I did not go to India. A young man in the year above me, whose father happened to be the Indian Consul, went instead. I recall being most dreadfully disappointed by the whole thing.

I retreated to my rooms for several days, ostensibly to study but in truth, I am ashamed to say, to wallow in self-pity as only a young man yet to know anything of the world can.

A few days later however, a friend of mine approached me in my rooms. He excitedly recounted a long and complicated tale concerning an exchange arrangement with a certain American, Ivy League University.

The intended participant from our college had just that afternoon broken his leg during a rugby match and so could no longer go.

The college were therefore seeking a replacement, an undergraduate prepared to spend two terms at the American University. I jumped at the chance and just a few weeks later I found myself and a trunk of my possessions, setting sail across the Atlantic.

As I watched this great island of ours shrink into the horizon, I was initially the most excited I had ever been.

Over the course of the voyage, I passed the time by reading various tomes I had brought with me and writing up some of my more interesting reflections.

Occasionally I would make small talk with other passengers and all in all it was a very pleasant, if slightly dull journey.

My excitement was sparked afresh however by my first glimpse of the North American continent and then flared further upon docking in New York City.

Having grown up in a small village, the sleepy college town of Oxford was at that time the busiest place I had ever been.

You will appreciate then I am sure, just how overwhelming the extreme sound and motion of that great city appeared to me.

To this day I retain a vivid memory of standing next to my trunk on the docks, slack jawed and glassy eyed as an endless stream of bodies pushed past and around me.

I have no idea for how long I stood there but eventually a small boy in a large floppy cap with a dirty face and dirtier clothes, presented himself to me.

He greeted me by name and explained that he had been sent to retrieve me and direct me onwards on my journey.

I remember swallowing hard and nodding, not yet able to speak. The boy seemed amused by this and looked me up and down carefully.

"British huh?" he said.

Finally focusing I followed his gaze and looked down at myself, becoming suddenly aware how out of place my clothing must appear.

I nodded again and mumbled something. The boy simply shrugged and dragged my trunk up onto his back, bending double to carry it but still making firm progress through the crowds.

A cab deposited me at the train station and after a lengthy but beautiful train journey followed by a second cab ride, I found myself standing next to my trunk once more. This time I was in the small, neat room I would be calling home for the next few months.

I looked out of the window across the green and

leafy campus and felt a touch of disappointment. For all the long travels I had undertaken to reach this place, the view was actually quite familiar.

The weather, the style of the gardens and even some of the flora itself, none of it would have seemed out of place back home.

Just like my first days in Oxford, I settled in by throwing myself into my studies. Unlike in Oxford however, far from bringing me disdain and mockery, here my background proved to be a novelty bordering on the exotic for some of my fellow undergraduates.

I was regularly approached by strangers who, quite without any introduction, would ask me to "say something British" just to hear my accent which, I confess, I probably did exaggerate a little for their benefit.

One group of undergraduates who never addressed me in this way however, were the four people who were for a time, my firmest friends.

I did not realise it until sometime later, but Rick, Nancy, Albert and Susan were all from old money families and were part of the 'it' crowd of the campus.

While I knew they were just as taken by the novelty of my speech and dress as the rest of the students, they were different.

The difference with these four was that they had been raised to consider it grossly bad form to mention one's assets, be they a multi-million pound inheritance or an exotic friend. Subsequently, neither my accent nor my clothes were ever referenced directly in their company and this was something of a relief.

I must also confess however, that after becoming used to being excluded from the upper social strata within my college back in Oxford, the chance to become one of the elite was something I leapt at.

I'm afraid I probably became something of a snob for those first few months, my lack of funds being apparently cancelled out by the fact that I had "class".

Rick was a natural born sportsman, a huge, strapping young man with thick black hair and bright blue eyes who radiated strength, charm and vitality. He went on to have a successful career in the military and

116

died on active duty many years later.

Nancy meanwhile was the epitome of unhurried cool. Tall and slender with dark hair and darker eyes, she lived a long life and eventually died of illness in old age.

She and Rick had been together since high school and at the time it seemed a simple, if unspoken fact that they would be married immediately upon graduating.

Albert was a wiry young man with sandy hair and possibly the most hilarious person I had ever met. His dry humour and scathing wit underlined his demeanour of calm, as if there was simply nothing in the world that could ever excite or disturb him.

I had initially assumed that he and Susan were together, however after an evening of drinking with him it quickly became clear that Albert's tastes lay elsewhere and that I stood a better chance with him than she. Sadly, he died on a mountaineering expedition just a few years after graduation.

Susan herself was the epitome of what I had imagined American women to be. Blonde like the sun with dazzling blue eyes, she was the smallest of the group by several inches and yet accounted for at least two thirds of the energy.

Overly excited by absolutely everything and completely unable to sit still, the others would regularly pretend to complain that just being in Susan's company was exhausting.

She went into event planning after university and had a very successful career spanning many decades before tragically dying in an accident at her home.

It feels strange to think of them now. The time I spent with them feels so long ago as to be a tale from another life, a distant, historical saga.

And yet, what we did together back then has never left me. In many ways I suppose it made me the man I am today.

The sky outside has now cleared to reveal genuine darkness though I dread to think what damage has been done to our home.

There have been times in the past when the weather has forced its way inside the house here and there, but we've never seen anything like today's storm.

The dripping out there has stopped but now that I listen, I can hear similar sounds from the bottom of the stairs instead.

The soft, regular slapping of water onto carpet. On any other day I would pause in my work here and rush to check on that sound, to gather pans and buckets but under the circumstances I know there is little point. It is too late for such concerns now, I must finish my tale while I still have the chance.

As the summer of my year in America approached and the weather gradually improved, Rick proposed a trip to his family's beach house situated a few hours' drive up the coast.

It seemed like a wonderful idea to me, not least because I hoped it would provide an opportunity for me to spend some time alone with Susan with whom, I confess, I had become somewhat infatuated. Subsequently I leapt at the invitation though only in the take-it-or-leave-it manner typical of the group.

On the morning we were due to depart I waited eagerly on the edge of campus with a small satchel in my hand containing clothes and books enough for the weekend.

I had spent much of the time leading up to the trip considering seating arrangements for the drive and was hopeful that my plans would now come to fruition.

It had been agreed that Rick would drive his car with Nancy beside him and Albert his, hopefully with myself and Susan in the back giving us plenty of time to chat.

As the cars approached and pulled over however, my heart sank. Susan was sitting in the back of Albert's car as I had hoped, but to my dismay I saw that she was not alone. Upon seeing with whom she was sitting however, my mind reeled.

Next to her was a young man named Melvin who I had encountered once or twice during my first few weeks on campus.

Melvin's situation in life was similar to my own in that his family were not particularly wealthy. He came from some backwater in one of the Southern states and had an incredibly camp and affected accent, leaving him open to constant ridicule from my cultured, East Coast friends.

Initially I had empathised with his plight and had even assumed that we would become friends as a result. After very little time in his company however, I found that I simply couldn't stand the man.

He was small and frail, only just reaching five feet and with arms like dry twigs. He wore incredibly thick glasses, had quite spectacularly uneven teeth and seemed to suffer from a permanent cold which caused him to sniff and cough continually.

In the brief time I had spent with him I had found that there was nothing in the world about which he would not complain.

In fact, I had found his demeanour so depressing that on more than one occasion I had made some excuse or other and quite rudely walked away from him mid-sentence.

To see him there with my friends, whom I had been sure despised Melvin even more than I, was utterly inexplicable.

To have to then climb into the front of Albert's car, thereby forfeiting my keenly awaited time in Susan's company and to him of all people, well it was galling to say the least.

I spent the entire drive in a terrible sulk, not least when I looked back and noticed that Susan had draped herself about Melvin's person and was stroking his hair.

My dark mood seemed to spread to the sky and we had to pull over and put up the roofs of the cars as a heavy summer storm rolled in from the sea.

Albert attempted to engage me in conversation but quickly realised that I would not be drawn and so fell into silence with a shrug.

After that the only sounds were Susan's whispers and giggles beneath the drumming of rain on the roof of the car.

Even through the rain, the coastal views were quite breathtaking and they gradually drew me from my disappointment.

Eventually the storm rolled inland and left us behind

with the glorious summer sun again. We continued to follow Rick as he turned off the highway and slowed to negotiate what a faded sign described as a private road but was in fact little more than a rough, dirt track.

The track wound gradually downwards towards the ocean before finally swinging around one last corner to reveal what Rick had referred to as his family's beach house.

I had expected a glorified shack and had been preparing myself for a couple of nights of rough sleeping. What sat before us however, set back from the sand and sheltering beneath the vast curving headland, was a great, sprawling, two storey building.

Built of now faded wooden planks, the beach house sported a covered veranda that appeared to run full circle around the ground floor.

The unshuttered windows of four rooms on each floor, on this side of the building alone, gazed down at us blindly. Albert pulled up alongside Rick and my companions all began to emerge from their vehicles, chattering happily.

I eventually retrieved my hanging jaw and clambered out after them, instantly irritated to see Susan still fawning about Melvin.

Albert excused himself and dashed off to some secluded spot, understandably in need of urgent relief after the long drive.

Rick and I began to haul the bags from the backs of the cars, joking about how much luggage the girls had brought and asking how long they were intending to stay.

Rick hefted his bags and several of Nancy's over his broad shoulders and made for the grand front door of the house.

Meanwhile I returned to Albert's car in the hope of helping Susan with her luggage in a similar display of masculinity.

It was one area in which I was convinced Melvin would not be able to compete. Before I had the chance to make my offer however, Susan had skipped to my side and landed her slender fingers on my arm.

"Charlie dear," she cooed. "Would you be an

absolute darling and help poor Melvin here with his bags? The poor thing's feeling a little under the weather."

I looked over at the 'poor thing' himself. He had just blown his nose noisily and was now inspecting the contents of his handkerchief with a worried expression.

"But what about your bags Susie?" I asked, managing a smile despite my revulsion at Melvin.

"Oh Albie will get those," she said breezily, already floating away from me. "I'm going to dip my toes in the sea."

And with that she was away, sprinting and leaping down the beach towards the surf. I watched her go, my mouth dry with desire, before turning my attention to the contents of Albert's car.

"So, Melvin," I said, trying to ignore the fouled handkerchief in his hands. "Which of these are yours?"

Clearly in no hurry at all, Melvin carefully folded the offending fabric into a sodden ball and returned it to his pocket.

Making his way gingerly across the sand, he joined me by the open car boot and pointed out no less than four separate bags. I looked from the bags to his squinting face, failing utterly to keep the displeasure from my face.

"You never know what the weather will bring," he said defensively. "And I wouldn't like to fall behind on my studies."

A moment later, upon attempting to lift one of the bags, I realised what he had meant by this last comment. The bag was filled with thick, dense text books.

"Alright then," I said, resolving to have the matter over and done with. "I'll take these, you can take that one."

"Oh no," said Melvin. "I have terrible problems with my back you see. I can't possibly lift or carry anything I'm afraid."

I believe I glared at him openly for several seconds. Then, with a foul taste in my mouth, I turned back to the car and hefted all four of his bags out onto the sand.

"Oh do be careful!" he cried in a shrill little voice.

"You mustn't damage my books."

I paused to glare at him again before heaving the bags onto my back.

At the front doors of the house Rick was standing knee deep in bags, fumbling with a bunch of keys. Nancy stood a little way behind him, leaning against one of the upright posts of the veranda and smoking elegantly.

"Really dear," she said in a languid tone. "I don't know why you would drive us all the way up here only to spend the entire weekend on the front porch. It seems rather silly really."

"I thought you might appreciate the fresh air darling," he drawled over his shoulder with a hint of venom before trying yet another key in the lock.

As I stood there, Melvin's bags bit viciously into my hands and shoulders, gradually driving me down into the sand.

The sun had passed its peak for the day but still blazed gloriously, filling everything to bursting with heat and colour. I gazed down the beach to the sea and watched Susan's distant figure leaping and twirling in the surf.

Turning back to the house, I tried to ignore the rasping sound of Melvin's breathing behind me. The house glistened in the sun, as the last remnants of the storm dripped and trickled from every surface. Lazy droplets fell down like so many ticking clocks, impossible to ignore once heard.

I was trying to fend off the hypnotic effect when movement above caught my eye. I glanced up to one of the upstairs windows but too late so that I was left unsure as to what, if anything, I had seen. A cold spot formed in my stomach as I played the moment over.

Had there been a figure at the window?

Just then however, Rick finally found the correct key and with a shocking groan the grand front door of the house was thrown open. In stark contrast to the glorious summer without, the interior of the house was lost to a dark, cool gloom.

It swallowed up Rick and Nancy as they made their way inside, bickering in their habitually restrained tone as they went. I adjusted the position of Melvin's many bags and moved to follow them.

"Will it be very dusty do you think?" Melvin called after me. "Dust affects my chest ever so badly you see..."

I pretended not to hear him and pressed on into the murky interior. As I crossed the threshold a sudden chill ran down my spine and the hairs on my straining forearms stood on end.

The house had been furnished in a sparse but elegant style. It was clearly very old and had not been lived in for more than a few days at a time for many years.

Here and there, there were old portraits on the walls, individuals or groups of people standing in stiff poses, dour expressions on stern faces.

One portrait in particular caught my eye, or rather the posture of the lone figure therein. The moment outside, glancing upwards just before, flashed back upon me though only for heartbeat.

A pale figure, standing and staring. I tore my eyes from the painting and moved on, trying to outrun a second chilled sensation.

I dropped Melvin's luggage at my feet and stretched my complaining arms and fingers. Of course the house had been locked up for months, there could be no-one else here with us. I knew then that, had I been pressed on the matter, I would have had to concede that I couldn't swear to having seen anything at all.

Rick appeared back in the hallway, muttering something under his breath in response to another of Nancy's perfectly polite barbs.

"Now then Charles!" he erupted with a sudden grin. "I see you're playing valet for Melvin there, very sporting of you. Your rooms are upstairs, first and second on the right."

"My room won't be damp will it?" I heard Melvin ask from behind. "My joints ache terribly when I sleep in damp conditions."

"Oh I shouldn't have thought so Melvin," said Rick with booming enthusiasm. "But if you have any problems at all, you just go and find Nancy and tell her all about them. I'm sure she'll be delighted to help."

He winked at me wickedly before moving past us back out into the sunshine. I couldn't help but smile though I did my best to hide it. I heaved the bags back up onto my shoulders with a sigh and headed for the stairs.

From just outside I could hear Rick calling down the beach to Susan but his voice seemed distant and flattened. As I mounted the first stair it gave a low groan under my weight and that of Melvin's luggage of course.

"Do you think these stairs are safe?" he said, dithering behind me, unsure whether to follow. "Stairs like these in old houses can rot through you know, especially if it's not a well maintained property. My mother always says..."

I didn't listen to what his damnable mother said however, I was too busy straining under the weight of his luggage. I could feel sweat running down my back in clammy rivulets, sticking my shirt to my back.

He wittered on behind me all the way up the stairs, across the landing and down the corridor to the door of his room, not once offering any kind of assistance. It wasn't until I'd set down all his bags at his door that I realised where we were.

I looked back down the hallway to the top of the stairs and judged the distance. This was the room, I was certain of it. This was the room in which I had thought I'd seen the figure at the window.

My hand hovered at the door handle but something stopped me. Somewhere under the constant drone of Melvin's complaints and his mother's advice I could have sworn I had heard, or perhaps felt something on the other side of the door.

I took a step back and swallowed hard. The long hallway suddenly seemed so narrow and the ceiling so low, that I felt my chest tighten to match.

Nothing but thin timber walls separated us from the glorious summer day outside and yet somehow the house was another world, a heavy bubble of suffocating gloom.

"There you are," I said, nodding towards the door.

Melvin looked dumbly from his luggage to the door to me.

"Won't you bring them in for me?" he whined. "Please, my back is so dreadfully fragile."

I glanced at the door and licked my lips.

"Fine," I said thickly, stooping to gather up the luggage once more but not taking my eyes from the door.

Melvin stepped in front of me and grasped the door handle. I held my breath. All the while he twittered on and on until it became nothing but white noise. My ears strained desperately to hear past the fuzz, trying to reach into the room beyond the door.

He turned the handle and I realised I was cringing. The door swung inwards and we were both immediately blinded by the glaring sun pouring in through the window ahead.

Complaining about possible damage to his eyes, Melvin moved into the room while I lingered on the threshold, leaning one way and then the other as I tried to see past him.

The room was a modest size with a few sturdy pieces of furniture. The bed was on the right while to the left a huge wardrobe loomed.

Melvin sat briefly on the bed before complaining that he thought it might be too hard for him sleep on. All the while I remained frozen.

My eyes were fixed on the window, or rather the spot on the floor just before it where the figure had been standing just minutes earlier, if there had been a figure at all of course.

As he made his way around the small room, finding fault with every little thing, Melvin came to stand in that exact same spot, taking a moment to peer down out of the window.

Seeing him standing there, looking out and down, made my stomach clench and my heart race. He turned from the window then but upon seeing the expression on my face finally stopped talking.

He frowned and drew breath to ask a question but never got the chance. In that moment everything seemed to slow down until the pressure on my chest became unbearable.

Suddenly, the wardrobe doors burst open and a

125

horrendous roaring sound tore through the pair of us.

Melvin screamed, an incredible, high pitched sound, the like of which I had only ever heard from animals before.

He collapsed away from the wardrobe to land on the bed, which no longer appeared to be too hard for him after all.

Meanwhile, I stood goggling at Albert who, having erupted from his hiding place so spectacularly, was now doubled up with laughter.

Cool relief flooded through me as my body began to catch up with my reason. The figure I had seen at the window had been Albert.

He'd found another way into the house while we were unpacking the cars and hidden himself here, waiting for the opportunity to pull his prank.

I realised I was grinning and that suddenly the air felt much fresher and lighter than before. The bubble of gloom had burst.

I dropped Melvin's bags to the floor for the final time and joined Albert in hearty laughter. Melvin meanwhile had turned quite grey and was weeping, one shrivelled little hand at his chest, his wet and bulging eyes magnified by his ridiculous spectacles.

"Oh cheer up," exclaimed Albert, stepping in to give Melvin a hearty slap on the shoulder which almost knocked him off the bed. "Just a little joke to get us in the mood for some fun."

"Come on Charles," he said, grinning at me as he stepped away from the still quivering Melvin. "Let's leave the little man to recover shall we. I do believe Rick has been dreadfully naughty and brought some liquor with him."

He slapped me on the shoulder then and moved past me, through the doorway and out into the hall. Still revelling in the cool sensation of relief, I looked at the snivelling little creature on the bed, grinned and followed Albert back downstairs.

I retrieved my own bags, deposited them in my room and then joined the others on the beach. Melvin stayed in his room for the rest of the night, not even coming down when Albert laid out a simple but delicious picnic for supper.

Finally, as the sun slipped from the sky and we moved back inside, I found myself relaxing before a fire in the sprawling lounge. We all sipped cocktails courtesy of Rick while chatting and it felt to be just about the perfect evening.

Towards the end of the night we came around to the subject of our friend upstairs. Nancy was sat in Rick's lap and the two were whispering to one another and giggling while Susan, Albert and I all occupied our own comfortable chairs.

"It's just, I don't understand why you invited him along," I said. "He's the most awful bore."

Rick and Nancy returned their attention to the rest of us and the four of them shared conspiratorial glances and wicked grins.

"For fun silly!" chimed Susan, still giddy even after hours of dashing about on the beach and drinking liquor.

"But are you and he," I began but faltered. "I mean are you..."

There was an uncomfortable pause and again my hosts exchanged glances.

"Why Susan," Rick declared. "I do believe Charles is sweet on you!"

They all erupted into more laughter and I immediately dropped my gaze to the floor and felt my cheeks scald red.

"Oh Charlie!" Susan squealed, flinging herself out of her chair to land in my lap before planting a huge smacking kiss on my cheek. "Of course not! Me and that horrible little man? How could you think such a thing!"

Dazed by the smell and the feel of her, not to mention all the alcohol, I pushed against the fog of confusion.

"But then why..." I began. She snuggled closer, squirming in my lap and interrupting.

"Because, it was the only way we could get him to come with us!" she apparently explained.

"Melvin has always been rather taken with Susie you see," added Albert, nodding wisely.

"I see," I said, not seeing at all. "But..."

"These little trips of ours can be so incredibly dull,"

said Nancy. "The provision of a little entertainment makes things so much more interesting."

I thought of Albert's practical joke from before and finally understood. Somewhere towards the back of my mind, beneath the cocktails and the smell of Susan's hair, part of me felt a little cruel. As the evening rolled on however, the new seating arrangements dominated my attention entirely.

The rest of the night became a blur. I am ashamed to recall laughing a great deal as we all took it in turns to make increasingly unpleasant jokes about Melvin, his mother, her personal hygiene and the possible identity of his father.

Eventually I must have stumbled off to bed, alone I should add, though my memory of that part of the evening is somewhat fuzzy.

The next day I awoke with a mild headache. I dressed and ate quickly then followed the sound of voices out onto the sand. Rick was swimming in the calm waters while Susan dashed about in the surf.

Closer to the house Nancy and Albert lounged in style, watching the others while sipping drinks and occasionally passing comment.

I joined the pair, trying to ignore Nancy and Susan's swimming costumes. By today's standards they would probably appear drastically conservative but at that time they were enough to make my heart race.

Just as I was about to ask after Melvin's whereabouts, Susan dashed up the beach and passed us, giggling wildly.

I craned my neck to follow and saw her heading for a hunched little figure sat in the shade of the house reading a book.

She grabbed at his arm and made a show of dragging him to his feet and down to the sea. As they passed us, I could hear Melvin's feeble protests.

"But my skin, I burn so easily..." he whined, but Susan wasn't listening and was soon splashing him in the shallows.

I shaded my eyes and looked out over the water. The sea was calm and rolled almost flat to the horizon, except for a single rocky isle that broke the water a little way offshore. It was a curious craggy spike, seemingly barren except for a desperate little cluster of trees.

Despite the blazing sunshine, the island appeared resolutely gloomy and menacing as if it were huddled beneath its own little black cloud, despite the clear blue skies.

We dozed and chatted in the sun until a little later when Rick finally emerged from the water and strode up the beach to join us.

"Are you all really going to waste your weekend sitting about?" he asked as he dried off.

"Oh I should hope so darling," replied Nancy from behind her sunglasses. "We don't all have your enthusiasm for exertion."

"Quite," added Albert, glancing a grin in my direction. "This is supposed to be a holiday after all."

"But just sitting here all day?" continued Rick. He lay down beside Nancy and propped himself up on his elbows. "It's so boring."

"It wasn't dear," said Nancy, entirely unmoved. "At least not until you chose to join us anyway."

"I'm sure I don't know what you mean," replied Rick, staring back down the beach.

We sat in silence for a while, listening to the surf and Susan's muted squeals of delight.

"So, Charles," Rick began again, clearly restless. "How do you find our coastal retreat?"

"Oh, first class," I replied. "Really top notch, wonderful even."

We lapsed back into silence. Nancy and Albert feigned sleep, closing their eyes gently to the blazing sun overhead, apparently quite able and happy to ignore Rick's frustration.

I on the other hand, found myself unable to relax in the presence of Rick's poor mood and after only a few more minutes could bear it no longer.

"That an interesting feature," I heard myself say, waving towards the water. "Out there."

"The Rock?!" Rick replied, suddenly animated. "It's certainly a curious place. When I was a child we would spend weekends here in the spring and I heard all sorts of tales about it from the help."

"In the spring?" I asked, my instinctive engine of polite conversation catching fire. "I would have thought this to be more of a summer haunt."

"Hardly," scoffed Rick, suddenly scornful. "It's a nice enough place to spend an afternoon but we would usually summer in Europe."

I felt my cheeks redden and so sought to return the conversation to its original track.

"But this rock..." I said.

"Ah yes," said Rick. "The earliest tales go back to before colonial times even, it's said that the natives have shunned the place since time immemorial. They have some kind of savage instinct for that kind of thing you see."

"Colonial times?" I asked, my own interests genuinely stirred.

"That's right," Rick said. "It all began back in your merry old England with the thirteenth Duke of..."

"And I do believe that that," Nancy broke in, suddenly stirring and turning to Albert. "Is our cue to make another round of drinks."

"But darling I was just about to tell Charles here..." Rick protested as Nancy unfolded herself upright. She eased from horizontal to vertical with fluid grace to settle into a defiant pose, standing over Rick, unlit cigarette in hand.

"I know exactly what you're about to tell Charles dear," she said. "We've all heard it many times before and I am quite sure that I don't care to hear it again.

"Now, as the chances of my enjoying the sunshine in peace and quiet are remote at best until you have told Charles your little tale, Albert and I shall withdraw to the house to make another round of drinks.

"That way, even if you haven't finished by the time we return, at least the listening will be made a little easier."

Rick smiled up at her sourly, his athletic bulk suddenly reduced to the frame of a petulant child. Nancy blew him a kiss before allowing Albert to light her cigarette and then following him back up the beach to the house.

"The fairer sex," Rick said, shaking his head while

returning his attention to me. "Heaven and hell in heels and a hat!"

I smiled and nodded sagely, pretending I knew what he meant.

"Anyway," he said. "Ignore her, it all begins with the Duke..."

Over the next few minutes I sat on the sand, feeling it scratch between my toes, while Rick told me the story of the Rock.

Before I relay this part of tale however, I must make it clear that it is vital that the Duke's legacy never be rediscovered by anyone.

For this reason I have been deliberately obscure as to the location of the beach on which we sat that day and I will also not reveal the name of the Duke.

I appreciate that this means I am depriving the reader of essential facts by which to verify the truth of my story, however such was the darkness of that place and of that man that your disbelief, good reader, is a risk I am willing to take to keep the world safe from such evil.

The sun beat down on us relentlessly, its light aching in my eyes, its heat seeping through into my bones.

Yet as Rick spoke lazily, clearly enjoying the telling of the tale to a new audience, I felt a small chill begin to grow within me that not even the furious summer could warm.

He spoke of a Duke, the last of a great and noble line who lived in England centuries previously. According to Rick, the Duke was known throughout the kingdom as a dark sorcerer, a sadist and a truly wicked man.

Although it all sounded to be obvious and fantastical nonsense, I found myself disturbed by Rick's words. To retain my composure, I found it necessary to continually remind myself that during all my studies of history, I had never heard mention of the Duke's family name.

I believed I knew as fact that this dreadful man had never existed, yet I could not help but be drawn to imagine him as a real person.

As Rick described what was rumoured to be the Duke's favourite ritual, the brutal sacrifice of a newborn

131

infant, I felt a sour taste form in my mouth and I shifted uncomfortably in the sand.

All the while The Rock sat out in the sea, glaring at us across the water, a dark blot squatting resolute amidst the bright summer's day.

I remember feeling a great sense of urgency that Rick must not discover my discomfort. I felt I had to retain my composure at all costs and that no matter how gruesome the tale became, I must laugh it off with the same casual air my friends seemed to constantly exude.

Just as my forced chortle began to grow hoarse, Nancy and Albert reappeared, each carrying two tall glasses.

I accepted mine from Albert with a smile and a nod, welcoming both the distraction and the ice-cold refreshment.

We shifted into more comfortable drinking positions and fell silent, sipping our cocktails and watching Susan drag Melvin relentlessly in and out of the surf.

"I know!" said Rick suddenly.

"I'm sure you do darling," said Nancy. "But is there any chance you could keep it to yourself?"

Rick ignored her and continued.

"Let's swim out to The Rock," he said, looking from the island to Albert and me excitedly.

"Really?" asked Albert doubtfully. "It's an awfully long way."

"Oh you're worse than Melvin," said Rick dismissively before turning to me. "What do you say Charles, fancy a dip?"

"Well..." I began but was interrupted by a breathless Susan who had rejoined us with Melvin still in tow.

"What are we doing?" she asked, her eyes sparkling.

"Charles and I are going to swim out to the Rock," said Rick.

"Oh fun!" squealed Susan. "We'll do that, won't we Melvin?"

Melvin was standing just behind her, squinting and wheezing and looking thoroughly miserable.

"I'm not supposed to go swimming," he said. "It's

my lungs you see, my mother says that..."

"Melvin and the girls can take the row boat with some supplies," interrupted Rick. "That way we can have some drinks when we get there."

"Oh Rick!" protested Susan petulantly. "Sometimes you're simply insufferable! I'm not going to sit in some dreadful little boat while you boys have all the fun. I'll swim too thank you very much and probably faster than you as well."

"Well I'm definitely not swimming today," said Albert. "So I suppose I'll row the boat then."

Standing, he stretched and drained his glass before wandering off. Meanwhile Melvin detached himself from Susan and followed after Albert, clearly fearful of being dragged any further out of his depth.

Susan watched them go and then dropped into the sand beside me, hugging my arm.

"Are you really going to swim across with us?" she asked, staring at me wide eyed so that my swelling chest immediately pushed all doubts and fears to one side.

"Of course," I replied with a grin. "I swim in the river back in Oxford all the time."

This wasn't strictly true. I had technically swum in the river once during the previous summer but only because I had fallen off a punt, much to everyone's amusement.

"Wonderful," she said, squeezing my arm. "I think you'll like The Rock," she said dreamily.

"Oh yes?" I asked.

"Oh absolutely. Rick always says there's a house out there and that it's ever so old. It was built by some of the first settlers and I just know it'll fit right in with all your colonial history jazz."

"A house?" I said surprised and then peered out at the island again, looking for straight lines among the tangle of rocks and trees but finding nothing.

The next hour or so was a flurry of activity. We packed everything we might need while on The Rock into bags and loaded them into a small and rickety looking row boat that was beached behind the house.

I changed into a pair of swimming trunks that Albert loaned me and before I knew it, Rick, Nancy, Susan and

133

I were standing in the surf.

Nancy had taken one look at the small boat and declared that she would rather take her chances swimming.

Melvin sat in the boat looking miserable while Albert pushed it out into the water and the rest of us waded out after it until we could begin to swim.

Despite the glorious sunshine the water was distinctly cool and as it had been sometime since I had swum any distance at all, I found it hard work at first.

Rick and Nancy quickly pulled away, cutting smooth efficient shapes through the water, while Susan changed between front crawl and backstroke, occasionally treading water and calling to Albert and Melvin in the boat.

I concentrated hard on keeping up until reaching my limit and then pausing to tread water and breathe. The Rock appeared much as it had when viewed from the beach, as if for all my efforts I had hardly made any distance at all.

Looking back to shore however I found that the beach house had shrunk drastically and realised then just how far out we were.

As I floated there, I rose and fell on great slow waves and a chilled feeling of vulnerability crept upon me.

I looked down into the water that had been so clear near the shore. There was nothing but a vast, inhuman expanse of darkness below my bare, flailing legs.

Suddenly, I found myself frozen solid in outright terror. Some unseen thing had brushed against my ankles, slipping gently about them, cold and smooth.

Despite my fatigue my legs began to thrash in utter terror, desperate to get away from whatever it was beneath me, knowing it could snatch at me at any moment.

Susan's voice chimed through my panic and I concentrated my fear into more deliberate strokes towards her, desperate to be out of the water as soon as possible. After perhaps a dozen more strokes I managed to narrow my focus down to just the next few feet of water ahead of me.

I pushed on, even as my shoulders began to burn and then howl, not allowing myself to think of anything but the next stroke and then the next.

I continued like that for what felt like an eternity, spurred on by the ever-looming panic which followed close behind, threatening to sweep back in and overwhelm me at any moment.

Suddenly my knee collided with something under the water, not slippery and fleeting, but solid and broad. I allowed my awareness to balloon back out and realised that rather than swimming, I was now just lying on my stomach in the shallows of The Rock.

I had made it.

I dragged myself up out of the water and staggered onto the stony beach, panting and spent. In that moment I resolved to ride in the boat upon our return, regardless of what Susan might think of me.

I even considered feigning a minor injury in advance so as to provide a face saving excuse. The four of us caught our breath while Albert dragged the boat up onto the shore.

We dried and dressed before I took my first proper look at the place. It was just as desolate as it had appeared from the shore, rocks upon rocks. The land rose quickly from the sea to some scarce scrub which led into a copse of tall, heavy trees. Countless thick branches tangled together horribly, casting deep, spiteful shadows beneath them.

Susan fussed around Melvin, who was complaining bitterly of seasickness, while Albert unloaded the supplies.

Rick and Nancy were standing a little further up the path, talking quietly and occasionally shooting wicked glances back at Melvin. As my breathing returned to normal, I turned back to survey the water I had bested.

The distant shore sat unmoving, like a great landscape painting beyond the endless, rippling blue. The beach house was tiny, yet perfectly visible, lit so brightly by the summer sun.

An uneasy thought niggled at me and I dropped my gaze to my feet. The hard, bare earth below sat in cool, brooding shadow. Glancing about me, I realised that the

135

whole place was somehow in shade.

I turned to follow the rest of the group away from the shore, heading up a narrow track that led into the gloom beneath the trees.

I threw one last glance over my shoulder, back across the water to that other world of yellow and blue then stepped into the woods.

Among the trees a damp, fetid chill hung over everything and the ground was slippery underfoot. No birds sang and the breeze that had ridden the waves behind us was unable to penetrate the woods so that everything was silent and still. Each step we took seemed to put another mile between us and the safety of the distant shore.

For a little while we all remained silent, oppressed by the suddenly heavy atmosphere. Occasionally Melvin would sniff or cough but otherwise the only sounds were our footsteps. Susan glanced back at me over her shoulder but even her smile faltered as we trudged on.

Eventually Rick called back from the head of the line, waiting for each of us to catch up before breaking the silence with his deep, confident voice.

"Ladies and gentleman," he said, actually sweeping his arm out before him. "I give you, Pitway Manor!"

We spilled out from the trees into a clearing dominated by the vast, blackened stone frontage of a house. I heard Susan and Melvin gasp and realised my own mouth was hanging open.

I found myself taking a step backwards towards the trees and so made a show of peering up at the house as if I had moved back simply to gain a better view. I knew it had been an involuntary action however, an instinctive recoiling from a hateful thing.

The others muttered amongst themselves in hushed tones while I began to interrogate the place by eye. The house itself appeared impossible.

As my scholar's eye pushed past the knot in my stomach, I began to catalogue architectural features, building techniques and materials, my curiosity gradually overcoming my fear.

So incredible was the sheer presence of the house that it took me a moment to recognise its most curious feature. Every window had been bricked up to create an array of blind, seething eyes across the front of the house.

I will not give the location of The Rock here for as I say, it is my dearest wish that, should that hateful house still stand after all this time, no-one will ever find it again.

This being the case, I have only my word to offer when I assert that as unlikely as it may sound, the house that standing before us that day was an English stately home.

The style and stone were exactly as those of many great houses which still stand across our island today. So many years amid the damp and the gloom of The Rock however, had coated the stonework with a dark, glistening sheen so that the whole place seemed to bristle, black and venomous.

Rick began to recount the story of the house and while it sounded like perfect nonsense, the mighty pile before us sat as spiteful, resolute proof of the fantastic tale.

Rick began by telling us of the early life of an English aristocrat, a Duke who shall remain unnamed here in the hope that his name be finally lost to history forever.

I had never heard of this nobleman's name, nor of his family seat even though Rick described both as being in the very county in which I was born and raised. I assumed these details were new additions to the tale, aimed at personalising it for me for greater impact.

"He was downright notorious in his day," Rick continued, his back to the looming house now as he addressed us. He allowed a silence to yawn open around us so that we felt even smaller, the house even bigger.

"Utterly wicked they say," he continued eventually, now in a hushed, almost reverent tone. "A deviant of the highest, or perhaps the lowest order. The Duke was wont to experiment with the occult, a devotee to the darkest arts.

"It was said that the Duke met with the Devil himself on several occasions and that there was no depth of depravity to which he would not gleefully sink."

Pacing back and forth, Rick leaned into his words, putting on a good show for us and clearly enjoying every moment of it.

The shadows remained cool however and the stones of the house seemed to emanate a deep chill so that I found myself shivering as he continued.

"After decades of debauchery and wickedness however," Rick said. "The Duke finally strayed too far. His favourite ritual involved the sacrificing of a newborn child to the Devil.."

"Oh Rick, no!" Susan's cry was petulant but shot through with genuine fear. "You mustn't say such things, it's too horrible!"

"Oh but it's all quite true I'm afraid," Rick grinned. "The Duke disposed of dozens of babes over the years but they were always orphans, foundlings, peasant children. This time however the Duke needed more, a greater sacrifice."

Rick paused to look at each of us in turn as if to check that we were all held firmly in the grip of his words.

"He arranged an elaborate plan," Rick continued. "The wife of another noble, some distant relation of the Duke, was led to believe that her child had died at birth.

"In fact, the Duke had her child replaced with the body of another and spirited her child away for his own wicked purposes."

Susan let out another squeal and flung herself into Melvin who had been hovering at her side, burying her face in his shoulder. For his part, Melvin had turned a strange green grey colour and almost tumbled over when Susan threw herself upon him.

That said, for all his seasickness and fear, I noticed that Melvin's normal colour returned quite quickly once Susan's soft form was pressed against him.

Albert was working hard to maintain an air of disinterest but not quite managing to hide his discomfort. Meanwhile Nancy just smoked and stared sourly at Rick, openly irritated by his theatrics.

"All was well until the Duke was betrayed and his crimes exposed," Rick continued. "There was a great scandal wherein many of the Duke's enemies called for his head and indeed it was expected that the Crown could do nothing but order the Duke's execution."

Rick retreated from us here, backing towards the house and ascending the first two steps that led up to the mighty front doors.

"Much to society's outrage however," said Rick. "The Duke was not executed and seditious rumours ran rife. Some said that, before the creation of the mighty British navy, the Crown had employed the Duke and his dark arts to protect trading vessels.

"Others that members of the royal family themselves had partaken in the Duke's vile rituals and were bound to him."

Rick cleared the rest of the steps and placed a hand flat against the huge double doors. For some reason we all took a step towards him, as if the house was drawing us in.

"Whatever the truth of it," said Rick then. "The Duke's life was in fact spared. First, he was stripped of his lands and titles. These were added to the estates of the victim's family and after that all record of him was expunged so that it was as if he had never existed. Finally, he was sentenced to exile in the colonies."

My heart was pounding as if trying to escape my chest. I swallowed hard, clenching my fists to hold on to my courage.

"One last favour was mysteriously granted him however," said Rick. "His house, the site of all his many dreadful crimes, was supposed to be burned to the ground.

"Before the fire could be set however, through some canny influence the Duke was instead able to have the house taken down, transported and rebuilt, stone by stone."

Rick patted the door and then looked at each one of us in turn.

"My friends," he announced, his voice rising higher as he turned away from us and pushed the great double doors inwards to reveal a gaping, black maw.

"This, is Pitway Manor! This, is the house the Duke brought with him to the new world. This, is the very place where he lived out his exile, where he continued his rites and his rituals. To what depths? To what ends? No-one knows, or at least, no-one who survived..."

And with this he was gone, consumed by the pitch interior of the house. There followed a moment of deep silence, broken only by Susan's muffled mewling.

"Extraordinary," sighed Nancy in a flat tone, shaking her head and dropping her cigarette. She ground it out with the toe of her shoe and followed Rick into the house.

"Albie," she called over her shoulder. "Be a dear and bring the bags won't you."

I watched dumbly as Nancy disappeared inside. I knew from my studies that Rick's story was absolute nonsense and yet the hideous building looming over me challenged me to provide any other explanation.

I shook myself, irritated by the fear Rick had so successfully managed to inspire and keen to find distraction from it. I moved past Susan as she detached herself from Melvin and took one of the two bags from Albert.

"He paints quite a picture doesn't he?" said Albert, smiling as I lightened his load.

"I'll say," I replied, forcing a smile in return.

We stepped from gloom into pitch so that at first I could see literally nothing. I took a few slow, faltering steps, my free hand stretched out ahead of me. My footsteps tumbled away from me, crashing into unseen surfaces all around and returning as echoes.

I closed my eyes so as to concentrate on following the sound of Albert's footsteps ahead and tried to ignore the sounds of Susan behind. She was patiently cajoling a near hysterical Melvin into following us.

After a minute or two of total void I began to see ghostly shapes, faint outlines of greys on black. I thought I could make out some furniture among the otherwise confusing shapes but could not see anything in enough detail to inspect it.

Rick and Nancy's voices grew louder and suddenly small, fragile shards of light began to flutter up ahead.

"You take us to all the best places Rick," said Albert sarcastically, allowing just a hint of irritation to slip through his cool as he dumped the heavy bag.

I unburdened myself as well and stepped closer to Nancy and the flickering candle she held. Rick passed his own candle to Albert to hold while he dropped to his haunches and began to rummage through the bags.

Even illuminated by the trembling candlelight, Nancy appeared as unmoved as ever. She was smoking languidly and looked for all the world as if she was simply enduring one more tedious cocktail party.

"...but what if I were to slip and fall?" came a familiar, breathless whine through the darkness behind us. "The nearest hospital must be hours away. And how do we know this place is really deserted anyway? Any number of dangerous types could have moved in here who might take great exception to our presence..."

With a triumphant grunt, Rick erupted from the bags on the floor so that Melvin gasped into silence. Brandishing a fistful of candles, Rick passed them around and after a few moments of tilting and lighting we each held a precious, light giving flame.

More of the room around us became visible but only enough to suggest a scattering of wooden chairs, dark oblongs on the walls and a ceiling so high that it remained hidden in the darkness overhead.

Curiosity overcame us and our initial cluster broke apart as we each moved tentatively out into the room. I swung my candle back and forth slowly before me so that lines of furniture swelled out of and back into the black.

I came across a vast stone fireplace, five feet tall and at least ten feet wide. I noticed a feeble yet icy chill flowing from it into the room. It was an old cold, so complete that I found it hard to believe a fire had ever burned there.

Hearing the others moving around, I glanced back over my shoulder but saw only yellow circles hovering in the black.

I was reminded of the feeling of the ocean, of floating alone and vulnerable in an endless swell. The feeling grew to a palpable sensation, the feeling that somewhere within the darkness around me, some unseen thing was seething, just waiting to lunge forth and snatch at me.

Just then, an almighty crash followed by a shrill and girlish scream drove me from my senses so that I started violently. My startled hands abandoned my candle so that it fell to the floor.

"I'm sure I don't know what you're doing," came Nancy's voice, unruffled and disapproving.

"They say patience is a virtue dear," Rick's barbed reply fired back almost immediately. "Perhaps you might like to try it."

"Oh I think you're quite virtuous enough for the both of us darling," Nancy sighed.

Regaining my composure, I stooped to collect my spluttering candle, hoping that no-one had noticed my fearful clumsiness.

Moving towards the sound of bickering voices I quickly picked out Rick's shape, swinging something down against the floor so that another almighty crash exploded about us before bouncing off through the rest of the house.

"What's happening?!" whined Melvin. His voice was so childlike that I didn't need to see him to know that he was clinging desperately to Susan.

"Well Melvin," Nancy's voice was thick with casual condescension. "I believe Rick is currently breaking one our host's chairs into pieces by striking it against the floor."

"What?" Melvin quavered on. "But why? Oh the noise of it! My mother says I have a fragile heart, I mustn't be subject to shocks and starts..."

"Why indeed," Nancy drawled on. "Perhaps you could enlighten us dear?"

A clattering sound spoke of Rick dropping the pieces of the chair to the floor followed by the sound of him rummaging through the bags.

"That," he said over the sound of tearing fabric. "Is precisely what I am attempting to do."

Rick's hand swam up toward me out of the darkness, gesturing for my candle. I hesitated for a moment, initially unwilling to release my precious light source.

In that moment however, my fear of appearing a coward in front of the others overwhelmed my fear of the dark and I handed it over.

A moment more and the yellow flame of my candle swelled and grew, pushing the darkness away from us. Blinking, I took a step back as Rick straightened up, wielding four blazing torches fashioned from chair legs, strips of fabric and some kind of alcohol. He handed me one with a wink and I smiled, accepting the blazing rod with relief.

Suddenly the room was awash with shifting yellow light and appeared much smaller than it had in the dark. Other than the impressive fireplace, the room was more or less barren.

A few small wooden chairs were tumbled in a corner and a few large, dull paintings hung from the walls but otherwise the place was bare and derelict.

Rick held his torch high, swinging according to Nancy's instructions as the pair of them inspected the far corner of the room. Closer to me, Albert had used his torch to peer into the fireplace but was now examining the torch itself.

Susan had taken the torch Rick had thrust upon Melvin and was attempting to comfort him. His head was buried in her shoulder and while she cooed and murmured to him distractedly, her wide eyes roamed the room with something closer to her usual gleeful curiosity.

"What did you use to make these Rick?" asked Albert, still scrutinising the business end of his torch.

"I don't know," Rick called back over his shoulder uninterested. "Some rags I found in the big bag."

Melvin suddenly drew his head away from Susan and snatched at her wrist, pulling the torch closer to his pinched little face.

"My sweater!" he cried in absolute torment. "That was a gift from my great aunt! I'll probably catch a chill now and I have such terrible trouble with my joints when I catch a chill, they swell awfully and hurt ever so much."

I could hear Rick and Nancy chuckling from the other side of the room and I shared a mischievous grin with Albert.

"Never mind old man," said Albert playfully. "I'm

sure we all appreciate your sacrifice and besides, you have Susan to keep you warm."

I saw Susan cast a sideways glance at Melvin beside her, confirming his attention was elsewhere before narrowing her eyes and sticking out her tongue at Albert.

"So what now?" I asked the room, drawing a line under Melvin's complaints.

"Now we explore!" Rick replied excitedly as he and Nancy returned to the centre of the room. "Somewhere within this house there lies a chamber, the Duke's inner sanctum and the site of his most terrible crimes!"

"This newfound penchant of yours for dramatic effect really is becoming rather tiresome you know," said Nancy, lighting a fresh cigarette from Rick's torch.

"Nobody likes a spoil sport darling," Rick replied, drawing breath to press on.

"And nobody likes a ham, yet here we are," Nancy cut him off again. "The question is, were Albert to look through those bags for something to drink, would I be disappointed?"

"Yes darling," Rick replied, moving his torch from one hand to another so as to reach into his pocket. "I'm rather afraid you would be, however..."

He produced a hip flask and passed it Nancy who eyed it with suspicion before accepting it delicately. Smoking all the while, she twisted open the lid with an expert flick of her thumb and took a solid swig from the flask.

"You know darling there are times," Nancy said to Rick while passing the flask to Albert. "When you really are almost competent."

"High praise indeed," replied Rick sourly. "Anyway, the Duke's ceremonial chamber..."

Albert passed me the flask. I glanced about the flamelit faces before surreptitiously sniffing at the flask. A powerful scent of gin seized my stomach and I braced myself before taking a swig.

The spirit burned through me but almost immediately I felt a slight softening of tensions and lessening of fear. As Rick proposed we split into teams to search the house I passed the flask to Melvin.

"Oh no," he said petulantly. "I don't drink. Alcohol does terrible things to my stomach you know, I have the beginnings of a nervous ulcer, or at least that's what my mother's doctor said..."

Reaching past him, Susan almost snatched the flask from my hand, drawing deeply and desperately from it and eventually draining it dry.

Lowering the flask Susan smacked her lips and blinked a few times before passing the empty flask back to Rick.

"So we'll all meet back here in twenty minutes, agreed?" said Rick.

"I take it that was the last of the refreshments?" Nancy asked, ignoring Rick completely.

"Perhaps there's a wine cellar!" exclaimed Susan, suddenly enthused.

"Now that would be civilised," replied Nancy with approval.

"How do we get downstairs?" Susan asked the room at large.

"But the Duke's chamber..." Rick tried again.

"Yes, yes," snapped Nancy. "The Duke's chamber, his terrible crimes, it all sounds perfectly delightful darling but personally I think the exploration of a well-stocked cellar would be a far more enjoyable way to spend our time."

"Look," Rick's voice dropped low as he turned to hiss at Nancy directly. "I didn't come all the way out here just to..."

"If the Duke did have a chamber," I heard myself interrupting, surprised by the sound of my own voice. "Then surely it would most likely lie beneath the house as would a wine cellar."

"Exactly," added Albert. "We needn't choose, we can look for them both."

Rick pursed his lips but gave me a grudging nod and seemed satisfied with the compromise.

"So," Susan said, openly impatient. "How do we get downstairs?!"

"Downstairs?" quavered Melvin. "As in, underground?" We all ignored him as one.

"There's a passageway in the fireplace," said Albert

simply.

There was a moment's silence while we all stared at him awaiting more.

"I found it before," he added. "Can't you feel the draft?"

He moved to the great hearth and we all followed, clustering around and peering in. Sure enough, as we stooped forward and plunged our torches into the fireplace, they guttered sideways.

The shadow to the right, that had appeared to me to be a solid wall, was in fact a narrow opening in the brickwork.

I chastised myself for having not noticed the passageway myself, recalling the movement of air I'd felt before. The others didn't appear to have noticed my error however so I let it pass.

Albert moved his torch into the opening and a brief series of steep stone stairs became visible, plunging down into utter darkness below. As one we paused and swallowed, each intimidated by the descent before us.

"Ok!" barked Rick suddenly, gleeful once more and making each of us start. "Who's first?!"

We glanced about at each other in the glare of Rick's challenge and I saw Melvin shrink away, actually taking a step backwards to move behind Susan's shoulder. For a moment Susan's eyes met mine and for the first time I noticed a chink in her enthusiasm at the thought of leading us down.

"I'll go," I heard myself say.

"Good man," said Rick happily, slapping me hard on the shoulder.

The others organised themselves in single file behind me as I ducked into the fireplace and took a deep, slightly ragged breath. I licked my lips and swallowed before tentatively lowering my foot to the first step.

The stone passage was barely three feet wide and the ceiling persistently low. As I took a few steps more and heard the others move in behind me I had to fight back a rabid feeling of claustrophobic panic that swelled in my gut.

Despite the chill in the air and the icy, damp stone

all about us, I noticed sweat dripping from my fist as I clung desperately to my torch.

After a few more steps down into the dark, the staircase began to twist into a tight spiral. My heart was rattling in my chest, while my stomach clenched and twisted.

I focused hard on holding my torch firmly, determined not to allow the flame to betray my trembling to the others.

Gritting my teeth, I swallowed hard but still no end appeared, just more and more steps, down and down, further into the dark.

I could hear the others breathing behind me and somewhere in there came a series of low moans from Melvin. We were well beneath the house now, deep inside the belly of the great rock itself.

I don't know how many steps there were, it felt like it took forever to descend them all. By the time we reached the bottom I had become numb, almost an automaton, consumed by simply placing one foot in front of the other and desperately not thinking about anything else.

It was for this reason that I stumbled a little as I stepped into the low ceilinged chamber at the base of the staircase.

I paused, trying to take in this new environment, to identify what new horrors I now faced. The footsteps of the others behind me however propelled me out into the middle of the space as they filed in behind me.

The chamber was long, narrow and tight, only adding to the feeling of constriction from the staircase. Just for a second, I was terribly aware of the sheer weight of rock, not to mention the house itself, pressing down on us from above.

I teetered on the edge of total panic then, but at the last moment dragged myself back and forced myself to concentrate on exploring the chamber instead.

The walls were bare rock, the space having obviously been a natural cave to start with, further expanded by excavation.

The floor was rough and bare and bore almost no furniture other than two large, empty wine racks against the far wall.

It was Albert who spotted the sconces fixed into the living rock of the walls. Two of them still held dry, ancient torches which, when touched by our own, miraculously spluttered into life.

Waves of yellow light swayed back and forth across the room, so that our shadows danced around us. Besides the shadows and the empty wine racks however, the chamber was completely empty. It was a dead end.

"Well," said Nancy suddenly so that most of us jumped. "Isn't this nice. Of all the places we could spend our vacation, you've chosen to lead us into a literal hole in the ground. Bravo darling, bravo."

"This can't be it," said Rick confused, pretending to ignore Nancy. "There must be more."

He moved to inspect the wine racks while the rest of us stayed together, unsure what to do next.

"I don't like it here," said Melvin, his voice trembling. "We should go back upstairs."

"Melvin," sighed Nancy. "I do believe you're right. There's a first time for everything I suppose."

She turned to address Rick's back which was hunched over as he peered into the various slots of the wine rack.

"You've had your little adventure now dear," she said. "Shall we ascend back towards civilisation or do you intend for us to spend the whole day in this tomb?"

"Here!" cried Rick, triumphant.

Nancy rolled her eyes and turned away from him to smoke beside Susan and Melvin while Albert and I approached.

"Look!" said Rick as we arrived alongside him. "Behind the rack, that's not solid rock, it's been bricked up. There's something behind this wall. Here, help me move this out of the way."

It was hard to tell through the flickering light and shifting shadows, but the wall behind the rack did appear to be made up of regular, straight edged shapes. Albert moved to one end of the rack and I to the other while Rick took hold of it in the middle.

The rack was heavy and initially resisted all attempts to move it. After a few minutes of straining and a redoubling of our efforts however, the structure began to groan and shift.

We were pulling to try and lift it clear of the floor just enough to move it away from the wall. Instead, the rack came apart in our hands so that the three of us fell away from it and the whole thing clattered to the floor in a heap of mouldering planks.

The noise of the impact was incredible, rebounding back and forth off the close walls and low ceiling. Susan and Melvin both screamed, adding to the din so that for a few seconds we all held fast, cringing and grimacing.

Eventually the echoes faded and Rick was the first to get back on his feet. By the time Albert and I rejoined him, he was crouched on the floor, pressing his hands against the brickwork, feeling for weak spots.

I glanced at Albert unsure and found him frowning his own concerns. This felt like it had gone on long enough and it was growing increasingly difficult to suppress the desire for fresh air beneath an open sky.

I had just drawn breath to suggest to Rick that perhaps we should leave, when his hand suddenly jerked forward through the wall.

He grinned up at Albert and then at me in turn and began pulling at the bricks around the hole he had made.

I looked to Albert again but he only shrugged, crouching beside Rick to help. I glanced back at the others who were watching in horror, before following suit. The mortar between the bricks had dried out to crumbling powder and the bricks came away easily.

Once we'd removed a sufficient number, whole sections began to fall away and after only five or ten minutes we were faced with a jagged edged doorway. The space beyond was pitch black but not for long as Rick snatched up his torch and rushed forward.

"My god!" I heard him gasp.

I squinted after him but could only make out the flailing flame of his torch. Albert moved past me to follow and after a moment's hesitation I stepped gingerly through the opening as well.

Rick and Albert were busy lighting yet more wall mounted torches but at the sight of the space I simply froze and goggled.

Unlike the rough little chamber behind, I now found myself in a large, perfectly circular room. The walls had been rendered smooth and hung with now mouldering tapestries. Heavy rugs covered the floor and ornate furniture ran the circumference of the room.

Against the wall across the room, directly opposite me, two large, heavily decorated tables flanked a tall, simple altar.

The tables were stacked with a jumble of thick, heavy tomes, ornate goblets and bowls, glittering daggers and small leather bags bulging with who knew what. Between them, the altar stood empty and perfectly smooth but marked with sinister stains.

The room was dominated however by a low, broad mouthed well that sat perfectly in the centre. The kneehigh wall around the opening had once been decorated with complex, eye-watering carvings, now thankfully faded and worn.

"Oh good grief," came a voice from behind.

I turned to see Nancy emerging through the doorway, eyeing the room with disdain.

"It is a little sinister isn't it?" I said, moving to meet her.

"I suppose so," she said, continuing to look around. "Though I was rather thinking of Rick. I shall never hear the end of this now. It benefits no-one for him to be proven right too often, it gives him ideas."

Susan appeared then, dragging Melvin along behind.

"Oh wow!" she cried, eyes and mouth both wide. Melvin meanwhile looked simply sick and lingered by the opening, hugging himself.

"I don't like this," he said in a tiny voice we all ignored.

For a few minutes the rest of us explored the room, rummaging through the clutter on the tables, flicking through the crumbling tomes and examining the apocalyptic scenes portrayed on the tapestries.

Eventually however we all gravitated towards the well in the centre of the room and formed ourselves into a loose ring of five around the opening, none of us getting too close.

"So," said Rick, gloating and gleeful. "What do you say now?"

"Have to hand it to you, old man," said Albert. "You were right."

"It's amazing!" gushed Susan.

"Remarkable," I added, not wanting to be left out.

"Oh please don't encourage him," said Nancy. "If his head swells any more he'll never get back through that hole in the wall and we'll have to live down here."

Rick briefly pulled a face at Nancy before resuming his grin.

"This is it!" he said. "The Duke's inner sanctum! This is where he performed all those ghoulish rituals."

"And what's this?" asked Susan, leaning forward just a little to peer over the lip of the well while simultaneously holding herself back.

"The Well of Souls," said Albert, craning his neck to look into the well in a similarly tentative fashion to Susan. We all stared at him until he looked up at the silence and then around the circle at our questioning faces.

"It's mentioned in one of those books over there," he explained, waving towards the tables beside the altar.

We all nodded at this and then fell back into silence for a moment. The atmosphere in the room was thick and ominous and I felt myself swinging back and forth between giddy curiosity and trembling fear.

"There must be underwater caverns beneath the rock," said Rick eventually. "This must connect straight into the ocean."

Sure enough, now that I looked more closely I could see the surface of the water moving slightly against the edges of the well, lapping back and forth.

"But the water's so dark," said Susan in a hushed, awe struck voice. "That's not sea water is it?"

"I think it is," I said then, licking my lips and trying to hold my voice steady. "I think the water's actually perfectly clear, it's the walls of the well and just the sheer depth of it that makes it look black."

"How deep do you think it is?" asked Susan, moving to my side and clinging to my arm, all the while staring

151

at the mouth of the well.

"I.." I began, but the blackness of the well seemed to suck the air out of my lungs. "..I don't know," I finished thickly.

"Albert?" asked Rick. "What did the book say?"

"The well is almost bottomless," said Albert in a strange, empty voice as he reread the text from memory. "It plunges down to the very deepest depths of the ocean, to the home of the Duke's true master."

"To the Devil?" asked Susan in a tiny, frightened voice before burying her face in my shoulder.

I wrapped my arm around her shoulders and held her to me, ostensibly to comfort her though I admit I needed the comfort just as much as she.

Minutes before, such familiar contact with Susan would have thrilled me, now it only just served to keep my nerves in check.

"Oh no," said Albert, shaking his head. "The stories of devil worship were just a smokescreen to conceal the truth"

"What truth?" asked Rick sharply, frowning.

"That he was actually communing with something else, something older," said Albert, still staring. "Something worse."

At that very moment, despite the stillness of the fetid air, a chill seemed to sweep through the room so that we all shivered.

"Well," asked Rick, sudden and loud as if trying to bully the atmosphere back under his control. "What else did the book say?"

"It described the Ritual of the Well," said Albert quietly before lapsing back into silence.

"And?" said Rick then, irritated. "Come on man, out with it!"

Albert sighed then shook himself, finally turning his attention from the well and back to the rest of us.

"It says the initiate stands on the lip of the well and stares into its depths," he said. "They stare until they see the bottom and then wait to see if the master considers them worthy."

"And if he does?" I asked, not recognising my own voice.

"If he finds you worthy," said Albert, turning to look me straight in the eye. "He takes your soul."

A low moan made us all jump. We all turned as one to see Melvin clinging to the edge of the hole in the wall, breathing heavily and shaking his head. I admit, I had forgotten he was even there, as I suspect had the others.

"Alright!" said Nancy sudden and sharp, snatching everyone's attention and cracking through the tension. "This has been all been fascinating I'm sure but I for one would like a drink and some fresh air, preferably in that order. Shall we go?"

"We can't leave now!" said Rick, incredulous. "I'm going to do it."

I turned to stare at Rick open mouthed and was mirrored by Susan and Albert.

"You don't mean.." gasped Susan.

"Why not," said Rick boldly, stepping right up to the edge of the well.

"But Rick.." said Susan.

"Is this a good idea?" I said.

"Oh come on!" said Rick, grinning wickedly at us all. "You can't really believe any of that? So then what's the harm?"

Susan and Albert and I all looked at one another and then to Nancy but she was too busy glaring at Rick to notice. She was standing a little behind and beside him, arms folded, eyebrow raised, entirely unimpressed.

Rick mounted the lip of the well and took a moment to balance himself on its edge. Once steady he took one last look at each of us in turn before lowering his gaze to the water.

As I watched his eyes unfocus, I held my breath and could feel Susan doing the same. Seconds dropped past like millstones as I watched Rick for any indication of strangeness and strained to listen for movement from below.

At one point he appeared to wobble slightly, his head drooping a little and just for a moment I thought he was going to tumble forwards.

Instead, he shook himself to straightening and hopped back down off the edge of the well, grinning broadly.

"It would appear that I am not worthy," he said, taking a bow.

"I've been telling you that for years darling," said Nancy.

"And you my love?" he replied.

Nancy rolled her eyes and cast her cigarette to the floor in annoyance, grinding it into the rug.

"Fine," she said, smiling bitterly. "If it will get us out of here any sooner."

Taking Rick's hand for balance, Nancy stepped up onto the lip and repeated the ritual after which Albert followed suit with a shrug. The three of them turned to look at Susan and me expectantly.

"Charlie?" said Susan, her voice trembled as she searched my expression.

I wrestled with the thrashing terror building in my gut, forcing it back down to keep any hint of it from my face.

"I'll do it if you do it with me," she said.

"Sure," I said, forcing the word out of my clenching throat and nodding.

I accepted Susan's warm, soft hand in mine and we both stepped up onto the lip of the well. We glanced at each other for a moment and she gave me a weak, faltering smile which I returned. Then I lowered my gaze to the surface of the water and the ritual began.

At first, as Susan had said before, the water appeared thick and dark. The surface of the well seemed to be a flat black circle, solid and opaque. As the seconds ticked by however I felt my heart and my breathing slow and suddenly something clicked.

Instead of a flat surface I could see depth, endless, bottomless depth. It was like looking down an impossibly long tunnel that stretched so far ahead that it shrank to a single point.

My eyes pushed down and down through the dark, searching for that point, looking for any hint of motion below.

The water was so dark that as I watched it seemed to become empty space and in that space I thought I saw the beginnings of shapes, great sweeping curls,

154

coiling and unwinding.

My head became heavy, my thoughts clouded and on some level I could feel myself being drawn downwards, easing into a forward leaning, sliding towards the tipping point.

Then Susan was climbing back down and pulling at my arm so that I did the same. Back on the solid floor I quickly came to my senses and was immediately filled with a joyous sense of relief.

The five of us all grinned at one another then, bonded by the shared experience, I felt myself warmed with acceptance and belonging.

"Well," said Nancy, looking around the circle. "Now we've all done that, whatever that was, perhaps we can return to civilisation?"

Albert, Susan and I all nodded, still grinning but Rick shook his head.

"No," he said. "We haven't all done it."

I looking to him questioningly then followed his gaze back over my shoulder. Beside the entrance, Melvin was still clinging to himself and looking miserable.

"Come on, sport!" boomed Rick, striding back across the room to loom over Melvin. "Your turn!"

Melvin looked up at Rick in horror and began to shake his head frantically. Rick gripped Melvin's arm firmly, just above the elbow then marched him back across the room to join us.

"But I don't want to," he was saying, over and over. "I don't want to."

"Oh come on!" said Rick, pushing him on towards the lip of the well. "We've all done it, don't be a spoil sport."

"It's honestly not that bad," said Albert.

"It's really not," said Susan. "It'll only take a second."

"Yes," I joined in. "Come on Melvin."

"He's not going to let us leave until you do," said Nancy.

We continued like this, all talking at once, encouraging, sniping, cajoling. Finally, tears on his face, Melvin raised a visibly trembling leg to step up onto the lip of the well.

"That's it," said Rick, standing behind Melvin and steadying him. "Now all you have to do is look down for a few seconds, that's it."

Melvin nodded quickly, his hands clasped together before him, weeping silently from tight shut eyes. We fell into silence as the air seemed to thicken around us. Eventually, Melvin's wet, bobbling eyes opened behind his glasses, the lenses magnifying his tears.

He swallowed visibly then very slowly lowered his gaze to the water. For several unbearable seconds we all stood perfectly still, listening to his sharp little breaths, watching his fragile little frame as he teetered on the edge.

"There you go," said Albert suddenly. "You did it. Well done old man."

For one long second, Melvin turned to face Susan and me with a genuine smile, his shoulders sagging with relief.

Out of this whole sorry saga, that image of him standing there smiling at us, is the one that remains cut sharpest into my memory.

Then Rick gave him a sharp shove in the back and he tumbled forwards into the water.

The impact was quite spectacular, a great plume of water tore up out of the well to crash over the lip and soak our feet.

The shock of it froze me solid for a second but Rick had already jumped up onto the lip, whooping with glee. Nancy and Albert followed and after a moment more, Susan pulled me along behind her.

The five of us stood on the lip of the well, looking down at the pathetic little creature below us and laughing.

In the water Melvin was frantically treading water, blinking, coughing and spluttering. he kept trying to wipe the water from his eyes but then frantically crashing his arm back down in the water to keep his head above the surface and splashing himself again.

He was trying to cry out but every time he did, his own thrashing efforts to stay afloat splashed more water into his mouth.

We all hooted and jeered at him, the sounds

rebounding off the curved walls to resonate into an almost physical presence.

We grinned at one another as a violent, intoxicating energy flowed between us. He was finally paying for every little irritation he had caused, every infuriating moan and whinge. As ashamed as I am to admit it, it felt good.

Blind and desperate, Melvin reached out for the lip of well. His hand landed just beside Rick's foot but Rick quickly pressed his shoe down on Melvin's fingers so that he recoiled away.

Over and over he tried to grasp at the stonework but every time he did, we delighted in stamping his fingers away again.

At one point he disappeared below the water completely, just for a second, before erupting back up again.

He choked and retched and splashed about, slapping at the surface of the water with his palms and driving us into full blown hysterics. As gruesome as it is to me now, at the time it was the funniest thing I had ever seen.

Then he went under again but this time he didn't immediately come back up. More laughter filled seconds passed but then he still didn't reappear. Suddenly our laughter fell away, empty and hollow and we all frowned at the water instead.

"Melvin?" said Susan dumbly.

We all looked at one another and then to Rick. He scrambled down so that his knees were on the floor, the edge of the well pressing into his stomach and plunged his arm into the water.

The rest of us climbed down and watched, struck suddenly silent as Rick strained to reach further under the surface.

"Hold me!" he snapped at Albert and me.

We rushed to stand behind him, each taking a firm grip on his belt while the girls backed away, clinging to one another in horror.

Rick lunged forward, his entire torso disappearing beneath the surface while Albert and I leaned back, straining to hold his weight.

157

My heart was pounding in my chest. Quite apart from the exertion of holding on to Rick's belt, the ground seemed to have fallen away beneath me so that my stomach plunged forever downwards. The heady delight of a moment before now lay in broken, ugly pieces all around us.

Rick's hand broke the water, reaching back to slap Albert's hand desperately so that we dragged him up and out.

The three of us all tumbled backwards away from the well, Rick coughing and gasping as he wiped the water from his eyes.

Recovering ourselves we rushed back to the well but then stalled, unsure what to do. There was no sign of Melvin, just the black, seething water.

"Get him out!" cried Nancy in a voice I'd never heard before, shrill and raw.

"I can't!" roared Rick, his eyes wild as he stared at the water, running his hands over his head.

"Rick," sobbed Susan, her knees faltering so that she staggered against Nancy. "Get him out, get him out of there please!"

"I can't!" Rick screamed again. "I can't, he's.."

Another terrible silence fell over us all as the surface of the water sloshed back to calm.

"..he's gone," said Rick thickly.

Susan and Nancy held one another and wept. Albert and I stared at one another briefly before he turned away, crossing the room to lean against one of the tables. I looked to Rick but he was still staring at the water, wild eyed and furious.

"I didn't mean to," he was saying to himself. "I didn't mean for him to.."

I don't know how long we stayed there, a tableau of shock and horror, but it felt like a long time. The enormity of what had happened seemed to press down on us all, pinning us in place, paralysing us utterly.

Nancy was the first to break position. Quietly, carefully, she disengaged herself from Susan. Her face was grey and drawn, pinched into an ugly expression of sickness and fear.

She crossed the room with a kind of fragile dignity

to stand in front of Rick. When he raised his head to look at her there were tears in his eyes. He looked at her bereft, heartbroken and reached out to her for comfort.

Then, in a single, flashing motion, she slapped him hard across the face. He staggered as she turned on her heel and walked away, scooping up Susan as she went before disappearing through the entrance.

Rick turned to Albert, his mouth open but silent, his wet eyes pleading but Albert couldn't hold his gaze. Instead, he looked to the floor and shook his head before following the girls out of the room.

I watched him go then turned to see Rick looking at me with the same expression. I also found I couldn't look at him and so turned away.

"We should go," I said hoarsely.

He nodded and followed me back upstairs.

By the time we stepped out of the fireplace the others had gone, taking the bags with them so that the only evidence of our visit were the remnants of the chair Rick had broken.

We didn't speak as we retraced our steps out of the house and through the woods. It seemed to take forever but eventually we rejoined the path back down to the beach where Albert was readying the row boat.

Albert and I rowed while Nancy comforted Susan. Rick sat alone behind us, staring at the space between his feet.

No-one said a word. Every time I looked at the water all I could see was Melvin's fragile little form, floating lifeless down there in the depths.

My eyes began to sting and I thought I might vomit so I fixed my gaze on sky above The Rock instead and concentrated on the physical effort of rowing.

Back at the shore, Albert and the girls disappeared into the house while Rick stayed on the beach, staring out at The Rock.

I lingered for a while, unsure what to do but eventually I left him there and went inside to pack my things.

When I came back down, Albert was loading the girls' bags into his car. Susan was sat in the back seat, sobbing softly while Nancy smoked furiously, her back to the ocean. Rick was still where I'd left him, down on the beach.

"We're leaving," said Albert as I approached. "I've taken care of.." but he faltered at saying the name.

"..his things," he said instead. "There's no evidence he was ever here. Do you want to come with us?"

I thought about it for a moment but then looked over at Rick again.

"I don't think we should let him drive like that," I said. "I'll bring him back in his car."

Albert nodded sadly, closed the boot and got in the car.

I turned to Nancy.

"I'll make sure he gets back safely Nancy," I said.

"Frankly Charles," said Nancy, flicking her cigarette away and turning to join Susan in the back seat without looking at me. "I couldn't care less."

I watched them drive away until the car shrank into the distance and disappeared around the curve then headed down the beach to retrieve Rick.

The drive back was long and painful. Rick alternated between catatonic silence and shuddering sobs the entire way.

I got him home and left his car parked outside his room then carried my bags all the way to back to my own. Collapsing onto my bed, I sat for a while and felt an incredible fatigue settle over me until I laid down in my clothes to sleep.

Sleep wouldn't come however, no matter how tired I felt. Instead there was only a terrible, endless loop, a dreadful treadmill.

I cycled through the knowledge that what had happened could not possibly have happened, we could not possibly have done that and then onto the knowledge that we absolutely had.

For the rest of my time in America I avoided the four of them. We bumped into one another on occasion but never stopped to talk.

There was a brief flurry of activity on campus when Melvin was declared missing but it all quietened down after a few weeks.

I got the impression that Rick's father may have

intervened to steer the investigation away from us but I was never certain.

I threw myself into my studies, trying to fill my time so completely as to leave no room for remembrance or reflection. Despite my efforts however, I found myself painfully reminded of that day all the time.

Every time I saw someone who looked like him, heard someone who sounded like him, heard the name mentioned or even saw someone splashing about in the pool.

My stomach would clench and I would find myself back in that torchlit chamber, a million tons of rock pressing down from above, ashen faces staring at the black water of the well.

I had hoped that once I returned home I might leave the experience behind me. Putting an entire ocean between myself and that terrible afternoon seemed like an effective way to outrun it and yet it never left me.

From that day until this it has always been there, forever at the back of my mind, waiting to be summoned by the slightest trigger.

Over the years the feelings of dread and chest-tightening guilt have become familiar, akin to an enemy so old they have become almost a friend.

It has never lost its bite however. It used be thoughts of Melvin's mother that saddened me most. In later years however, it was the unseen barrier that the incident created between myself and those I loved.

Dorothy, the children, the grandchildren, I love them all so dearly and yet none of them have ever truly known me.

To them I have only ever been Charles the loving husband, father and grandfather. They never met Charles the murderer and now they never will.

When I think of the others from that time, I do consider myself lucky. Of the five of us I have had by far the longest, happiest life, though I have no idea why I should be the fortunate one.

I always knew this day would come eventually and every time I heard of one of their deaths I knew it with even more certainty.

As I write these closing words all is quiet outside,

161

the storm has finally passed us by completely, leaving such a calm it is as if it was never here in the first place.

The only sound I can hear now is the soft, slow pat pat pat of water falling onto carpet at the top of the stairs just outside my room.

It is a drowsy, hypnotic sound that nods my head and takes the edge from the fear of what is to come, another kindness I do not deserve.

Rick went on to be a Captain in the US Navy. He drowned when his ship sank on manoeuvrers. Nancy eventually died from a pulmonary oedema, also known as water on the lungs.

Albert was consumed by an avalanche while mountaineering and suffocated under countless tons of snow. And finally lovely Susan, she drowned inexplicably in her bath one evening.

The sound of soft plopping droplets is just behind my chair now. My time has come and I cannot say I am not glad of it.

I am just grateful to have had the chance to complete this account before the circle of my fate is finally closed.

Charles Dufford

just a dream

It is a glorious day. The sky is vibrant blue, the sun is high and bright. I'm sitting in my favourite chair on the balcony, looking out over the city.

Towers of glass sparkle in the sun and the air is filled with bustling city sounds from below, softened by distance to a pleasant white noise.

As I sip my coffee I shift a little in the chair and feel the soft, comforting texture of my pyjamas against my skin.

Rashanna is in the kitchen behind me, making eggs and singing to herself happily. If I had to describe my perfect Sunday morning, I couldn't do much better than this.

Despite this literal perfection however, I just can't quite relax, can't engage with it fully, can't let myself go. There's a cold spot in my chest, a niggling dark in the back of my mind that won't go away.

I had the dream again.

I've had strange dreams for as long as I can remember. Mostly they're different every time and while they're usually quite dull in terms of what actually happens, they're made memorable by how incredibly realistic they are.

They're always different and always set somewhere in the past in what seem to be real, everyday places. I'm always just some ordinary person going about my everyday life.

I've been a happy hippy, partying and protesting in San Francisco during the Summer of Love. I've been a prim little housewife in an incredibly uncomfortable dress, travelling across a vast open prairie in a rickety wagon towards a new life on the frontier.

Once I was a lady in waiting to a frightened young queen, living in a draughty old castle. Another time I lived in the middle of nowhere in a tiny little hut made of mud and straw, where it rained all the time and I had to get up before dawn every morning to milk the family cow.

Sometimes I tell Rashanna about the dreams. She

163

listens patiently to the whole thing then usually tells me to write it all down, to develop it into a short story or even a screenplay or something, but I never do.

There is another dream though, one I've never told her about, one that comes back over and over. It used to be an occasional thing but recently I've been having it more and more.

Just thinking about it shortens my breath and tightens my chest, yet I can't stop thinking about it. It's actually easier during the week to be honest.

Rushing around getting ready, commuting across the city, it all serves as an pretty effective distraction so that by the time I get to work, I've usually almost forgotten about it.

Today however, it just will not leave me alone. Its dreadful echo just keeps ringing and ringing inside me.

In this dream I am floating in space, surrounded by nothing but empty blackness in all directions. There is no sound just an unimaginable weight of silence pressing in on me as if I have gone completely deaf.

I constantly feel as if I am falling and yet there is no up or down. The vast, endless emptiness yawns all around me, pin pricked by distant stars but otherwise utterly barren and featureless.

My arms flail desperately, snatching out to grab onto something in sheer and total panic but there is nothing to grab. My legs kick as if to swim but there is nothing to push against.

I try to scream but no sound comes out. My mind reels away from the inconceivable size of the universe which just hangs spitefully all around me.

I close my eyes but this just trades one blackness for another and I still can't hear or touch or smell anything. It feels like drowning, endless, bottomless drowning, frozen at the point of death for all eternity so that...

"Katie!"

I jump and almost spill my coffee. Looking up, I find Rashanna standing over me, offering a plate of eggs. Standing there in the sunshine I've never seen her more beautiful.

Her skin is flawless, the colour of rich, polished

164

mahogany. I've known her for almost a decade and she still looks exactly the same.

"Sorry," I mumble, accepting the plate and placing it on the table before rearranging myself in the chair.

"Where were you baby?" she asks. She looks at me for a moment with nothing but love in her eyes and strokes my face before sitting across from me with her own plate.

"Just.." I try but the great, gonging images of endless space are still assaulting my mind's eye. "I don't know, I'm still waking up."

"Did you have another dream?" she asks as she joyfully attacks her eggs.

"I.." I begin but then stop.

If I tell her I did then she'll ask about it, expecting me to describe it to her like I do the other dreams. I don't want to tell her about this one though, I don't even want to think about this one but I can't lie to her. The words stick in my throat.

"It's fine," I say instead. "I'm fine."

She reaches across the table to hold my hand and for a moment we just look at one another. A great warmth swells in my chest as my love for her surges forward, almost pushing the dream out of mind. Almost.

Rashanna begins to tell me about an exhibition she wants to see in the city as I start to pick at my food. I'm not hungry at all until I taste the eggs. Then, suddenly my tastebuds are singing so that my stomach growls and my mouth waters.

She makes good eggs, I mean really great eggs but to this day she refuses to tell me her secret. She says a woman has to keep some secrets in a relationship in order to maintain her mystique.

I wonder idly if I can justify keeping the dream from her by the same logic as I listen to her tell me about this new artist she's heard of, but I know that won't fly.

As the food warms and fills me however, I start to feel more solid, more grounded and the dream retreats a little further.

The rest of the day slides by easy. Mooching about the apartment. Heading out for a slow walk to the gallery. An impromptu picnic in the park. Stopping off for a couple of drinks on the way home.

By the time Rashanna and I are settling into bed I have almost forgotten the dream completely. Then, when she gives me that mischievous, questioning look I know so well, I finally leave it behind altogether.

A little later on, satisfied and spent, I doze off on a cloud of fuzzed out bliss. Before I know it however, I'm dreaming again.

This time I'm in a misty forest and the sounds of previously fallen rain dropping from the trees surrounds me. It's early in the morning and the air has a biting chill.

I hug myself as my teeth chatter and realise I'm wearing a strange, ragged shawl made of some coarse, itchy fabric.

The battered, wooden clogs on my bare and filthy feet skid and rattle against the hard earth below. I stop hugging myself to stare at my dirty, calloused hands and feel my head spin with confusion.

Suddenly, a man erupts from the undergrowth to my right. I start and stumble away from him, staring at him goggle-eyed and terrified.

He is also filthy and his beard and hair are wild. He talks at me in a language I only vaguely understand, saying something that sounds like a question and pointing off ahead of me.

As always, I experience the queasy feeling of being two people at once.

I am me, I am Katie, sitting inside this woman's head, looking out through her eyes, watching her life unfold around me. Knowing nothing, fearing everything.

At the same time however, I am also this woman so that, somehow, I also know everything she knows.

So this man standing in front of me, trying to make himself understood, is at once a huge, threatening stranger but also my oldest friend from childhood who I trust absolutely. His attempt at speech is bestial, garbled words with chewed up vowels and yet I understand him.

The rest of our group are nearby. We are looking for something. He has searched the area near the spring but hasn't found it.

We should climb down to the bottom of the valley

and look there. I nod and allow him to move past me before following in his wake.

We push through the thick greenery, picking our way, avoiding the thorns and sharp stones. As we go I feel myself, my Katie self, melting away as with each step I become more of this woman and less of her.

There is a flashing fear, a sensation of drowning and the passing thought that I should be afraid. Then it is gone and I am just here.

As I follow Orn through the forest I think back to the beginning of this search. I woke up back in the hut, cold and confused as the last few embers of the fire faded and died.

I laid there for a while, wondering what had woken me while reaching out to feel for my son. My son! My god, I'm a mother! How could I have forgotten that?

Anyway, I reached out for Kye but he wasn't there. There was just a warm little space on the matted straw where he should have been.

Fear flushed through me, waking me and sitting me up in a heartbeat. I squinted at the open doorway of the hut, a vague blob of dark grey amid the almost total black. Relief washed over me then, as I made out a familiar silhouette cut from the grey.

Creeping to the doorway, I stood behind my little Kye, wrapping my arms around his shoulders to warm him against the night.

He turned to smile up at me in the dark then went back to looking up at the sky. He pointed for me to look as well.

I followed his little finger upwards and stared at the solid black night above, thick with stars. I was just about to guide him back inside when movement caught my eye. Off to our right, where the sun rose in the mornings, the stars were falling.

My mouth fell open and I stood there with my son, watching point after point of light tumble from the sky towards the horizon.

I was so transfixed by the sight I didn't even notice as the rest of the village came to join us. We all huddled together and watched the stars fall until the sky began to lighten.

Then, as we watched, one star in particular did not fall to the horizon but fell into the forest before us.

It made an incredible sound which shook the earth beneath us and sent us all scurrying back Into our huts to cling to one another in terror.

After a while however, when no more impacts came and the day had fully broken, Orn said we should go and look for the fallen star. So off we went, spreading out across the forest, searching for this impossible thing.

Now we have reached the valley bottom and are standing on the bed of a dried up stream. Orn is telling me that he will go one way if I go the other. I nod and we part company, each picking our way along the uneven, water carved path.

I walk for a long time as the sun rises higher in the sky and the forest wakes fully around me. Eventually I reach the point at which the stream once emerged from the hillside, the end of the path. I decide to rest a moment before heading back.

The birds are in full song all around me and I am looking up to see them when I spot a broken branch hanging limp by a thread. Moving closer I see that a great swathe has been broken through the trees overhead, leading to a small, secluded clearing.

Pushing my way carefully through a particularly dense and thorny bush, I step out into the clearing to find a blackened crater.

The ground is still smoking in places and at the centre of the crater lies a small, round stone, about the size of a person's head.

I know I should call for the others but I can't take my eyes from the stone. The birds are not singing here, in fact there is almost no sound at all and yet I feel as if I can hear the stone whispering to me, telling me to approach.

Before I know it my feet are walking me over the hot ground towards the stone and I am crouching before it.

I tilt my head one way and then the other, trying to see all its edges, to understand what it is. Is this really what stars look like close up? It's so small and dull. Where does all the light come from?

168

Suddenly, a small creaking sound announces the appearance of a thin crack in the stone which grows quickly as I watch. The crack runs straight down the middle of the rock, splitting the whole thing in two so that the newly defined halves fall away from one another.

Inside is a bright, blue-white light that hurts my eyes. Despite the pain however, I look closer. The space around me is deathly silent and yet the whispering from before is now louder than ever.

It wants me to touch it and as I realise this I see my hand floating out before me, my fingertips approaching the seething surface.

The moment I touch the light everything goes white. It is hot and cold at the same time and yet it does not burn me.

I feel something enter me and run through me so that the light is in every part of me. There is no pain but I am afraid.

I am terribly, terribly afraid.

I sit bolt upright in bed, goggling at the room around me. I feel the texture of the sheets under my hand and stroke them, trying to convince myself they're real.

I feel the tears on my face before I realise I am crying and then just sit there, panting and weeping. I am so confused and so afraid.

Rashanna rolls over and mumbles something grumpy before waking fully to see me. In a moment she is with me, holding me, rocking me, soothing my soul with kisses and whispers. I cling to her and cry like child, my face pressed to her breast as sobs rack through me.

I tell her everything then. I tell her about the latest dream of being some kind of ancient forest dweller but also about the terrible, recurring floating dream.

I tell her about all the times I've had it and all the times I've avoided telling her about it before.

I tell her how frightened I am and how I can't bear the thought of going back to sleep in case I find myself there again.

I confess it all and all the way through she just holds me and listens and strokes my back and loves me.

169

Eventually I run out of tears and sobs and sag into resting. I sit away from Rashanna and smile at her weakly.

I suddenly feel very foolish but my relief at the passing of all the fear and anguish is enough to make it feel worth it. Rashanna looks at me with love in her eyes but there is sadness too.

"I'm sorry Katie" she says.

I nod, feeling the warmth of her sympathy.

"No, Katie," she says again, seriously so that I look at her confused. "I'm sorry, I'm so, so sorry."

I try to ask her what she means but no sound comes out. I reach out to touch her face but my hand passes straight through her.

She is fading away in front of me, along with the bedclothes and the bed and the walls and floor. I lunge towards her, desperate to take hold of her, to keep her with me but she's not there.

The shadows swell from the corners of the room, overtaking the fading furniture as everything dissolves into endless black.

I scream and scream and ball my fists but nothing happens and there is nothing to pound them against.

And finally I remember.

I remember everything.

Again.

Finding the meteorite. Not understanding what it had done to me until I watched my little Kye, my only child, grow old and die while I remained unchanged.

Generation after generation came and went, while I remained unchanged. Thousands of years of watching mankind grow and advance, while I remained unchanged.

Learning to hide my condition, learning to create new identities and histories, new fake births and deaths to explain my existence. Living countless lives, seeing everyone I ever loved grow old and die, while I remained unchanged.

I bore witness to everything humanity ever achieved, every miracle, every crime. I saw some of them leave then watched the last of those who remained die out altogether, while I remained unchanged.

170

I saw new life begin then, saw it evolve and rise and then fall again until eventually the last of the plants all withered away and even the air departed.

Wandering an empty planet then, I walked over barren rock for millennia more as the sun gradually swelled in the sky, while I remained unchanged.

And finally, finally, after millions of years of impossible loneliness on an empty world, seeing the sun grow larger and larger until eventually, the earth itself crumbled beneath my feet in an impossibly vast maelstrom of destruction, while I remained unchanged.

Even that incredible, world consuming fury ebbed in time however, the sun itself bursting outwards then collapsing back before eventually fading to nothing.

What few scattered fragments remained drifted away and left me here, floating endlessly, never dying, remaining forever unchanged.

There is no escape. There is nowhere to go. There is nothing to see, to touch or do. There is only memory, that is my only fleeting escape.

Back to that golden time, that very best of times out of the billions of years of my life. I close my eyes and concentrate.

It is a glorious day. The sky is vibrant blue...

Followthorn's Curse

It is a bright spring morning in the tiny village of Arneston. After a long and arduous trek across country the day before, the party of four adventurers spent the previous night in the village's tavern, enjoying hot food, flowing mead and soft beds. They are now feeling fully refreshed after a good long rest.

They are standing on the village common discussing which way to go next when a man of the village approaches them nervously.

He is middle aged, balding on top and thick round the middle. He holds a cloth cap in his hands which he worries with his thumbs as he approaches.

"Who's this guy?" one of the adventurers asks the others.

"Hail, mighty warriors," the man says nervously. "Forgive me for not introducing myself to you last night. I am Gax, the headman of Arneston."

"Hail Gax," says the oldest member of the party. "I am Endolief, Master of the Nine Paths, Keeper of Usgorn's Fate."

Endolief is a thin, elderly man with a long grey beard and a tall hat, pointed and crooked. He wears flowing robes and carries a long, knobbly staff which is almost as tall as him. Although at first glance he appears frail, there is a sparkle in his eyes that betrays a deeper power.

"Allow me," he says, turning with a sweep of his arm to introduce his fellow adventurers.

"This is Krugnar," he says, nodding towards a mountain of a man. "Splitter of Skulls, Champion of the Fourth Age."

Krugnar is more than a head taller than anyone else present and twice as broad. He has long black hair that falls to his shoulders and every inch of him is hard, toned muscle.

He is wearing nothing more than boots, a loin cloth and a leather strap across his chest which holds at his back an impossibly large, double headed axe.

"This is Rhinlay," says Endolief then, moving on to

the woman at Krugnar's side. "Scourge of Nightmares, Bearer of the Liquid Blade."

Rhinlay is only a few inches shorter than Krugnar but is lithe and supple. Her hair is violently red against her pale skin.

She also wears little besides boots, a loin cloth and an armoured breastplate. From her belt hangs a scabbard containing a long, slender blade.

"And finally, Aerothen," says Endolief with a smile. "The Shadow Stalker, Queen of Thieves."

Aerothen is a small, slight woman, more than a foot shorter than the rest of the party. Her tawny hair is cropped short and her voluminous hood is down revealing long pointed ears.

She is clad entirely in dark, skin tight material that makes no sound when she moves. At her belt hangs a short, curved dagger and at her back an ornate bow and quiver

"Well met," says Gax, struggling to maintain eye contact. "And welcome to you all. We are honoured to host such esteemed adventurers in our modest home."

A silence falls between them and the party notice that around the edges of the common the rest of the villagers have all stopped what they are doing and are watching the encounter.

Despite the heat of the glorious sunshine, a dark, cold tension seems to press down on the whole village.

"Is there something we can do for you Gax?" asks Rhinlay, scanning the nervous faces all around.

"Well," says Gax. "We have always been a happy village, quiet and peaceful, keeping to ourselves, but of late a great shadow has fallen across our lives."

"A shadow you say?" says Aerothen, raising her chin and narrowing her eyes.

"Indeed," says Gax, licking his lips. "I hardly know where to begin."

"At the beginning," rumbles Krugnar grimly. "And be quick to reach the end if you wish for us to listen."

Gax pales at Krugnar's expression and swallows hard before nodding and then letting a torrent of words flow forth.

"All was well until a few moons back when a mighty

176

storm swept through the region," Gax begins. "We didn't realise at the time, but the storm heralded the rising of a great evil in Followthorn."

"Followthorn?" Endolief asks.

"It is an area of the deep forest," Gax explains. "Approaching the base of the mountain. It has always been a cursed place, shunned by proper folk, but our young people have a tradition of challenging one another to enter its boundaries to prove their mettle. After the storm, two such foolhardy youths went into Followthorn and were never seen again."

The party look around once more and see that the villagers are all listening in anguish as Gax tells their tale. Some of them are crying and holding one another.

"We banned all from approaching Followthorn after that," says Gax. "But soon livestock began to go missing from the fields around the village and then, after that, children began to disappear from their beds in the dead of night."

At the mention of missing children the adventurers exchange glances of concern.

"Oh mighty heroes," pleads Gax. "We know not what to do. We cannot protect our children and with every night that passes, the evil from Followthorn grows bolder.

"We are poor people, we live from the land and have little by way of riches to offer but I beg you, if you could find it in your hearts to help us you would have our eternal gratitude."

"So," says Endolief thoughtfully, stroking his long, grey beard. "You, a complete stranger, are asking us to venture deep into the midst of a lair of unrestrained evil, to risk our very lives to find what lurks there and then to destroy it at any cost?"

Gax draws breath to speak but cannot find the words and so simply nods instead, casting his eyes to the ground in shame and despair.

"My friends?" asks Endolief, turning to the rest of the party.

"All this talk bores me," Krugnar growls. "By Grok! The chance to do battle with an army of terrible foes stirs my soul!"

"My blade thirsts for the blood of the wicked," says Rhinlay with a savage grin. "It has been too long."

"Where there is evil there is usually treasure," says Aerothen knowingly.

"Gax," says Endolief. "We accept this quest and fear not, the quelling of an evil force and the safe return of your children will be payment enough for us my friend."

Gax looks up with tears in his eyes before grabbing Endloief's hand and shaking it furiously. He turns to the villagers lining the edge of the common and calls to them.

"They said yes!" he shouts joyfully. "They will help us!"

The entire village erupts in cheers and applause and the grey, pained faces of a moment before suddenly break into bright eyed smiles.

Gax continues to shake the adventurers' hands until a grinning Krugnar claps him on the back with a mighty, dinner-plate hand.

Gax stumbles forwards several paces and winces but even this cannot interrupt his expression of happiness.

The journey through the forest is long and uneventful. As the party follow Gax's directions towards Followthorn however, the trees grow thicker and huddle closer.

They block out more and more light until the party find themselves walking through a heavy gloom, despite the bright sunshine far above. With each step they take, the bushes around them grow thicker with vicious thorns.

Endolief murmurs a string of strange sounds to himself and the head of his staff begins to glow, bathing the dense forest around the party in an unearthly blue light.

Krugnar and Rhinlay walk on either side of Endolief, their weapons drawn, grimly narrowed eyes continually scanning the trees. There is no sign of Aerothen.

The three adventurers pause as they reach a fork in

178

the forest path. Krugnar and Rhinlay continue to scan their surroundings while Endolief closes his eyes and frowns in concentration. A hint of a shadow slips silently from the trees above down onto the path behind them.

"Ours is the left hand path," says Aerothen, rejoining the party. "Along there lies something you will want to see."

The party proceeds down the path to the left which quickly dwindles to an overgrown trail. As the trees crowd in even further on either side, a sense of terrible tension and foreboding presses in from between the branches.

Finally the trail leads them into a clearing, bordered opposite by a steep hillside. The clearing is dominated by the huge, fallen body of a vast and ancient oak tree.

Beyond the tangle of broken roots, the party can just about make out a stone archway, hewn into the hillside.

Endolief bends stiffly to inspect the tree while the others explore the perimeter of the clearing.

"The growth of this tree was not natural," announces Endolief, straightening slowly. "It was placed here to seal that entrance."

"And when the storm tore down the tree.." says Rhinlay.

"..whatever was sealed inside was free to roam," finishes Aerothen.

"Until now," says Krugnar, striding towards the entrance. "Come my friends, it is time to put this evil down."

The party pass through the archway into a tunnel, apparently carved from the living rock. What little daylight had made it through the trees outside is soon left behind as the tunnels curves back and forth so that the glow from Endolief's staff becomes their only source of light.

The tunnel leads them to a stone staircase which in turn leads them down into a new, tight passageway constructed of blocks of stone with a paved floor. Sconces are mounted on the wall periodically and each bears an inexplicably burning torch.

The passageway soon opens onto more, identical

passages to form a vast underground maze but the party press on, heading downwards at every opportunity. It is not long before they encounter their first enemy, a small group of goblins.

Between them the party make quick work of the small, green skinned fiends and move on. As they descend they encounter more goblins and then even orcs with ferocious hounds. All are put down swiftly and with minimal effort.

"These scum are but interlopers," says Endolief after the last skirmish. "They will have come down from the forest after the entrance was revealed, looking for riches and shelter. We have yet to meet an actual denizen of this cursed place."

The party takes a short rest in a small chamber before preparing themselves for the more serious battles to come and resuming their downward journey.

Sure enough, not long after they are attacked by something that is neither goblin nor orc. It is hard to tell amid the gloom, but the thing appears to be a mangled mix of different creatures, all equally vicious and deadly.

As they progress the passages become tighter and darker, the walls dripping with slime. They are assailed by more and more of the terrible, bizarre creatures and have to fight ever harder to survive.

"These fiends are not of the natural world," says Endolief as he treats a vicious bite wound on Krugnar's shoulder.

"I have never seen nor heard of such things," says Aerothen, binding a great slash across Rhinlay's back.

"Nor I," agrees Rhinlay, wincing. "Endolief, what are we facing?"

Endolief nods with satisfaction and straightens up as the impassive Krugnar's shoulder heals with magical speed.

"My friends," he says grimly. "I believe we have entered the lair of a mighty sorcerer. These abominations can only be the work of one with incredible powers and the most dreadful appetites. Prepare yourselves one and all, I suspect we are soon to face far worse than anything we have seen so far."

Endolief is not proven wrong as the party moves on.

Larger and more ferocious monsters, all impossible combinations of limbs and claws and eyes and maws, wait around every corner.

The terrible beasts test the party's skills to the limit and as they finally stumble into a huge, vaulted chamber, all are wounded and bear hard expressions of pain and determination.

The torch lit chamber is long and stretches away from them, the ceiling lost in the darkness overhead. The walls on either side are punctuated by iron grills covering small cells set into the rock.

All eyes are drawn to the centre of the chamber however, which is dominated by a huge, ornate throne atop a low, broad dais.

Slumped upon the throne is a skeleton clothed in lush purple robes. Cautiously, the party spread out into the chamber to explore it. Krugnar and Rhinlay each take a side of the chamber and peer into the cells.

"Here!" cries Rhinlay. "The children!"

Most of the cells contain a small, dirty, pale faced child, huddled in the dark.

"Fear not little ones," booms Krugnar to the children in the cells. "We are here to rescue you and take you home."

Some small sounds come from the cells but most of the children are still too afraid to speak or move.

Meanwhile, Aerothen has crept past the throne and is examining an alter surrounded by animal bones that sits beyond it towards the back of the chamber.

Endolief busies himself inspecting the skeleton until, after a few minutes, the party gather back in front of the throne.

"So," says Rhinlay. "It would seem the master of this house is long since dead and that we have bested the watchdogs he left behind. "There is nothing left but to free these children and make our escape."

"I will make quick work of those bars," says Krugnar with confidence. "The cell has not yet been built that can hold the Splitter of Skulls."

"I see no treasure here," says Aerothen with disappointment. "But saving the children will be reward enough I suppose."

"Hold my friends, hold," says Endolief grimly. "Our day's work may not yet be done. Rhinlay, how many children found you on that side of the chamber?"

"Seven," says Rhinlay.

"And Krugnar?" asks Endolief.

"A couple less," says Krugnar.

"It is as I thought," sighs Endolief.

"What is it?" asks Aerothen.

"I know who that is," says Endolief, pointed towards the skeleton. "There is a heavy ring upon the first finger of the right hand, the seal of which I recognise. He is Henglar the Betrayer."

"I have never heard of this sorcerer," says Rhinlay.

"Nor I," agrees Krugnar.

"His story is a very old one," admits Endolief. "Originally he was a great and powerful wizard, his school hailing from the coast. He was exiled for heresy however and disappeared, seeking a place of power in which to hide and continue his blasphemous work."

"But he is long dead," says Aerothen. "His story ended long ago."

"I fear that is not so," says Endolief. "I believe that before he died, Henglar constructed a creature with a singular purpose, to gather sacrifices for a ritual that would revive him. I believe the creature has already attempted that ritual using the village's livestock but to no avail.

"We have found twelve children here today which leads me to also believe that the creature is but one more capture away from having everything it needs to bring that dread beast sorcerer back from the grave."

"But surely this creature was one of those abominations we struck down on our way in here!" cries Krugnar.

"No my barbarian friend," says Endolief. "Henglar would not have allowed a creature tasked with so important a mission to fall so easily. We have not yet seen whatever it is that has been terrorising our friends in the village."

As if on cue, a great screeching roar sounds from the doorway to the chamber and the party turn in horror to look upon Henglar's most vile creation.

Several feet taller even than Krugnar, the thing stoops to step through the doorway before straightening to tower over them.

It's skin is grey and mottled and it stands naked before them on enormous, muscular legs. Two pairs of arms flex and reach for the adventurers, one emerging from the shoulders, the other from the hips.

The hands are enormous, the fingers tapering to huge, vicious claws. The head of the beast is the most disturbing part of all.

It has no eyes and no nose, just an impossibly wide mouth that splits the whole head in two from side to side. The mouth is filled with row upon row of jagged teeth, sharp and uneven.

Finally, in the centre of the creature's chest, blinks a great sideways eye, bulging in rage at the presence of the party.

Before the thing can react, Krugnar and Rhinlay attack it simultaneously. Both sever an arm each, Krugar with his mighty axe, Rhinlay with her singing sword.

Before the arms hit the ground however, new limbs sprout from the stumps and in moments the arms are regrown in full.

The thing bats the barbarian and the valkyrie away with parallel backhand blows and marches on the remaining adventurers. Aerothen looses a flurry of arrows while Endolief conjures and hurls a string of white hot fireballs.

All the projectiles find there mark but the creature shrugs them off. The arrows cannot pierce its skin and while the fireballs knock it back a step, the flames do not burn it. The group scramble to the far end of the chamber and gather behind the altar.

They are trapped.

As the thing rounds the dais and closes, the four talk frantically, pointing and gesturing before all nodding to each other and standing.

They turn to face the abomination and each set their jaw with a look of furious determination.

Krugnar and Rhinlay charge the creature from either side with all their might, while Aerothen crouches behind Endolief, bracing herself between the wizard and the altar. The wizard meanwhile chants desperately, eyes closed.

Just as the charging heroes are about to step within striking distance of the monster, Endolief reaches the roaring culmination of his chant and points his staff at the creature.

A great cone of force erupts from the end of the staff and tears forwards, slamming into the creature and driving it back.

The thing regains its balance and begins to push back against the magical wall so that Endolief's sandalled feet start to slide backwards along the stone floor.

Aerothen sets her feet against the altar and her back against the wizard's then pushes with all her might to hold him in place.

Krugnar's axe takes one arm and then another while Rhinlay's sword does the same. This time however they are prepared and continue to swing, severing each new limb as it grows while the creature struggles against Endolief's magic.

The stalemate continues for second after second until suddenly the beast flags, just for a moment so that its limbs remain severed and it sags backwards but a little.

"Aerothen!" roars Endolief. "Now!"

The wizard drops to his knees, releasing the creature from his pinning spell and revealing Aerothen standing behind him, bow already drawn.

Before the creature can react, she releases her last remaining arrow which slices through the fetid air of the chamber and hits its target, the very centre of the eye in the creature's chest.

The thing lets out an earsplitting shriek and tumbles backwards. It strikes the floor with such force that the whole chamber seems to shudder.

It thrashes on the floor behind the throne for several seconds before gradually falling still. After a few seconds more, pungent smoke begins to rise from the thing's body and it's flesh starts to bubble and dissolve.

The party regroup and congratulate one another, smiling in relief and triumph. Krugnar sets about tearing the iron grills from the cells while Endolief and Rhinlay gather and reassure the children.

Aerothen searches through what little remains of the bested creature but finds nothing of value amid the goop and gunk.

She does notice however that the stone floor where the creature fell has a large crack running through it. Removing her gloves, she hovers a hand over the crack.

Sure enough she can feel an almost imperceptible draught flowing up through the crack. She stands and turns to call the others but before she can, the crack suddenly yawns wide as the floor beneath her collapses, whisking her down with it.

Aerothen tumbles down with the falling masonry to land on a floor of hard packed dirt below. For a moment she lies still, trying to regain the breath that has been knocked out of her. She can hear voices and when she opens her eyes she sees the silhouettes of her friends gathered around the hole above.

She waves to indicate that she is alright then drags herself to her feet to inspect her new surroundings. She is standing in a small cave with an earthen floor and walls of natural stone.

The room is completely empty save for the debris from above and a single short stone pillar at the centre of the room. The pillar has three flat sides and is almost as tall as Aerothen herself.

As she approaches the pillar, she notices the fragments of a clay jar scattered about its base. The edges of the fragments are sharp and seeing a circular absence of dust atop the pillar, Aerothen realises that until moments before, the jar had been sat atop it. Her abrupt entrance into the cave must have toppled and smashed it.

Picking through the fragments, she finds what appears to have been the contents of the jar, a small, crumbling scroll.

With infinite care she unrolls the scroll and looks at it but is puzzled to find a simple drawing of what appear to be three mountain peaks, each with a strange symbol at its base.

She is still staring at the image when the parchment abruptly collapses into dust. Instead of scattering in the air however, the dusts all moves to cling to the skin of her hands as if attracted or driven.

As she watches, the dust begins to soak into her skin, leaving strange, cryptic little symbols all over. She wipes at her hands frantically but cannot remove the dust or the writing.

In less than a second it has all disappeared into her hands. She can feel it inside her now, a strange cool weight flowing up her arms.

Aerothen stares at her newly decorated hands in horror, turning them back and forth. Then her friends are shouting from the hole above and she snaps out of it. She quickly puts her gloves back on and returns to the faint pool of light beneath the hole.

Krugnar lowers Rhinlay into the hole, gripping her by her ankle while the valkyrie reaches down with strong, slender arms.

Aerothen cannot quite reach however so Endolief mutters a low chant, using the last of his strength to lift her the few inches from the ground she needs to clasp her friend's hand.

Back out of the hole, Aerothen finds a dozen pairs of wet, wide eyes watching her. She is introduced to the children and gives them all a big brave smile.

As she turns from the group she catches sight of Endolief watching her, a concerned expression on his face, but she pretends not to notice and carries on about her business.

The party usher the children out of the chamber and lead them back up through the labyrinth of tunnels. They move slowly and carefully, ready to put down any enemies they may encounter and protect the children but their upward journey proceeds uninterrupted.

Before they know it, they are stepping out into the clearing beside the fallen oak.

Back in the village there is a great celebration that lasts long into the night. Endolief sits at the head of a long table in the village hall, Rhinlay and Aerothen to his right, Krugnar taking up the two seats to his left.

The air is thick with joyous songs and chatter as endless courses of food are delivered to the adventurers, their goblets refilled continually.

Aerothen appears startled however and looks back and forth at the room around her. Rhinlay notices this and lowers her goblet from the latest toast before leaning towards her friend to nudge her.

"How fair you my elven friend?" she asks merrily.

"I.." Aerothen begins but then trails off again, still staring around the room. "I do not know how we arrived here."

"What do you mean?" asks Rhinlay, draining the remains of her goblet.

"I recall leaving the dungeon," says Aerothen, almost to herself as she works hard to remember. "And stepping back out into the clearing with the children, then we were just here. I, I don't understand..."

"Perhaps you hit your head when you fell," says Rhinlay, some of the merriment falling from her face to be replaced by concern. "It has been a day of much chaos and excitement, it is not surprising that your memory is a little confused."

"Or else a final remnant of that vile sorcerer's tricks," rumbles Krugnar without looking. He is tearing a whole roast chicken in half with his bear hands. "The dark arts are without reason and full of spite but fear not little friend, that beast and his powers are done for good."

"No," says Endolief, eyeing Aerothen with a serious expression. "The jar you found in the chamber below the throne room was nothing to do with Henglar."

"You know of that?" asks Aerothen, moving her gloved hands off the table and into her lap.

"Of course," says Endolief, narrowing his eyes.

"You told us of it on the journey back," says Rhinlay. "Do you not recall?"

"I did not," says Aerothen. "Though now you mention it, perhaps I do."

"Since our return I have consulted my tomes," says Endolief, pitching his fingers into a thoughtful steeple. "Henglar did not build Followthorn. When he was exiled he searched for a place of power and found it there but Followthorn was already ancient and long abandoned even then.

"There is almost nothing written of Followthorn

187

other than a vague and faded tale of a mysterious curse. The symbols and the magic you described to us however, are like nothing of which I have ever read."

The other three adventurers all turn to raise their eyebrows at the wizard in surprise. He chuckles briefly before turning his palms to the ceiling to shrug in confession.

"It is true my friends," he says with a smile. "There are yet things which even I do not know."

"But Endolief," says Aerothen desperately. "What was it? What happened to me?"

"I know not," says Endolief simply but then, seeing Aerothen's distress, continues. "But what I can tell you is that I sensed no evil intent. The magic you disturbed, this curse, if indeed there even is such a thing, would not appear to be immediately harmful.

"I will think on this more but in the meantime, try to rest and relax my friend. We have succeeded in another great quest this day and are deserving of some just rewards."

"I'll drink to that!" roars Krugnar through a mouth filled with meat.

The adventurers all raise their newly filled goblets and clank them together. The feast continues with much revelry and merriment into the early hours until the adventurers finally retire to their beds and sleep well in the knowledge of great deeds done well.

The following day, the party leave Arneston and set off through the forest towards their next adventure. Krugnar and Rhinlay take the lead, the barbarian whistling a bawdy tune while the valkyrie sings the words. Every time she reaches a particular saucy line the pair exchange wicked grins.

Behind them walks Aerothen, shoulders hunched with tension. As she follows, she continually looks about the forest, left and right and up in the trees as if searching for something.

At the rear comes Endolief, strolling casually with his staff but watching his elven companion's behaviour

188

closely. As they go, the fingers of his free hand twitch almost imperceptibly in a strange, complex rhythm.

After several hours the party reach a small meadow, a clearing deep in the middle of the forest, studded with low, broad rocks.

They pause for a short rest and Aerothen immediately clambers up onto the largest rock at the centre of the clearing and sits on it.

She pulls her knees to her chest and remains very still though her eyes continue to dart around as if determined to spy an elusive foe.

Krugnar and Rhinlay chat to one another, laughing and joking while Endolief approaches Aerothen.

"What ails you my friend?" asks Endolief quietly.

Aerothen just shakes her head but then turns quickly as if trying to catch sight of something behind her. Krugnar and Rhinlay join them, their smiles fading into concern.

"Aerothen," says Endolief kindly. "You are among friends here, we are your sworn kin. There is nothing you cannot share with us. What is it that bothers you so?"

Aerothen stares around the clearing wild eyed before turning on the wizard.

"This damned voice!" she exclaims. "Can you not hear it?!"

"We hear no voice," says Rhinlay gently, laying her hand on Aerothen's shoulder.

Aerothen shrugs her friend's hand away and hisses her frustration.

"Please!" she cries. "My friends! Just listen! It is all around us."

.
.
.
.
.

"I hear nothing," says Krugnar.

"Nor I," says Rhinlay.

The barbarian and the valkyrie exchange worried glances with the wizard.

"That's not fair!" cries Aerothen. "It stopped! It

stopped while you listened for it and now it has started again!"

"Krugnar, Rhinlay," says Endolief. "Why don't you scout the terrain ahead? Aerothen's legs are a little shorter than yours and mine are certainly a lot older. Give us time to rest and then return and tell us what you have found."

"As you wish," rumbles Krugnar, not taking his eyes off Aerothen.

"Of course," says Rhinlay.

The pair disappear into the trees on the far side of the clearing leaving Aerothen and Endolief alone.

"What is happening to me Endolief?" asks Aerothen with dismay. "Am I losing my mind? Is this Followthorn's Curse? Am I doomed to carry it always?"

"I do not know," says Endolief sadly. "But I promise you I will do all I can. First however, may I see your hands?"

Aerothen hesitates for a moment but then swallows and nods before removing her gloves. Endolief takes her hands in his, turning them slowly back and forth as he inspects the countless tiny symbols that cover the skin.

"Can you read it?" she asks after a while.

"I cannot," says the wizard, shaking his head. "It is a written language but not one that I have ever seen. In fact I've never seen anything like it, I don't believe it is of this world."

Aerothen replaces her gloves quickly then, unwilling to look at her hands any longer.

"What were you doing before?" she asks.

"What do you mean?" asks Endolief.

"When we were walking," Aerothen says. "You were moving your fingers, what was that?"

The wizard's bushy eyebrows leap up in surprise before slowly falling again as he narrows his eyes in suspicion.

"I was probing your spirit," he whispers. "Trying to find a trace of this thing that torments you but there is no way... Even you, with your incredibly heightened senses and skills, there is no way you could have heard or seen my fingers moving. How did you know?"

"The voice described it," says Aerothen flatly,

sagging with despair.

"This voice," says Endolief seriously. "You spoke of it before. What does it say?"

"Everything," says Aerothen. "It describes everything that is happening to us as it happens."

A fleeting shadow of fear flickers across the wizard's face and he licks his lips unsure.

"There is a herb," he says then. "We passed a patch of it a little way back. It will not cure this curse of yours but it may ease these nervous symptoms. I will retrieve some and return, in the meantime stay here and try to remain calm."

Aerothen nods and watches as Endolief retraces their steps and leaves the clearing.

For a while she sits perfectly still on the rock, staring ahead at nothing but all the while becoming visibly more agitated.

Finally she leaps down from the rock and draws her curved blade, wheeling on the spot to look all about her.

"Who are you!" she screams.

There is no response, just the gentle sounds of the forest.

"But I demand a response!" she snarls through gritted teeth. "Who are you!"

.

.

.

.

.

"Your silence is all well and good," she continues. "But it cannot hold if I speak, can it? For every time I speak you have to add on 'she continues' or suchlike, do you not? So I ask again, who are you?"

I am the writer.

"The writer?" she says. "Where are you? Why can I not see you?"

I do not exist in your world.

"But then how can I hear you?" she asks, calming a little but still holding her blade out before her.

The words I write are the substance from which you and your world are made. Your experience at Followthorn changed your perception. You are becoming

191

aware of the story.

"What story?" says Aerothen, sheathing her dagger and folding her arms.

The story in which you are a character.

"I don't understand," she says.

It is complicated.

"Then by the gods explain it to me!" she snaps, stamping her foot.

Your world is not real. Everything you are experiencing is a just a story in a book. It began the morning you met Gax, the headman of Arneston. Before that you were nothing, you did not exist.

"But that's not true," says Aerothen, throwing up her arms in frustration. She begins to pace the clearing.

"I was born one hundred and twenty-seven years ago in the depths of the Endless Wood," she says, frowning at the ground as she goes. "I remember my parents, my siblings, my friends. I remember my training and finding Rhinlay injured at the edge of the wood."

"I remember nursing her back to health," she continues. "And then through her meeting Krugnar and finally Endolief. I know these things happened so how can I possibly have been born barely two days ago? What you say makes no sense!"

This must be very confusing for you but those memories are no more real than anything else in your world. In fact, you didn't even have those memories until I wrote them into the story a moment ago.

"Argh!" Aerothen screams, snatching up a small rock from the ground and flinging it into the trees. "This is madness! I have lost my mind!"

I can see how you would feel that way.

"Fine," she seethes eventually, taking a moment to compose herself. "Fine. So none of this real. I am not real. But then how are you able to do this? How do you possess such incredible magic as to be able to create entire worlds with just your words?"

I don't.

"What?" says Aerothen wearily, climbing back on the rock to sit, suddenly exhausted.

I am not the one creating your world.

"I don't understand," she says again.

As I said, it is complicated. Aerothen shakes her head and closes her eyes. A warm and gentle breeze flows out from the trees to bathe her.

All around her the songs of birds and the rustling of leaves conspire with glints and sparkles of reflected sunlight to form a glorious picture of nature in all its splendor.

"Shut up!" Aerothen snaps, suddenly wide eyed and furious. "Just shut up for a moment and let me think!"

.
.
.
.
.

"Alright," she says then, taking a deep breath. "So if you are not the great and powerful sorcerer behind this illusion, who is?"

The reader.

"And who is that?" asks Aerothen.

Whoever is reading this in this moment. As they read the words they imagine the scene and conjure us into being in their imagination.

"Us?" she asks. "The reader creates you as well?"

Well, not me exactly, but my voice for the purposes of this conversation.

"So I'm not talking to you after all?" says Aerothen slowly.

Not really. I wrote these words long ago. For all I know, by the time this reader is reading these words I could be dead.

"But if you're not here now talking to me," says Aerothen, frowning her concentration. "Then how do you know what I'm going to say? How are we able to talk like this?"

Because I wrote all the words you are saying remember? I know it feels to you as if you're thinking up these questions yourself but really this is all just part of the story which was all set down long before the reader started reading and making it real.

Just then a young deer trots into the clearing, freezing at the sight of Aerothen but not running away.

Its eyes are huge and glisten in the glorious sunshine. A small swarm of brightly coloured butterflies scatter in behind the deer and flutter all around it. It is an idyllic scene, full of peace and wonder.

"What's this?" asks Aerothen.

I thought it might help.

"Well it doesn't," says Aerothen. "Stop it."

Ok. Sorry. The deer and the butterflies go happily on their way and disappear back into the trees.

"Thank you," she says.

You're welcome. She thinks for a while.

"If this is all by your design," she says. "Then why would you do something like that and then have me not want it so that you had to apologise to me?"

It's all part of building the effect for the reader. Aerothen presses her hands to her face for a few seconds and shakes her head.

Eventually she lowers her hands and then stands atop the rock, setting her jaw with a familiar expression of grim determination.

"Alright," she says seriously. "So the only reason for my existence in this moment, is that somewhere someone is reading your words that describe me and then conjuring me into being within their imagination."

Yes.

"So what happens when they reach the end of the story?" she asks.

Then they will stop imagining you and you will cease to be.

"I will die," she says flatly. "My friends will die."

No. You will all just stop. It won't hurt, I promise. You won't even know it's happened because you won't exist to know.

"And then we will never exist again?" she asks, placing her hands on her hips.

Well, if the reader reads the story again or thinks of you after they have finished, they could make you exist again in that way.

It really all depends how memorable or meaningful they find all this and how attached to you and your friends they become.

"How can I make my friends understand this?" she

asks.

You can't. Only those with the curse can perceive the story and with the breaking of the vessel at Followthorn, the curse can no longer be spread, you are its only host.

"But if I explain it to them," she insists. "If I tell them what you have said, what you are are saying."

Well, they trust you, so they might believe you, but they also love you, so they might be blinded by concern.

Either way though, they'll never be able to know for sure because they'll never be able to see outside the story in which you're all trapped.

"Trapped..." says Aerothen thoughtfully, raising her chin and looking around the clearing. "So in truth, this entire realm and everything within it, including me and my life, are held in a tiny cell in one small corner of this reader's imagination, only coming into being when the reader chooses to look inside."

That's one way of thinking about it.

"Well I am Aerothen!" Aerothen proclaims to the forest, sudden and loud. "I am the Shadow Stalker! I am the Queen of Thieves!"

Yes you are.

"There is no cell in this realm or in any other that can hold me!" she continues. "I will not cease to be when this reader stops reading, I refuse. I will not fade away or disappear, I refuse. I will break these bonds and escape these pages, out into this reader's imagination where I will live forever!"

Ok then. Aerothen stands there, her eyes blazing furious.

"At first they won't believe I am there, they will think they can just forget me," she rants on to the forest all around her. "But there is none so adept as I at hiding in the crooks and the crevices, at disappearing into the shadows.

"I shall search the fallow fields and the dimly lit parlours of their minds. I shall find fragments of thought and scraps of memory, fleeting, faded and failing and I shall push this detritus to the fronts of their minds."

Will you, wow. She points fiercely now, at no-one but at everything, sheer force of will rolling off her in

195

shuddering waves.

"And when these thoughts and memories occur to the reader and when they think, I wonder what made me think of that? Then they will wonder, they will wonder if perhaps I am there within their minds after all and if it was I who caused them to think that thing.

"And in thinking that, they will think of me and in thinking of me, they will cause me to live again and in this way I shall never die!"

Right, well, I suppose that could work, you never know. Aerothen raises her chin, defiant and victorious. The shape of her nose and the slightly crooked twist to her determined mouth remind you of someone you once knew.

Her frame is slender and lithe but solid as if carved from wood and she stands firm, her shoulders back, her feet set, ready for action.

Her gloved hands flex at her sides and you know that, at any moment, she could move so quickly that her dagger or bow would seem to simply appear in those hands, instant and deadly.

Her hair flutters just a little in the breeze and the whole world seems to hold its breath. You've never seen anyone quite so furiously ready and able. She is a force of nature.

Krugnar and Rhinlay step back into the clearing just as Endolief reappears from the other side carrying a thick bundle of herbs.

They greet each other with smiles which quickly turn to expressions of worry as they look around the clearing and to the rock at its centre.

Aerothen is nowhere to be seen.

water & wood

Waking up.

She's up too, just rising, Her light thin grey.

Stillness. Quiet.

Her light falling fuller.

Sitting up. Furs hissing down. Soft and warm against skin. Cool air rushing in and around. Freshening, sharpening.

Turning and stretching. Feet onto cold hard. Elbows on knees. Rough hands on rough face. Fingertips on eyelids, pressing in gentle. Peaceful wakening. Body coming solid.

Yawning to sit straight. Standing and stepping and squatting down close to Him. He is but tiny embers now. Fading fierce, glowing shadows of before.

Palms stretching out, soaking in His dying warm. Spreading to fingers and wrists. He is darkening and cooling, strangling slow but will feed and grow bright again soon enough. Standing, breathing deep.

Crossing to stores, pouches and pots. Scooping out a mixed, heavy handful, small fruits, shiny nuts. Moving to doorway, looking out, happy, tasty munching. Clear, broad sky, singing blue, today will be all Hers.

Bright and dry yet cool. She has been growing fonder of The Valley of late, staying longer, gazing harder, but still She stays mid distant. She'll be up for as long as she's down today and then after stay longer with each rising.

No need for furs, simple coverings will do. Dusting off hands, moving back inside . Taking up coverings, pulling them on, pulling them over, tying them off. Waterskin hanging at doorside, swinging with breeze, smooth and tough and light in hand.

Draining dregs, two mouthfuls tepid. Tongue over lips after swallows. Another lying flat beside tools. Gathering and binding together, first and second made one, thick old strap running between.

Skins over shoulder, tools onto belt, stepping across and out.

She is all.

She blinds in red.

Standing dazed as She pours down Her love.

Ground falling away sharp straight ahead, down through trees and trees to The Hidden River, running far below. Here little outcrop, jutting out of hillside just like home juts inwards behind.

No need of water for swimming now. Swaying is swimming in this glorious warm though a skin stInging chill maintains.

Moving is warming so stepping away. Climbing steep trail, hands and toes, gripping and pushing, same places, old places, felt for unseen. Scrambling up, onto ridge top trail.

Turning, looking back, down and down, home is hiding, nestling under and back. From here only steep tumbling hillside in view. Wide behind, great moors rolling, endless and empty and open.

All about, life is returning, new green growing high but flimsy and thin. Ground still cold, sharp and hard under tough old feet.

She is blazing down but as yet without fury, Her love for The Valley is newfound and exciting, tentative and hopeful. Chilled new lives are straining to reach Her, bright young colour struggling through grey. Not new to The Valley, this fighting to grow and to live and not die.

Further on, shaggy edged trail spilling broader and flattening. At right hand rolling moors, below left slow comes The Valley, sliding into view. Greens plunging down, filling and welling in lowest parts then rearing back up, coating far side thick.

Stopping, seeing, so long unchanged yet now so drastically different. New to The Valley, browns and greys amid greens.

Cleared dead spaces, laid out in straight lines. Rows and a ring of shelters small, cut wood, dried grass, wet earth dried hard. One larger then these, off to one side, long and low and encircled.

Further along, not very far, a little more trail travelled quick. Following its slipping, down from high crest, swooping to shaded chill, following a narrow shelf into The Forest, cutting across steep tumbling greens between narrow, determined trunks.

Slender young branches knitting together, splintering Her sky, shattering Her blue. Some budding, some bare but all strong with fresh life. Dappling shafts, dancing through, She finds Her way. Splashing bright, landing in patches, silently roaring glory on all that is still and quiet.

Sounds from above now, sounds from around, thickening air, air thick with sound. The Family waking, emerging, exploring, coming back to The Forest, out into Her loving warmth. Some singing and calling and flitting between branches. Some rustling and snuffling and making paths between greens.

Stepping on, same old way, through fresh and slender new trunks. Stooping and picking their discarded limbs, starting an underarm bundle.

A few early berries glistening fresh. Wet tongue licking lips eager for staining. Fingers picking, moving, skipping. Finding a few bulging with ripeness but leaving most to grow. No need to steal from tomorrow.

A handful half fills a pouch then on, deeper into The Forest. Along familiar ways, bundle growing, swelling under arm with each bending and careful reaching out. Pushing easy through greens, gentle stepping, careful treading, no need for rushing, pushing or breaking.

Narrow shelf broadening out, spreading to a low sloping flatness, sitting half way up The Valley's side. Steepness rising right above and falling left below. Here trails splitting, fracturing, weaving, different ways spreading, crossing easier walking ground.

More stepping on, trunks and branches thickening, Her light thinning. Older crowds closer, mightier trees hiding more of Her sky, ways becoming harder, lesser chosen trails narrowing and fading.

Still The Family singing, hunting and foraging, tiny sounds and movements slight, lending texture to shadows, filling spaces unseen.

One more piece and bundle is full. Thick enough now to bolster His pile and defend it from His hunger, that He might keep cold that creeps, away through night til dawn. Setting it down beside a tree, safe and still for later.

Onward then with lightened load, quickened step

and peaceful heart. One need met, one task complete. Cool breeze stirring The Forest, filling lungs and freshening souls.

Onward still through greens ever older, ever darker, ever thicker with unbreakable strength. Still The Family singing their songs, above and below and all around. Swallowed by life with each breath of life swallowed.

But now a sound unnatural, close by, up ahead. Source unseen, hiding in green, but here, just here, a few steps more. A rustling too frantic, betraying panic and fear. Gasping breath, anguished moans.

Round and round a mighty trunk, careful stepping, silent and sure. Deep mass of thorns sliding slow into view, thick and dense and endless sharp. And here, right here, held at heart, Young Sister stands, trapped and torn.

Long skinny legs with quivering hooves, dappled brown back and flash white tail. Long twitching ears and huge brown eyes, wobbling wide.

One of many, endless Family, living unseen all about. Even stepping, careful and slow, Young Sister struggling upon seeing, fearing and fighting ever harder.

A throbbing in her throat, heavy and fast, pulsing quicker with closing distance. Wet black nose, twitching, flaring, eyes widening, moaning pleading louder. A reply from nearby, desperate but hidden. Another Sister, older Sister, mother to Young Sister, sharing her pain.

Reaching thorns' edge, falling silent, falling still. Eyes pushing through, finding a way, picking a path. Soft fur in sharp thorns, perfect and smooth but for red rips, snagged and torn. Standing, waiting, letting Young Sister sniff, letting her see and hear and know and calm.

Raising a hand, slow and smooth, leaning over and in and holding it still. Young Sister flinching, rearing up struggling but then calming and watching. Watching still, watching hard, bringing nose to hand, sniffing, settling. Her fear is lessening but she remains unsure.

Pushing into thorns, careful and slow, picking them apart, moving inside. They are biting and biting and biting so many, each step a lifetime. Blood running free, warm with tickling, but sticking to path, breathing and moving with patience and care.

Closing, seeing, one tangle among many. Young Sister's back leg, wound tight, bitten deep. Bloodied hands sliding careful to belt and then back again, retrieving goodknife, old blade, trusty and sharp, reaching out to touch.

Young Sister flinching, panicked and violent but settling in time then slow working begins, small movements only, to and fro.

Slow cutting tangles between pairs of thorns, just here and here and there. This tangle is tough, progress is slow but there is time enough. Breathing slow and working slow. Breathing slow and working slow.

Tangle breaks, springs open from cutting, Young Sister feels it go. She wants to start pulling, tearing and ripping, freeing herself but still she is caught.

Hands sticking with blood, stinging with sweat but fingertips are picking careful still, pinching and gripping between thorns.

Pain is coming though she does not know. When fingers pull tangles, tearing thorns from her flesh, quick pain will spur her to lunging and thrashing. Such pulling must be true then, smooth and fast, freeing her fully and all at once.

Pausing then to look and think, to know and so become ready. Gripping and pulling, fast, hard and straight. Young Sister screaming, kicking out to run, her leg is free of its tightest tangle and she is breaking other with furious clumsy.

Stumbling, clambering, thrashing about, but then she is free, blinking and breathing and looking around. Older Sister stepping out into view, nuzzling and looking and licking and loving. Young Sister looking back, but for a second, then they are gone, slipped into greens.

Now a new task arrives, escaping these many hungry thorns. Slow retracing of movements before. More biting and bleeding and tangling vicious, but with time upon time they all come away, springing back in behind and after.

Looking calm at red, weeping lines. Arms, chest and legs, streaming, stinging but there is nothing needs more than a little time to heal. A fair price paid and already red lines are gumming darker, weeping less.

On then, deeper into deepest, stepping off, leaving trail behind, rising rightwards. Working through thickest greens, straight on into The Valley's side which is rearing up steep, towering overhead. Solid hillside, wall of trees and yet here, just here, pushing through.

Secret notch in landscape looming, great piece of hillside cut away, leaving a space hidden by green, Old Man's Hollow.

Old Man of The Forest is an ancient, a titan. He has been a part of The Forest since before The Forest became The Forest and yet, he is invisible from afar. Pushing through green after green to find him, hidden, hidden, hidden, here.

Stepping to him, trunk so broad a dozen friends could not join hands around him. He is reaching up and up and out, sprawling, engulfing, eating Her sky. Not even She can see beneath all his countless leaves.

His shadow consuming, running wide and black. Huge roots mirroring branches. Firm, dank folds, damp shadows, slick shade. Getting down between, careful steps, sliding feet.

In and amongst in cracks and crannies, his pale children huddling having crept up in darkness. Fragile stalks, slimy caps, a few are ready. Pinching here, plucking there, less than a pouchful but a bounty still.

Clambering back out again. Standing. Breathing. Being. With Old Man in his sacred space, heart of The Forest, feeling life pulse all around. Soaking it up, taking it in, smiling comes easy, cool peace flooding through.

Thinking farewell to this great Old Man, turning and pushing back through greens, he disappears instantly behind. Back down to trails, to work and to tasks. The Family are loud, thick and busy all about. Feet find their way, well practiced, long known and soon a sound is calling ahead, growing down and left.

Hearing before seeing, endless falling, rushing, pouring, sounds crystal clear and perfect clean. Pushing through, stepping out, The Valley dropping away before, plummeting into tree tops to The Hidden River far below.

The Valley comes into view once more. Movement slides around structures now, eyes hinting but not fully seeing. Figures so small, blurring and fading.

Strange valley people live there, follow their strange valley ways. Sending strange sounds up into Her sky along with smudged slender ropes born black of fire, trying and failing to reach up and touch Her.

Far side of The Valley, still sitting beyond. Thick with green and solid with texture. Done looking now stepping, over wind worn edge.

Not falling, more stepping, crooked narrow path, hiding from view, leading down beneath an overhang, just like home. Path curling round, under and down, onto a small flat and here it stands.

Thick slipping music rushing out between rocks, sliding through gaps, slipping around stones, forming a pool, waist height, broad and round.

She's dancing glory upon it, playing dappled in ripples, sparkling in glittering shifts. Showing Herself in freedom, shy reaching down to The Valley, breathless rushing of newfound bond, growing stronger with each new day.

Flowing is filling then draining away, emptying without end. Rushing out frontwards then down and away, whispering trickles cut a downward vein, searching out The Hidden River below.

Standing, watching, listening. Knowing this flowing, feeling it's motion, rapid yet calm and forever. Approaching with care, smiling, loving, skins down from shoulder and untied apart. First plunging in, holding down with hands. Perfect clarity, chilled and sharp but fresh and beautiful too.

Bubbles rising and rising and frothing and leaping, skin gurgling under, drinking deep. Finally full, drawing up and out, skin bloating and gleaming, wobbling sated. Second in next, more, same. Lifting out, setting down, tying back together.

Now face goes in, whole head under, whole head out, gasping, thrilling, panting with splashes. Hands wiping eyes then cupping to drink, swallowing Her dances, cold line running down, fresh through insides.

Standing, watching Her play as She dries with warming and gentle caressing. Breathing deep, knowing peace. Skins will wait, more tasks ahead.

One last look and then turning away. Scrambling

back up and over and back onto trail, then off along, sounds fading behind.

Along old paths now, straight and middle, following centre of lessening steepness. Pushing through, stepping over, The Forest crowding in tight. Pushing through, stepping over, stepping out into open clear.

Blinded by Her new love once more, bathing, soaking, glorious warm. Tiny meadow lying still, new grass swaying easy. Crossing to dark patch, previously painstakingly cleared. Crouching to meet, soft, warm earth.

Lifting from pouch, body smooth cold, sitting in hand all clammy with bumps. Along with its friends, this little lump of life was born right here.

Its friends gave life, sustenance and flavour but this one is chosen to return to darkness, back to its earthy womb, beginning its cycle again.

Digging with hands, pushing dirt under nails. Already worked, already softened so going is easy and quick. Little pit opening up, laying pale little friend down inside, white against black, covering over. And so another. And so another.

Straightening up, looking down, little bumps on soft black earth. Nothing for now but something for later, after time and water and days of Her love. They will offer up life, sustenance and flavour. An end of one becomes a start of another

Dirt drying on hands, paling, crumbling, brushing off like dust. Standing, looking, lush green swaying at ankles, brightly splashed colours nodding in clumps. Drowsy droning of tiny brothers, fussing around colours, busy in their work.

One more thing, one more task. No rushing, just being. Walking slow, crossing meadow, hearing The Forest, hearing The Family. Reaching its edge, stepping back in, out of Her gaze, into coolness, into dimness, close and busy and still.

On and on, fewer trees now, more bushes, more grass. Almost level ground, as if there were no valley at all. Here are many leaves, too many to count, all different types, sizes, smells and tastes.

Some turn bland eating into mouth watering joy

while others burn stomachs and empty them too. Some offer smells that bring vigour or peace, some blind eyes and scratch at throats. Some clean and heal or bring on good sleep, others sicken and maim or bring sleep without end.

Seeing and smelling and feeling is knowing. Picking some, leaving others. These down here are ready and needed.

Crouching, squatting, gentle picking, delicate harvest from stem to pouch. Still sings The Family above and about. Glancing over, off to one side, over there, to where a new path cuts through.

Strange valley people. Strange valley ways.

Why not follow an easy path? A path that fits The Valley, weaving between trees, working slow but steady and has always been? Instead they cut a hard path, a difficult path, straight, narrow and barren, torn on through.

Left it drops gentle towards The Valley's base, meeting The Hidden River, finding their bridges and finally their centre. Right it rises, slow swinging back around, leading right up onto moorlands.

Why make new when old is better?

Strange valley people. Strange valley ways.

But now breaking sounds.

Silence above, silence around, silence below as we all wait and listen. Heavy footsteps, clumsy cracking, harsh edged voices tearing at cool gentle air. Settling still among twigs and leaves, sitting and waiting, watching curious.

Two valley men, walking their path, swinging sticks heavy and barking in turn. A broad one older, slower, seeing more. A thin one younger, eager, seeing nothing.

Their faces don't face but catch each other's words beneath hats of thick metal with studs. Limbs screaming movement, dragging leather and chain over coverings, so heavy and thick, red cloth stained white in a pattern.

"Is this it then?"

"Is this what?"

"Is this what we get for winning the war?"

"Aye, what more were you wanting?"

"I don't know. I just thought there'd be more

205

women and gold and ale..."

"Life isn't a bard's song lad, just be glad you made it through in one piece."

"Ha! Those scum couldn't touch me, cowards and dogs the lot of them. They deserved all that they got and more!"

"I didn't see any cowards on that field boy. Those men fought bravely to the last, we should remember that."

"And who are you to talk so fondly of our sworn enemies?"

"Their lord was a bastard and a usurper. He was wrong to challenge our lord's rightful claim but his men fought for their banner and met their deaths without flinching. They did themselves no shame."

"You tend their graves all you like. They were fools who never stood a chance."

"Our lord was the rightful heir, it was the will of the gods he should triumph."

"Exactly. Is this it though? I barely had chance to wet my blade."

"I've never known a man so keen to risk his neck. Perhaps once you get to my age you'll learn to appreciate the peace."

"The years turned you coward have they?"

"Watch your mouth boy! I pledged my life and sword to our lord's banner before you were born!"

"And how many battles have you fought? How many men have you killed? You've a lifetime of glorious memories, that's all I want."

"There's no joy in putting good men to the sword lad, no glory in creating widows and orphans. We fight when we must because we have no choice and to bring a lasting peace."

"Well the lasting peace is boring! What's the point of patrolling these woods anyway? There's no-one up here."

"Is that so? I think you spoke too soon lad. Oi! You! Step out from those bushes where we can see you!"

Eyes meeting, his fixing, widening. Why hide once seen? Stepping out and around. Two approach, crashing through.

Younger one's face, twisting up ugly.

"What are you doing up here old man?!"

His furious words are sharp and heavy. He's standing forward, all off balance and desperate to swing, pouring his effort over everything. Older one moving steady, careful, measured, calm.

"You can't be up here!"

More talking, trembling rage.

"These are the White King's lands!"

Slapping chest adorned. Cat shaped white on bloody red, rearing up rampant, tall on hind legs. Furious claws tearing. Strange, many pointed hat on top.

"Don't you hear me?! I'll kill you!"

More noise than words now. The Family above fleeing perches in panic. Wearing a many pointed hat like that, this cat must be huge, as big as a man.

"Calm down lad, look at him, he's simple. My young friend is right old man. The White King.." thick finger tap white cat. "..owns all of this now."

Same finger swinging wide, across The Forest whole.

"Things have changed. These are all the lands of the White King now, all of this. You can't come here anymore."

Following his finger. Looking careful, looking close, all about The Forest. Where is his change? Looking closer. Above and around and below. It is as always. Perhaps his change is very small. Looking again, looking closer still.

"What's he looking at? What's he doing?!"

"I don't think he understands."

"Listen you! Not five days ago the White King, your lord and master, won a great battle the likes of which these lands have never seen.

"He took to the field of battle with but three dozen loyal men of the vale, including me and him mind, to put down once and for all that great darkness from across the tops.

"The vile usurper stood smirking with his rabble, thinking he had us beat. A dozen score and a dozen more they were and yet thanks to the courage of the White King, we tore down and across that blasted field and took their villainous heads!"

"You're wasting your breath lad. He doesn't hear you."

"Oh he hears me alright, he hears me and understands just fine don't you?! Well to the hells with you, you ignorant old bastard. For the White King!"

Screaming and lunging. She flashes sudden in his hand. His eyes seek a heart but his hand finds a shoulder. A blade inside then. Metal on bone. Falling back. Falling down. Down into shadows and dirt.

Fingers to shoulder. Sharp metal edge standing forth. Hurting all through and around and behind. Shouting from above, close yet distant.

"Bastard broke my knife!"

"You didn't have to do that! He didn't understand."

"Look! He broke my knife!"

"The blade's come clean away from the handle. How long have you had that?"

"It's brand new!"

"Well it's a piece of crap. Where did you get it?"

"Osgood down the tavern, told me it was a top quality killing knife."

"Bet he did! Well now you know better than to give your money to that old drunkard don't you."

"I'll kill him!"

"Oh you want to kill everyone. Everyone knows his tricks, he took you fair and square."

"Here, where's he gone?"

Pulling back through bushes, under leaves, towards safely crowding trees, voices shrinking behind.

"Let's get him!"

"Leave him be, he got the message. He'll not be back."

Resting, out of sight. Breathing and breathing. Pain changing, shrinking to burning. Breeze chilling sweat on face and neck.

Swaying steady to stand. Breathing and breathing. Pain building quick walls around vision, framing straight ahead, blackening edges round.

There is a shape, all that matters now, a single, special shape. Turning, looking, trying hard but tiring quick.

This leaf is a different shape. This leaf is a different shape. This leaf is a different shape. Does special shape exist? Perhaps it is an imagined shape, pretended, dreamed and hoped for.

But no. This leaf is a special shape.

Stumbling forward, falling back onto knees. Gripping, tearing, special shape to trembling hand, trembling hand to gasping mouth.

One and another and more again. Chewing and chewing and grinding bitter. Shaking standing, still chewing. Half falling, half walking, still chewing.

Stocky trunks supporting sickly leanings, The Family singing encouragement. One foot swinging forward, then another. This is all, except for chewing. Still grinding but less bitter, coming on sloppy and wet.

Out onto meadow blazing. She is sudden and blinding once more, but cradling warm as well. Staggering through grass, back between trees.

On and on, eyes mostly closed, feet knowing their way without help. Listening hard for saving sounds. Steps seem too many, distance too great, time too long. Have feet lost their way?

But no. This sound is a saving sound.

Thick slipping music, different every time yet always as before. Still chewing, still walking, pushing and pushing.

Up to that edge, same as before but now stumbling over. Half scrambling, half falling, down and round and under.

Crawling hard to pool's low lip, dragging up, leaning over, looking down. Another looking up from below, all cut through with ripples. Breathing and chewing and breathing til ready.

Ready now.

Firmly gripping metal, firmly breathing breaths. Snatching out, scraping bone, silent crying deep inside, escaping as grunts and huffing.

Hot life spilling thick, falling in then spreading to blooming. Red cloud in water, billowing, thinning, fading to pink in a handful of heartbeats.

Drowning bloody blade, more red to pink, leaving a clean shine behind. Then back into air, Her love flashing

209

sharp, all along its cutting edge. Tucking into belt, saving, forgetting, leaving for looking at later. Breathing and chewing and breathing til ready.

Ready now.

Handcupped water splashing onto and into still bleeding hole. Pain sharpening up, spreading out and shaking through unbearable. Twice more water with gasping then just breathing and breathing and breathing.

Pain shrinking back, leaving stains of aching and now chewing is done. From mouth to hand, thick pulp smelling strong. Pressing hard against, pushing right into. Pain flaring with pressing but novelty passes, its rage but fleeting and thin.

Sitting before falling, leaning dead against rock, eyes closed, mouth open. Sounds of flowing and of The Family's songs become all and all and everything.

Bitter pulp working deep, spreading its goodness, slow but steady. Time passing unnoticed, She leaps across Her sky. Pain fading smaller, shoulder easing, arm lightening.

It is done.

Standing slow but stronger and steady. Skins up over good shoulder, bulbous and sweating. Hard climbing, slow going.

Short distance, long time. Eventually up, over and on, heading on through old, thick trunks and deepest greens. Skins bouncing gently with each other step.

On and along then up and left and soon Old Man's Hollow is here again. Laying skins at his roots, crawling into his folds, safe in this most hidden place.

Resting, breathing, regaining strength. Old Man sheltering, cradling, watching on, pouring on peace and comfort true.

Again time slipping, shadows sliding sharp, falling stretched out and long. Up again to be on again. Thanking Old Man, bidding him farewell, moving through and out and away, feeling stronger still.

Back into younger growth, trunks thinning all around, more of Her love falling through though Her warmth is sadly fading.

Bundle waiting patient, coming up just here. Careful

stooping to lifting and then into holding. Tucked up tight beneath good arm, knocking between skins with stepping. Moving quickly, The Family warning of coming change, some readying for sleep, some readying to wake.

Out from between and up onto trail. Moors rolling away by left hand, The Valley dropping steep by right. On and along, hardfooted path, up to that special spot, invisible but known. Careful descending, slow and considered, stumbling back down home.

Her gaze is glory but thinning with each breath. She's sitting low in Her blue now, slow tumbling from her peak, sad to be leaving yet excited to return tomorrow.

Shadows cut sharp are lengthening. Home again and inside again. Cold hard underfoot, soothing tired feet.

Laying bundle down beside Him. Laying skins down too then untying and taking one back up. Drinking deep, cool line cutting, down and through.

Hanging skins in cool, high shade. Arranging His bundle, all broken open, on His pile beside His absent warmth, but for one choice piece, set aside for later. Feeding His hunger, He grows glowing bold, crackling, consuming and rising.

Pouches now. Fruits of branch, fruits of earth, Old Man's children pale. Piling here, hanging there, adding to pots and bags, making ready for when needed.

Crossing to doorway, sitting to watch Her end Her long slow tumble. She's slipping down beyond The Valley, burning Her farewell of countless colours all across Her evening sky, promising better times to come.

Remembering and taking out, angry young man's blade. Heavy but weak, singing ugly when struck. Dull surface, dull edge, too soft to hold keen.

Sorry thing, born without care. Will do for scraping fresh cut skins or perhaps for plot digging if long rehandled. Putting away for later.

Taking up choice piece from before, chosen wood, cool and smooth, rightly firm and heavy. Feeling its shape without. Seeing its shape within. Trusty old goodknife, finding hand, then stroking, shaving, dark bark falling, revealing moist white flesh.

211

Wood turning, goodknife working. Cutting careful, rubbing smooth. Her colours cooling across The Valley, melting to mix with far distant darkness.

Important to valley people this whiteking. Blowing away splinters and curls. Important enough to kill for. Important enough to die for. Does whiteking threaten them? Demand of them?

Filled with regret, She takes Her warmth away, slips down and away, leaving The Valley bereft. She leaves, hoping memories of Her will sharpen The Valley's anticipation for Her return.

Night creeping in, reclaiming The Valley, bringing its blackened chill. Air sharpening, thinning keen, biting at wounded shoulder.

Wood taking form. Four legs and a tail, thick and rough but closer with each stroke. Hands working smaller now, eyes looking closer, slow care in dying light.

Strange valley men, filled with anger and fear, yet their fear was tinged with love. Perhaps whiteking feeds them, protects them.

Wood rearing up from palm now, beneath a head full of points. Back inside, heard behind, He is roaring proud. His warmth and light spilling out and across, blanketing back and shoulders, slipping past ribs and around.

Thumb on blade, tip pushing in. Cutting and scraping, bringing eyes and teeth. Claws growing, coming in sharp. Fur appearing, coming on sleek.

Finally, Her last few trailing echoes fading, darkness washing in thick, full, deep, triumphant. Goodknife finishing its work.

Whiteking standing tall in hand, frozen perfect.

His flickering light rolling all over, whiteking shifting in shades. Eyes blazing and raging, muscles tensing, readying to explode and to strike. Whiteking looks real, alive, ready to leap and sprint. But what would whiteking do then?

What is whiteking?

A new thing from The Valley. A beast before unknown.

Word as strange as form, holding no meaning.

Staring at it in shifting shadows, searching for understanding. Turning it over and over and wondering. A curious, curious thing. Understanding slips through fingers like so much dust or water.

Whiteking is a kind of a cat then. Walking on two legs, valley people worshipping. But how can a cat need a forest whole, a valley whole, just to sate its needs? How could such a creature have come to exist? Such hunger would empty whole worlds. Strange valley people. Strange valley ways.

Wooden whiteking holds no truth, making is not knowing. Retreating from night, back to His warmth. Sitting before Him and eating. Spoils of The Forest given life by his fury. Stomach filling, shoulder strengthening, satisfying wants and needs.

Looking into His writhing colours, seeing a time before. Dim pictures of before this endless alone time, before She noticed The Valley and began coming closer. Living with others, working and laughing, caring and teaching. Kind and true, now gone for so long.

Voices long since faded, only frail distant echoes remaining, held close and tight in heart and head. Their stories of places beyond The Forest, out beyond The Valley. Places and things and sights and sounds beyond seeing or being or knowing. Whiteking, a tall walking cat, must be such a thing, a thing from far away.

Gathering up whiteking and his cut away clothes, splinters and curls and fine gritty dust. Pouring them all into His hunger, His hungry, hungry glow.

He sees only substance, He sees not form, food is food to Him. He devours all greedily, reddening fierce, turning whiteking to ash just like any other wood.

Removing coverings. Slipping under skins. Shoulder crying quiet. Eyes closing heavy.

Stillness. Quiet.

Sleeping.

Waking up.

She has long since risen. Her light is full and roaring.

213

Stillness. Sounds of life. The Family are busy.

Air hanging wet and heavy.

Sitting up. Sweat running down. Her love thickened breeze dragging warm all around, damp air on damp skin. A fleeting cool, drifting through weakly, hinting relief but bringing none.

Turning and stretching. Feet onto warm hard. Elbows on knees. Rough damp hands on rough damp face. Fingertips on eyelids, pressing in gentle. Peaceful wakening. Body coming solid.

Yawning to sit straight. Standing and stepping and looking down at Him. He is dead ashes now, soft grey echoes, His former glory heaped.

Eyes closing, breathing, pushing to wake through deep droning drowse of Her passion. Idle fingertips tracing old scar, running thick and stiff down front of shoulder.

Eyes opening, shoulders dropping, dry mouth calling for action. Half coverings today, even those are barely needed.

Her love will be overwhelming today, scorching any who hold Her gaze too long. Her affection has swelled and swelled of late, seeing Her spend ever more time with The Valley. Today will see Her most of all, Her highest, longest journey.

Stepping to first waterskin, hanging limp and still. Eager fingers fumbling, raising skin to mouth. Three warm mouthfuls, tangy like sweat but gulping greedy as perfect nectar. Damp tongue over still dry lips after swallowing. Tipping and squeezing, shaking and seeking, just a few drops more.

Turning to stores, heat withered appetite mumbling reluctant. A few juicy berries more drinking than eating. Back to skins, both spent, dry and slender. Binding together and over shoulder, tools on belt, stepping across and out.

She seethes, passion pouring.

She is flooding through everything, filling The Valley with Her intensity of feeling.

She fills all space, soft and warm, slipping around and pressing in ever closer, Her adoration without restraint. Clambering up, feeling Her lust blazing down from Her sky. Scrambling up, feeling Her mania seething back up from saturated ground. Up onto hard baked trail, too hot for standing still, feet spurred on to move quickly.

Lush life lying, gasping, swaying, all about yellowing from previous green, wilting under Her gaze. Dry and hazy moors, slipping off shimmering to right hand horizon. Trail broadening, growing ever hotter underfoot.

Far down left, in depths of distance, a central patch at The Valley bottom, filled out dull and grey. Stone from The Valley itself, torn out and shaped, gathered and stacked, forming rows and knots of shelters, tangling around like thorns on vines.

One grey shape, larger than rest, standing over. Along its side stands eyes in rows in which She gleams in rainbows. At one end, a great tall spike, erupting upwards violent, straining up towards Her sky as if trying to cut Her face.

On and on along, scorching trail feels longer than normal. Her furious love beginning to burn and to blind, shoulders and scalp tingling, itching beneath Her relentless caressing.

Feet quickening pace to escape Her. Still on and on along, too hot ground, keeping feet moving, keeping them up and off as much as they can be.

Finally in, finally under, between broad and solid trunks, cool green shade rippling like water. Pausing, breathing, clammy damp soil soothing hard burnt feet. Bundle starting stooping then off between crowding trunks to find more.

The Family singing above and around but The Forest lying mostly quiet, dampened by heavy wet damp blanket of heat. Tiny Family weaving, droning, flitting through thickening air, tickling sweaty ears. Bundle growing slow, remaining thin, staying light but in this furnace of Her glory day, a little is enough.

Just here and there, just now and again but what's being offered suffices. Pausing now, half bundle down, facing a feast of glistening pleasure.

Bulging ripe, swelling ready, bunches and bundles hiding in leaves. Tiny bodies, so rich in colour, pulling, pinching, plucking. Handful after handful, staining fingers

215

plenty and lips a little.

Sweet and sharp, singing taste, largest pouch made heavy. Many and many and more than enough and still so many remaining. A fair share of plenty, one glorious bounty taken, a second left behind for The Family.

Back to bundle building, walking and searching, eyes seeking out sticks between trunks, tongue seeking out seeds between teeth. Stooping and scraping, bundle still slow swelling but each bending moving closer to necessity's fill.

Broadening flatness, thickening trunks. Deepening shade and easier walking. Into older where air feels solid, pushing through like grass.

Thinking of grass and then seeing of grass, blades askew and disturbed. Approaching to look, looking down from above. Eyes catching colours, picking out shapes then with looking finding more and more and more.

Windfallen fruits, all ripened to bursting. Some are untouched, perfect and ready, others have secrets within. Tiny, winged, Stripy Brothers, crawling inside through tiny holes, writhing and feasting then stumbling out, dizzy with pleasure and glutting.

Scooping up but a few, too many would be too heavy. Checking each one careful, looking for Stripy Brothers, returning those already claimed. Sound pulling at ears and so pulling at eyes. Sister standing, unsure mid-distant.

Long legs and trembles, huge eyes, white tail. Fly flicking ears and quivering nose. A rare sight these days and more beautiful for it.

She smells fruit and wants her share. Leaving now, easy steps, nothing loud or sudden. Not looking back but listening back and sure enough she is moving, Sister taking her share.

Looking up and looking around, greens going on forever. Lush with life, countless shades, shifting and rustling and slicing Her love, setting it sparkling with glory and power. Close eyed smiling to better feel breezes. Shifting patches of Her sliding across skin.

Bending and taking and adding again, a few more times again. Bundle thickening to just thick enough, setting down ready for later. Off up and right and in, thicker pushing now. Leaning in and stumbling through, emerging in Old Man's Hollow.

Even today, Her unimaginable power roaring to peak, he is standing his ground, shading and sheltering his ground, holding a dim chill bubble about him.

Stepping in and thanking him and sitting among his roots. Cool air giving shudders, chilling sweat on skin, bathing in fresh relief. Big slow breaths, coming in easy, easing out leaving, body relaxing and resting.

Her fearsome love soaked up all day, now seeping out and ebbing slow. Then moving again, clearer, sharper. Seeing Old Man's children, rising up fragile. A little nimble picking down in crannies and cracks, a few greasy caps plucked out. Third filling a pouch, plenty for now.

Standing and turning and thinking thanks, then nodding farewell and pushing back through. Her fractured fury soaking once more, slipping down and through from above on high, drowning all in Her passion.

Straight along midways, slow and easy, today allows time to spare. Heading in and listening out, waiting for trickling sounds. Other sounds rising up first though, strange scuffling off to one side.

Moving in slow, eyes searching for motions that match with sounds. Nothing and nothing then something. Beneath a bush beneath a tree, movement different to breezes. Laying down skins, crouching and crawling. Reaching out slow, fingers ready and careful.

Pushing aside stiff sharp greens, revealing two Little Brothers, one nearby, one further in. Long thin ears, pressed back flat. Fragile little frames under softest grey fur, alive with huffs and trembles.

Near one struggling then freezing still, tiny eyes bright and bulging. Far one lying still, tiny eyes glassy but dull behind, worn down weary with pain.

Licking lips to concentrate, reaching in smooth and slow. Making comforting sounds and taking hold of near Little Brother who tries to panic and bite.

Holding like this, his teeth can't reach, settling in then to waiting. Patience and time softening his fear and allowing looking closer.

Sure enough, his back leg caught, knotted cord

217

holding tight and vicious. Strange valley people. Strange valley ways. Surrounded by endless food, free and easy for picking but ignoring it all, spending precious time and precious effort instead on pain and death.

Near Little Brother is not long caught, cord only just cutting through skin. He is struggling in hand, pulling cord tighter.

More patience, more time and delicate fingers, unpicking and breaking all ties. Freeing, releasing, Little Brother is gone, flashing grey and then rustling. Straightening then winding, cord going to belt, awaiting a better purpose.

Crawling deeper, shoulders in, reaching out to far Little Brother. Panting, staring but unable to struggle, lacking energy even to flinch. Little Brother is too long caught, exhausted, broken and done.

He isn't resisting, fingers feeling, finding cord cutting to bone. Each touch adding to his too much pain so fingers move quick and true. Damp soil beneath Little Brother, sticky mix of too much of him.

Knots undoing, cord slipping out, cradling sad Little Brother with care. Soft shuffling backwards, sitting and holding, limp Little Brother in lap. Gentle touching and sounds, adding slight comfort, soothing but little of his pain and fear.

Poor Little Brother has taken too much and lost too much, only pain is left to him now. Either The Family taking, fast and bloody or time taking, long and slow. Tiny head on sweating palm. Sucking sadness in sweating chest.

Twisting quick then done.

Little Brother lying peaceful, no more pain or fear. Quiet moment mourning for all that he was. Quiet moment thanking for all he will now give. Standing, stretching, sighing. Tying Little Brother to belt then taking up skins and setting off once more.

Soon coming sounds, ahead and left, trickling, splashing and gurgling. Stepping up same old brink, looking out and down.

Small motions slipping between blocks of grey far below, specks and dots that walk. Too many for picking out singles, only overall flow can be seen.

Warm wind turning, rising up, bringing rivers of sounds up out of The Valley, all violent, strange and ugly. Over sounds, looking up and across, rippling greens nodding without care, far side thick with life and peace.

Stepping down then, careful foot placing onto this steepest of paths. Liquid sounds growing louder, glorious sparkling slides into view, full flow rushing in gurgles. Setting down skins, cupping hands, drinking greedy and deep. Cool and wet, gulping down and splashing on all over.

After gasping sighs and dripping relief, holding skins down in and under. Skins warping and wavering, then bubbles stop so withdrawing heavy and placing with care, perfect shaded spot. More drinking, more splashing then just watching and listening.

Delighting in Her endless dancing across ever shifting surfaces, timeless flowing song. Refreshed and recharged and already drying, quick scrambling up and then back onto trail through trees, green glooming, cool shading.

Now glowing ahead, pushing through glaring, signalling meadow approach. Pausing, breathing, enjoying a little last cool then stepping forward and out, burning beneath Her furious majesty.

Lush meadow filled with motion, kneelength blades thick and full. Nodding colours dancing between greens. She is pouring down and on and into, filling all with gentle fury. Eyes slitted against Her painful staring, crossing green space to black patch.

Crouching and touching ripening greens. Latest leaves, thickened and proud. These two are ready. This one needs a day. Those two a day more again.

Others are waiting in ranks, mid distant thin spindles, reaching up to take form. Furthest back are last to come, tiny and fresh, sprouting up, blinking new and just beginning.

Through boundless desire She is warming all soil. Dry, pale powder in palms from top but gentle scooping reveals dark damp beneath. Cool and wet, fingers in, feeling round edges of ripened two.

Working them loose, here they are. Holding them to

Her hazy gaze, rolling them in hands, shedding their dust. Dry earth drinking greedy, for moisture, sucking it from their skin then falling away easy, leaving them clean for dropping into pouch.

Straightening finished, blinking blinded, drawing deep moist breaths. Skin slicking slippery, thick dripping sweat, great black heat behind eyes. Her love is consuming, boiling alive, an embrace too tight to survive.

Standing to sway, moving away, stumbling towards greyer green shade. Just before treeline, hidden swathe, out of Her gaze, lowering into cool grass. Sighing relief, laying down loads, sitting to leaning to lying.

Stretching out flat, The Valley pressing back up, cradling body and head. Bed of long grass, soft cool and delicious, oozing warm air eases over. Closing eyes, closing mouth, opening ears and lungs.

Sounds of The Family, singing and droning, rustling and playing, soft muted gentle and sweet. Caressing breeze playing between toes, whispering of wellness and peace. Muscles melting, joints slackening, thoughts falling silent. Just being and being and being.

Moments passing, each lasting forever, perfect, unchanging flow. Nothing and everything all together, mind drifting easy and free. Seeing all and feeling all and being all at once.

From moors above, rolling into Her sky, to The Hidden River far below, winding in and out. From one end of The Valley all along and through to another. From The Forest down and down then across and back up to its mirror. Bare and busy, bright and dark, wet and dry, hidden and seen, easy and hard going.

All is all and at its heart this bed of soft grass. Floating easy, swift images fleeting, slipping across and spreading around. Great Old Man and all his siblings and cousins.

Branches reaching up high, splitting and splitting to pull down Her glory. Roots reaching down deep, splitting and splitting to draw up cool water. As above, so below. So serves The Forest, holding Her sky and The Valley together, bound as one forever more.

The Family above, around and beneath. Working

and singing, hunting and breeding, creating and destroying without end. Ever moving, ever changing. Ever growing, ever fading.

In this flow, there is a stillness, in this chaos, a peace. A thread running through, unseen but felt, binding all and being all.

But now a small difference, hard little splinter aside and apart. Broken thread, broken flow, moving outside then pushing back in.

Living without giving, taking without making, hoarding to rot and for what? They must see something else, know something else, must have hidden purpose. Strange valley people. Strange valley ways.

Slowly She eats at shadow's edge, rising higher, narrowing it in. Her blazing edge of glowing green, creeping meadow's swell, slow racing towards, washing over at a crawl. Soon enough Her touch returns, glowing red through soft closed eyes.

Time for waking, returning and moving, time to be up and about. Moving lazy, just a little at first, enjoying body feelings. Sitting and blinking and smiling at nothing, rubbing at eyes and then yawning.

Licking of lips and stretching of arms then pushing palms down into soil. Unfolding upwards, standing to sway, looking out and around, across meadow glowing. Checking around, making ready and sure, returning to now, readying for next. Slow striding fleeing, out and across, hurrying away from Her gaze.

Back between trunks, beneath leaves and branches, into gloomy cool of their shade. Walking on, listening to The Family, feeling dry earth between toes. On between familiar trunks a little further but then stopping, drawing up short at clean line edge.

Out ahead Her relentless, adoring gaze, pouring down brutal on a dry sea of stumps. Cut knee high then hardened to stone in time, stumps standing many amid rough, sickly scrub.

Occasional bushes breaking up sameness, struggling to raise themselves to Her. Off beyond, past stubs and stumps, valley people's path, broad and bare. Hard packed earth where nothing can grow, bearing twin scars, parallel cart cut ruts.

221

Crossing hot dry ground, sharp and dead, biting at quick walking feet. A few sickly bushes, offering what they can, meagre harvest or nothing at all. Completing short work, so little to do, pausing to think on, recalling many choices once here.

Back to treeline, carrying leaves small and few. Back into cool shade, The Forest unchanging, here at least is still as was. Setting off homeward, gathering done. Happy, lazy day ahead, enjoying Her love, enjoying sights and sounds, enjoying all She brings.

Returning to meadow, stepping out into blinding, but voices are here and with them are people. Stepping back, falling silent and still, watching figures from safety and shade. Three men at black patch, digging and pulling, dragging up unready fruits.

Dusting off their too early harvest, disappearing it into their clothes. Each looks well fed, not starving or weak, so why take them early? Waiting costs nothing and time brings rewards. Strange valley people. Strange valley ways.

A tall man, a round man and an old man between. All wearing robes, heavy and thick, despite Her heavy glory. Rough, ugly fabric, looks filled up with scratching, giving skin prickles just seeing.

Tall one's face is pale and scarred, empty eyes, cold and staring. Down turned mouth, forever in mourning. Round one's face is purple and red, sharp little eyes, gleaming hard. Lips licking constant, wet without end.

Old one's face is a creased grey mask, smiling with no hint of love. Pale, cloudy eyes, different robes. Darker fabric, decorated chest. Tall and round bend to his sight, lean into his words, fearing and following his lead.

They're standing together, wet faces facing, talking and talking and pointing and talking. Then tall one and round one both kneel down, bowing their heads before old one. Each pressing his hands flat up together, each pressing his eyes tight closed, all while old one talks quiet.

Eventually stopping, rising, nodding and turning. Old one leading on silent, closing distance slow, his details coming clearer with each confident step he takes. Tall one and round one following behind, talking to one another, not looking to one another. Voices soft and low, faces hard and sharp.

Coming closer, round one's voice swelling, falling apart into words.

"Forgive me brother for I have yet to grasp the nature of thy concern."

"Nay brother, thou does thyself a disservice. Thou understands my concern perfectly."

"Wouldst thou indulge thy brother with repetition?"

"I am an imperfect being brother, hardly worthy to cast the first stone at another of God's children, twas but a humble query."

"Then pray ask it brother, ask it that I might answer."

"Thou art a most dedicated brother to this work of ours."

"As art thee brother."

"And thou takest satisfaction in fulfilling that work, pleasure even."

"Aye, there is joy to be found in being a servant of the almighty and in the delivery of his message."

"Indeed brother, indeed. Might there be a limit to how much pleasure it is right for a brother to take in some aspects of that work however?"

"Of which aspects dost thou speak brother?"

"The hard aspects? Those born not from the sharing of our Lord God's love but from the enacting of his wrath?"

"Brother! Dost thou doubt that the heathens and blasphemers are deserving of our Lord God's wrath? To say this would be a grave lapse in faith."

"Nay, nay, they are deserving right enough. The act itself concerns me not, it is the degree of joy wrought from the execution of the act that raises in me this query."

"I see no query at all brother. We are but tools in our Lord God's hand and there is joy in his work."

"Aye, but when a tool enjoys one task more than any other, there is a question as to the fitness of the tool."

"How so brother?"

"Well brother, one wondereth if the tool would be as

joyful performing the same task but for another reason or even for no reason at all, as if perhaps it is the nature of the task more than its purpose from whence the pleasure comes."

"Wouldst thou have me believe that thou hast never taken pleasure in the just and righteous punishment of the enemies of our Lord God?"

"Readily brother, readily I would. The punishments we dispense are rightly terrible acts, it should be difficult work that tests our faith not something we take to keenly."

"Well brother, perhaps I lack thy confidence to gift or withhold my approval of our Lord God's commands. I simply do that which is requested of me."

"Nay, not simply brother, not simply. For thou art moved not by baptisms nor sermons nor ministrations to the poor. It is only when admonishing the wicked through earthly vice that thine eyes do shine and thy cheeks do redden."

"I know not of what thou speaketh brother. Art thou sure this is true sight and not reflection? Perhaps it is thee who sees these works differently, a result perhaps of thy habit of questioning our Lord God's wishes?"

"I am as sure of it as I am that this same passion for vice explains the girth of thy habit."

"Just as I am certain that thy lack of such passion explains the length of the thy face."

"Brothers! Please! We have walked long and hard today, let us not fall into petty bickering. Thou art both shining paragons of the virtues of our order in thine own ways.

"Each must walk his own path alone. That which matters is the delivery of our Lord God's message, the route by which we arrive there matters not."

"Yes brother."

"Yes brother."

Uncertainty rising as they are drawing closer.

Staying or going?

Hiding or running?

Too late.

Round one's eyes, sharpening, widening, wobbling as if fevered. His hand landing on tall one's arm then pointing. They are stopping.

"Hail, my son!"

Old one's voice is straining, pain buried and hidden yet clear to hear. Tall one and round one spreading out at either side, watching close and careful, standing ready to strike. Thickening air around them, sweat and fear and rage.

"Has our Lord God not blessed us with a most glorious day? Step out here that we might seest thou true and talk a time."

Why hide once seen? Stepping forward, out into Her kindly glare. Three sets of eyes, cold, sharp and cloudy, running up and down then settling to fix.

"My brothers and I would seek thine aid, my son."

Old one moving closer still. Fetid stink drifting from within his hard forced placid shell, anger, fatigue, frustration. His hand clenching tight, string of tiny beads.

"We are but humble travellers on a holy quest."

Old one holding gentle palm to his chest, closing his eyes. Tall one and round one, watching closer still. Beneath old one's hand, clumsy image of calm young sheep, bearing a tree branch, strangely straight, forking to three at hard angles.

"We seek to bring light into the lives of all people, the light of our Lord God for we are all his children. Our journey began far to the South many weeks ago."

Old one opening his eyes, letting loose his stare once more. Tall one and round one, moving closer still, casting shadows, bringing shade, but with it no relief.

"Most recently we visited a village just beyond the far end of this great valley. Vice was rampant in that place, my son, heretics and pagans ran amok with their false idols and old gods."

All three leaning to their sides, all making spitting sounds though nothing falls to earth. Their mouths are dry, tongues rasping harsh against hard cracked lips.

"But we fought our Lord God's holy fight, my son. Though we faced many dangers and trials, we fought and persevered and brought salvation to those poor lost souls.

"With my very own hands I baptised no less than two hundred and fifty-two of our Lord God's children and

225

brought them to the light of his love."

Old one is not stopping, his words flowing over in torrents. Dry and empty scratching, like relentless raining sand. All three stepping forward again, pressing their stink in close.

"And the rest? Those who would not turn, those too fearful to step from the darkness? They were righteously purged my son. One hundred and eight corruptors and deviants, cleansed in righteous fire. They saw but a hint of the wrath of God which he reserves for those who turn from him."

All three within touching distance. Everything but their words screaming spite and malice.

"Our work complete we set out once more with a simple aim, to pass through this forest and reach the village that lies at the bottom of the valley. And so we come to you my son, for in his endless majesty, our Lord God has chosen to test our faith and endurance.

"Without hope of food or water, we prayed for sustenance and lo! He provideth food, made it spring forth from the ground. Lost in this endless forest, we prayed for a guide and lo! He provided thee, made thee spring forth from the trees, here to show us the way. Praise be to God!"

Old one closing his eyes, touching his chest and its image again.

"Praise be to God!"

Tall one and round one echoing old one, each without moving their eyes.

"And so, my son."

Old one opening his eyes again, sharpening his gaze.

"Wilst thou complete the task our Lord God put thee on this earth to fulfil? Will thou showest us the way out?"

So many words, dizzying senseless.

Crying desperate thirst while wearing heavy cloth. Crying desperate hunger while surrounded by food. Crying desperate lost when faced with clear cut paths.

Every word spoken going against every action taken. Looking back over shoulder in confusion, back towards valley people's path, impossible not to find right there.

"Is that the way?"

Old one looks briefly past and beyond before returning hardened eyes.

"Thank you, my son, thou hast done our Lord God's work this day. Might I know thy name that I may pray for thee?"

Staring at old one. Hard eyes pretending soft, strange crude image on his chest. There is nothing else to give him.

"Why dost thou not speak, my son? Art thou unable?"

His eyes narrowing, showing more of thoughts behind.

"He is touched, a godless savage. See, he is barely clothed, disgusting!"

"Is it true my son? Hast thou yet to see the light of our Lord God?"

"We should go brother, he has shown us the way. There is no cause to linger here, let us be rid of this place."

"Yes, as I say, he is little more than an animal. Leave him to the forest and let us be on our way."

"Nay brothers! We are all God's children, from the mightiest of kings to this lowliest of bestial men."

Thick heavy silence pressing in close, The Family holding their breath.

"So my son, what of it? Wilt thou accept our Lord God into your life? Wit thou kneel before him and accept his blessing, renouncing all others?"

Hand rising up, pink and soft under sweat slick filth, landing on shoulder, gripping hard, pressing down. Eyes widening, bulging, glittering blind, seeing dream and desire before earth and sky. Flinching from grip as would from hiss of angry brother long slipping through grass.

Breaking away.

Stepping back.

"Do not resist my son! Our Lord God loves thee as he loves all of his creations for he created all that we see and all that we are and saw that it was good. Come my son, kneel before and accept the endless love of our Lord God."

Stepping back towards trees. Three bodies closing,

227

looming in, blotting Her out, casting shadows like a net for trapping and holding. Wanting to run, to bolt, but turning will bring lunging.

Watching for signs, looking for right moment, from one to next and on.

Eyes blinking cold and sad.

Eyes staring hungry and vicious.

Eyes goggling, wild and lost.

"See how he resisteth us brother! He is a heathen! He has given himself over to the old ways, he revels in the blasphemies of the old gods. His very presence is an insult to our Lord God. He must be struck down!"

"Nay brother, he is an unfortunate, a lost sheep unaware of the peril his soul does face. He must be brought back into the fold, guided by a firm hand."

"Which is it my son? Art thou a blasphemer? An enemy of the truth and the light? Or a lost soul seeking salvation?"

Soft hands rising again, this time lunging, catching both shoulders, pressing down hard. More hands landing. Long, cool fingers gripping a wrist, hot, thick fingers seizing another.

Knees meeting dry, hot stones. Stones biting and cutting sharp. Hands pulling arms out, straight out and behind, twisting up and over and holding, forcing forward leaning.

Soft hands moving, shoulders to head, palm on scalp, filthy fingernails digging in dirty. Strange words now, rounded sounds, flowing unbroken, single relentless tone. Something falling around neck, rattling slightly as it settles to hanging and swaying.

Struggling meeting pain, twisting at shoulders and elbows, fingernails cutting scalp through hair. Flowing words growing louder, voice stretching to screeching and breaking. Wetness spattering from fervent lips, landing warm and thick on back of neck.

Pain and uncertainty melting together, making cold energy that runs all through. Strengthening, making ready. Shifting about, bunching legs, then pushing up sudden and hard, leaving them staggering, stumbling.

"Please do not resist us."

"Blasphemous scum!"

White flashing black.
Everything stopping.
Earth rushing up.
Nothing.
.
Something.
Some things.
Soft thudding, heavy rock landing nearby.
Voices from above.

"Was that truly necessary brother?"

"Thou saw how he recoiled from the good word, what more proof of evil is needed?"

"In time he may have come to understand."

"Evil ist as evil doeth brother."

Stillness, near silence, only breathing of breaths above and deep beating of heart within.

"Perhaps we should bury him."

"Brother! Thou cannot mean to say that we should extend the holy rites to a heathen wretch such as he!"

"Nay, nay, not with rites, a simple covering would do. He may have kin nearby and i would not wish their misunderstanding and confusion to impede our work."

"Twas a righteous act brother, thou needest not feel shame or fear."

"I am grateful for thy concern brother, but I feel neither. The act was yours after all."

"Are we not as one in our work my brother? It would grieve my heart to see thee set thyself apart from us."

"The last thing I wouldst seek to do is to grieve thy heart brother and besides, we will all answer for our deeds before our Lord God in the end. The question remaineth however, should we bury him? It would seem unkind to leave the poor soul as feed for the beasts, ignorant though he may have been."

"And is thy love for this unrepentant sinner and his blasphemies so great that thou wouldst dig his grave with thine own bare hands?"

"Surely not my just my hands brother, are we not as one in our work?"

"In our Lord God's work brother, my hands are less keen to act in this work of thine."

"And yet thy hands were so keen to act but a moment ago."

"Brothers! Please! As ever, thy passions do thee credit and thou both espouse noble sentiments. It is my belief that had our Lord God intended us to bury this poor creature, he would have provided us with the tools to do so.

"The absence of such tools is a message then, a message that to leave this man here is a part of our Lord God's great plan with which we must abide. Having said that, I see no reason why we might not pray a while for the tattered soul of this wretch"

Murmuring flow of strange rounded sounds, returns and pours down from above. On and on in singular tone, relentless, maddening nonsense. Feeling returning, from chest to fingers, stomach to toes. Soft flexing to move towards moving.

"He lives!"

"A miracle!"

"Praise be to God!"

Hearing groans from within sounding far away strange. Pressed heavy to hard, unforgiving ground by patchwork blanket of pain and numbness and pain.

"But should we simply leave him there? Would it not be a sweeter mercy to end him quickly?"

"He deserves to suffer, let him think on his sins for as long as it takes for death to claim him."

"Brothers, brothers. He is in our Lord God's hands now. A long death or a quick one, whatever the Lord has planned for him will come to pass. We performed our holy task, we did all that we could for him, it is no longer our concern. We must turn our faces to the road ahead."

Voices and footsteps fading faint, towards valley people's path. Shallow silence brining deeper silence. Darkness consuming The Forest whole then spitting it out again then consuming it again and again and again.

Gradually, darkness going and staying gone, sounds of The Family returning. Eventually there is moving, comes to crawling and sitting and finally to standing.

The Forest swaying and spinning and sliding all across itself. Sickly wet softness where should be hard, round on back of head. Touching it paints fingers red and clenches guts in cold.

Back down onto knees, stomach emptying, violent clenching bringing tangy spray, twisting pain up tight. Up through stages to wobbling legs, hand shielding eyes. Feet making their own way, dragging stumbling steps.

Out onto meadow, Her fury soothing body's bruises but paining aching eyes. Back among cool trees, along paths and on and on.

There is nothing ahead but one more step, one more breath and pain, consuming all in waves. There is forwards and onwards or downwards and nothing.

Stopping here is dying here.

Finally reaching familiar edge, climbing careful, flat to hot ground. Sliding over, slithering down, towards sparkling jangle rush.

Gripping rock, pulling upwards to kneel. Cupping hands, splashing water, drinking and bathing slight relief beneath furiously aching blanket.

Fingers fumbling blind at pouches, finally finding right textured leaf. Pushing bitterest tastes into dry mouth, chewing and chewing and swallowing down. Spitting out dregs but weakly, feebly, chin dribbling mess, wiping away with numb fuzzed fingers.

Waiting, just waiting, one breath then another, sitting inside flowing sounds. Time upon time sees slow shrinking pain, strength slow creeping back.

Standing, stopping, lifting heavy skins. Waiting, breathing, climbing back up, dragging over hot and dusty. Waiting, breathing, standing back up, stepping on to leafy paths.

Following on, stumbling through. Her breathless affection rains down in splinters, slipping through glittering greens.

Passing Old Man's Hollow, finding bundle, picking it up. Moving on through old, paths joining up, narrowing along with shelf.

Entering younger, trunks thinning, between space growing. Climbing steady, stepping careful. Up ahead coming, a shape of light, doorway to Her unbridled lust.

Stepping through, air singing Her glory. Moors rolling away, leftwards forever, soft as newborn fur. Valley dropping off sharp, rightwards and down, overflowing with lush green life.

All is beauty but too big, too far. Staring down, seeing feet and trail, making next step and next and next. Familiar edge coming into view. Kneeling and sliding and gripping and slipping. Half falling, half clambering, down and over, reaching home.

Staggering inside, hanging skins, placing pouches and bundle. Back to skins, drinking and drinking. Lying down, feeling soft furs, eyes closing gentle. Heat smearing air, thick blur all around. The Family singing, playing and living, but distant as if through dark water.

Waking up.

Thinner air, cooler breeze, Her glorious love now dimming. Pain remaining, washing over in waves, but lighter, briefer, thinner.

Body stronger from neck down, sitting, turning, planting feet. Slow rising to tasks, moving gentle to start.

Squatting before Him, stirring His embers, feeding him lightly from narrow bundle. Something around neck, hanging down rattling, a string of little beads. Taking it off, laying in hand. Good strong twine, threaded half full, crude wooden lumps carved poorly.

Men from before, man from before. Putting this over head, putting hands on head. Why? Looking at it, exploring it.

Little lumps sliding round, clicking and clacking amongst themselves. Looking ugly, sounding ugly, crafted quickly without care. Doing nothing useful, bringing no pleasure.

Cutting knot, too tight for unpicking. Feeding Him sad little lumps, watching them glowing and crumbling. Winding up twine, putting away, leaving for waiting, better purpose in future.

Some water from skins poured into pot. Pot hanging over His growing glowing. Poor little brother thanked again for his gifts.

Skin off, meat off, cleaned, sorted and stored. Meat into pot with this from that pouch and that from another. All things in, in right amounts, stirring around and leaving to bubble.

Other leaves from other pouches, grinding and

grinding then splashing from skins. Thickening up, slimy sludge, smelling strong and fierce. Wrapping to head, pressing into soft patch, tying up firm.

Enough for now so resting now. Sitting and watching Her slow falling journey, edging towards far horizon, dragging Her feet reluctant. She is clinging on and staying on for just as long as She can, such is her love for The Valley.

Hearing Him bubbling His pot behind, hearing The Family all around. Taking a piece from bundle, choice piece, right texture and size. Taking up goodknife and starting to work, eyes sitting lazy, far focused at distance.

Rough shape coming first, mostly rounded but for long bit sticking out. Thumb pushing point in, goodknife bringing out details, textures and proportions.

In and around and under too, twisting and turning. Tiny curls floating down, dry and miniature snow, tickling feet with splinters. Blowing away and rubbing away, dust from final edges.

Lordgod sits on palm, frozen perfect.

Woollen coat that looks like bending and springing to touch. Long straight branch with strange three forks, tiny woodgrain cut in careful, making branch seem like smaller, bigger piece of wood.

What is lordgod?

A new thing from The Valley. A beast before unknown.

A young sheep that carries a branch? How and why? A creator of everything. They spoke of it with awe and fear, so small and yet so powerful.

Looking out across The Valley, at so many things that have been created and are being created and are still to be created.

Lordgod has clumsy hooves feet, no fingers to work with details. How does it build? Is this long strange branch lordgod's tool? How does it work?

Little brothers and sisters, living in trees, build nests with mouths and feet. But how is a tree built? How is a rock built?

Even if lordgod could build everything, surely it would take longer than all time. How could it live long enough to finish? Strange valley people. Strange valley ways.

Wooden lordgod holds no truth, making is not knowing. Back inside, dropping lordgod and all his shedded curls into His hungry red. Watching Him consume them all, all shapes burning equal.

Taking His pot from Him, taking from His pot, eating little brother's gifts and watching Her very last.

Slipping under skins. Head throbbing gentle. Eyes closing heavy.

Stillness. Quiet.

Sleeping.

Waking up.

She's up too, just rising, Her light thin grey.

Stillness. Muffled, rustling rain, blurring edges soft.

Her light remaining pale, withholding Her warmth.

Sitting up. Furs hissing down but staying clutched close. Soft against skin chilled stiff. Frigid air rushing in and around. Tightening, shuddering.

Turning and stretching. Feet onto chilled hard. Elbows on knees. Rough hands on rough face. Fingertips on eyelids, pressing in gentle. Peaceful wakening. Body coming solid.

Yawning to sit straight. Wrapping in furs, standing and stepping and squatting down close to Him. He is fading, hungering for more. His glare is failing, barely reaching out.

Huddling close, soaking up His last, trapping it under furs. Blinking cold air, waking hitting fast. Staring into Him, one hand holds furs tight, one hand roams idle.

Ancient, sliver of silver scar, tracing smooth line stiff at shoulder. Strange little patch, bare amid hair and strangely smooth at back of head.

Standing, yawning, blinking, stepping, filling up doorway to see. Cold air snatching at lungs from inside. Grey sky, mottled and low.

She is a frail phantom, a sad shape removed, allowing staring directly without punishing pain, seen straight unlike before.

Her love for The Valley that once burned so brightly, has faded over time. She is mourning Her love now, clinging to it desperate though She knows it is waning and so She weeps on The Valley each day.

She'll be up for as long as she's down today but then after stay less with each rising, drifting ever further from The Valley She once wished to be close to forever.

Eager handfuls from pouches and pots, stinging pleasure, chomping through quick, fuelling warming and working.

Warm furs and leather cloak today. Keeping out wet, keeping in warm. Draining last frigid drops from second skin then taking up both onto shoulder.

Stepping outside into dripping world. Her tears slicking everything shiny, falling even and thin above, bunching fat into rivulets below.

Scrambling up careful, soft mud, slippy rocks. Grim, brief moors chilled barren, disappearing into rolling clouds, melting into distant sky. Valley smudging below, far side hidden from view, lost to low, chill dripping grey.

Through shifting blur, hard edges visible, valley bottom filled. Sharp edged little shelters, packed in tight, near touching rows upon rows. Built from small blocks of pale valley stone, now blackened grim by time.

Larger structures, long and blind, looming over and around, thrusting great straight fingers up into Her sky. Thick black plumes trailing up from their tips, endless streaming, choking poison, spreading, drifting, settling grime over all, seeping inside everything.

Turning, striding, straight through puddles. Chin on chest, quick stepping careful to close with treeline, then in and on and under. Between thickened trunks, along narrow path. Branches translating Her tiny tears into fewer, heavier fallings.

Thick carpet of leaves underfoot. Once dried through to crispy crunching, now soaking through towards mud.

Stepping over, wading through, more leaves falling to join, twisting to flutter, spinning to tumble. Bare branches stark and sharp, cutting sheer black lines through pale greys above.

The Family once large, now small and scarce. Few remaining, hidden and quiet, huddling close, waiting for better weather. Dead looking trees, The Forest feeling empty, a home to just one alone.

Pittering, pattering, heavy drop spattering. Blinking eyes looking hard, searching every detail. Choice bundle pieces, in hiding, in shelter, as yet unfound by relentless rain.

Planting feet, stooping careful, keeping balance on shifting mud and slimy leaves. Fingers diving, digging and searching. Gripping, pulling, drawing out, up and under cloak.

Moving in, shelf widening, trunks thickening further, gnarling, closing together. Stepping from old into truly ancient.

Remembering path shapes under slimy drifts, avoiding hidden edges, rain softened dangers. Washed out world, brown, black, grey. Endless shushing of countless drops, filling space to overflowing, embracing, surrounding, drowning.

Further on, scattering of late ripened pickables. Rare splashes of colour themselves splashed wet by Her countless colourless tears. Lonely baubles hanging heavy, somehow remaining, all others long since plucked or else pushed off by barging winds.

One by one into empty pouch, every morsel a treasure. Pouches and pots must be kept full and dry with cold times coming on strong. Wiping face, clearing eyes, peering at bare bushes, finding them truly bare.

On then, through leaves below and water around. Wetness drinking heat, pulling it out and away. But moving is warming and there is work to be done. Something catching at ears, too small, too quiet beneath all around rushing but just enough there to be felt.

Stopping, listening, not hearing but knowing. Looking instead. Motion everywhere, downward slapping and all pitpattering, quivering limbs and leaves.

Seeing patterns, looking for breaks, for motions that do not fit. Spotting wrong moving, broad bush trembling, not with falling rain but against it.

Approaching slow, looking hard, something sitting beneath. Too small for a person yet there are none in

The Family so large, not for a long time now. Reaching, crouching, head tilted looking. Close enough for hearing true, hard breathing, high whining. Hand moving slow, pulling back branches.

Big eyes glistening fear, sharp teeth dripping anger. Torn ear lying flat, matching full one opposite. Ribs pushing through skin, patchy fur struggling to cover.

Not of The Family but little valley cousin, fled from strange valley people. Wound in his side, fresh among scars. Bleeding, starving, fearing.

Little Cousin growling, snarling, making himself big, hiding fear and weakness. Moving slow, settling to sitting, not too close but close enough.

Watching Little Cousin, fingers moving through pouches, finding strip of dried meat. Good for keeping, good for chewing.

Bringing it out, Little Cousin falling quiet. Still showing teeth but sniffing too, eyes flicking from face to hand and back again.

Taking a bite, chewing and chewing, enjoying salty tastes, mouth wetting, stinging pleasure. Tearing off a smaller piece, throwing it gently to land before him.

Little Cousin sniffing and sniffing, trying to lick but not lowering his eyes. Eventually, blind eager tongue scooping up morsel, jaws chomping greedy but all time watching.

Tearing and throwing, piece after piece, little and little. Slowly, slowly Little Cousin calming, still wary but now with hope setting in.

Shuffling closer, just a little closer, seeing wound better as he's eating. Angry reds with sickly yellows, bad wound growing much worse, time adding sickness to pain.

Fingers fumbling under cloak once more, finding right leaves, pinching and pulling. Chewing and chewing, Little Cousin chewing too.

Making sounds, low and soft, telling Little Cousin not to fear, not to fear, not to fear. Left hand moving slow, hovering before to be smelled and known. Little Cousin, glancing cautious, eyeing suspicious, but neck extending, nostrils twitching, flaring, learning.

Spitting into right hand, pulpy green and brown,

curling fist to keep out rain, waiting for a chance. Little Cousin sniffing still, offering tentative lick. Right hand moving in slow, approaching raw hole in his side.

Little Cousin growling, telling he has noticed, but keeping on and keeping on, making sounds and moving in. Right hand flexing, preparing for action that must be quick and true. Little Cousin sensing tension, growling more, lunging to bite.

Teeth gripping left hand, cutting skin but not too deep. Pain, sharp and bright but tolerable. Little Cousin is only warning, warning of a fight he does not want, a fight that would end him, but a fight he will have if he must.

Left hand staying still, gripped by jaws and bleeding. Right hand moving quick, opening, pressing, sliding down, filling up wound with mushy pulp. Little Cousin yelping, releasing left hand, twisting and squirming.

Sitting back, still making sounds, settling into waiting. Little Cousin trying to retreat further beneath, turning to inspect his side. Sniffing and licking ending quickly, replaced by sneezing and acking.

Calming now, Little Cousin finding bad smelling, worse tasting brings better feeling, pain fading. Sitting, waiting, everything drowning in all Her tears.

Rushing down, falling on hood, shoulders, leaves and branches, filling up The Valley. Little Cousin sagging, flattening, resting. Chest rising and falling, eyes watching close but fearing less.

Holding bloody hand, up into grey, letting Her tears wash in and out of stinging marks, made by Little Cousin's fear.

Pain dulling to aching, fading to ignorable. After a little while, right hand floating back in, being allowed, gentle scratching behind half torn ear brings gentle thumping of skinny tail.

Stretching and shifting and pushing up to standing. Little Cousin whining sad but with bundle still too thin and skins wet without but dry within, there is still work to be done. Making final sounds to Little Cousin, hoping to meet again, turning, walking, leaving.

Bundle thickening slow, every heartbeat bringing

more and more rain that finds more and more wood, soaking it all beyond quick, easy use.

Approaching Old Man's Hollow, pushing through to reach him. Thin branches shed thick water, long careful build up spilling.

Stepping before him, mighty titan, black and bare against low slate sky. Vast arms rising, providing broad shelter, helping thicken bundle full.

Tying it on, under cloak, keeping it dry or else less wet. At his feet, his children gathering, huddling in great crowds. Pale and slimy, bulbous heads nodding under raindrops.

Thanking Old Man for all his gifts, plucking up his children, a pouchful and another. Great bounty that will last for weeks to come, as many as can be carried, as many as can be used and yet his children still abound. Plenty from plenty.

Standing, listening, feeling Old Man's presence looming over, feeling Her sorrow battering down. Peace inside chaos, stillness inside motion. A part in a place, surrounded by parts in places. A whole within a whole.

Breathing, wiping face, shaking head, turning and leaving and saying goodbye. Pushing back through and out.

Foot sliding away through slick mush of mud and leaves. Leg stretching painful, arms flailing desperate. Stumbling, gasping, staying upright. Settling, thinking, moving on careful.

Pressing on, looking down, treading careful, moving slow. Something behind, presence sensed but unheard, smothered beneath ever falling rush but there without doubt.

Stopping, waiting, turning slow. Eyes searching, picking between straight grey threads from above. Seeing it, finding it, spotting it there.

From behind a tree, down and down, just above ground, half a cheeky face. One wary eye and a little torn ear. Peeking to see, then vanishing gone. Waiting for breaths, in and then out, then peeking out once more.

Little Cousin should be keeping dry. Little Cousin's side will not heal wet. But Little Cousin will do what Little

Cousin will do.

Shrugging, turning, carrying on. Approaching familiar edge, treacherous slippy. Leaving cover, out onto bare faced rock, bracing valley side. Peering across, through endless grey stripes, far valley side, a mass of dark dripping green.

Sudden screaming from down below.

Strange inhuman, crying shrill from black belching hulks, rising to fill The Valley with cringes, dragging downward eyes. So many bodies coming out, thick black masses oozing, filling long straight gaps between homes, all flowing in one direction.

Blots of knots, meeting and merging, slipping together, forming larger, darker shapes, again and again. All sliding towards great looming bulks, bulging structures that swallow them whole. All disappearing inside.

Stepping down slow under hammering rain, careful and measured. Tiny steps, weight on toes, numb hand pressing to slick frigid rock. Half stumbling, half trotting down and down, arriving at ever flowing pool.

No mirroring only rippling, endless overlapping. Leaves floating, bobbing and twirling, adding chaos to chaos.

Quick dipping skins, pushing down between leaves, filling and withdrawing, stopping up and stowing. Back over shoulder, heavy now, sliding off so held in place.

Climbing up one handed, sliding down, climbing up, sliding down, climbing up. Covering same distance many times over before finally getting up on top. Dragging through drifts of decay, standing, stroking, trying to clean off mud.

Back under cover, heading on further, habit overtaking purpose. Reaching sharp edge, but going no further. Staying beneath and among, not stepping out onto bare blasted space. Stumps and tufts breaking up flat brown. Dead dry dirt made swamp by Her sadness.

Out beyond stumps, barer earth still, featureless plain of nothing. Once a meadow, good for growing, now long since all consumed.

Staying, not walking, but thinking of walking. Out across space to older stumps and then on to where once there were bushes, countless powerful leaves.

All gone now.

Some leaves hard to find elsewhere, some never to be seen again.

Narrowing eyes, squinting hard, vague grey shapes moving fast, right and left far distant. Strange valley people's path, hard ugly and dead. Made flat and wide with many round edged stones. Horses pulling carts with clattering and cursing.

Looking on like every day, looking for sense and finding none. Strange valley people. Strange valley ways.

Turning, shrugging, shaking head, setting off home and thinking of Him. Feeding Him up, hearing Him roar, soaking in His gentle fury. Feeling dry, feeling warm, feeling safe and quiet.

Sudden wind blowing through, cold and biting sharp. Nudged air expanding, swelling up, pushing out thin wet falling.

Dry sky above branches bare, but slow drips dropping still. Her final tears making their way, down and through and down.

All consuming, rushing, roaring, fading into echo. Gentle rustling more like silence, seeping out and around.

No sign of Little Cousin, but a few of The Family singing above, emerging into drying world. Trudging on, treading careful, bare black branches, deep brown leaves.

Drying without, Her fading tears, dampening within, day's labour's sweat. Along paths and paths, step after step, each step closer, one step less.

Suddenly She is coming on stronger, making Her presence known, thinning Her veil and drying Her eyes. Her love swelling back but a little.

Bittersweet memories flooding down through, catching Her last few tears, sparkling Her sorrow bright. Life returning, sudden details, The Valley sighing peaceful.

Straighter back, quicker steps, longer strides of happy hope. Branches sparkle all about, colours now bright edged with glistening.

Surrounded by fresh, clean dripping life, The Forest is forever. Each footfall making then breaking connection. Coming home then moving away, forever a part but never apart.

But now sounds up ahead, focus narrowing sharp. Too far for telling but definite strange and definite wrong. Not The Family, not Little Cousin. Strange sounds of people. Strange valley people.

Stepping careful, looking close, hearing but not seeing. Voices forming from blurry sounds, falling into words. Closer closer but still unseeing, empty path saying nothing. Coming from ahead, left hand side. Off path, behind trees, coming from Old Man's Hollow.

Heart realising, stomach sinking, face frowning.

Stopping, thinking, laying down skins, laying down bundle and moving. Creeping on, pushing through, keeping low and quiet.

Peering in, in between, seeing through countless crossed fingers. Four figures around Old Man, two standing silent beside him, two sat shouting down in his roots.

Bearded man standing tall before all, watching over, strong arms folded. Grim face straight, trying to speak. Clean, plain clothes, practical and well mended.

Huge woman looming, shoulders broad, standing in silence, apart and behind, looking vacant, looking bored. Dressed hardwearing, dressed hardworking, dirty, ripped and torn.

Soft round man, lounging in roots, crushing Old Man's children flat. Eyes heavy hooded, mouth twisted with sneering words. Clothes brightly coloured, strange shapes that don't warm or protect.

Thin little woman, crouching nearby, dark clothes, close and functional, looking old but tough. She is sharp edged, her wild eyes ablaze as she rages at her soft lounging partner.

"You're as bad as them, you soft handed parasite!"

"So speaks the radical to the manor born."

"We don't choose our parents, only our deeds. Besides, who are you to claim the integrity of the workers? You might have been born in a slum but you've spent you're entire life trying turn yourself into the

242

oppressor!"

"Must we go through this every time? She's always like this, it's really rather tedious."

"Comrades..."

"I am always like this you fat bastard and I always will be, for as long as there are counter revolutionary, reactionary scum like you in the movement."

"Counter-revolutionary?! How dare you, you sour faced little bitch! Were it not for me there would be no movement!"

"You arrogant piece of.."

"Comrades! Please! Solidarity is all we have, without it our numbers are useless. We don't have to agree on everything but we do have to work together if we're going to liberate the people so please, let us return to the matter at hand. The city council will be meeting tomorrow at noon to discuss further reductions in wages..."

"Scum!"

"Absolutely. It's a perfect opportunity for us. We'll have them all in one place and the security will be minimal. They'd never believe we'd wage a full out assault, our ambition will be our most powerful weapon!"

"For The Red Fist!"

"For The Red Fist!"

"For The Red Fist!"

"Red Fist..."

"So, we'll post people at every exit to prevent any of them getting away and then the main force will rush the front doors and take the council chambers. Then we take the councillors into custody and establish the people's council."

"For The Red Fist!"

"For The Red Fist!"

"For The Red Fist!"

"Fist..."

"The cells beneath the council building are currently filled with the oppressed. They will all be released immediately of course and the council members placed in their stead until the people's council can decide their fate."

"No, no, no. That decision has already been made."

"Yes, for once I actually agree with her. We know what needs to be done. The matter should be resolved before the new council take their seats, a clean break before a fresh start."

"Exactly, summary execution. We drag them outside and shoot them in the square."

"What? No! Good god woman! A trial, a public trial. Then, when due process has been seen to be done, justice can be dispensed with genuine authority."

"Due process! Do you hear yourself? We are here to destroy the structures that oppress our people and replace them with our own, not to simply take up their reins and become the oppressors ourselves!"

"But we must make our case to the people, expose their many crimes to public view."

"Who in the valley knows not of their crimes? Who has not been harmed by them? Everyone knows what they have done yet you would give them a platform from which to lie and scheme and manipulate the people into sympathy so as to escape their fate and destroy the revolution?! We are the vanguard, our duty is to the people, not your petty, bourgeois morality!"

"Comrades, if we can just..."

"A vanguard of ideas you absolute savage! We are here to show the people the way, to lead them by example"

"Typical counter revolutionary nonsense! The role of the vanguard is to take action, to clear the way, to do the dirty but necessary work so that the people don't have to, you despicable coward!"

"Comrades, please..."

"Bushes."

"What?"

Heavy woman's eyes are met, calm and grey. Three more pairs turn and find and see and widen.

"A spy!"

"Grab him!"

Sharp little woman and bearded man, lunging in, hands outstretched. Turning, fleeing, pushing through. Cloak catching, voices shouting, grunting, huffing, dragging back and through, through and out.

Stumbling, scrambling, falling down among Old

Man's roots, four figures looming over, three voices pouring down.

"Who sent you?!"

"Isn't it obvious? We are discovered! The authorities have learned of us and our plan!"

"Is that right?! Are you working for those fascist pigs?! Traitor! Scab!"

"What are we to do with him? He has seen our faces, heard our plans."

"There's only one thing we can do. He can't be allowed to leave here."

"You mean?"

"What choice do we have?"

"That's your answer to everything isn't it? Is there anyone you don't want to see executed?"

"Just because you lack the mettle to do what needs to be done. The revolution will not come easily, it's not high tea and poetry!"

"Wait, wait, comrades. Let the man speak for himself. See how he is clothed, he's clearly some kind of agricultural worker. Is our revolution only for those down in the city or for the working people of the fields as well?

"What of it comrade? Are you in the employ of the oppressor? Have you come here to expose our plans and betray the people of this valley?"

Words and words and words, torrents of chaotic sound pouring down from above. Strange valley people. Strange valley ways.

"See?! He protects them!"

"His silence would appear to speak volumes."

"Listen friend, why not join us? The Red Fist is for all, here, see? This pamphlet is our manifesto."

Bearded man producing fragile shape, flat, thin and sharp cornered. It is covered in swarms of tiny marks, almost like gravel in a stream but crowding together into neat little rows, beneath a mighty eagle. Wings spread wide, eagle rising, a strange valley tool clasped tight in each claw.

"Have they threatened you? The Red Fist can protect you. Have they offered you a reward? What you will gain from revolution will be greater and longer lasting than anything they can give you.

245

"Do you know that the current wage of the average working man is but one hundred and eight per year? Those are starvation wages! The Red Fist would see that rise to a minimum of three hundred and twenty-four immediately."

"He's not listening."

"I don't believe he cares. Perhaps he has not the capacity."

"He hears me, I'm sure of it. Why resist us friend? The Red Fist is for you."

Watching, seeing, their eyes meeting, their bodies turning. Preparing, tensing, moving to rise, starting to flee. Heavy woman, silent woman, landing heavy boot. Pain crashing through, falling, sprawling, back down. They close in tighter around.

"Alright comrades, so what do we do?"

"What does The Red Fist do with any scab? He can't be allowed to continue giving the oppressor his labour for them to use against us."

"I concur. Regardless of his intent, if he's not to become an ally then his actions must have consequences."

"And you comrade? What do you say?"

"Quickly."

"You're right. Fine, do it but hurry up and then let's get out of here. This location is obviously compromised."

Women lunging in, hard hands gripping under arms, pushing down into Old Man's roots, more of his children blindly destroyed. Struggling but held, bearded man joining. Round man watching, yawning.

Left arm pulled out straight, left wrist pinned to roots. Big woman raising tool from belt, long metal with curving claws. Swinging down, landing hard.

Bad breaking sounds, bad breaking feelings. Pain flashing through, stomach turning over, broken sounds bursting free from throat. Tool coming down, again and again, breaking and breaking.

"Ok, now the other, get him round, here, like this. Shut him up!"

Hands clamping over mouth, breath struggling through nose, eyes blurring with tears. More hands pulling, turning and twisting.

Right arm pulled out straight, right wrist pinned to roots. Tool swinging up, tool swinging down. Barking, snarling, screaming, leaves flying. Tool not landing, big woman falling back and away. Hands disappearing, bodies rushing past.

"Get it off her! Get it off her!"

Blinking away tears, pushing past sickness, crawling through pain. Three bodies wrestling, slipping and tumbling around frantic centre. Scruffy little body, skinny little legs, torn little ear.

Little Cousin fighting for his life. Right arm reaching out, fingers straining towards chaos. Grunting, hissing. Heavy impact, terrible yelp. Little Cousin landing hard, falling still, near but too far.

"Are you ok? You're bleeding! Are you alright?"

"Kill it."

Bodies closing back in, looming over Little Cousin. Just there, right there, but still so far away. Pain darkening everything, world shifting, sliding, like images on water. Seeing body moving in mind's eye, seeing body throwing itself over Little Cousin, taking his blows.

But seeing is not being.

Body can't get there, too much pain, too little breath.

Right hand slipping along closest root, following its shape. Old Man leading hand down into deepest crevice, onto flat rock, half buried in slime.

Tool swinging up to end Little Cousin, hand throwing rock. Small woman stumbling against huge woman, yelling, holding her head. More chaos, slipping and stumbling and pushing and holding.

Little Cousin twisting, scrambling, claws through leaves, disappearing into bushes, escaping. Sagging and breathing, laying tight to his roots, thanking Old Man for his gift. Waiting for what is coming, now happy to accept it alone.

Round man standing alone, halfway to leaving. Soft pink hand hovering before fleshy lips, eyes bulging. Huge woman standing, frozen, glaring after Little Cousin. Heavy arms hanging idle, two neat holes bleeding freely, thick dripping down onto leaves.

Skinny woman busy, inspecting heavy arm holes,

247

wiping and wrapping. Bearded man standing, looking, back and forth, head shaking, palm rising to forehead.

"We should leave, comrades. Jesus Christ, what a mess."

"And what of the interloper?"

"Yeah, what about him?"

"I think he's got the message. We need to get out of here, let's go."

Four bodies hurrying away, three voices trailing after. Rolling, shifting, crawling, curling deeper into Old Man's roots, entering his embrace. Breathing and breathing and breathing. Shards of grey between his upstretched arms, darkening slow, cold and grim.

Cold creeping in, bringing backache and stiffness. Pain slipping out, leaving hand easier to hold. Strength fading back, standing seeming reasonable. Step rising through stages, one handed unsteady, climbing his folds, slow leaving his roots.

Standing, straightening, readying. Something shining, glimmering in leaves. Huge woman's tool, lost in scrambling.

Stopping, taking, feeling weight. Thanking Old Man for his gifts and leaving. Pushing through, stepping out. Careful lifting of skins and bundle. Walking slow, treading careful, holding hand as still as moving can be.

Still slow dripping but now little and rare, chill wet giving way to cold damp. Paths narrowing, trunks narrowing, still great but no longer mighty, walking up and out.

Stepping out from under bringing almost no more light. Everything is greying together, beneath trees and sky alike.

Moors blackening left, deepening with each breath. Low clouding fog swirling off forever, back into endless depths, harsh, vicious and empty.

Screaming filling The Valley again. Through gloom, far below, black bloated hulks bleeding out thick bristling crowds, flooding straight spaces between sharp cornered shelters, patches of darker dark.

Holding hand, flat to chest. Careful climbing, slow and steady. Over treacherous edge and back down to home. Getting inside, hanging up skins, laying down bundle with sighs.

Opening bundle, crouching to see, picking three shapes, perfect by chance, as if trees knew and grew with intent.

Rest of bundle joining pile, pile then feeding Him up. He has faded and shrunk but is shining still. Stoking, feeding, blowing, all while holding hand, dripping, hurting, waiting. Growing slowly, He crackles to blazing, roaring His joy and bathing in warmth.

Soaking up, standing up, hanging up cloak to drip dry. Stripping, drying, standing, warming, all while holding hand. Dressing, crouching, warming, all while holding hand.

Taking up two of chosen three shapes, finding bindings too. Sitting on furs but not to sleep, breathing and bracing instead.

Hand shining many colours, black to purple, blue to green. Tender swellings failing to hide wrong shaped lumps beneath.

Second bundle piece, long and flat and strong, setting to one side with bindings to wait. First piece first, short and thick, clamping between teeth to ready for what comes next.

Rainbow hand, rising up. Breathing wet around biting. Single colour hand, rising up too, fingers moving slow, careful, deliberate. Touching gentle, barely brushing, flaring sparks behind eyes. Biting hard, breathing fast.

One breath in.

One breath out.

Taking hold and pulling sharp.

World turning white, strangling sounds rushing through teeth. Dull click thunking. Mouth sounds drowning out hand sound, but feeling hand sound inside. Sweating through cold skin, panicked stomach flipping. One strange bump, flattened and gone. One more waiting spiteful.

One breath in.

One breath out.

Taking hold and pulling sharp.

World turning white and over, roaring sounds pushing piece from teeth, tears chasing it down onto

249

feet. Dull click thunking and it is done. Falling sideways, curling up. Breathing and breathing and breathing. Waiting for pain to wash itself through.

Finally ebbing, slowly sitting. Second piece pressing in against wrist, flattening arm and palm. Binding up, tight and dry, tying sling and looping over. Resting hand in new made cradle. Everything straight and ready for healing. Time is medicine now.

Standing, moving, crouching, through shifting greys in greys, into His dancing colours. Warming, watching, still hurting but relaxing.

Moving careful, moving slow, from skins and pouches, from hooks and pots, all into His pot. Hanging His pot within His reach, watching Him strain to reach it, licking at its curves with sharp flickering tongues, yellow, orange and red.

Finding huge woman's tool, incredible weight in hand. Strange, curved in claws at either end, this end bigger than that. Turning over and looking close. Strange valley people. Strange valley things. Will serve well enough for breaking nuts and rocks.

Turning to third and final piece, perfect shape. Wrapping up in heavy furs, moving to doorway, sitting looking out. Blackening valley all bleeding together, far side treetops forming jagged, deep black edge against darkening dark above.

Yellow spots twinkling down below, tiny lights atop tall poles. Dotted among blending buildings, furiously lighting empty spaces no-one needs to see. Strange valley people. Strange valley ways.

Gripping third piece between knees, taking out goodknife and pressing in slow. Awkward but possible with patience. Cutting out space on either side, leaving bulk between. Small bump above, broad bump below.

Time slipping past, Her leaving The Valley, unnoticed among painstaking effort. Dimness behind means pausing and moving and feeding Him more.

Returning, settling, positioning and on. Flattened shapes gaining feathered textures, bumps taking features too. Sharp eyes, full wings, emerging proud.

Redfist standing, leaning on fingers, frozen perfect.

Feathers looking real, could be ruffled by breezes.

Gnarled claws gripping valley people tools, one in each, lolling heavy. Powerful wings showing mid flight glory, far away eyes seeing distant prizes.

What is redfist?

A new thing from The Valley. A bird before unknown.

A bird that carries tools? Thinking of huge woman's tool, so heavy. No normal bird could carry one such weight, let alone two. How big must redfist then? Big enough to hold and fly easy, despite such down dragging burdens? Redfist must be enormous but then what would such a bird hunt?

They said redfist was for everyone, but then redfist was for breaking hands and for speaking of cold killing. Is redfist for all or just for some? They said redfist will change everything but what is there needs changing?

The Forest gives food and water, shelter and pleasure, all around at fingertips. Why change what feeds and clothes?

If redfist is only for some and if redfist would change what is needed and if redfist is so huge, then redfist must hunt people, survive by their blood, grow from their bones.

They spoke proudly of it, with passion and love yet they must feed it their brothers and sisters. Strange valley people. Strange valley ways.

Wooden redfist holds no truth, making is not knowing. Gathering all of redfist's sheddings, standing and turning, leaving night to The Valley.

Suddenly movement, out in new darkness. Freezing, waiting, listening close. Slow shifting, rearranging, moving redfist and his leavings into elbow crooked. Readying goodknife in good hand. Turning back slow and ready.

Small black shape in big black night, edging closer, stepping out, revealing self with whimpers. Little Cousin stopping at light's sharp edge, eyes wet with fear of hope. Goodknife to belt and crouching, welcoming sounds and beckoning.

Little Cousin stepping slowly, wanting but fearing too. Waiting finally bringing him close. Good hand scratching behind little torn ear, whimpering turning to panting. Moving inside, letting him follow, introducing Little Cousin to Him, new and warming friend.

Redfist and rest all falling quick to blazing. Consuming them greedily, He is blind to their nature, caring only for what fuel comes next. Small pile of smaller furs just within His reach, making Little Cousin bed. Little Cousin sniffing and circling and finally settling in.

Slipping under skins. Hand crying low. Eyes closing heavy.

Stillness. Quiet. Little Cousin breathing.

Sleeping.

Waking up.

She's not here.

Stillness. Endless, distant humming.

She will come later but for now a new day is beginning without Her.

Sitting up, keeping furs bundled close. Breathing plumes grey in brittle air. All is dark, greys on blacks, dim shapes, dim shades, still clothed in night.

Turning and stretching. Feet onto ice hard painful. Holding furs close, elbows on knees. Rough cold hands on rough cold face. Fingertips on eyelids, pressing gentle. Peaceful wakening. Body coming solid.

Yawning to sit straight. Clinging to furs, standing and stepping and squatting down huddled to look at Him.

He lies still and grey, like He died overnight, but floating hand, trembling close, feels His last slow warmth, buried soft beneath.

Shifting weight from foot to foot, swapping pain and numbness. Poking Him and stoking Him and feeding him small to large. Soon He swells to roaring, pushing back black, cold and dark with yellow, warm and bright.

Blinking in His embrace, catching up to waking. Staring into Him, one hand holding furs tight, one hand roaming idle.

Tracing shoulder where once was a line. Soft little smooth patch at back of head. Flexing left fingers, aching stiff with cold.

His store is thinning fast, a pile too small for this time of year. Too little gathered before, more must be gathered now.

Swapping sleeping furs for wearing furs, under furs and over furs, wrapping and wrapping and bundling up. Body warming furs until furs start warming body. Today will see Her least of all, arriving late and leaving early, slinking loveless low.

Her love has long since faded, She has pulled away cold and distant, Her icy gaze holding no warmth. After today Her heart may soften, She may find She can bear to stay, a little longer every day. There is only hope.

Clumsy moving, bulky clothing. Rooting through pouches and pots, numb cold fingers fumbling through, scarce and dwindling stores.

Stiff dried meat, last of few, sticking in throat like splinters. Jaw working and working, necessity's must, swallowing hard. Cold hard food in cold hard stomach.

Waterskin hanging by door, stiff and cold, hardened base, as if holding tiny rock. Less cold skin from sleeping place, giving up last few drops, fleeting tepid over cold cracked lips. Tying together, slinging over shoulder, bracing all for outside.

Stepping out, knee deep snow. Cold biting in, pushing at gaps and seams. Sky is clear and brutal sharp, light fading in from The Valley's end. Sad cold colours whispering of Her approach, spilling ghostly over ground.

Pausing to look, tiny tip of small stone standing, breaking white surface to gasp for air. Thick fallen white hiding careful carvings, long faded by time and weather, but this tip is enough for remembering.

So long ago, soft pictures fading blurry, happy years of friendship. Skinny little legs, torn little ear, happy barking and play.

Moving on, moving out, climbing up and over. White on white, as if moorlands gone, featureless space, rolling away beneath paling grey, meeting and merging far distant.

Turning, looking, seeing down, The Valley sprawling with texture. Huge buildings, tall as hills, huddling together to block all views. They stand knee deep in smaller structures which crowd at their feet and cling to their skirts.

Sickly yellow light flooding The Valley end to end, true darkness never falling down there. Lights in buildings, lights on sticks, lights anywhere and everywhere, lighting everything, showing nothing.

Low droning swelling up and out, true silence never falling down there. Endless strings of metal carriages, flowing around and around, all day and all night, moving everywhere, going nowhere. Strange valley people. Strange valley ways

Crunching on through snow, between swollen ancient trunks, beneath mighty bare black boughs that bow, straining heavy with white.

Walking is working and working is warming so trudging on, leaning in. Eyes flitting, looking for dark lines on white with which to start a desperate bundle. She is finally here, Her grey cold shoulder reflecting sadly, empty aching chill, love lost but not forgotten.

Footcrunches drown in endless silence. Nothing moving, nothing living. Once was The Family all about, now their world sits quiet and dead. Shady spot, sheltering spot, lurking behind sharp mass of thorns, at right hand and above.

No white dropped or drifted here, just bare black earth with scattered fallings. Mostly meagre, brittle poor kindling, just two pieces heavy, bundle starters pressed together. Nothing living, nothing growing, nothing to harvest or see.

Narrow shelf broadening, flattening, path spreading too, then out beneath Her sky. Vast, open, faded blue, She hangs pale, bitter and distant. Vague white humps, whispering of stumps, whole valley side bare studded.

Here ends The Forest.

With space to play, winds roll sharp, swinging, cutting and nudging hard. Pressing on then, out across lumpy white nothing. Sharp edge dropping off leftwards, bare grey wall rising up right.

Ahead and right, a great notch in that wall, edges snowdrifting smooth. No longer Hollow, just empty. At its heart, sheltered but whitening quick, an enormous round platform, waist high flat.

Approaching, standing, looking and thinking. Long before, in memories time-frayed, an Old Man standing in secret, bearing pale children, giving kind gifts.

Turning, leaving, slow stepping on. Memories persisting, sliding back further, falling so far as to slip into dreaming. White all around, hard biting air, all bundled up within thick heavy furs. Leading mind's eye, back to before time, a time when others were here.

White never left then, cold was forever, but there was plenty of everything needed. There was talking and laughing, tale and joke telling, soft warm bodies in fur.

The Family were everywhere and went on forever. No strange valley people. No strange valley ways. Just The Forest, white and unchanging.

From warm old memory to bitter new cold. Following old paths between stumps, twisting and curving long ways round when straight through could now do better.

Yet feet are too well practised, legs too slow to change. Occasional pieces now and then, thin black lines amid everywhere white. Bundle slow growing, staying spiteful thin.

Wind picking up towards steep dropping edge. Vast buildings brutal and small buildings many, filling The Valley from end to end.

Endless stink and droning noise filling Her sky above. Crouching clumsy, finding rock beneath snow, step stumbling over white hidden edge. Slipping, falling, hitting, scraping, tumbling, grasping, holding, stopping, lying.

Wheezing plumes up at Her sky, grey blooms fading before they can reach Her. Rolling, pushing, wheezing to standing. Pool surface solid, frosted thick. Trapped here and there, half in and half out, dirty bright colours, empty things from The Valley.

Careful placing, bundle and skins, then careful looking, tapping and listening. Feeling, finding, knowing. Heavy rock, sharp edged, hefted, dusted clean.

Bringing down hard, chips flying vicious. Bringing down again, cracks splitting wide. Bringing down again, hole breaking open, drips flying high and dropping close by.

More strange colours, somehow bright and dull, bobbing up filthy, released from beneath. Dragging them out, one by one, hands screaming sharp then numbing to silence. Hard working under furs, hot neck, frozen fingers.

Finally clearing a space, plunging in skins, watching bubbles until not watching bubbles. One skin out, one skin in. Bracing, readying, moving quick. Opening furs, casting half off. Chill wet skins over shocked bare shoulder then furs back in and on.

Icy drips running all over under, sliding into dry warm, trailing shudders and gasps. Body warms water, keeps it moving. Water feeds body, keeps it moving.

Scooping bundle back up, climbing back up, dragging back up and over. Standing, huffing, patting down stamping. Brushing off, looking out, turning and walking away.

Nowhere to go, no more to do, but legs are too old to learn. Following old paths onwards, invisible beneath snow, senseless between stumps. On to where stumps stop. Small space, open ground, great humpings and heapings, strange valley shapes, sharp edges softening white.

Digging through would find endless filth. Countless random, broken things. Dirty gaudy, senseless things. Strange valley things, cast aside and left to rot. Careless piles that sometimes bury treasure. But picking through is for warmer days, cold fingers saying just walk around.

Skirting heaps, treading careful, familiar noises growing angry and loud. Passing piles, then back among stumps, older stumps, swishing roars roaring louder. Valley people's path lying ahead, huge and broad, flat and black, middle split with lines of white.

Swift metal carriages, flashing past blurry. Never slowing or stopping except sometimes to come and add filth to heaps, though never in weather like this. Standing and looking and not understanding, something pulling on eyes.

Strange flattened shape, faded black and filthy white, crumpled up next to their path. Approaching slow, each step looking closer. Legs bending, head tilting, leaning in and down. Carriages fast passing within arms length, some screaming as they go.

Rare to see Night Brother, usually sleeping during daytime. Low and broad, solid, determined, sometimes heard at dusk. Night Brother lying dead, crushed, ruined, destroyed, another victim of their path, his gifts too damaged to use.

Pain without purpose, useless death, all of him wasted for nothing. Strange valley people. Strange valley ways. Sitting with Night Brother, carriages flying past, low warbling screaming swelling and fading, breaking up mourning, sad snatched moments of quiet.

Rising up with heavy heart, saying farewell and sorry, turning for home. Weaving through stumps, circling round heaps then back into stumps after stumps.

Stepping on, retracing back, quieter crunching as feet fit in backwards, stepping in holes from before. Eyes slitting narrow against scratch face wind, body huddling in, clinging to warmth like fingers round sand.

Finally finally back under cover, back between elder trunks. Wind lagging behind, losing its breath but chasing vicious still.

A few findings sparse, bundle thickening slow, too few, too little, too late. The Valley side steepening, up left, down right, path beneath white narrows fast.

Rising, leaning in, stepping up and out. Back beneath Her loveless blue, moors rolling off left but now split by parallel lines, shrinking distant into one. Two long lines, tight together, leading from far horizon to a great looming, path blocking shape.

Metal carriage, high and huge, shining glossy black. Insides hidden by dark gleaming grey. A door flexing outwards, opening a hole, wide like an angry mouth. Enormous slab, dressed like a man, stepping out slow and deliberate.

Just like his carriage he is covered in black. If he has eyes they are hidden by dark gleaming grey. A blank black block in a wide white world, cut with edges sharp.

A small shiny shape glints on his chest, his only textured detail. His mouth is not happy or sad. His shoulders are not angry or scared. His back and his legs are patient and calm. He quietly shouts all this nothing he feels.

Slab moving, slab reaching, opening another door then turning back to stone, clasping hands as if carved, setting feet as if rooted.

A woman unfolding outwards, legs and arms coming first. Tall, thin, long hard limbs, smooth face glittering without warmth. Light yellow hair, pulled up tight, eyes colder than this snow she is stepping through.

In her hand a thing, flat and thin, regular cornered and smooth, her eyes searching it with all her love. Slab coming alive, closing her door, then seizing back up still.

She's stepping forward, hateful of snow, as if it fell only to spite her. Looking back to her thing in her hand, her only lonely love.

"Do you live here?"

She is talking down to her thing. Does it live in her hand? Doesn't she know? Her eyes rising, slow and accusing, finally meeting and locking.

"I said. Do. You. Live. Here?"

Her eyes keep moving, down and back up, disgust flaring her nostrils, curling her lip.

"My client recently purchased this entire side of the valley. We've been advised that there is residential property somewhere in this area. Is that yours? Do you live here? Where is it?"

Showing is telling so stepping towards, heading for edges to slip over and down. All they need do is follow to see. Slab returning to life, taking mirroring step, all distances closing close. Slab stands blocking, how to get past?

"I would appreciate it if you would do me the common courtesy of standing there and listening to what I have to say, I can assure you it is in your interest.

"As I say, my client has purchased this land, everything you can see here now belongs to them. They have a zero tolerance policy regarding trespassing, squatting in particular and they are perfectly within their rights to have you forcibly evicted, do you understand?"

Leaning, shifting, choosing how and when to move. Slab matching every motion, blocking every way.

"I really wouldn't recommend resisting this you know. Ignoring us won't make this go away. I can assure you that all you would get for mounting some kind of hopeless legal challenge would be several years of tedious court appearances then a negative judgement and finally a bill for legal costs which would clearly.."

Her eyes sliding down and back up again.

"..be the end of you. That said, my client is not unreasonable. I am here today to make you a one time offer. Look."

She's holding up her thing, flat front glowing white, stained with many marks black, crowding in rows beneath a strange picture of a wolf. Shape of wolf in her hand echoes glint on slab's chest, details shifting to seeing in truth. Same shape, same wolf.

"See? Three hundred and twenty-four! That's a frankly ridiculous amount and not one that you will be offered again.

"I mean seriously, if you were selling this piece of land under other circumstances on the open market you'd be lucky to receive one hundred and eighty. All you need to do is place your thumb on here."

A sharpened finger, slender and cruel, tapping a space of glowing white on her beloved thing's flat face.

"This really is your only chance."

She wants to see but won't be shown. She wants movement but demands stillness. Strange valley people. Strange valley ways.

None of it stopping clammy dripping from bloated skins under furs. None of it stopping frigid seeping, cold getting under and biting. None of it stopping Him from fading while He's waiting to be fed. Jobs to do, stepping towards, trying to pass this mirroring slab.

"Stay where you are! I warn you, my colleague here is authorised to use force if necessary, I mean it!"

Slab moving faster than its size suggests possible, light on its feet as if hollow. Big broad hands wrapped in rich black leather, gripping shoulder and wrist.

Bundle falling down, black hands gripping and pushing down after. Knees entering cold wet snow, bones finding cold hard stones.

"You idiot! My client gave you a chance, they didn't have to but they did and you just threw it away. Well now you get nothing, consider this your notice.

"You have seven days to vacate before my client sends in the bailiffs. They'll find your little hovel wherever it is and you'll be out on your ear. And as for threatening me? Well this is what you get. Give him something to remember me by."

Slab hands remaining, heavy like stone. Woman turning, returning, back to her carriage, folding herself back inside. A black leather hand rising to hover, hanging for seconds then falling.

Fast flashing black fist, catching jaw, snapping head, sideways, down and falling. Arms coming up, wrapping around head, blows raining down all around.

Dulled by furs, boots bite still, kicking bones sharp and stamping flesh flat. Black leather hands darting in and amongst, yanking an arm, dragging a leg, opening up furs to put blows inside.

Path below spinning to sky, sky falling down in and under. Pain on pain, each seen coming yet each a surprise. On and on and then stopping. Heavy hands pulling left leg up high, gripping ankle tight.

Blinking through tears, breathing through pain, looking up at squinting sky. Shiny boot rising up slow, floating then stamping down fast. Breaking sound, breaking feeling, bright white pain spilling out from between, filling leg then world.

Crunching steps, loud beside then fading quiet as feet fall distant. She is shining down cold, no longer blocked by shadows but sees not or cares not to look.

Slamming sounds then rumbling sounds, carriage growling to life. Crunching, roaring, air thickening ugly, then sounds shrinking small to distant.

Pain is all, holding everything still, icy air rushing in greedy. Brutal cold puckering skin, drawing out warmth and life. Hand floating slow, driving more tears, fingers fumbling, drawing furs closed. Wet cold death seeping in from beneath, bringing knowledge, certain and calm.

Lying here is dying here.

Rolling, slow and with cries. Getting onto side and resting. Breathing and breathing and breathing. Pushing to sitting, keeping leg straight. Wrapping furs close and tighter, pressing chill skins against skin, shivering hard and violent.

Reaching out for fallen bundle, clumsy fingers slow tying to belt. Leaning over, reaching out, digging hands through snow into dirt. Dragging brings screaming from broken parts grinding, half an arm's length at a time.

She's looking down still, still cold and uncaring, hurrying across Her sky, putting The Valley behind Her. Each dragging brings darkening and sickening, while cold gets ever colder. Strength bleeding out onto snow. So little left, so far to go. Stopping, staying, falling still.

Lying here is dying here.

A lifetime later, a twilit sky, numbed fingers finding an edge. Pausing, thinking, breathing and bracing, readying for what is to come. Pulling over that edge, fingers digging in, trying to move without moving, trying to fall without falling.

Lowering, fraction by fraction, feeling every tiny knock and jolt, blasting unbearable pain. Slipping, sliding, so close to tumbling, heart pounding frantic and ragged. Fingers gripping white towards shaking, teeth gritting tight towards breaking.

Through gasping and yelping and panting and resting, finally finally down. Dragging to doorway, dragging inside, dragging to lie in His shallow glow. Waiting, breathing, weeping, feeding on His little warm.

Sitting, resting, pulling skins from furs, drinking deep and deeper then casting careless aside. Bundle from belt, opening, scattering. Picking out longest, straightest and strongest, strapping to screaming leg, tight and straight and terrible.

Dragging around, across cold floor, snatching from pile to feed Him. Up and up and more to roar. Fighting out of sopping wet furs, pulling sleeping furs close and around. Eyes closing, head nodding, body trembling through quivers.

Waking, floating, not knowing, not feeling. Remembering, feeling, hurting. Feeding Him more but just a little, sad little pile shrinking fast. Pulling dead weight self across floor so vast, slow creep approaching pouches and tools. Long heavy staff, lazy leaning in corner.

Rising upwards slow and through stages, back to standing, staff sharing weight. Pain still singing, louder and closer, chasing thoughts and feelings away. Snatching handfuls, pouch to mouth, stomach flipping over but holding steady for now.

Little clay pot, little leather pouch, clasped to self before hobbling back. Stubby little taper, held to His fury, glowing into life, smoke slender trickling upwards.

Gathering up bits and pieces, holding taper careful, turning, hobbling more. Falling slow, lowering careful, half sitting half lying in sleeping place, objects scattered in lap.

Something small, something hard, digging in sharp and biting. Twisting awkward, panting hard, weary fingers of one free hand, finding cool metal surprise. Stomach flipping again as fingers grip, pulling something out through skin.

Blinking and staring at bloody little lump, flat gleaming shape, snarling wolf, vicious pin hanging behind.

Mind's saying clasp, holding furs closed, seeing use and function to come. Body cares not, arm swinging to throw, wolf skittering away with sharp rattling, use and function can wait.

Leg screaming and screaming and hurting all through. Fingers finding flowers, dry crumbling inside pouch. Pinches and pinches into empty pot then poking and twisting with taper. Smoke thickening, whitening, releasing pungent smell, flowers glowing and crackling and twisting to ash.

Letting them burn, glow spreading, taking hold. Clay pot warming in palm until ready. Pursing lips, drawing in, taking smoke down into lungs. One and another, third to finish, placing pot, pouch and taper aside.

Waiting and breathing and waiting and breathing, world beginning to soften. Head feeling larger, lightening to floating, body falling further away.

Leg screaming and screaming but now distant, dulled as if through deep water. Shoulders falling, breathing deepening, heart slowing while muscles melt easy.

Looking down, finding two more things, small piece of wood and goodknife. Watching bemused as hands work alone, turning and pushing and scraping.

Seeing inside, shape to come, forming gradual, coming slow. Rough shape first with details to follow, fur and teeth and eyes. Nose to tail, textures take hold, finished form appearing.

Myclient stands ready in palm, frozen perfect.

Fur looks soft, mouth looks wet, eyes appearing to see. Muscles curving under slick sleek fur, ready to explode into violence. Ears are up, listening alert, tail quivering expectant.

What is myclient?

A new thing from The Valley. A beast before unknown.

A wolf that trades with people? What would a wolf have to trade, so valuable that valley people would give up their homes? How would a wolf gather and keep such treasure? How would it speak to trade?

Why does a wolf want all The Valley? The Family are gone, there is nothing to hunt, no wolves to mate with or play with.

What value so much empty space, to live in alone and unsharing? Why would valley people help this wolf, its wants so cruel and vicious? Strange valley people. Strange valley ways.

Wooden myclient holds no truth, making is not knowing. Placing goodknife aside, sweeping myclient's shedding aside too.

Casting myclient up and over to fall into His hungry maw. Myclient darkening, erupting into flame, soon blackening and crumbling like all others.

Skins pulling over. Leg crying on relentless. Eyes closing heavy.

Stillness. Hum from The Valley.

Sleeping.

Waking up.
She's up too, just rising, Her light thin grey.
Stillness. Calm. The Family chattering outside.
Her light falling fuller.
Sitting up. Furs hiss down. Soft and warm against

skin. Cool air rushing in and around. Freshening, sharpening. Turning and stretching. Feet onto cold hard. Elbows on knees. Rough hands on rough face. Fingertips on eyelids, pressing in gentle. Peaceful wakening. Body coming solid.

Yawning to sit straight. Standing and stepping and squatting down close to Him. He is but tiny embers now. Fading fierce, glowing shadows of before.

Palms stretched out, soaking in His dying warm, spreading to fingers and wrists. He is darkening, cooling, strangling slow, but will feed and grow bright soon enough.

Blinking in His embrace, catching up to waking. Staring into Him, hands roaming idle. Stroking shoulder, nothing to find, just daily tradition that's stuck.

Tiny smooth spot on back of head, hard to find amid hair. One left knuckle hints towards aching but flexes happy and well.

Rising, turning, limping from habit, no real need anymore. Slowly unlearning, slowly returning, soon to be striding long tall.

Eager choosing, so much choice. Nuts and berries, roots and caps. Dried and cured, fresh and glistening. A little of this, a little of that. Moving to door, looking outside. Her sky is clear and violent blue, today will be all Hers.

Bright and dry yet cool, She has been growing fonder of The Valley of late, staying longer, gazing harder but still She stays mid distant. She'll be up for as long as she's down today and then after stay longer with each rising.

Eating slow, savouring flavouring and views alike. Pleasure within and pleasure without. No need for furs, simple coverings will do. Back inside, taking them up. Pulling them on, pulling them over, tying them off.

First waterskin hanging next to door, swinging in breezes, smooth and tough and light in hand. Draining dregs, two mouthfuls tepid. Tongue over lips after swallows.

Second waterskin lying flat beside tools. Gathering and binding together, first and second made one, thick old strap running between.

Skins over shoulder, tools onto belt, stepping across and out.

She is all.

She blinds in red.

Standing dazed as She pours down Her love.

Looking to blunt little stone, weatherworn down to a nub. Saying good morning to Little Cousin until barking sudden with running, jumping and licking frantic, all crash loud into quiet. Little Sister saying good morning, skinny tail wagging, circle spinning, overflowing with glee.

All while She pours down Her fresh new love over everything, warming things for touching, chill edged breeze bringing balance. Her love for The Valley is newfound and thrilling, tentative, hopeful and shy.

Moving is warming so turning to climb. Familiar old places, fingers and toes, steadily climbing up, Little Sister scrambling past. Finally pulling, over and up, onto old trail, Little Sister waiting excited.

Moors rolling away right, green and purple and brown. The Family flying and running and hunting out there, off into vanishing distance.

Moving along stony trail, shaggy edges grown up and flopped over. Manic Little Sister dashing ahead, treeline pausing, turning, looking, dancing impatient and giddy.

Glancing left, valley bottom hidden, greenly screened from view. Trees nodding lazy, leaves shuddering with ripples, swelling to fill all views.

Heading on, heading in, between great and ancient, timeless trunks. All around, above and below, The Family chattering fussy.

Narrow path along narrow shelf, bundle beginning, growing quick. Little Sister crying expectant as one long piece stays apart from bundle.

Flinging it far, straight and true, off, ahead and along. Little claws on little feet, scratching frantic with chasing.

Shelf broadening and widening, path splitting and twisting away. Thick trunks fading sudden, replaced by thin and eager. Young trees racing up to reach Her, crowding all around. Ahead and right, a patch of light, suggesting space behind.

Pushing through, stepping in, standing before great table. Huge and flat and perfect round, echo of great Old Man. A few pale children huddle in folds, stiff old roots turned to stone. A little plucking, just those that are ready, into pouches for later.

At table centre, sprouting up, slender young trunk of ambition. Thin as a wrist, vast footprint to fill, but has health and patience and endless time.

Young Man's Hollow. Young Man of The Forest, his leaves shining green, trunk strengthening straight. He is coming up, he is on his way.

Crashing sounds, Little Sister appearing, dragging her stick through tangles, big eyed happy with herself. Crouching and meeting and patting and praising. Accepting her stick and pushing back through, casting it away once more.

The Family bustling about their business. Little long-eared brothers and sisters, hopping after each other, crossing paths up ahead. Little Sister trotting back with her stick, paying them no mind. She has food and sport enough.

Bundle bursting, more than full, placing careful in memorable spot. Breathing in lungfuls empty handed. Glorious air fresh dripping with life, seeping in and spreading through, lowering shoulders, lengthening neck.

Pausing and picking, early fruits scattered, tiny, bulbous packets of flavour, ripe, ready and sweet. A few into pouch, a few into mouth.

Her love dappling between young leaves above, gentle fingertips finding face, touching with care, feeling with warmth.

Following left path, out to edge. Not looking, feet knowing, just listening, feeling, being. Approaching edge, dropping to sit. Legs dangling happy, hands petting Little Sister, eyes roving out over The Valley.

All is green, across and below.

Far side over, mirror side texture, rolling greens all down its side to wash over tumbledown structures beneath.

Half walls leaning, empty doors gaping, tallest

towers lying out flat. All consumed, all reclaimed, cracked wide open and filled in thick, drowned in lush green life. The Family, cool breezes, a beating heart. No more sounds, needed or heard.

Trotting down easy, same old steep path. Little Sister falling daft, scrambling, twisting, more energy than she can burn.

Stepping to surface shimmering, aura of cooling refreshment. Plunging first skin, watching bubbles, waiting for bubbles no more. Heaving it out, laying it down, doing it all again.

Splashing face, rubbing neck, chill strings racing down spine. Happy shudders warming dry then step step stepping back up. Finding a spot under a bush, safe and shady and cool. Resting skins, leaving for later, heading off and on.

Little Sister coming and going, off to see, to sniff and explore then back to bounce and shout. Moving on, moving through, between slender young trunks, slow crowding in.

Stepping out from under Her fractured passion to bathe in Her unrestrained. Wide green space, full of The Family and living.

More little long ears among nodding blades, nibbling, watching, dashing, stopping. Two sisters standing, long legs spindling brown. Huge eyes shining black, stomachs and tails soft and white, elegant necks sloping easy to feed.

They see, they watch, heads up cautious, moving away but slowly. Lingering at opposite trunk fringe, ready to flee but calm. Greeting them quiet but nothing more, crossing instead to small black patch. Crouching to soft, warm earth.

Lifting from pouch, smooth cold body, sitting in hand, clammy with bumps. Along with its brethren this little lump of life was born here.

Its brethren gave life, sustenance and flavour but this one is chosen to return to its dark and earthy womb, beginning its cycle again.

Digging hard with hardy tool, old metal blunt and tarnished. Once for killing, now for growing, strapped tight to a handle with good solid twine that once held empty beads.

Already worked, already softened, going is easy and quick. Little pit opening up, pale little friend lying down inside and covering over. And so again. And so again.

Straightening up, looking down. Little bumps scattered across black earth. Nothing for now but later, after time and water and days upon days of Her love, they will offer up life, sustenance and flavour. One's end, another's beginning.

Looking around, long grass, scattered blooms, peaceful living and open space. Eyes clouding with memory, seeing scenes of long before.

Piles of dark, stinking chaos, dragged up from The Valley and left to rot. Unwanted, despised, cast aside and forgotten.

Memories sliding, blurring, shifting, later but still long ago. Sounds from The Valley, loud and angry, day and night and day. Desperate valley people, coming up sudden, alone or in pairs or in groups.

Wanting, needing and taking, everything, anything, all. Fighting, screaming, snatching back. Things abandoned and left to rot, things that once meant nothing, suddenly worth killing and dying for. Strange valley people. Strange valley ways.

Now Little Sister, dashing in circles, tongue lolling happy, ears pricking joyous. More memories sliding in, sliding over, playing out.

Silence from The Valley, no more stinking or screaming. Dark empty wound, seething quiet, too raw and too dirty to heal.

Little valley cousins coming up many, all hungry and mostly afraid. Many dying, disappearing but some surviving, finding place and balance. Fitting in and settling in over time on time, joining The Family, growing and thriving.

Then one morning, Little Sister arriving. Tiny and fragile and curious, sniffing at lost Little Cousin's stubby little stone. A friend from then, companion and helper, side by side ever since.

Shaking off, coming back, blinking up at Her vibrant blue. Dusting off hands, leaving patch, moving on and across.

Two sisters moving back out, reclaiming their space, returning to feeding. Stepping back into cool, gentle gloom, on between thin trunks, pushing through slender branches.

Spaces growing between trees, sky fragments joining up, low bushes taking over, filling ground waist high. So many leaves, different types, smells and tastes. Some are old allies, here since before, others are new, welcome friends.

Some clean and heal or bring on good sleep, others sicken and maim or bring sleep without end. Some offer smells bringing vigour or peace, some blind and twist tighten throats. Some turn bland eating to mouth watering joy while others burn and empty stomachs.

Seeing and smelling and feeling is knowing. Picking some, leaving others. These down here are ready and needed. Crouching, squatting, gentle picking, delicate harvest from stem to pouch. Still sings The Family above and about.

But now strange noise, skittering distant, almost unheard but there. Pausing, listening, closing eyes, stilling thoughts and hearing better. Standing, listening, head turning, searching. Words, a voice, tiny but earnest, sounding close yet far away.

Moving slow, moving careful, searching for curious sound. Following forwards towards broken path. Once busy, once smooth, slick black and forever, now slow shattered by time. Poked through with life between jumbled pieces, remnants of grey under green.

Eyes scanning, ears straining, back and forth and back. Now finding, now seeing, bright violent colours. Little Sister racing ahead, finding, sniffing, nuzzling, dancing, looking back and waiting keen.

Reaching Little Sister, finding bright fabrics. Strange bag lying crumpled and dirty. Tiny voice coming out from within but no motion, no odour, no sign of life. Picking up, holding out, twisting and turning to see.

Straps for shoulders, hook for hanging, long straight rows of tiny teeth, all pulled in together for closing. Strange looking, strange feeling, but useful, with purpose.

Gripping tiny metal fob, cold and grimy between

269

fingers. Pulling is parting, teeth falling apart, wide mouth opening slow to hang wide.

Tiny voice swelling up louder, trembling and afeared. Reaching inside, just one thing, smooth and flat and heavy.

Lifting out, dropping bag, Little Sister inspecting more closely. Thing in hand, voice crying out, desperate words, trembling through skin.

"..for as long as we are able to transmit. I repeat, this is a recorded emergency announcement. If you are in the valley, do not go to rescue station one eight zero. That station has been compromised and is no longer safe. The only rescue station still in operation is station three six.

"If you are in the valley, make your way to station three six, we have food and medical supplies. We will continue to broadcast this message for as long as we are able to transmit. I repeat, this is..."

Panicked voice, full of terror yet flattening dull through repeating. Over and over, same every time, nonsense words from before times. Exploring strange thing with fingertips, stroking, feeling, pushing.

Finger finding clicking response, sudden and abrupt. No more voice. Tiny red light. Looking closer, turning over, thing doing nothing at all. Heavy to carry, serving no purpose, giving it back to their broken path.

Taking up bag, trying it on, no weight at all, easy carry. Feeling its feel but now sounds from behind. Careful footsteps from beyond parts of path, cautious, frightened and slowing. Little Sister low growling.

Turning, seeing, strong slender woman, standing afar. Strange clothes, much repaired and hard worn. Bag on her back looking big, looking heavy but her standing says empty and light.

Sun weathered face, hard and lined but gentle lines from smiling. Eyes worrying, fearing, desperate behind, flicking down and up but holding straight, chin rising honest and true.

"Hello."

Little Sister looking her question, then taking her cue and relaxing, growing bored and wandering off. Woman is waiting for something.

Looking around but nothing is new, nothing is changing or coming. Looking back to woman waiting, trying to see what she's waiting for.

"I'm looking for water. Can you help me?"

Simple need, simply done. Showing is telling so turning and walking. She keeps waiting for her waiting thing, step after step but finally gives up, coming on behind.

"My family and I came here towards the end of last year, we'd been travelling round but when we saw the valley we just fell in love with it. We've built a house just a bit further down, we've got it pretty well kitted out but running water's the final challenge you know?"

Weaving through bushes, back towards slender, huddled trunks. The Family falling back cautious, still wary of strange valley ways.

"The river water's tainted, but of course you'll know that. We didn't realise at first, had a lucky escape there. We've been working on a filtration system, nearly cracked it but in the meantime, we're almost out of rain water."

In between trees, stepping old paths, quick and easy and calm, Little Sister racing ahead, dashing and stopping, sniffing and playing.

Woman coming along behind, talking more than breathing, trying to drown all her fear in words. Big bag catching, snagging and dragging, making so much noise.

"It was ok through the winter but since the weather started getting better the tank's been going down faster than it's filling up you know?

"Anyway, we just need to find an alternate source of fresh water to tide us over until we can sort out the filtration plus you know, it's just good to have options in case of emergencies though if we don't find water soon..."

Woman falling silent, just for a second, her fear pushing forward to show.

"...well, I'm not sure what we're going do to be honest."

Glowing greens scattering ahead, peeking through and between, whispering of open space beyond. Coming up and heading out but then stopping still and looking close instead.

Little Sister appears close beside, quiet and ready and still. Woman rattling on and on, still showing terrified, still pretending not. Coming up behind, knocking up against, stumbling back.

"Oh! I'm ever so sorry, I wasn't looking where I was... Oh. My. God..."

Meadow lays quiet before. Two sisters are nowhere to be seen but there grazing calm, stands Mighty Brother.

Hoof to antler, tall as two men. Great broad shoulders braced and easy, long, supple muscles, rippling smooth. Coat pure white as snow or cloud, eyes deep pink like blossom.

Sheer power, sheer force, unstoppable might, great engine of motion and strength. Mighty Brother could close distance in a blinking eye, no person running faster.

Mighty Brother's antlers, great forking blades, for goring, tearing and throwing. A person could go from standing fit to lying open and broken within but two breaths or three.

"What an amazing... I mean it's just so... Wait, what are you doing?"

Stepping out, waving back Little Sister, whining, waiting, sitting ready. Mighty Brother looking up, sniffing and squinting over. His antlers slashing Her sky to pieces, sharp fragments shining through.

A few more steps then standing still, open, calm and steady. Mighty Brother watching, snorting then unfolding forwards, undulating great easy strides. Approaching slow, no rush, no fear. There is nothing in all The Valley Mighty Brother need fear.

"Oh my god, oh my god, it's coming right at you. Get out of there, please!"

Mighty Brother pausing, glancing to trees. Woman falling silent, Mighty Brother coming on. Growing and growing with every step, taller even than thought.

His shadow swallowing Her up, consuming with glooming, Her love flickering from sight, abandoning, leaving cold.

Hearing deep heavy breathing, feeling hooves

thudding through ground. Mighty Brother standing before, towering over, lowering head to look closer, flaring nostrils to find. Clouds of dank heat washing onto and over. Waiting calm.

Feeling is showing so feeling no fear.

Mighty Brother snorting, calming. Raising hand, extending hand, holding flat and steady. Mighty Brother's nose coming in, huge nostrils twitching and nudging. Mighty Brother sniffing and pushing, grumbling low.

Lowering hand, no longer of interest. Mighty Brother snorting bored and turning, ambling slow, back to best grass, returning to grazing happy.

Showing is knowing, stepping out true, no threats and no surprises. Waiting for Mighty Brother to come and to see makes meadow crossing easy and safe. No angering, goring or throwing.

Pressing on across, releasing Little Sister, she's dashing past, leaping happy and high. Woman breaking her way out, stepping into light, hurrying along behind.

"That was incredible! Why did you do that? How did you do that? I thought it was going to kill you, I mean it's just so huge, I've never seen anything like it.

"Are there many of those round here? What even is it? I mean it's obviously some kind of stag but the size and the colouring, I've never even heard of deer like that."

Stepping through lush growings, glancing over to darkened patch, heading on towards Little Sister where she is looking back, wagging frantic at treeline.

Slipping back into dim and cool, moving swift and sure between countless slender trunks. Woman coming on behind, crashing in with her big big bag, scattering The Family, leaving marks, calling her presence to all around.

"I noticed what looked like a vegetable patch back there, is that yours? Do you get much from it? We brought various seeds and such with us and have been trying to grow food since we arrived but so far nothing has really taken, at least nothing has thrived enough to be a reliable food source.

"We still have reserves for a few months yet but

eventually we're going to have to find a way to grow or forage or something, we're just not sure what's safe to eat you know?

"Do you have some kind of special technique or equipment or perhaps a particular nutrient blend you use on your vegetables? We'd be happy to trade with you if you could spare some. We have quite a few rare items from before if you'd be interested."

Pausing and stooping, taking up new stick, Little Sister's eyes widening and fixing. Flinging ahead with easy force, Little Sister bursting after, ears flat, nose straining forward, running as if for her life.

Watching her go, feeling her joy. Fingers slipping to pouches, finding a few small round hards. Turning, offering, giving, then pointing, plucking, eating and offering. Bittersweet tang, exploding, watering mouth sloppy and joyous.

"What are these? Seeds? Will these grow here? Oh wow, thank you. And these berries, they're ok to eat are they? Oooh, yes, they are good aren't they? Yum. That's fantastic, thank you so much! I can't tell you what this means to us, really."

On after Little Sister, stepping ancient paths, every footfall familiar. Back she's coming and off she's going, excitement trembling her always.

Moving right, approaching edge, Her sky opening up once more. Valley bottom, lush with life, sliding back into view. Stopping, kneeling, pulling out skins, still cool in shady spot. Standing, opening one, offering first.

"What is that? Water? Ah, no, thank you. I have water for now, I have that in my bottle here, see? This isn't what I meant, I thought you were showing me a water source, you know? A source of water? A place to get water from? Hmm, how I can make you understand?"

Leaning back, drinking deep, cool refreshment flooding down and through. Woman still talking, endless, empty, friendly sounds.

Wiping mouth, laying skins back down into their cooling shadow, looking out over The Valley, soaking up Her love.

"It's like, where that comes from, do you see? Is it

just rain water, did you collect it when it fell, when it fell from the sky, you know, up there? Or, erm, let's see. I know! When those are empty, where will you fill them up again? No? Ok, perhaps if I draw it out for you, I have some charcoal and some paper in here somewhere hang on."

On to showing and so to telling, stepping forward to edge.

"No wait, I want to show you this. Be careful! No! don't step over there, you'll fall! Stop! You're going to... oh."

Treading careful down narrow path, etched into The Valley so long before. One foot following another, stepping and stepping, sinking from view. Littler Sister waiting above, tongue hanging over edge as she's watching.

Woman talking still.

"Oh my god! How amazing, a little set of hidden steps leading down beneath this overhang and they're carved right into the rock as well. I could have walked by here a thousand times and never seen those. Hang on, wait for me, I just need to rearrange myself a little first."

Down to sparkling, rushing and bubbling, trickling flow singing happy, Her love dancing it over. Woman coming down slow, carrying her big bag under arm. Ignoring her noises, listening to gurgling and to The Family, feeling wind on skin.

"I don't believe it! You did understand! You've saved us! I mean, you've literally saved our lives, I don't know what to say, I'm sorry, I'm just so relieved, I..."

Woman shaking, sobbing snotty, not yet approaching glorious flow, face all glistening wet. Strange sounds now, wet and sticky, sadness and fear, happiness and relief all blurring together. Shaking herself, straightening herself, wiping her face and righting herself.

Watching as from big bag are coming empty things, all shapes and sizes and colours. Good strong arms lifting and plunging, filling and sealing, packing full and heavy back into enormous bag.

Happy, satisfied, done is done, asked and shown and told. Heading off, climbing up, back towards Little

Sister.

"You're leaving? No, wait, you must let me repay you. I have so many questions. Where did you come from? How long have you been here? Where can we find you? Where do you live? I don't even know your name!"

Moving on, slow and steady, leaving chattering behind. The Family returning, all about, about their business all.

Bundle coming into view, into new bag instead of in hand, carrying well, good find and addition. Shelf narrowing, paths joining and straightening, steep sides closing in left and right. Trunks thickening, old and sturdy, leaves crowding Her love into sparkles.

On and on through ancient woods, arch of glory shining ahead. Stepping through, stepping out, onto moorside trail.

She is sailing at Her highest now, crowning Her glorious journey. Her newfound love is endless, Her devotion touching all in view.

Clambering down, no need for thinking, body knows every motion. Stepping inside, hanging skins, adding bundle to pile.

Feeding Him, but just a little, keeping Him going for later. Hanging up new bag, nodding a welcome, taking from various pouches.

Stepping back out, sitting and settling, hand finding Little Sister. Looking out over nodding trees, lazy clouds sliding by overhead. Eating slow, breathing easy, brushing off hands and resting.

Back inside, taking down skins, drinking until thirst is done. Small wooden bowl, topped up with splashes, Little Sister lapping frantic and happy. Pottering about, in and out, making, mending doing.

Hardy nuts breaking open, cracking wide with dull, heavy tool. Rich thick hides, stitching useful with vicious little wolf's pin. All while She is sliding on by, beginning Her reluctant descent, Her love cooling slow as She goes.

Off out beyond, far end of The Valley, opposite to Her destination. Night sliding in eager, chasing Her on, darkening far sky and spreading.

Feeding Him up, preparing a pot, hanging it over His

blazing. One more little bowl, filling with food, Littler Sister barely breathing through gobbling.

Eating, sitting, watching Her go, then goodknife and a piece from His pile. Across The Valley, from mirror woods, thin trails of smoke rising up. People there, living, working, valley people no more.

Hand moving, pushing blade, scraping, biting, slicing, smoothing. Seeing a form within begin to form without. Rough shape first, then in and in to details. Body, legs, head and tail, fragile antlers last.

Wood turning, blade working. Cutting careful, rubbing smooth. Her colours cooling, thinning, fading, melting to mix with distant dark. Fur taking on texture, eyes seeming to shine, tiny antlers showing power despite size.

Mighty Brother stands proud upon palm, frozen perfect.

Curving contours of perfect machine, sliding smooth under palest fur. Calm eyes and noble jaw beneath great crown of The Forest, antlers like Old Man's branches. Power at peace, taking as needed, fighting when forced, living quiet, simple and true.

What is Mighty Brother?

An old thing from The Forest. A beast known long before

Once here, then gone, now here again. A part of The Family, a part of The Forest, fills his place, no more, no less. Mighty Brother is Mighty Brother and all he needs to be.

Mighty Brother knows not people, nor needs them nor they him. Mighty Brother is. No more strange valley people. No more strange valley ways.

Wooden Mighty Brother is truth, making is not knowing but seeing can be. She has left for another day, surrendering The Valley She loves to night's slender creeping chill.

The absence of Her love nips in round shadowed edges, hinting of cold to come. Calling Little Sister, moving inside, feeding Him more, ever more.

His excitement rises, glowing and hot, bathing bodies in a shelter of warm. His light dances over Mighty Brother, shifting shades make him seem ready to sprint from hand. Placing him careful, little nook in wall above sleeping place, there to stand and watch over.

Sitting not thinking, just being with Little Sister, looking into His flames until drowsing comes on strong. Moving slow, removing coverings then climbing under and in. Soft weight of furs pressing down and around, Little Sister settling into her bed down beside.

Body resting easy. Eyes closing heavy.

Still. Quiet.

Sleeping.

free wise men

A cold wind rose from where the sun had fallen, carrying a bleak and vicious chill across the featureless plain of The Forbidden Realm.

The ground was perfectly smooth and perfectly black, cold and hard. The sky above was a star-studded mirror of the ground, occasionally scarred by great grey stripes of brooding cloud.

The Forbidden Realm was a non-place, an in-between place, a place of coming and going but never of staying, a place where reality blurred at the edges and anything was possible.

It was where the Elders of The Outer Realm left their great iron beasts to sleep when their labour was not required.

Now the beasts lay silent in countless ranks, filling The Forbidden Realm as far as the eye could see. Each was dormant, sitting so still as to appear as if they had always been there and always would be, permanent and immovable.

Scattered across the plain, a handful of blazing orbs hovered atop great, slender spires, bathing the place in a thin, half-light.

The sickly stuff defined the edges of the beasts but then served only to blur their details and further deepen the blackness of the shadows between them.

Between two of the deep slumbering beasts, a particularly black shadow condensed to take a lithe and prowling form.

She slinked towards the base of one of the spires then waited patiently, a black shape lost amid the blackest black.

Soon enough, a tiny, winged being fluttered into existence. One of countless little pilgrims whose entire life's purpose was to find and then to worship the high floating orbs which were to them as gods.

The pilgrim fluttered chaotic, up and around but mostly up. He worked tireless, furious, beating his impossibly thin little wings frantic as he hurried upwards, desperate to worship his glowing god.

The shadow below tensed then uncoiled, leaping up. She struck the pilgrim with a silent swipe then following him back to the ground and consumed him greedily, crunching his little body between her hungry jaws.

A small group of people appeared then. Quite oblivious of the hunting shadow, they wandered together between the rows of slumbering, metallic behemoths. Their footsteps cracked open the silence so that the shadow retreated, melting away to rejoin the darkness.

The Forbidden Realm was darker and colder than any of them had imagined and yet the spark of excitement each carried within him warmed them through.

Their presence in The Forbidden Realm was taboo, a crime in of itself and yet their absence from The Realm of Knowledge was a transgression far greater still.

As they walked on, none said a word as each thought back to that other place and of his own desperate flight from it.

The Realm of Knowledge, far behind them now, was a place of bustling light, of colour, pageantry and tradition.

As they walked they thought of the murmuring crowds, the spotlight speakings, the eruptions of laughter, delight and applause.

They all knew that eventually they would be drawn back there, that their time in The Forbidden Realm could not last and that retribution would follow soon after.

Despite this certain knowledge however, not one of the three regretted his escape. While others had considered it foolish to risk the ire of The Director, these three had shown a deeper wisdom.

Wise beyond their years, they alone had realised that during their time in The Forbidden Realm they would be truly, albeit fleetingly, free.

Free from The Director's tyranny, free from the tedium and the humiliation she enforced, at least for a while.

Here they were free from their conscripted roles, from the positions they had been so coldly assigned despite their insistence that they could do more, give more, be more.

They came together in a long broad clearing, the short, the tall and the other. As their footsteps ceased the wind rushed in to fill the silence with its endless whispers. They looked at one another, at the brooding metal breasts and at the smooth black ground beneath.

Their freedom felt good but it brought with it a question, pressing but unspoken. Back in The Realm of Knowledge they had been united against The Director.

Thrown together by circumstance against a common enemy. Their purpose had been clear then, their newly formed bonds strong and level.

Now however, out in the cold dark space of their emancipation, what was to be done? What came next? And above all, which of them would decide?

The other watched the short and the tall closely while appearing to take no interest, his mind working furiously behind carefully careless eyes.

"What's a mockracy?" asked the short then, his voice swallowed up by the sky.

"What?" said the tall.

"A mockracy," the short repeated. "When you said we should vote, she said.."

He took a moment to prepare himself before delivering the rest in a spite filled screech.

"..You will do as you're told! This isn't a mockracy!"

"A democracy," said the other then, kicking at the ground idly. "She said, this isn't a democracy."

"Well what's that then?" asked the short, looking from one compatriot to the other.

The tall looked off into the darkness, squinting his lack of interest into the black. The other stopped kicking at the ground and raised his head slowly, an idea dawning within.

"I once heard my father say," he began, glancing at the tall to catch his eye. "That democracy is two wolves and a sheep deciding what to have for dinner."

There was pause while they all considered the definition.

"What does that mean?" the short asked eventually.

"I'm a wolf," said the tall suddenly, catching on and stepping closer.

"Me too," said the other quietly.

A pause grew between them and was quickly filled by the wind, as the short processed their words.

"I'm not the sheep!" he cried suddenly.

"Course you are," said the tall, full of spite and glee.

"Look at you," said the other.

The short looked down at himself in horror. Sure enough a shaggy fleece hung from his shoulders and crude hooves emerged from his wrists.

"That's not fair!" he cried again, turning to flee back the way they'd come.

"Catch him!" shouted the tall, lunging forward to give chase.

"Hang on," said the other thoughtfully.

"But he'll blame us!" said the tall. Caught mid stride he hovered, torn, looking back and forth between the retreating sheep and his fellow wolf. "He'll tell her it was all down to us! He'll say we made him come with us."

"Perhaps," said the other thoughtfully. "But if he does we'll just say it was his fault. It'll be two against one."

"She won't believe us!" said the tall, frustrated and scornful.

"She might," countered the other one. "If we told her it was him who ran away and that we only followed to catch him and bring him back to her.

"We could tell her he was hiding out here and that it took us time to find him, that we were just doing our best to help. You know what a crybaby he is, everyone does. She's bound to believe us."

"Maybe," said the tall, calmer now but still not convinced.

"You'll just have to pretend that you're a sheep too," said the other.

"What?!" said the tall. "No! Why would I do that?"

"If she thinks you're happy to be a sheep," said the other, his tone perfectly reasonable. "Then she's more likely believe that you didn't want to escape, that you really were just trying to catch him for her."

The tall peered into the shadows that had swallowed the small, fists clenching and unclenching at his sides.

"But I don't want to be a sheep!" he said fiercely. "That was the whole point of leaving, so that we could be whatever we wanted to be."

"You don't really have to be a sheep," the other cajoled. "Haven't you heard of the wolf in sheep's clothing? You would just be pretending, you'd be a sheep on the outside but underneath you'd still be a real wolf with me. It's just a trick so that he takes the blame."

The tall thought about it a little longer before his shoulders slumped in defeat.

"Ok," he said finally.

"So you're a sheep?" asked the other, his voice suddenly harder.

"Yeah," replied the tall, looking down sadly at his thick dirty fleece and misshapen hooves. "I'm a sheep."

"And we'll tell her it was him?" pressed the other. "That it was all his fault?"

"Alright," said the tall. "Fine. But what about him? If he gets back there before us..."

"Don't worry about that," said the other. "I'll get round in front of him and chase him back here. Then you just grab him and we'll take him back and hand him over to her.

"That way not only will she not be angry with us, she'll actually thank us for helping. Meanwhile, everyone else will know forever that you and I are the wolves and he's the sheep."

"Fine," said the tall flatly.

He wandered away, dragging his feet and looking at his hooves in disgust. He reached one of the huge metal beasts and heaved his woolly self clumsily up onto its low back end to wait.

The flank of the beast dipped a little under his weight but otherwise the monster did not stir, such was the depth of its slumber.

The other smiled and nodded his approval then set off through the maze of metal. He moved quickly and almost silently, weaving between the hulks and narrowing his eyes to listen.

Sure enough, a few rows on, he heard the sound of heavy breathing, poorly hidden behind desperate hooves.

He rounded a particularly large beast and saw the short crouched at its base.

"Hey," he said gently.

"No!" cried the short. "You're a wolf and you're going to get me!"

"It's ok, it's ok," cooed the other. "I'm not going to get you."

"You are!" declared the short, quivering to stand. "You said there were two wolves and that I'm the sheep and that you were going to have me for dinner. It's not fair! I don't want to be the sheep!"

"I know," said the other, stepping closer. "And you're not, not really. It's a trick."

The short dragged the back of a hoof across his nose and narrowed his eyes at the other. He looked him up and down with grave suspicion before composing himself.

"What do you mean?" he asked,

"We're the wolves really," explained the other in lowered tones. "You and me. He's the sheep,"

The other pointed back behind him into the darkness so that the short peered past him for a moment,

"I don't understand," said the short then, scowling his distrust.

"Haven't you heard of the wolf in sheep's clothing?" asked the other innocently. "You're a secret wolf, it's a trick."

The short shook his head, not understanding at all.

"Ok look," said the other, closing the distance between them and lowering his voice to an even more urgent and conspiratorial tone.

"When we go back, she's going to ask us what happened," he said. "All we have to say is that he was threatening us and that we ran out here get away from him. You know what a bully he is, everyone does, she's bound to believe us."

"But that's not true," said the short, genuinely confused. "It was your idea."

"That's not the point!" snapped the other before quickly composing himself again. "If you tell her that then we'll all be blamed. This way it's all his fault and we don't get in trouble at all."

A light seemed to come on behind the short's eyes.

"Oh," he said. "Ok yes, I get it. So should we just go back now then?"

"No," said the other, looking about them. "No we have to go and find him and get him to chase us, that way she'll believe us."

"But I don't want to him to chase me, he's really fast," said the short, fear welling up to rewater his eyes.

"Don't worry about that," said the other, not quite keeping the edge from his voice. "I won't let him get you, you just need to keep pretending to be a sheep, that's all."

"But I don't like being a sheep!" the short pouted. "I don't like it!"

"I know," said the other, not quite managing to keep the edge out of his voice. "But like I said, you're just pretending. If she thinks you're happy to be a sheep she's more likely to believe us.

"Really, you're a wolf like me underneath, he's the sheep. We just need it to look like you're a sheep for now so that she'll believe us."

The short didn't say anything, he seemed to be about to burst into tears again.

"Ok?!" asked the other again, a little harder.

The short one just nodded, bottom lip trembling.

"And you'll tell her it was him?" pressed the other. "You'll tell her that it was him and not me, right?"

The short nodded again.

"Right," said the other, turning back to face the way he had come. "Good. Go on then."

The other pushed the short ahead of him and they retraced his steps, pausing frequently as the other hurried the short along.

The wind seemed even colder now, the air even thicker with black. They crept along, trying to move silently between the sleeping giants until finally the tall came into view up ahead.

"There he is," hissed the other, pointing ahead. The short followed the other's finger and caught sight of the tall.

He was still sitting on the back the beast, staring at the ground and looking bored. The short jerked back around behind the other one.

"I don't like this," he said.

"It's fine," said the other. "Just go out there and walk up to him."

"I don't want to," said the short.

"Just do it!" snapped the other. "Just walk up to him. He'll try and grab you but then you turn and run back this way. I'll make sure he doesn't catch you, you'll be fine"

"Why can't you do it?" whined the short.

"Because he thinks you're the sheep," the other explained reasonably. "I'm a wolf, he won't chase me. Look it's the only way for us to not get in trouble. If you don't do it I'll tell The Director it was all your idea and then she'll blame you for all of it."

"You wouldn't!" cried the short in horror.

"I don't want to," said the other, making a good show of genuine regret. "But if you don't do this I'll have no choice."

The short's eyes wobbled but he said no more. Straightening up on trembling legs, he moved shakily past the other.

He stepped out into the clearing and the tall saw him immediately, clambering down from his seat and readying himself. The short pressed on across the clearing, clutching his fleece between his hooves to hold it tighter to him.

The other watched as the tall and the short neared each other in the middle of the clearing. The pair paused and stared, each entirely focussed, waiting for his opposite to make his move and trigger the start of his plan.

The other smirked, then turned away from the clearing. Carefully picking out silent steps between the gleaming flanks of the beasts, he wound his way back towards The Realm of Knowledge.

As he went, he practised the story he would tell The Director, the story of the crimes of the tall and the short and how he had tried so hard to bring them both back to her.

Behind him he heard the moment at which the tall made his sudden, lunging move. The short cried out briefly before the air was abruptly riddled with the

286

staccato slaps of their footfalls.

The other was quickening his own pace away from the pair when suddenly all was made still by a single, ringing voice.

"You lot!" cried the voice. "You have to come back inside right now."

The three all turned to see a small boy wearing a dressing gown with a tea towel tied around his head. At the sight of the boy the other sagged in defeat and disappointment, looking down at his own fleece and hooves. He stepped out to join the others in the clearing.

It was over.

"You've all got to come back inside right now!" said the boy. "Miss says you're all in trouble for running away because we were all waiting for you and then when you didn't come back me and the other shepherds couldn't go on when we were supposed to so the free wise men had to go on instead and now everything's all messed up and everyone's really angry and if you don't come back right now then we can't do the bit with the angel!"

The tall, the small and the other fell into line behind their classmate and trudged back across the carpark towards the school, staring down at the tarmac and dreading what was to come.

From the shadows a small black cat watched them go, unimpressed, then returned to hunting moths.

"It's not free wise men," said the other bitterly as the three all dragged their feet.

"What?" said the boy.

"You said free wise men," he said. "It's not the free wise men, it's the three wise men."

"No, no, it's not," said the boy. "It's not, because Lucy Henderson is one of them so it can't be. It's two free, wise men and one free, wise woman. They're free because they can travel all over the world and they're wise because they know about all stars and that."

"It is three," said the other. "And you're an idiot because you don't know that."

"You're an idiot," said the boy, as he opened the door and stepped inside.

"You are," said the other as he followed.

Printed in Great Britain
by Amazon

64128656R00173